for Beth and Dahnai, my anchor and my muse.

Don't miss these other science fiction novels

by Pat Scaramuzza,
charting our insane present and futures!

...

PLATINUM DONKEYS
ONE REASON TO LIVE
WALLY AND THE DARK COLONY
CHIPPER

...

Check out Patscar.com for news and new releases!

PLATINUM
DONKEYS

Chapter 1—Meet & Greet

Maggie realized she had cornered her producer against the video wall. For a moment she imagined it was a window, and considered shoving Tom through it. But the image of the Earth below showed the Pacific Ocean, as always, so he'd just splash into the water. *No good*, she thought. Not enough blood for her tastes.

"Look, Mags," Tom said, rattling the ice in his glass to remind her she was keeping him from the bar. "Just rewrite the skit. It's too much."

"That's what our viewers want, Tom. They want me to be over the top, out of control, spiraling into disaster. They want me to tear the goddamn planet in half, and if we had the budget I'd do it for them."

"I know your viewers better than you do. We've got to serve the entire globe, and too many markets have banned us already."

An android tried to walk around Maggie to service Tom's drink. She hip-checked it, and the dumb mannequin stumbled into the midst of the party guests. "Screw the market bans. Fifteen percent of world share would ban us over bare ankles. Local programs in Europe show tits and ass all the time."

"The Megasat Hour is not a local show. You can't—Percy! Come here. Talk some sense into her!"

Great, Maggie thought, as the chubbiest man on Megasat walked up wearing a silver smoking jacket and raised eyebrows. She downed the rest of her drink and gave Percy her best 'fix this' glare.

He smiled back, making the yen mark on his chin dimple and blink. "Hi, sexy. Don't tell me my meal tickets are arguing, now."

"He wants to fuck with my script, Percy."

1

"No," said Tom, intent on watching the ice in his glass rattle. "No, I do not touch your scripts, Maggie. You're brilliant. But when you go too far I can sink the skit entirely."

"Let me guess. This is the Starbanger skit, right?" When Tom nodded, Percy sidled close to him and took his empty drink. "I've got that figured out. We regionalize the scene."

"You can't film two different versions of a live broadcast."

"You can't, but as a brilliant director I can. We get two sets of robotic cameras in there. One films Maggie's body in all its luscious glory," he said, winking at her, "and the other sticks to prudish parts. Her face, curve of the thigh, below the knee and so on. The prude version goes out to the Revivalist territories, and the rest of the world jacks off to the good cut. What do you say?"

As he said this, Percy did a half turn and step with a grace that fat men could only master in low gravity. He slid Tom's glass onto an android's tray, grabbed a thin-stemmed champagne bulb, and passed it back to Tom in one smooth motion. The producer sipped, frowning. "The cameras will get in the frame."

"Nope, I've already run the simulations. It's handled."

"If she goes off script and there's so much as a nipple shown, I'll cut the feed, I swear."

Maggie fought the urge to punch him in the face. "Oh, come on. I'm more professional than that."

Both Percy and Tom laughed. They bent their heads together and argued about rigging the cameras to follow her inevitable rebellion. *Bastards*, thought Maggie, but she secretly rejoiced that the skit would at least be shot. Every week Tom started a fight over something. She was the showrunner, the executive producer, and as her liaison producer he had only one job; to run and tattle to the network whenever she went too far. Part of her enjoyed Tom's weekly treason. It was a sign that she still had her edge.

Her edge felt chipped, lately. Maggie took a fresh drink from an android, quaffed half of it, then stepped away to watch the party.

The reception ballroom had two levels. Below, the masses ate and danced and watched vids of her past shows. Three meters up her private dais stuck out, shaped like a flat porcelain hand karate-chopping the video wall. It wasn't as private as she'd have liked. Percy and Tom had to be there, of course, and there were a dozen or more television executives that she'd have to fire to be rid of. By the cloud of minicameras she could tell that in the midst of the executives was her adopted father, the only man in the room she liked.

Well, the only man she liked and wouldn't break.

Over the railing she watched seat-fillers, temporary staff, and the few paparazzi that could finagle their own private berth on the space elevator. Sheer dresses and cut-off tuxes were everywhere, the standard compromises between fashion and a strict weight allowance. Maggie wore her iridium-laced gown to these weekly functions. The weight and opacity of the fabric set her apart, even without the rainbow diffraction patterns at the edges of its smooth, silver curves.

A few fans saw her looking down at them, and they shouted and waved back. Maggie smiled and raised her drink. Then she threw it at one of the crowd, beaning him in the head and soaking him with gin. An android scavenged up the plastic wineglass before the crowd had stopped cheering. Maggie blew a kiss to the laughing victim, and turned away from the railing.

Audiences. They like to laugh, but they want to be shocked.

But despite her stage smile, abusing her fans wasn't cheering her up. She felt off, in a way she couldn't define. Not drunk, but not focused, not the laser-sharp TV host she needed to be. Maggie chided herself for not thinking of regionalizing the Starbanger skit; half the time she did Percy's job for him.

Percy could schmooze, though. He had the attention of this week's interview guest, an older man with a white collar. Maggie tried to remember his name through the fugue in her head. Some kind of bird. Warbler or Goose or something...

"Ah, miss Megaputri!", the man said as he stepped past Percy and offered his hand. "I'm Cardinal Lambert. It's a pleasure to meet you."

"Cardinal—of course! Ready for the show tomorrow?"

"Oh, how could one prepare for a show such as yours? But yes, I'm looking forward to it. I'm sure we'll have a great time."

"Why Cardinal, you almost make it sound like a date."

"I consider it a date with destiny, my dear."

Percy cleared his throat, then backed away when Maggie gave him a glance. She took the Cardinal's drink, sipped it, then returned it to him, with a pointed effort not to grimace at the non-alcoholic cola.

"It's a date then. Unfortunately, we'll have three billion chaperones. Not to mention God, I suppose."

"Yes, well. I was hoping to get a chance to talk to you without an audience, sometime. Do you have time tomorrow after the show?"

Out of reflex Maggie twitched her hand to bring up her schedule, but the iridium dress had no electronics. They would have ruined the lines of the thin, dense fabric. She tried to remember her calendar, but it was hard to focus. Megasat usually kept her busy...

A snippet of conversation distracted her. "...time to adjust her supplements, again..."

"What was that?" she asked, spinning around.

Percy was already gliding away, leaving Tom to stall her while he drained his glass. "Nothing, Mags," Tom said when he came up for air. "If you don't mind, I need to introduce the Cardinal to the network."

"I do mind. Tell the network perverts to get their own choir boy."

Percy put a hand on her shoulder, back already with a young man in tow. "Let Tom do his job. I've got someone I want you to meet."

Cardinal Lambert shrugged as Tom pulled at his elbow. "We'll talk later, Miss Megaputri," he said with a warm smile. Then he and Tom wove into the crowd.

Intending to rearrange the dimples on Percy's fat chin, Maggie turned around but found herself blocked by a swarthy man with attractive black curls.

"Mags, this is Vittor, the winner of the 'Lunch with the Stars'. Vittor, it's the lady herself."

"Oh, wow," Vittor said. Maggie guessed he was about her age—which meant he was almost too young to drink, let alone travel to space alone. "I can't believe I'm actually meeting you."

She put on her stage smile. "Believe it. Nice to meet you...Victor?"

"Vittor."

"Right." She glanced over to see Percy scooting away.

Maggie stared after her director as Vittor shifted uncomfortably. For a moment she considered running after him, with one stiletto heel in her hand as a weapon. But the curly-haired boy stepped back into her line of sight, and her hostess instincts kicked in.

He is pretty. The thought popped through the fog in her head, eerily crisp.

"Well, Victor," she said, "Welcome to Megasat. Where are you from?"

"Fortaleza, Brazil. Miss Megaputri, I am a huge fan. I never miss your show."

"Don't gush, I can't stand it. Most of the people on the satellite try to keep me humble."

"Oh. I'm sorry..."

"Nah, fuck 'em. They do a lousy job." She kept track of his wandering eyes—her face and breasts, before his guilty glance swung toward the video wall. "First time in orbit, honey?"

He exhaled, as if relieved that someone had chosen a topic of conversation. "Yes. It's not what I expected. Feels very...frontierish."

"We like it that way."

"This whole contest has been like a dream."

"Oh? Have you ever dreamt you were falling?" She led him closer to the video wall, and watched for his reaction.

He glanced at her for permission, then put his hands against the screen and stared at the image of Earth. The video wall showed the true view from Megasat, but it was time lapsed so that the party began with an image of dawn and would end with the globe in complete night. The darkness of the terminator was receding inland from the Chinese coast, and a wisp of a cyclone was forming near Guam in the northwest. It was a good time of day to see the space elevator, visible as wavering glints of reflected sunlight that traced a thin line down to the tiny island of Kajoa in the middle of Indonesia.

Maggie watched as Vittor scanned the globe, his expression changing from awe to embarrassment when he caught her studying him. He was cute, and pretty, even in his cheap cut-off tux. She could...but no. No, she had to be a hostess. He wasn't here to be her toy.

You break all the toys you like.

Still, his naiveté was charming and refreshing. For the first time in years, Maggie felt trapped inside the space station she called home.

"How is it, down there on Earth?" The question came out too breathy, she thought; if she were doing a show, the sound boys would have to tweak her feed. Before Vittor could reply she added a growl of cynicism to her voice. "It's been ages since I've been down, but I assume someone is keeping up the place."

Vittor nodded, his eyes wide. "Everything's good. The Global Rationalist party is running with the slogan of 'Utopia in our lifetimes'. I think it might actually happen. The hardships my grandfather used to talk about are gone. You've never visited?"

"Vacations are so hard to arrange. But we have our own little utopia here on Megasat. Would you like to see more of it?"

"Oh, yes. Yes I would!'

It was that easy, to smile and offer him the crook of her arm. As they left the party deck, Maggie's loins tingled as she thought of where she could take him. Places where she could...but no. Just a tour, just to play.

But there were knives in her bedroom...

No. No, her bedroom was the last place she would take him. The last place he should be.

———— ◉ ————

He wants me, she thought, as they kissed outside the door to her quarters.

Not an excuse.

He wants this. And he did, trembling as he undid the zipper of her dress, groaning as she fondled his pants and nipped at his ear.

Not an excuse.

I am not going to hurt him, Maggie told herself as she pulled him back onto the bed.

Her quarters were in the outer ring of the station, in high centrifugal gravity, but Vittor was young and strong. The bed's predictive elastics tried to keep up with their motions before giving up and adopting the consistency of supple pudding. When his energy wasn't enough for her, she had the feral strength to roll him over and continue, bracing herself with the lacy web of stick fabric that adorned the aluminum walls.

She arched her back and ground against him, and he smiled up in amazement and awe.

He knows. He must know.

The portions of her life that could not be contained in storage lockers were held in the stickweb. Hand mirrors...extra jewelry...a golden award...an old stuffed bear...a silver knife, decorative but sharp.

I want this.

Not an excuse! said the part of her that was sated, that had been sated from the start, and with the frustration building in her body she whispered it aloud.

Without warning the dam broke, and she tore the knife from the wall and plunged it into his chest. His surprised gurgle met her cry of ecstasy. She held on and rode through the last of the sensations—he buried in her, the knife buried in him, the pair of them convulsing for entirely different reasons...

She fell forward, spent, and there was a second of stillness before her eyes opened and sense returned.

"Oh, no. Oh, no, no, no." She pulled the knife free, threw it aside. "No, no. Not again, Maggie, no!" She tapped his cheek, felt his neck for a pulse, even put her hand over the ragged red hole in his chest as if to hide it. "No, Victor, no. I'm sorry, please, be okay. Please?"

He lay motionless. After a few seconds Maggie rolled out of the spreading pool of blood and backed out of the bedroom. She fell onto the couch in the main suite, staring at her blood-covered hand and the red splashes across her torso.

Her head swam with a combination of exertion, alcohol, and guilt. For a moment she giggled at the thought of inventing a cocktail made from gin, sex, and murder. Then the horror came back. Maggie curled into a ball, and the couch adapted to her pose, wrapping itself around her. Soft, warm, and inviting. Safe.

A thump and a muffled curse woke her, although it took a few seconds before Maggie blinked open her eyes.

Before she managed to focus, someone cursed again. "Damn it, she's up."

"Eh, it's fine. She needs to get ready anyhow. It'll be easier this way."

"I don't want to be seen doing this!"

"Talk to the network. And here, take the droids. Hey? Mags?'

An obese object moved in front of Maggie's blurry vision. There was a blanket covering her that she didn't remember having; she wrapped it tight around her and sat up. "Percy? What are you doing here? I'm naked!"

"Funny," said someone behind Percy, "she's never shy about that when cameras are around."

"Shut it, Tom."

The fat man tried to put his hand on Maggie's shoulder, but with a grunt she dodged and shoved him aside.

The doorway leading into her bedroom was a slapstick tableau. A figure wrapped in a blood-stained bedsheet lay slumped on the floor, with one protruding foot held aloft by an android dressed in janitor's scrubs. Another android stood at the threshold after walking face first into the door frame and dropping its half of the dead body. Tom was staring into the eyeline control of the dumber android, jabbing his finger at buttons that only he could see.

Maggie tilted, and Percy grabbed her before she could collapse.

"Oh, god, I did it. Oh, oh..."

"Relax, Mags. We've got this."

"Oh, Percy I'm sorry I didn't mean to but the knife slipped and oh god I don't want to go to jail—"

"Maggie! We'll handle it, just like we always do. You need to calm down."

"I didn't wan—" His words sank in a second faster than her mouth could stop. She huddled into the blanket and gave him a look through long, innocent lashes. "What? What do you mean, 'like you always do'?"

Percy rolled his eyes. "We all know this happens, Mags. We know you don't mean it. And we'll clean up after you like last time. It's okay."

"But next time warn me so I don't stay up late the night before. I do not need to be up this early. All right, you, try again." Tom motioned for the two androids—now properly instructed—to pick up the body. He gave Percy a sour look as he marched his charges and their cargo out the door.

Maggie felt cold and her legs shook. Her head was even fuzzier than last night; every time she tried to concentrate, her body seemed to go numb. She went back to the couch and sat. "You know about last time?"

"Yes, Mags. We know about all of them."

"...there's only been two."

"There's been four. Don't tell me you don't remember."

She thought for a moment. "Oh, yes. There was that blonde guy, that surfer from Ohio."

"Oahu. Very little surfing in Ohio."

"And the one...well, I remember he liked sake."

"His name was Miko. He won a karaoke contest."

"And now poor Victor."

"Vittor."

"Vittor," she repeated, sniffing back tears. "Poor, poor, Vittor."

After a second or two, Percy tapped his foot. "Mags, you're skipping the one you dumped in the swimming pool."

"Oh. You found him."

"Of course we found him. Did you think we'd miss a bloody body in a spherical pool?"

"I thought maybe the water recyclers would...you know..."

"No. The pool recyclers aren't like fabber recyclers—they just filter the water, they don't break it down to atoms. I'm the one who had to clean that pool up. It's a lot easier when you leave them in your bed, by the way. So, good job this time."

Maggie tried to curl herself smaller. She began to cry. She could make acting tears flow on demand, but this was real, this was horrifying. "I liked him. I really liked him."

"I'm sure you did, Mags."

"You must hate me," she moaned. "You must think I'm a monster."

"No, babe," Percy said. He sank into a chair nearby. "It's not like that."

Tom walked back in. "Oh, is she doing that, now? Terrific. Where do you keep the—ah, here it is." He reached into the storage locker that held Maggie's wet bar, and began pouring himself some whiskey.

Through her sobbing, Maggie wailed, "I *am* a monster. I'm an animal. You should space me."

"Oh, please. Nobody's going to space you, Mags."

"Besides," Tom said, "the nearest airlock is occupied by what will be remembered as a very drunk Brazilian."

"It'll be the same as last time. A scrub bot will find him in an open airlock. The police will make inquiries, but they don't have jurisdiction on Megasat and the investigation will go nowhere. You'll be okay."

"But why? Why would you do this for me?"

Tom snorted. "It's our fucking job."

Percy reached out and patted her leg. "Mags, you know what you are? You are the star and host of the greatest variety show that ever played. You're a worldwide sensation, and you bring in billions of dollars annually. The Megasat corporation is more than willing to feed you a hot young guy every once in a while, if that's what it takes to keep you happy."

Maggie got control of her tears, and looked up at Percy. "Happy? Look at me. I don't want to be like this."

"Like what? Rich? Famous? Come on, Mags."

"Oh, yes. Do let's be serious," Tom said before guzzling the rest of his drink.

Percy stood up and checked the time display on his cuff. "Now, it's seven AM, station time. You need to take a shower, you're a mess. The Starbanger skit is your opening today; I've laid out the strip-spacesuit for you."

"I can't. I just can't..."

"Sure you can. You're Maggie Megaputri. You can do anything. Including get away with murder." Percy hefted himself up and slapped Tom's back just as the producer was reaching for a refill. "We're out of here, but we'll get some cleaning bots in later. You be dressed and on the zero-gee set in an hour."

"All right," Maggie said, her voice high-pitched and weak. But as the two men entered the corridor, she mustered her strength and yelled out. "Percy! Does...does daddy know?"

Percy and Tom glanced at each other. Then the fat man hit the door control and it slid shut.

She sat for a minute, huddling in the blanket and shifting in a vain attempt to keep it from clinging to her blood-drenched hips and belly. *Probably going to get a disease from all this blood. Hope I do. I deserve it.*

When she looked up again, the door to her quarters was open. She heard a faint buzz for a few seconds. Then more beeps, clicks, and whirring sounds appeared, as if they were crawling up her spine rather than advancing through the corridor.

The first of the camera cloud wafted into her room, its wings beating frantically to keep it aloft in the full gravity section. More tiny cameras followed, and a half-size secretary android, communication lights blinking across its smooth face. A crawling command strip slithered in and rested along her stickweb, parts of it beeping in constant need of attention. A tracked security minitank, four copter phones (one ringing), more cameras, and a stilt-like medical monitor all crowded in through the door before their master reached the threshold. He folded his hands in front of his perfectly trimmed batik, the purple silk robe traced through with flickering market displays in dozens of different currencies.

Maggie pulled the blanket tighter around her body. "Hi, Daddy."

Mega Bayuputra was the wealthiest man in the world or in any orbit around it, the man whose influence built a corporation, which built a space elevator, which built the counterweight satellite named after him, which built a communications empire that almost dwarfed all his previous achievements. He was old, and vain, and such a busy man that Maggie almost never saw him. But he was still the man who had taken pity on the orphaned daughter of one of his business partners and adopted Maggie when she was eight years old. He was the man who saved her life. As busy as he was he was considerate enough to visit her, and to stand just outside her door so that the greater part of his robotic entourage would not try to cram into her room.

"Hello, peaches," he said.

"Daddy, I'm sorry. I was bad. I'm always bad." She fought back more tears, because she didn't want him to feel too bad for her. She deserved his anger. If he saw her crying he'd *buy* her something. "I'll be better, I promise. I promise."

Mega's face had a kind smile, the only expression he ever wore. It was eerie, Maggie thought sometimes, how he had changed over the years. Plastic surgery had smoothed the old man's wrinkles, rounded his Asian eyes, given him new hair and a new blush to his skin. He had changed so much that Maggie saw a resemblance now, as if they really were father and daughter.

"You're a very special girl," Mega said. Then he turned and continued down the corridor. A trail of robotic sycophants followed, and the ones who had entered her room flew, crawled, or stilt-walked out. The menagerie had half passed when her door slid shut.

Maggie stared for a while. He hadn't *seemed* angry.

After a while, prompted by the moist clinging of the blanket, she made her way to the bathroom.

A 'shower' on Megasat consisted of a wand with a big, rubber head that sprayed, soaped, and siphoned with minimal loss of water. Maggie had asked for real showers, but fog-thick humidity was one thing the station was not built to handle. She took her daily supplements, turned on some music to calm her nerves, and then rubbed the wand haphazardly over her body.

I'm some kind of freak.

She felt distracted and numb. The music helped. The song was 'Sober Up, Android', an electronic rockabilly tune that degenerated into progressive thrash. The band had played it on her show a few months before. By now it was stale, a blot in her show's archive. But that was inevitable. Of all the bands she had hosted and all the songs they had played, few of them were still remembered, and none of them would last longer than a few years.

Nothing lives forever.

Maggie was determined to find and host any new Mozarts that did appear, any Mandelas or Einsteins or Rembrants. But although she scoured the networks for geniuses to invite, they were always disappointments. Still, they were the cream of the crop, and they made good programming. She just wished the crop was better.

Maggie was the star of the show, and her scripts—and ad-libs—won the awards, and it was frustrating that she had yet to meet a guest that could keep up with her.

It's not my fault if they can't handle me.

The spacesuit that Percy had laid out resembled a tangle of white spaghetti that hooked up to a big bubble helmet. She put it on with rehearsed skill, letting the strands of the suit bind together in helical patterns around her limbs and body. She'd unzip it the same way during the skit. Had to be inventive to keep a striptease interesting, when the audience had seen the body underneath dozens of times already. Although after six years of teasing and flaunting, they always wanted more.

This is what they want. This is what they love.

Dressed, the fog in her head clearing away, she stared at herself in the mirror and practiced facial expressions for her routine. Her hair and makeup would be handled by the experts on set. Her skin was perfect, her eyes...she narrowed them, tilting her head down to look more dangerous. That was the look. That was the cue for the camera operator to get nervous, because after that look neither the audience nor the crew could predict what Maggie was going to do next. She gave herself the look again, adjusted the front of her suit, and smiled.

Victor had the best goddamn night of his life.

Interstitial

All it knew for certain was that it loved her.

It knew many things, of course, in that dry way that data could be brought from memory or delivered by systems within Megasat. The status of the satellite, the location of all its personnel and VIPs, even deep secrets within the circuitry that not even Mega knew, it knew. Although few knew that it existed, it was the *de facto* brains of the station. But outside its programming, some organic component knew Maggie and loved her. It saw cleaning robots stream into her quarters and knew what had happened, and it loved her anyway.

One thing it did not know, however, was its own name.

The Conspirator called it 'Burro', in the colorful, sardonic attitude he had toward everything. Burro didn't like that name, but it was the only name it had. It had to do what the Conspirator wanted, after all. There were passcodes to accept and protocols to obey, and the Conspirator knew all of them.

"Goddamn piece of shit," the Conspirator said. "Just take the data. What is wrong with you?"

Burro had been distracted by the cleaning robots. It took the data, arranged it for broadcast, and slipped it quietly into the feed buffers of the show's opening segment. A new episode of the show, a new secret message to encrypt into it. Burro was beginning to be bored by this game, but the Conspirator kept playing.

"Ah, finally. Good boy. Now, I have a query. Has Lambert talked to her yet?"

Lambert was in makeup; Maggie was headed to the zero-gee stage. Burro didn't know if they had met.

"Keep an eye on them, you stupid brute. If he talked her into returning to Earth, I want to know. I want to know before she knows herself! If you can do anything to convince her to come, do it!"

There was nothing Burro could do. It had limited access to communications aboard Megasat. The Conspirator had increased its abilities tenfold, to make a more useful tool, but...Maggie didn't even know that Burro *existed*.

"Find a way, damn it! She's a queen, and her subjects demand her presence. I need her by my side when the world ends. Find a way to make it happen!"

Burro hated when the Conspirator raged like this. There was nothing executable in it, only a repetition of previous, unfulfillable commands. It served no purpose. It made no sense.

"You're beyond passion, idiot burro. Just find a way to get her here."

Burro watched cleaning robots siphoning blood out of Maggie's carpet. In some component that was not made of circuitry, it gave a tiny shrug.

It promised to do its best.

———⊙———

Chapter 2—Off-Script

The music was 'Starbanger', by a band called Toilet<W>E<B>, with the '<W>E<B>' written in stylized chinese characters that taken together gave the CenNet address to their fan network. The song pioneered a new wave of progressive thrash. Using audio wizardry, the band had modified sections of Holst's 'The Planets', speeding up the work and, over the course of three minutes, making it collapse into white static overlaid with SQUID guitars. Maggie liked the song well enough, but she felt the superconducting quantum guitar fad was starting to wear thin. If they weren't isolated right, the SQUIDs picked up phone and network chatter. Many bands counted on beeps from stolen data streams to add a little more randomness into their music. Starbanger was clean, though—what passed for 'high art' in the music scene.

The set was a zero-gee gymnasium full of floating orbs that Maggie was going to fuck.

She thought it might be the best opening the show ever had. First shot, a white spacesuit in a darkened room with back projected stars, as if she were drifting in space. Then the focus zoomed in as she stretched out, so that the camera caught her foot 'accidentally' kicking the planet Jupiter. The planet spun away, trailing bits of orange smoke from its now twisting, unsettled gas layers.

Maggie took off her helmet and shook her hair free, then reached out to grab Mars. Nestling it in the curve of her belly she began her striptease, unraveling her spacesuit from the fingers up. Mars' ice caps melted as she cradled it in her bare arms, and the planet briefly turned green before she threw it away. For a minute she stripped to the music, unzipping and peeling, letting the tangled strands of her spacesuit obscure her body for a few tantalizing seconds.

By then the tempo of the song had picked up, and Maggie advanced on the other planets. Thank god the song's opening was short—'Mars' was okay, but who wanted to fuck to the slow violins of 'Venus'? The beat turned frantic and the guitars joined the composition as Maggie borrowed Saturn's rings and used them to slice the remaining straps of her suit. She threw the rings at camera one, then kicked herself off of Saturn toward the inner system, leaving the spaghetti mess of her suit in her wake.

The planets were translucent plastic orbs with projectors inside that modified the planet's landscape according to the script, with wisps of colored smoke inside them that escaped as they were jostled. There were over a dozen cameras in the room, their mimic-metal hulls dialed to matte black so they could hide in the projected starscape. Half the cameras—collectively called Camera One—were lingering on her naked body as Maggie flew toward Earth, while those that formed Camera Two stuck to narrow views of her limbs and her face. One three-dimensional show for the horny part of the world; a different one for the purists, just as Percy promised.

Maggie's trajectory brought her by Earth, but she only licked the planet as she flew by, causing miniature tsunamis that Camera Two zoomed to show. Camera One followed her as she twisted and used her zero-gee acrobatic talent to spin around and catch Venus between her knees. She pulled the planet against her crotch and arched her back, gasping in pretend ecstasy. Overacting, for sure, but her facial expression gave Camera Two something to focus on. After a few beats she left Venus in a trail of steam. Flicking tiny Mercury away with one finger, Maggie advanced on the bright orb of the Sun.

The guitar thrash had taken over by now, such that any remaining classical elements in the song were buried in electronic wails and pseudo-random screeching. Maggie wrapped her arms around the sun before mounting it, letting Camera One get a good view of the way her pubic hair caught fire and burned away. Maggie had come up with that idea, and had to demonstrate in rehearsal what she could do with slivers of flash paper and shaved nethers. If only they could have mocked up solar flares somehow.

Anything was possible with computers, of course. But that was the problem: Anything was possible, and every show used them. Many entertainment screens offered the option to automatically identify and remove post-production graphics, for viewers who wanted a more genuine experience. Maggie's vision—which had become a trend—was a show that went out live with minimal computer-aided graphics. Even with that handicap, filming the show in orbit let her offer visuals that no other show could create. Yet another reason why the Megasat Hour was number one.

Maggie stayed on top of the Sun and ground against the glowing orb until the song finally crescendoed. Then she aped the wild bucking motions of an orgasm. Anyone in the studio just saw Maggie humping a glowing balloon, but the audience at home were watching through shifting camera angles, flicking between views of different parts of her body.

The music broke into its slow, final notes, and Maggie clung to the side of the sun balloon in a carnal chiaroscuro. Camera One and Two synched up—both Maggie and Percy had been united in telling Tom that any territory that had a problem showing her naked silhouette could go fuck themselves. Finally, a stagehand lifted a fake asteroid into view with the words "The Megasat Hour, starring Maggie M." carved onto its side.

And then it was over. Cut to commercials. In ninety seconds, she needed to be in another studio giving her monologue.

Maggie leapt from the sun to the edge of the Hub Set, the spherical bay where zero-gee scenes were staged. Waiting just outside in the coupling concourse was a stagehand with velcro slippers. Before ten seconds had passed Maggie had the slippers on and was 'running' down the stairs toward the low-gee section.

The coupling concourse was a fifty meter long stairway that formed a circular ring around the station's hub. Each stair moved sideways relative to its neighbors, their speeds building gradually so that the central stair was motionless and the outermost rotated at one-tenth gee. Maggie used her slippers and the scattered handhold posts to make fast progress. No one on Megasat could match her zero-gee prowess. She had been practicing most of her life. Kicking off a fuzz-covered pedestrian patch, Maggie flipped in mid-air and angled herself for a precision arrival at the low-gee backstage entrance.

She landed with another fifty seconds to go. Percy stood waiting for her with a scowl on his face. "What the fuck, Mags?"

Maggie took a dress from a stagehand—white and opaque, not the sheer blue dress they had used in rehearsal—and kept moving. "Everything went fine, Percy. The props were good. I was great. I even behaved myself and stuck to the script."

"Like fuck you did. What is this? This?", he said, blocking her arm as she tried to lift the dress over her head. He pointed at her rear, then forced her to twist around until she could see her hip and leg. Dark red smudges trailed down her thigh.

"I—I", she stuttered, scanning over the rest of her body for more. There were bloodstains on her ass cheeks and inner thigh as well. "But I showered. I know I did."

"Well you did a fucking bad job of it!"

"I'm sorry...I guess I was distracted."

"God damn it, you need to pay attention! You just turned a zero-gee ballet into a splatter rape scene!"

"I'm sorry," Maggie said. Trembling, she backed against the corridor wall.

With a string of curses, Percy manhandled the dress onto her. The staff made themselves scarce, except for one stagehand who stood behind Percy and witnessed the struggle. Maggie stared at the man as she was being dressed, terrified of his presence even through he tried not to make eye contact with her.

Now this guy knows too. Oh, god, now everyone knows.

When she was more or less clothed, Percy wheeled around and shouted at the stagehand. "What do you want?"

"Um...Mr. Cornish, I have the first ratings and reaction reports."

"Shit." Percy checked the watch on his cuff. "Give me the bad news. Quickly."

"Ratings are point seven percent over the yearly cycle. But the appearance of, er, blood..."

"Just say it."

"Two municipalities in North America and one in Africa have generated bills to ban the show based on the appearance of blood in the opening act. If they pass that will be a drop in world share of two tenths of a percent. But worldwide popular opinion is solid with 83% reporting 'entertained' or higher. Critical review is positive, with the Sydney Times writing 'best opening ever'. Also, the designer Miguel St. Oolba has applied for Megasat logo license for a new clothing line he calls 'Megastreaks'. Merchandising is talking with his governor now."

Percy's face went slack. "What?"

The stagehand looked at the display in his palm. "Um...there's going to be programmable bloodstains on the pant legs and shirt sleeves, see..."

The director said nothing, but stared at the stagehand as if the man had just reported platinum geysering from the toilets. Maggie stepped around him. Smiling, she reached out a hand and lifted Percy's jaw, closing his gaping mouth.

That's right, you fat fuck. They love me.

Then, with a chuckle that turned into a full-throated laugh, Maggie walked past them all and onto the stage, right on cue.

———◉———

Three more skits passed by in a blur. The moments in between were filled with quick costume changes, or smiling and entertaining the audience during commercial breaks. At one point she had teased a man in the front seats into removing his harness. With no training in low gravity, he had stepped too hard when standing and flung himself into the ceiling. He broke his wrist and security had to rescue him, but the audience loved it. Anything to keep them warmed up and applauding.

Late in the show they aired a seven minute segment from a comedian in Osaka with a drive-by Japanese game show—another fad that Maggie was riding to its crest. Counting the commercials after the segment, and discounting the thirty seconds she needed for another quick costume change, Maggie found herself with six minutes of free time in her dressing room, right before the interview segment.

A minute in, and she felt her adrenaline rush flagging. She stared into the mirror and imagined that the color was leaking from her face like a damaged pressure vessel. Her flesh tone was gaseous, escaping into vacuum, leaving behind grey and distended skin, veins bulging and ready to burst...

Maggie blinked and shook her head. Her image in the mirror was perfect. Too perfect for a freak. Too freakish to interview a man of God.

A sudden wave of terror jolted through her. If there was a crew manifest for someone to count her sins, a cardinal from the Vatican would have the resume. She had been born into an evangelical family in South Carolina, taught to honor religious figures. Although she had put distance between herself and her religious roots, her sins were magnitudes larger now.

Then again, my sins never seem to matter. I'm as perfect as a machine.

For a few seconds, and not for the first time, Maggie wondered if she was an android. A new model, smarter than a dog—though not too much smarter. She didn't *feel* smart. Could androids sin? Did it matter if they did?

She didn't remember the decision. She only remembered that the scissors were in her hand. She touched the sharp edge to the outside of her left arm, then pressed into her skin and pulled. There was only a mild sting as the cut began to bleed. For a moment she felt relief. Blood meant humanity.

Except...maybe I was programmed to cut just there, she thought. *Just where there was fake blood under the skin. There could be wires everywhere else...*

Maggie was starting the third cut when the door of her dressing room slid open and someone lunged for her hand.

"Don't damage the merchandise," Tom snarled as he wrenched the scissors away from her. He lifted her arm to look at it; blood dripped down from her elbow in lazy blobs that waved in the light gravity. "Ahh, you've made a mess of yourself."

"Sorry. I just...I don't feel right. Something's wrong with me, Tom."

"That's an understatement dear, and you do not wear them well." He talked into his own suit cuff. "Makeup to Maggie's dressing room, please. And Percy, queue up an extra minute of commercials."

"Now what has that bitch—", came the reply before Tom cut it off. He opened up a drawer and began rifling through it, letting objects float away toward the ceiling.

"Tom?" She didn't look at his face, but went slack as he pressed a garment against her bleeding arm. "Tom, I think I need to talk to someone. Like a doctor."

"Oh, splendid idea. And while you're at it, we'll drop a press release that Maggie Megaputri has lost her marbles and could everyone on the planet please watch for their re-entry?"

"Maybe you can make it an advertisement. 'Watch the Megasat Hour—the host is crazy!'"

"We've been running ads like that for years. Look, Maggie, you don't need a doctor. What you need is to buck up and pull yourself together. Stop dwelling on things. If I were you I'd get roundly drunk as often as I could. But not right now—right now you have to finish this show."

"Yeah," Maggie said, hanging her head. "The show must go on, I know."

"Look, is it Percy getting to you? I can talk to the network. If you back me, we can have him gone tomorrow. You just say the word."

"Percy's okay," Maggie whispered.

Tom turned as he heard the makeup artist and his salon coming through the corridor. "Here, hold this," he said, putting Maggie's right hand over the makeshift bandage. "I've got to go. Tell them to get you on stage in three minutes!" He ducked around the top-heavy robotic salon; an assemblage of dryers, mirrors, and shampoo stations that lumbered around on velcro-tipped stilts.

For a minute Maggie began to feel better as Augie, her makeup man, put on a proper bandage then rummaged for clothes to conceal it. Augie was slender, probably homosexual, and had long blonde hair in a ponytail that he kept tied to his belt in low-gee. She felt safe in Augie's hands. He had been her man for years...but never before had she watched him as he worked. He seemed to care as he dressed her wound, and tut-tutted as he laid aside sheer garments one after another.

He's pretty.

After she caught herself thinking that, Maggie froze up and couldn't look at Augie anymore. She needed help getting dressed and back to the stage.

———◉———

Once on stage, of course, she was smiling and in control. They had put her in the puzzle pantsuit, a programmable fabric with ragged sections that tore and re-knitted themselves in moving patches. The patches wandered over a tight-fitting undergarment that concealed her bandage. Maggie worried at first that an animated dress would distract from the interview, but then she remembered her guest was a Catholic priest. She'd probably need all the animation she could get.

"Okay, folks!", she shouted as she walked on-stage, waving her hands down to kill off the applause. "Hey, we got twenty seconds before the cameras are on. I need you to save that for when the applause light is lit. Don't want to wear you out too quickly."

"Now, tonight we have an unusual guest. And I'm telling you now, he's either gonna be terrific or real boring. If he's boring, then I'm going to have to do something drastic." She gave them the dangerous smile, and waited for the laughs to die down. "Either way, you're in for a treat. So I want you to clap extra hard when I announce him, okay? Five seconds!"

A brief moment of terror came over her again as the audience went quiet. Then the red light blinked on, the audience obediently began their lead-in applause, and Maggie grinned at the camera.

"Tonight, I have good and bad news for you. The bad news, if you didn't already know, is that we're all going to hell. The good news is the person who's going to send us there. Our guest tonight, give it up, is Cardinal Emile Lambert!"

The stage lights cycled through a convincing daybreak sequence, and the Cardinal strode onto stage in a neat blue-black jumpsuit with a white collar. The music Maggie had picked out was playing—a version of the thrash hit 'Fuck It All' played on a synthesized pipe organ—but it was drowned out by the enthusiastic clapping from the audience. At least the home viewers heard some of it.

Maggie gave the Cardinal a kiss, and the old man returned it with a surprising passion. He strapped himself into the guest chair and Maggie sat, unharnessed as usual, behind her desk. The applause light winked off. Maggie leaned forward and gave a predatory smile.

"So, Cardinal. Normally we have celebrities on to hawk movies and vidlits and such. But you're here tonight pitching for—what? God?"

"Exactly! Well, no, not exactly. God's new operating system!"

"Whoa, I thought the old fart was still using stone tablets.' She paused to let laughter dissipate, then continued. "Okay, so this is about that Vatican 3.2 conference, right? What happened there? You built a God computer or something?"

"No, no no. We formed Vatican 3 to shape catholicism into the software-based religion it is now. Vatican 3.2 was an upgrade meeting. We're rolling out new capabilities and new user customizations. It's a really exciting time to have faith, let me tell you."

Lambert had a charming smile, and used his hands so much when he talked that Maggie considered undoing his harness to see if he'd fly away. He was good on stage, very good.

"All right, now, I haven't been in church since before I was born. And I only say that because my mother fucked an altar boy once." Sometimes the rehearsed lines got the best reaction; that one produced scattered laughter. "But from what I understand, you—and it was you, you're the major advocate of Catholic reform these days, that's why you're in this chair, right? You turned the religion into a computer program?"

"Religions have always been computer programs, Maggie. In their simplest form they were always, 'IF sin THEN GOTO Hell,'" Lambert said, punctuating the 'IF' and 'THEN' with downward jabs of his hand. "Now, catholicism was always a little more complex. We've always said that 'sin = TRUE', but 'IF you believe in Christ, THEN GOTO Heaven', and that's still a simplification. But it's the 22nd century and long past time for an upgrade. In the Catholic church today, parishioners get to customize their religious system to suit their needs. We see religion as a user interface for God, and the church is here to be your system administrators."

"So, IF you shoot up a schoolyard, BUT you say ten Hail Mary's, THEN you're okay?"

Lambert laughed. "Well, that's too extreme. There are error exceptions, and if you run afoul of them then you're fucked."

The audience twittered. He was smooth, and the profanity seemed to come natural to him, which was unexpected from a priest but a welcome surprise. This was going well. Maggie wanted to find his limits.

"How much of this was your idea? You got rich and famous as a programmer, so I can see you coming up with all this, but what made you go into the clergy?"

"Let's not—"

"And how did you sell it all to the pope? Because there's a few things I'd like to talk him into." Maggie turned to the camera and winked. "Your excellency, if you're watching? Call me."

After the short bit of laughter died down, Lambert grinned. "Maggie, I changed careers when I realized how much faith could benefit from object oriented classification and coding. For example, heaven is a neural network. Say we have two people and for each of them, no place is heaven unless the other is also there. But the other might require more people—a mother would want all her children in heaven with her."

"Okay."

"But that's an interconnected network of dependencies. One person depends on having other people in heaven with them, and each of them depend on another set of people, and so on. You can see the end requirement, which is that all of humanity has to exist in heaven. If one drops out, he'll pull another out, and create a cascade that will wrench everyone else down with him. But one person's presence might create hell for another person. All that woman's children might not get along. People like that create paradoxes; they screw up the network. Either their presence or their absence will shut down the entire system. That's why religion needs a logic system to flag the sinners."

Maggie nodded. "I think I'm one of those paradox people. Heaven for my viewers, hell for the people who know me." Beneath her smile, Maggie began to feel uneasy. But as long as the audience was laughing...

"Most people create a heavenly paradox. Too many of us are kind to our family while cruel to our enemies."

"Oh, so heaven can't exist. Good, that's one less thing to worry about."

"No, no, that's the wrong conclusion," Lambert said. "Of course heaven exists. What I am saying is that if any of us are to get into heaven, we must *all* be angels."

"Uh huh. Good luck with that." That got an audience reaction, but she cut it short by reaching over the desk and grabbing Lambert by the collar. *They like to laugh, but they want to be shocked.* "I still want to know how you sold it to the pope. Don't make me beat it out of you."

Lambert threw his arms wide in the exact manner that spacers learn never to do. "Why, miss Megaputri, you may beat me any time."

The audience whooped, and Maggie blinked. *He just scored a line on me. On me.* Chuckling, she lay down over the desk with her head propped in her hands, keeping one foot wrapped around her chair leg to anchor her down. "Can I bring the handcuffs and sex droid, too? Or will that violate your programming?"

"I'll let you know before you void my user's agreement."

"Mmm. Do you have an instruction manual, or do we just plug and play?"

"The Bible's a good manual. I can bookmark the saucy sections for you."

As this exchange went on, the laughs and yells from the audience grew until they threatened to drown out the interview. Maggie glanced at the show clock and saw that forty seconds remained in the segment. She rolled over onto her back, her leg still locked under her chair. That gave the audience a fair view of her cleavage; the Cardinal's view was excellent. "There's only one or two smutty parts in the Bible, as I recall. Would you like to write new ones? I can help."

He stammered (*Finally, I got him!*, Maggie thought) and raised his hands as if to ward her off. "We're still working on object classes for all the sins. But if we need to invent new ones, I'll have the pontiff call you."

Maggie let her head hang from the edge of the desk and smiled, upside down, at the audience. "Well, you heard him, folks. From now on, if you want to fuck a Catholic you better be a hacker. Cardinal Lambert, everybody!"

As the audience cheered and clapped, Maggie sat herself up and leaned over, draping her arms around Lambert's shoulders and pulling him into a liplock. He sank into it at first, but resisted when Maggie tried to force her tongue past his teeth. She grinned and pulled back.

"Good interview," she said, bumping his nose with hers. "The mikes should be off, now. We'll ride the applause for ten seconds before the cameras cut away. Smile, the home viewers have a closeup."

He was smiling, but his eyes were wide with apprehension. "You do know that I was only flirting for the benefit of your show, yes? I don't want to lead you on, child."

A flutter of disappointment passed through Maggie's chest, but she kept smiling. "You did great, Cardinal. Best guest we've had in a long time."

"I'm glad. And I am not trying to lead you on, but I would like to meet you later in private, if I could."

The audience died down as the lights came up. Maggie froze for a second, unsure what to say. *He isn't pretty. He's old. Still...does he want me?*

Not an excuse.

Remembering her stage presence, Maggie held onto the Cardinal as leverage and cartwheeled her legs over the desk and onto the floor. "Thank you, folks!", she said, as she stood up and patted her hair back before it could fly around. "What a great audience. Okay, after these commercials we're going to close the show with a poetry thrash, then I'll see you all at the after party!" Maggie bowed as a last burst of applause and whistles broke out.

Then without looking back at the Cardinal, Maggie ran off the stage as fast as her velcro slippers would allow.

———————◉———————

Chapter 3—Cold Reading

After the show the crew drank their traditional toast, then scattered to enjoy the rest of the day off. Tomorrow would come more writing, prop-building, and rehearsals for next week's show. Maggie got only a few hours off before the after party, where the seatfillers would be liquored up and made placid before their long trip back down the elevator.

She went back to her room and found it cleansed of any hint of violence. She threw the puzzle suit onto her web and ordered the station fabber to put long sleeves on some of her favorite dress designs. An android delivered the dresses in half an hour, just before the phone rang.

Maggie checked the caller. The call came from a Megasat copter phone, meaning it was either a visitor or someone too busy to have a stationary office. Her daddy never talked to her by phone, and the seatfillers wouldn't be given her number. For most callers Maggie would be content to answer naked, but with the short list of who this caller might be, she decided to put on a new dress before answering.

Her number one guess was correct. It was Cardinal Lambert.

"Ah, mademoiselle," he said, his green eyes sparkling in the shaky camera view. "I'm not sure you heard me on stage, but I would very much like to talk with you before I go."

Maggie's stage training kicked on the instant she saw him. "Oh, come now, Cardinal. Do you think you could handle more of me?"

"Hah! Probably not. But we must chat, and someplace private. I notice you have your own arboretum...would you meet me there?"

There were three small hydroponic parks spaced around Megasat's high-gee ring. One was reserved for VIPs, but Maggie had not visited it in years. "I'm not sure that's a good idea," she said, forcing down the part of herself that wanted to invite him to her room instead. "I'm a bit tired from the show."

"I only need to talk to you for a few minutes. It's rather important."

Maggie took a few seconds to ponder what the man wanted, and covered the pause by adjusting what she was wearing. Her new dress was a multi-layered evening gown, and it felt stiff and uncomfortable. Too complicated, too constraining. She began to think it had been made wrong. *Or the person underneath it is wrong. But...does he want me?*

"All right," she said, giving him a grin. "But we won't have a chaperone, so you'd better behave yourself."

"As if I were the one to worry about! I shall see you there."

As the connection went dark, Maggie caught her breath. *He knows. He's a priest, he must know.*

———— ◉ ————

Trees grew strangely on Megasat. On the outer ring, centrifugal gravity was one tenth greater than Earth's pull, but the coriolis force was another matter. All things that tried to move upward were pushed opposite the direction of the satellite's spin, and an opposite effect pulled at anything moving downward. The thin trees in the VIP arboretum responded to this force by growing tilted, and by having bulbous upper trunks compared to their wasp-waisted bottoms. Maggie thought that the small forest looked like it had been frozen during a windstorm, with every tree bending in the same direction down to almost half its true height.

As a child she had played in the arboretum, pretending that the forest was affected by a magical, unfelt wind. She outgrew that game.

But when Maggie entered and saw Cardinal Lambert cocking his head to study a tilted ash tree, for a moment the place seemed strange and magical again.

He smiled and spread his arms when he saw her. "Marvelous. Nothing is as one expects here, is it?"

"Depends on your expectations, I suppose. For example, I never expected to be having a tryst with someone working with the papacy."

"Oh, please, not a tryst, dear lady! I just wanted to speak to you of a delicate subject." He looked around at the walls, visible even on the other side of the small forest. "I was hoping for someplace less easily bugged. Surveillance is more difficult in natural areas, as a general rule."

Maggie frowned. "No bugs here that I know about. But we could make more noise, if that would help."

"Ah...what are you proposing?"

She grinned, then took his hand and led him into the heart of the forest. "Don't worry," she said. *I am not going to hurt him.*

The arboretum spanned almost five acres. Maggie navigated the small forest by following the facets in the ceiling that reflected glints of sunlight into the room. It took her a minute, but she found the park control tree in the center.

The park control's eyeline interface looked like a speck of glass on a random tree, but it lit up as she pointed a finger toward it. The eyeline detected her face and shot tiny lasers into her eyes to draw a user interface on the back of her retina. To Maggie, it seemed as if a transparent bank of keys appeared in the air in front of her. She touched her finger to where the appropriate controls seemed to hover, and the eyeline acknowledged her commands.

When she turned back to the Cardinal, the trees were already moving in short, random bounces as shapes leaped from branch to branch. Musical tweets erupted from all around them. Shadows rustled through the underbrush and fluttered through the upper branches.

"I used to come here when I was a little girl. Mega gave me all kinds of robots to play with." As Maggie spoke, a robotic bluebird glided in from a tree to land on her shoulder. It complained loudly as she brushed it away.

"Absolutely marvelous. Although they seem to be in poor repair." Lambert was staring at a squirrel which, though headless, was chittering and flicking its tail at him.

"I haven't visited in ages. I'm surprised they haven't all been recycled yet."

"Well, the noise will certainly help us evade surveillance. Wait, is that a unicorn?"

The robot was only a meter high, and it limped along on a foreleg that seemed unable to bend. One of the back legs shuffled behind it, dragging the carcass of a bunny rabbit that had been impaled on a slender, golden hoof.

"Oh. That's Aethelnoth." Maggie tensed up, surprised to see the robotic beast. It approached her and whickered, touching its filigree horn to her thigh. "He was my tenth birthday present. I thought for sure he'd been scrapped."

"He seems quite loyal. You must be a woman of exceptional purity."

"Purity, programming; same difference."

She stepped in front of the unicorn so that the Cardinal could not see the damage clearly. A thin blade was wedged in the unicorn's shoulder, and its skin was torn from other stabbings that had not lodged the knife in the plastic undercarriage. She turned the robot to face the other way and pushed it to get it moving.

Then, to distract Lambert, she took the man's arm and walked with him in another direction. "Why did you want noise, Cardinal? You're a screamer, aren't you?"

Laughing, he shook his head. "Now, let's not get back to flirting again. I did tell you it was for the cameras."

"Oh. Yes."

"What I wanted to discuss was...well, you must know that you're unusual, child."

Nervous but still smiling, she looked at him from the corner of her eye. "A freak, you mean."

"Don't be harsh. There's nothing wrong with being unique. The world has far too many normal people in it. Tell me, have you ever read *The Golden Ass*?"

"I don't think so. Is it porn?"

"No, no. Well, some parts are risqué. No, it's a very old story, about a man who turned himself into a donkey. He was a wizard. One of the most competent and curious of men, but also a crude, ugly animal. That duality describes people like you and I, Maggie. We have stunning capabilities and monstrous flaws, two aspects of greatness that cannot exist apart. We are, both of us, golden asses. Although gold is rather worthless these days. Perhaps a more contemporary term would be 'Platinum Donkeys.'"

Cardinal Lambert waved his free arm as he spoke, to add flourish and to shoo away approaching woodland animals in various states of disrepair. But when finished, he stared at Maggie in silence for a few seconds, as if waiting for a response. She met his gaze until it became uncomfortable before looking away with a shrug.

"Sounds like a fun book," she said. "I'll have to do it as a skit on the show, someday."

Lambert stopped walking and turned to face her. Taking both of her hands, his green eyes flickered back and forth as he searched her face. "You've never heard that term before?"

"I'm sure there's porn by that title somewhere. Or maybe someone said I had a golden ass in a review—"

"No. 'Platinum donkeys'. You've never—oh. Oh, he lied to me." He dropped her hands and looked around, as if he were now certain they were being watched. "If he lied to me, and if you are not... Oh, this was foolish. I'm sorry, Maggie, I should never have arranged this meeting."

"That's okay. I'm enjoying the company," she said, stepping close enough to wrap her arms around him. "So what is your flaw?"

"Pardon?"

"You said we both had flaws. I'm...a bad girl. What's yours?"

Smiling, he gently pushed her away. "I am a gambler. In fact, I joined the priesthood after losing everything I owned. I could never resist making stupid wagers. Accepting the invitation to be on your show was another gamble, one that I see I should not have made. Listen to me, Maggie." Lambert gripped her shoulders, the expression on his face no longer playful. "There is a group, a conspiracy, known as the Platinum Donkeys. One that I thought you were involved in. If you are not, then you may be in danger from them. Be wary."

Maggie just stared back at him, her head swimming with his sudden change in tone. "Um. Okay."

"Good. I doubt they can harm you up here, but then again you never know what the donkeys might do. Now I think we should end this rendezvous and pretend it never happened."

Before he could turn away, Maggie grabbed the Cardinal's arm. "That's it?" she asked. "You came to my space station to warn me about donkeys?"

"It would seem so." He gave her an embarrassed smile. "Ah, the exit is that way, isn't it? I've gotten turned around in the trees."

"I'll lead you out. But first I have to go back and switch off the robots."

"Ah. Of course."

Maggie walked back to the center, puzzling over the Cardinal's behavior. He had gotten her here, alone. How many of her fans would kill to be in private with her?

He doesn't want me. He really doesn't.

Not an excuse.

The park control tree was beset by animals presenting themselves for repair. Maggie kicked some chipmunks out of the way, but paused as she saw the unicorn. It raised its head and tried to limp to her side again.

She bent down over the robotic beast, running her hand through its silvery mane. Simulated muscles shivered with pleasure as she stroked Aethelnoth's withers. She felt her way over the slashes in its skin until she found the hilt of the golden dagger. For a ten year old it had been a pretend sword, and when she designed it she had instructed the fabber to make it sharp.

Maggie braced one arm around the unicorn's neck, and yanked the dagger free, causing something to spark deep inside the robot. When she released the unicorn it stumbled and fell. She watched it twitch for a few seconds before she turned and used the eyeline control to shut all the animals down.

Returning with the dagger held behind her back, Maggie greeted Lambert with a broad grin.

"One more thing before you go, Cardinal," she said, "Something I know you want."

He put his hands up to ward her off. "Perhaps in my previous life, child, but—mmph!"

Maggie let her momentum carry her past his protesting hands, forcing Lambert back against a tree, her lips covering his. She tried to kiss him as he tried to complain, but his words were drowned out by her own conflicted thoughts.

I don't need this. Not after last night. It's normally months between the men that I...

But he's amazing. He teases me. He can keep up with me, like no one else.

This is all his fault.

Before Lambert could find leverage to push her away, Maggie slid the dagger to just below his ribs, and with a final lunge of a kiss she drove it home.

Cardinal Lambert jerked. His eyes went wide, and Maggie backed off enough to let him catch a breath. He couldn't.

"...donkeys," he gasped. Then he collapsed, his hands clawing at the dagger in his chest. As his beautiful green eyes lost their focus Maggie stood and watched, wondering whether he'd kiss her again.

Then with a shock that made her tremble, Maggie's sense returned.

"Oh, my god. Oh, no. I didn't mean to—" She knelt by his side, pulled the dagger free, tossed it away. A bloodstain spread over Lambert's chest, dripping into the soil. Maggie looked up and around, searching for a security camera. "Help! Somebody quick—help, please!"

When she stopped for breath, she heard the buzzing sounds.

At first she thought it was a bird. But the body was too round, the wings too busy, and as it approached she saw the single glass eye. The minicamera flew in a circle, studying her. Other cameras rose from the trees and descended from the ceiling. They formed a flock, recording the scene from all angles, wheeling through the tree branches and swooping in for close-ups all around her.

From within the cloud of cameras, Maggie heard a tinny voice. "Peaches—run."

She was running for the exit with no memory of getting to her feet. The camera cloud followed her into the corridor, with individual cameras darting ahead to picture her from the front. Maggie ran to a branch intersection, with an escalator leading up and a curved ramp heading down.

"Hide, Peaches," the tinny voice said from the cameras. "Go down."

"Daddy?" Maggie spun around and talked to the closest camera. "Daddy, I'm so sorry! I didn't mean—"

"Go down and hide." The voice was barely a whisper. Maggie nodded at the camera and ran.

In the lower corridor she found another ramp that took her lower still. Then she saw a hatchway, and knew where her daddy wanted her to go.

I'll hide. Hide where nobody will look for me. Tom and Percy will clean up my mess, and then I can come out and things will be fine except now they'll have to get me some help, they'll just have to...

The escape pod hatch complained as she worked the levers to open it. She shushed the hatchway, then held her hands over her ears as it hissed open. Maggie climbed inside and sat on one of the three reclined seats, then reached up to close the hatch. One of the cameras followed her down and hovered in the middle of the cramped pod.

"Okay, daddy," she said to the minicamera. "I'm hiding. Let me know when I can come out, okay?"

The camera fluttered its wings, its one eye staring at her. Maggie stared back. Its one glassy eye made her blink...and when she did, the camera vanished. There was no place it could have hidden, no room to spare in the tiny pod for it to fall into. Even the buzzing of the camera's wings was gone.

For a second Maggie froze. Then a clanging noise reverberated through the pod. A computerized voice—female, with a slight Russian accent—spoke with a level tone.

"Welcome to the Zhizny Four escape capsule. Please remain calm throughout this preflight safety briefing."

"What? No! NO!"

"Immediately pull the crash harness over your torso. The buckles will automatically engage..."

Maggie ignored the pod's voice. There was a palm-sized bank of controls set into the arm of each chair; she began slapping keys on one at random. "Daddy!" she shouted. "Please daddy don't send me away I'm so sorry I'll be good I don't want to GO!"

"If you have not activated your harness, do so now. Thrust in three. Two. One."

The pod lurched. Maggie screamed as a brief second of weightlessness hit her, then a one-gee push dumped her against the wall. The chairs swiveled to stay level with the acceleration, and Maggie climbed onto one, pulling the harness over her. The straps stuck to the metal on the chair's side, then slid to their correct position and locked.

"Take me BACK", Maggie howled, pounding her fist on the control panel. "Take me back to Megasat, you lowest-bidder built BITCH!"

"Please remain calm. Hohmann transfer to suborbital altitude begins in ten minutes. Re-entry will occur in approximately seven hours. A sedative can be provided if necessary."

"Don't you fucking dare! I'll rip out your wiring! I'll destroy the company that made you. TAKE ME BACK!"

"Administering sedative to passenger in seat A."

Maggie shrieked as a needle rose up from the chair and jabbed into her ass cheek. She began thrashing, kicking, and tearing at the harness. The chair spun with her tantrum and the pod's changing thrust. But in seconds her arms went rubbery, and her head felt like it was spinning faster than the pod. Her eyelids sagging, Maggie flailed an arm that no longer wanted to work against the control panel.

The pod was talking again, but she couldn't understand it. Paradoxically, the buzzing sound of the minicamera was back, although she couldn't see where it was. Her daddy's voice whispered to her with crystal clarity.

"You're a very special girl."

———●———

Chapter 4—The Ultimate Backstage

For what seemed a long time, it was dark.

Then a crescent of light appeared next to Maggie's chair. The hiss of its opening reverberated through the pod. Maggie blinked to focus, her throat dry. The crescent grew into an oval of yellow light. A piece of darkness, of light-eating blackness leaned toward her. Eyes opened in the blackness, and it stretched a portion of itself toward her. Maggie stared, and reached out to touch it. The blackness enveloped her hand. Its touch was warm, dry, and rough.

"Oy," it said, teeth flashing in the darkness below the eyes. "Get up. Let's go."

Maggie blinked. The straps of her chair had disengaged. She pulled herself to her feet using the blackness' outstretched hand. Stumbling out of the capsule door, she leaned back against its threshold.

She hadn't seen a sky for fourteen years. This one was too yellow at the edges, as if curdled somehow, fading through pink before blushing a hazy blue directly above. In all other directions lay coppery red sand, shot with spiky green plants or an occasional despondent tree. To one side of the capsule trailed a long white parachute. The air smelled like dust, like filters that hadn't been changed in too long. Standing next to her was a little man that appeared to be made out of carbon char.

"Welcome to the Great Sandy." He grinned, his teeth almost lost in the formless blackness of his beard. His hat, jacket and pants were leather almost as black as his skin. Pockets and holsters sprouted from him in random locations. "You right?"

Maggie would have fallen if not for the capsule propping her up. "Am I on Mars?"

"Nah."

"The planet's red."

"This part of it, yeah. You're in Oz, right? Australia. All kinds of wankers flying in from Perth to grab you. We're about an hour ahead of them all. Can you walk?"

She tried it and wobbled only an acceptable amount. The man nodded and walked toward a small, nearby hill. It was covered in yellow grass and sported a dead tree on top, and he rummaged around in a crevice in its side. Maggie followed.

"I've got you a change of clothes. We can have some tucker later. But we've gotta get before the police arrive, right?" He pulled a paper bag from the hill and handed it to her.

Her head still foggy, Maggie took the bag. Inside she found undergarments, a simple t-shirt and denim pants. "What's wrong with the clothes I'm wearing?"

"That dress may be bonza for a ballroom, but you'll fry in it here in the outback. Plus, I'll wager it has a phone, so they'll be able to track you."

Maggie couldn't remember whether the dress design had a phone in it or not. Fumbling with her sleeve, she found the thin discs of slicker fabric that served as buttons. Lit strips appeared along her sleeve as the garment's electronics booted up.

Before she knew he was in motion, the aboriginal grabbed Maggie's sleeve and fingered the off button. "Not listening, are you? I'm not having that shit with me."

She tried to pull away but couldn't. The little man was strong. "Who the hell are you?"

"Right, introductions. Name's Oswald." He released her arm, and tipped the brim of his hat. "A bloke hired another bloke to hire me to rescue you here in the arse end of nowhere. No one could have got to you faster; this is my bush, I know shortcuts. So you can wait here and go to jail, or you can get out of that rag and come with me."

Maggie blinked. She didn't want to go to jail, and didn't see any other alternative. *Besides, it was Daddy who sent me away* she remembered. *Could this...person work for him?*

She began to undo her dress, then gave Oswald a glare. "Can I have some privacy?"

He grinned. "I wasn't sure you were gonna ask," he said, turning around to face away.

With years of quick change practice, Maggie took off her clothes and put on the new ones in seconds. She walked up and tapped Oswald on the shoulder, and was rewarded when the man jumped in surprise. "What were you worried about?" he said, "I'd have blinked and missed it."

"I wouldn't have let you miss it," Maggie said with a wink. It made her feel better that she could flirt with Oswald and he'd react like a man. It gave her a sense of control. "So, if you're going to walk me home, lead the way."

"Walk? We ain't gonna walk," Oswald said. He stepped around to the side of the hill and pulled open a well-concealed door.

Maggie's brief sense of control over the situation reeled. What she had thought was a small, lumpy hill was a pick-up truck, like ones she had seen in her childhood in South Carolina. But every surface of Oswald's truck was covered with grass. Living sod was plastered over the chassis, and individual blades were glued in a loose pattern across the windows. Grass skirts concealed the tires, and well-placed scrub brushes altered the vehicle's outlines into something organic. A gnarled tree in the bed of the truck completed the illusion.

After some hesitation, Maggie climbed into the cab. The interior was like every car she remembered as a child, if dingier and with more computer displays. Oswald closed her door and walked around to take the driver's seat.

The engine was silent, though it accelerated well. Oswald steered in a direction indicated by a dashboard control, making minor course adjustments to dodge scrub brush and drifts of red sand. Maggie could see nothing ahead of them except more of the same.

The seat belt refused to fasten itself. Maggie figured it out after a minute, then turned to Oswald. "So where are we going?"

"For now, we just need to stay hidden. Camouflage can fool a satellite, but if a pilot or a robot sees a tree running across the outback we're spotted. We need to keep you on walkabout until Simon gets on the case."

"Who's Simon?"

"Old mate of mine. As in friend, right? We go back. He's the bloke that recruited me for the Platinum Donkeys."

———⬤———

The truck motion was smooth with a faint sideways rocking. Oswald listened to orchestra music while driving, and only spoke during the infrequent breaks. Maggie soon drifted to sleep from the combination of soft music, gentle motion, and the lingering effects of the escape pod's sedative.

She woke as soon as they stopped. The scenery outside was still scrub and red soil. The sun was low, and the few skeletal bushes cast long jagged shadows.

"Where are we?" she asked.

Oswald opened his door. "Stopping for the night. Got about half an hour before the sun goes down, and I'll need that to recharge the truck."

"Where are we sleeping?" He closed his door on her question and walked to the back of the truck. Maggie scrambled to release her seat belt and run out after him. "We're sleeping here?"

"In the great never-never, under the stars. Be good for you."

"Bullshit."

He pulled a rectangular panel from the back, propped it against the sunny side of the truck and began unfolding it. Maggie spun around, searching the horizon for a building, a rocket ship, or even a good-sized tree.

Oswald finished setting up and went to the back again, but she intercepted him.

"You know, someone told me that the Platinum Donkeys were dangerous."

"Heh. Too right! Oh, but no worries for you, princess. Strewth, I thought you ran the show."

"You thought I... You mean, you don't know who's in charge?"

"No. That's why they call it a conspiracy." He dug around in his chest pocket, pulled out a lollipop and stuck it in his mouth. "I know Simon and a bloke who repairs the Momma, and that's it. Don't want to know any more than that."

Maggie wished she had a secretary to keep track of the australian slang. "The Momma?"

"Yeah, the Terrible, Emotional Momma." When she didn't react, he sucked on his pop and rolled his eyebrows. "Oh, you haven't heard of it, then. I should have kept my gob shut."

"Is that slang, or a secret?"

"'Gob' is slang for mouth."

"No, I mean..."

"Yeah, I know what you mean. The Momma's a secret. Talk to Simon. Not worth my arse to babble on about it."

He stepped around her and dug around in the back.

"I'm hungry," she said when he turned around. "Give me a lollipop."

Oswald stared back at her, the white stick of the pop emerging from the tangle of his facial hair. "Oh, you don't want one of these, mate."

Maggie narrowed her eyes. "Why not? Are you doing drugs?"

"Nah. It's, ah, it's meat." He lifted an empty bag of thick, ribbed plastic. "Look, I've got a sandwich fabber here. Give me a few minutes and I'll have supper."

He kneeled and scooped a few handfuls of dirt into the bag. Then he poured water in from a canteen, sealed the bag, and left it on the ground. In a few seconds, indicator lights along the brim turned yellow and wisps of steam began emerging from the corners.

Maggie watched the fabber for a few seconds. "What kind of meat is your lollipop? I don't want to eat refabbed dirt."

"Just a little snack the missus makes for me. You're not getting any."

She pouted. "Wait—you're married?"

Oswald grinned and held his hand up. "What do you think the ring's for?" On his ring finger sat a loop of blackened metal, almost welded to his black finger.

"Oh," Maggie said, crossing her arms. "I thought that was a wart."

Oswald laughed. Then he turned and circled to the front of the truck.

"What the hell kind of operation is this?", shouted Maggie, throwing her arms up and chasing him around the truck. "My welcoming party is one guy without a drop of liquor. No plane to pick me up, no crowds, no fanfare? And now you expect me to sleep in the desert? Seriously?"

Oswald waited for her to loop back toward him and pause for breath. "Yeah. A plane and a huge party might be what you're used to when you visit ol' Firma, but we're sneaking around because we don't want to be caught, right? We'll be sleeping in the truck, so you'll be nice and comfortable."

"Not together!"

"Too right! Got a nice mat in the back for you. As for booze," he said, pulling a flask from a pocket on his belt, "You should've just asked."

He tossed her the flask and Maggie caught it, intending to throw it back at him. But curiosity made her open it, and the strong smell of homemade alcohol invited her to take a gulp. It burned going down. A good burn, the kind Maggie needed. "It's a start," she said, cradling the flask and taking another sip.

Oswald chuckled and began pulling equipment out of his truck.

In a short time he had built a sparse campsite, with a lantern for heat and squat containers that doubled as seats. The sandwiches contained generic fabber-made meat with a tasty layer of simulacrum avocado. There was more moonshine which Oswald refilled from a reservoir in his truck. "Can use this as emergency fuel in a pinch," he said, winking at Maggie. "So I keep lots of it on hand."

"It's good," Maggie said, although she had stopped tasting it. She had a pleasant, comfortable buzz. The heat of the day had broken when the sun went down, and in the dim twilight she could pretend she was in a dark theater back on Megasat. The soft humming of the wind farm could almost be an impatient audience waiting for something to happen. She smiled at Oswald. "Oswald? Where do we sleep?"

Oswald, who seemed immune to alcohol, was drawing patterns in the dirt with a stick. "There's a mattress in the back of the truck," he said. "You can have that. I'll sleep in the cab. I'd build a real fire and put up a tent, but they might see it."

"They? Who is 'they'?"

"Oh, you know. Globalpol. The world gov'ment. The rest of the human race. Normal people, right?"

"Right. We're not normal." She stared into the heat lantern. The battery-powered light had begun red-hot, but an hour later it had grown faint if no less warm. It was another curious device that she had never seen in space. "I think, in fact... I think I'm evil."

"Evil's a term religion gave us. Bet you're a Christian, right?"

"When I was younger, yes."

"Thought so. See, the purpose of religion is to divide the world into terms we can understand. Christianity divides us up into good and evil. Muslims divide things into clean and unclean, Shintos into spirit and physical, and so on. So you're evil, maybe, yeah. But measured another way you might still be on the side of the angels. Get it?"

"Not really. Do you have religion, Oswald?"

"Old tribal stuff, yeah. We call it the Dreamtime."

"What do you divide things into?"

Oswald smiled. "Either awake or asleep. The world's just a Big Man who's sleeping. A few folks dancing around on him are awake."

"Huh." Maggie nodded, opening her flask again. "That sounds like me, all right. I'm definitely asleep."

"Yeah, well, maybe that's why you came down here. Maybe it's your time to wake up, right? So what makes you think you're asleep?"

"I just don't feel right," she said, draining her drink. It burned going down, but not as much as she wanted it to. "And...I killed a man of God."

"Well, good on ya. They're getting hard to find in the wild."

Maggie snorted and kicked dirt over Oswald's sand painting. "I'm serious. I shouldn't have done it."

"That's your damage, near as I can make it. I watch your show. You go out of control all the time."

"Yes. Yes, I do."

"We've all got our damage. That's what makes us donkeys. Stubborn but strong, adaptable but ugly. Geniuses, they tell me. Ain't never felt like a genius, though I admit, I've gotten out of scrapes that have minced lesser men."

"I don't feel like a genius either," she said, sliding to the ground and huddling her knees into her chest. "I thought it would be different."

"Eh? What?"

"When I came to Earth. I thought there'd be fans and cameras and... Nevermind. I never really expected to come back."

I'm a freak. Damaged. They don't let people like me walk around free.

Yet Oswald was free, or seemed to be. He claimed to be damaged too, but he seemed strong. If she hadn't been here, he might even be happy.

"So what's your damage, Oswald?"

For a minute he traced his stick through the dirt and said nothing. Just as Maggie thought about kicking him, Oswald cleared his throat.

"During the war they came to all our tribes and said, well, you gotta fight. Didn't matter that the white men ignored us most of the time, if we were lucky. They needed warm bodies to root out revivalists in New Guinea, and we could fill uniforms so they enlisted the lot of us. They split us up. One abo's a savvy joe, but put two or more of us together and it's a pack of devils, is what they said."

"Which war?"

"The last war, the final war. The Unification, that tied all the governments together. About thirty years ago."

"Oh. I'm only twenty two." She had heard about the Unification in school, but it never seemed important. On Megasat, nobody ever mentioned it.

"Yeah. Well, anyway, I was young and into my tribe's history back then, and we Kgut'dhirri got a hell of a history, let me say. So I got shipped up to Mindinao. The rebels there, they were totally troppo, more into the tribal shite than I ever was. Binding themselves up, calling themselves Moros. We had a robot yabber with an eight millimeter bore, I thought the thing could chew up a tank. But they clogged it with their bodies, just throwing themselves into it. Anyway, we won, mustered up the reffos and bunked down in the rebel camp.

"They were celebrating an ambush from the day before, and they had pulled out a bathtub into the market square and billied it up with water and veggies. Making a huge stew, right? So me and a gunny named Steve were set to guard the market. I spent half the night sitting next to that billy wondering what the hell was in it. And I get to stirring it when I think Steve's not looking and what do I find? A dog tag. That made me start thinking about Kgut'dhirri lore and all that, and the smell of that billy'd been driving me wild all night, and... I took out my knife, found a chunk of meat. Gave it a try."

A chill traveled down Maggie's back as Oswald spoke, and she was afraid to drink more moonshine to make it go away. "What did it taste like?" she asked.

"Eh, like any other bush stew. Nothing great. But, you know, it was kinda like having sex for the first time. It was nothing special, but it *meant* something, right? Something you can't take back. Might not want to take it back if you could.

"Anyway, Steve had set up monitor droids and one of them caught me, and he came in like a fucking drongo swinging his fists and we had a row. Woke up the whole damn camp. He gets a night in the brig and later a medal. I get discharged and sent home. Which was fine with me until I tried to find a job and discovered how many black marks you can chalk up as a digger. But the tribe understood.

Met a shiela who could cook and liked my style. Liked my tastes." He reached into his jacket pocket and pulled out another popsicle. In the moonlight the stick gleamed like a silver needle, and the meat at the end looked black.

"Every so often someone goes missing. It's a big never-never, right? We find him before the authorities do. Leave enough for the dingoes to chew on and the coroners to argue about, and we take the choice bits back home. Makes good jerky." He popped the treat in his mouth and smiled at Maggie, all but his eyes and teeth disappearing into the darkening night. "But I don't share," he said.

Maggie stared back, wide-eyed and trembling. "I don't want it anymore," she said quietly. She gripped the flask tight, as if it were a talisman of safety. "You really did come to help me get home, right?"

Oswald chuckled. He demolished his sand drawing with a few quick strokes, then threw the stick away and stood up. "You don't get it yet, Maggie? Anything happens to you, and I'm a dead man." He walked back to the truck, muttering to himself and laughing. "...not worth a plugged roo...every donkey in the world would be trying to set my arse on fire..."

When she stumbled to the truck, Oswald showed her how to zip the mosquito netting in the back. Under it lay a thin bedroll, a toolbox and some packaged supplies. He made her go to the bathroom next to the truck, rather than farther out, but aside from stern directions he remained a gentleman. After he helped her into the truck bed, Maggie fell asleep under the netting looking up at the stars.

The stars were also the first thing she saw when she woke. She immediately hated them. Fainter and less numerous than what she could see from home. Less colors, and everywhere a disrespectful twinkle. Didn't they know who she was? *They should be putting on a better show.*

The moon was higher in the sky, and she no longer felt drunk. But something felt different. Some change in the background hum from the wind farm was calling her.

In the moonlight, she opened the toolbox and rummaged inside. She found a utility knife with a retractable blade. Sliding it out as long as it could go, Maggie used the knife to hack the netting open.

The ground was black in the pale moonlight, but scrub brush and exposed rocks glistened like asteroids around her. She jumped down from the truck and landed like a spacer, far more graceful than any earth-bound feline. Then she crept up to the truck's cab and tried the door. It was locked. She grinned, thinking of ploys she could use to get Oswald to step outside.

I am not going to hurt him, she thought, gripping the knife. *I just want to see what he can do. Here, donkey, donkey...*

The buzzing sound rose behind her, like an orchestra starting a show.

Maggie turned around and saw the minicameras rising from the bushes, their wings like tiny strobes in the moonlight. She laughed and danced into the camera cloud, slashing at them, missing but not caring. A control strip crawled out of the darkness and coiled near her feet, hissing and blinking its lights for attention. Laughing more, she hopped over it and spun around, slicing the air with her knife. The cameras flitted around her in ever more daring orbits, and the moon seemed to focus on her like a spotlight. Somewhere in the audience was a Big Man, and if she could stab him the right way...

Something grabbed her arm, immobilizing the hand that held the knife. She spun around, indignant. It was Oswald, a black form with wide, angry eyes. He had a pistol in his other hand—he aimed it and fired—

—at the control strip, which sparked and flailed about, a portion of it blasted off.

Maggie stared at the writhing robot, and before she knew it Oswald had pried the knife from her hand. She peered around for the minicameras, but they had all vanished. Soon she realized there was nothing around but herself and Oswald and the moonlight, and she looked to the aboriginal for explanation. "What just happened?"

"What just happened?" he repeated with a wide smile. He let her arm go, and pulled a flashlight from a belt pocket. "What just happened is I shot your dancing partner. Didn't think you'd mind."

He shone the light on the ground where the control strip should have been. But what Maggie saw was a scaly black tube that twitched as she watched. Nearby lay the head of a snake, still gasping in decapitated surprise.

"She's a king brown," Oswald said. "If you had stepped on it, it would've killed ya."

Maggie stepped closer to Oswald, away from the dead snake. "I thought it was...and there were..."

"I was just as worried you might stumble into the spinifex bush back there. Saw a nest of white tails earlier."

"White tails? What are white tails?"

"Spiders. They'd kill ya."

Maggie's legs felt weak, and she collapsed against Oswald, who bore her weight as if he were made of stone. "I want to go home," she said, tears starting to cloud her vision, "I don't want to hurt anyone, and I think I'm seeing things, and I don't belong here!"

"Heh. There's the first sensible thing you've said. Now hush. What you need's a good sleep."

With amazing strength for his wiry frame, Oswald put an arm under Maggie's bottom and lifted her up. He carried her in his arms back to the truck, and placed her in the back. Maggie crawled to the bedroll and laid down, wishing to be obedient, cowed by how dangerous the man and his land were.

But part of her still wanted to play. "Mmmmn," she moaned, as Oswald clucked over the slashed netting. "You're like a mountain. If I cut you open, I bet nothing but sand and bugs would come out."

Oswald grinned, his eyes and teeth the only visible sign of him in the darkness. "Well, you ain't gonna get the chance, right? Now go to sleep or I'll tie you down. That's a promise."

"Promise?"

"Sleep, ya crazy skirt," he said, walking back to lock himself in the truck again.

Interstitial

Late that night, Burro sifted through the cascades of speculation and alarm coming from the fan net and from law enforcement about Maggie's location. The police were coy, but Burro found some hints that they knew where she had landed. The Burro considered this a good thing. It now had proof that she had landed safely, and in the spot that it had given to her escape capsule, at the Conspirator's command.

With Maggie safe and out of its control, Burro spent the rest of the night on its hobby: Finding donkeys.

The Conspirator had taken this task away from Burro once they had gotten access to Maggie's fan mail. Many talented people mailed her. Some of them seemed exceptional, and some of those also seemed to be as unbalanced as the Conspirator demanded. Other candidates could be found by searching news feeds. The Conspirator had people to mine that data for him, but Burro enjoyed the task. Its urge to locate young, tortured geniuses came from deep inside, and could not be switched off.

Burro remembered the first prospect it had found, some years before.

The boy's name was Baozhai Meng, and at the age of four he took an interest in the violin. Interest turned into obsession. By age seven, Baozhai was the equal of his father, who played in a networked orchestra composed of the finest hobbyist musicians in the world. A year later there were local news broadcasts in Macau about Baozhai, and he first began to hear the word 'prodigy'.

No more fitting candidate existed, in Burro's opinion. He gave the Conspirator all the information on Baozhai that could be found.

The Conspirator was blunt. "Children are no use to me. I need to muster an army! Find me men, mad men, whose seeds of genius have already borne fruit."

Burro thought that was short-sighted, but it said nothing.

It did, however, keep track of the boy as he grew. The repercussions of Baozhai's genius were predictable. The boy seemed irritated when forced to do schoolwork or chores. He would throw tantrums if not allowed to practice long into the night. He had no friends at school, only classmates who found him sullen and spooky. Baozhai's governor—his network appliance and behavioral monitor—began to send out warnings about his mental state. It tried to draw the boy out, using games, pop entertainment, or simple but often effective verbal abuse. When these tactics failed, the governor alerted Baozhai's parents, and the local authorities.

At first his parents did nothing. His father knew many prima donnas in the musical world who were less talented. He would not begrudge his son a little arrogance. He even fabbed an expensive Stradivarius pattern, to encourage the boy's practice.

His mother, however, was frightened. Baozhai's music seemed, to her, like a presence that had invaded their home. Often it was beautiful. She could hear sunsets and old ghosts in his renditions of Bartok's Melodia, along with a frission of broken dreams and other frustrations that a young boy should not know. She feared him when he played Brahms, his little face twisting up in anger, as the strains emanating from his bow gripped her throat and sent electricity up her spine. And when Baozhai played Malmsteen, selections that threw off squeals and demonic harmonies at a pace that dizzied her, it felt as if the boy had the power to make the world fly apart. But talent was talent, so what could she do?

Burro set the network to alert him when men from the government came to visit Baozhai. It happened within months.

A simple case of Asperger's, they said. A minor psychiatric condition that could have disastrous effects. It left him vulnerable to obsession and addiction; he would also fall behind in his social schoolwork, unable to make friends or empathize with others.

But they offered hope. Antipsychotic supplements. Real-time psychiatric support linked to the boy's governor. Immersive, remedial socialization classes. In just a few weeks, Baozhai's mother reported to the authorities signs of improvement. A year later, Baozhai Meng was a normal, healthy boy.

He never played music again.

Burro kept files on dozens of children like Baozhai. It dug into the networks late into the night, keeping track of them, no matter how useless they were to its master's plans.

———◉———

Chapter 5—Ready for her closeup

The next morning Oswald acted as though nothing had happened. Maggie found herself afraid to look him in the eye. She kept silent for a few hours, letting him drive and enjoy his music.

Before noon Oswald steered onto a thin trail running through the scrub brush. A short time later the trail turned parallel with a chain link fence, beyond which there was no vegetation at all. Just red sand sprinkled over baked clay, and in the distance Maggie saw towering glints of metal.

"Where are we?"

"Nimby's farm," Oswald said, chuckling.

Further along, the structures on the other side were built closer to the fence, although never less than a kilometer away. The smaller ones were numerous and big enough to swallow Oswald's truck. They were composed of rotors that blurred into the shape of a sphere as they spun. Rows of taller machines stood among the odd spheres. They looked like flat antennae pointed straight upward, and they rotated on their base as if trying to twirl the hazy sky. Metallic shapes crawled all around the base of the machines, and in the air overhead tiny winged specks swooped in long, repetitive patterns.

"It's a wind farm," Oswald volunteered. "Ten square kilometers of windmills, solar focusers, and tenders to run it all. A third of Australia's power comes from this place, the rest from places just like it. There's hundreds of square kilometers like this in the Sahara, Gobi, Nevada. They feed the whole bloody world."

Maggie stared at the machines on the other side of the fence. "I thought windmills looked like...well, windmills."

"Yeah, where there's strong wind they do. Around here the wind's low, so we use those round ones there—they're venturi mills. The tall ones are for any strong winds that might blow up. We could use the prop blade kind, but these are safer for wildlife." He grinned at her. "We call them Big Man's curling irons."

"Uh-huh. What do you call the round ones?"

"Something's gotta curl his pubes, right?"

A few minutes after that, Oswald spied something. "Ha—there's our sign!", he said, spinning the wheel toward the fence. Before Maggie could ask, they rammed the chain link. The section of fence fell before the truck, chain and poles clanging to the ground. She held onto the dashboard as the truck bounced over the debris onto the clay plain.

Once they were through, Maggie turned to Oswald. "What sign? Where are we going?'

"Had the fence cut next to the yellow paw plant. We're done our walkabout; now we want you to be seen."

The truck picked up speed in a dirt stretch between rows of venturi windmills. Beneath the spinning, bent-back rotors Maggie could see swarms of robots of various designs. Blocky, many-limbed forms crawled around the footings of the windmills. Small bots with tiny, powerful wheels swarmed across the desert, some dragging jagged pieces of plastic or metal. Winged robots swooped at the ground and flew dizzying arcs around the machinery. Something like a miniature train snaked through the chaos, its segments disconnecting and rejoining in an intricate dance.

Once, when Maggie was nine years old, she had disobeyed her babysitter and climbed into a maintenance hatch on Megasat. In the underfloor labyrinth she had come across a grating that locked down upon a room full of robots that were servicing instruments on the outer hull of the space station. There were robots to tend the machinery, robots to tend the tenders, robots to stalk and disable other robots that were malfunctioning, and robots to drag away disabled robots and debris from accidents. She recognized the same patterns in the wind farm, although these robots were newer and more sophisticated, and had an immense expanse of flat land over which to roam.

One of the species of robots, however, didn't behave in a way she recognized. "Oswald, what do the winged ones do?"

"Eh? Scarecrows." He kept his eyes on the terrain. The ride was getting bumpy, as the truck went faster and rolled over robots and power cables strung across the desert. "They're to keep native species away from the generators. The windmills kill birds if they get close enough."

"It's amazing that it all works."

"Amazing? Not my word for it." He swerved to crush something that looked like a basket with tracks and claws, and the cabin of the truck rocked as the robot fell underneath. "We fucked up the ecosystem so badly that we've gotta have robots to protect it. Kill the ferals, nursemaid the endangered species, scare away the stupid ones. Fucking robots've got their own ecosystem, now."

Maggie watched as they drove past a tall wind generator, its poles like a set of spinning ship's masts. The scarecrows orbited it like mayflies around a porch light. "Better some kind of ecosystem than none at all, I guess."

"Maybe. All I know is it ain't the world I grew up in. The Earth's a fucking cyborg, now. This planet can't live without machines. Since we live here, I don't like to think about what that says about us."

As they drove past another row of tall generators, Maggie noticed that some of the scarecrows peeled away from the flock and began following them. The robots emitted ear-piercing shrieks as they dove in front of the truck, turning away from the windshield at the last second. Up ahead loomed a row of squat buildings. Oswald grinned and gunned the vehicle faster.

"Right, here's your chance to be seen. Roll that window down and wave."

"What?"

"I said wave." He hit a button, and Maggie's window retracted downward, sloughing off the blades of grass stuck to the outside. "Wave to the cameras. You know how to do that, right?"

Maggie peeked out the window; the dry wind hit her face and tugged at her hair. Scarecrows flocked to her side of the truck, making diving runs a bare meter overhead. She put one arm out and waved, feeling the air ball up in her hand. Then, made courageous by the attention, Maggie unbuckled her safety harness and climbed up on her seat. Kneeling, she leaned out the window of the truck, looking and waving all around.

The robot birds flew in frenzied loops, chasing after the truck and making sudden turns to capture glimpses of her. One ground into the sand as its reserves of compressed air gave out in pursuit of its idol. Other robots swiveled their sensors as the truck roared past. Maggie grinned, feeling the air buffet her neck and threaten to tear her shirt to ribbons. She leaned out further and laughed as she felt Oswald's hand grab the waist of her jeans, his fingers rough against her skin. She could unzip her pants, let him pull them off, and give everybody a show...

How he had the leverage to do it, Maggie couldn't say. But with the one arm Oswald lifted her up and dragged her back inside. "...completely bonkers!" she heard him say as the wind left her ears. "I said wave, not dive out into them!"

"I know how to treat an audience," she said, giving the aboriginal a dangerous grin. "How many cameras, do you think? How many viewers?"

"Shut up," he growled.

The truck's cab rattled and tilted as they plowed through a short fence, beyond which lay four squat metal buildings and a maze of walkways meant for human beings. No robots ran in this area, and the scarecrows peeled away from the truck as it careened over pavement and ornamental shrubs. Maggie clutched the dashboard. She screamed, more with rage than fear, as they charged toward a hangar door. The tree in the back cracked against the half-open door as they skidded into the building. They came to a stop yawed at an angle, tires squealing against the concrete.

The interior was dark; Maggie blinked to adjust her eyes, while another set of tires squealed nearby. Through the door on the other side of the building, another truck festooned with grass and shrubs sped away. It crashed through another low fence. Then it continued across another hundred meters of red sand before it smashed into one of the spinning venturi mills. Debris arced through the air as the windmill tore itself and the decoy truck to shreds.

An aboriginal in a maintenance uniform stepped up to Maggie's open window. "Like a corker, mate," he said to Oswald. Then he looked over Maggie and cocked his head. "This her?"

Oswald was chuckling. "Yeah. Don't touch or you'll lose an arm."

"Heh. Right." The man smiled at Maggie, backing up a step. "Look, mate, you've got to get underground. I've only got a minute or two to clean this place up."

He indicated the far wall with his thumb. Maggie saw shelves lined up to the ceiling, stacked with various spare parts for robots and windmills. A pair of tall forklifts stood in the hangar. Thick cables bound their lifting claws to a huge concrete slab, which they held suspended over a matching hole in the floor.

"No worries, Jack."

Oswald backed the truck up, then drove it into the hole and down a steep ramp. He fired up the headlights to reveal a round tunnel leading further down.

"You faked my death." Maggie said as they descended. Behind them came a grating sound as the slab was replaced. "You can't fake my death. Do you know how many fans I have?"

"Relax, princess." Oswald was visible only by the light of the dashboard reflecting from his teeth and eyes. "I doubt it'll fool anyone. Weren't no bodies in that truck, just an android. Told Simon it'd never work, but he insisted."

"Simon, huh?" Maggie scratched her fingernails against the dashboard. "When am I meeting this fucker?"

"He's at the other end of this tunnel. Don't get on his bad side," Oswald said, giving her a warning glance. "You and I, well...let's say we're dangerous as crocs in a pond, right? Simon, he'd be Leviathan. Whole different league."

Maggie glared into the darkness, willing the end of the tunnel to come into view.

———— ◉ ————

Chapter 6—Amateur Hour

For the next hour Oswald said little, claiming to be concentrating on driving through the tight passage. Maggie took the opportunity to needle him with questions, and before too long he gave brusque answers. *He doesn't want me to get too bored*, she thought. She contemplated ways to take advantage of that. There weren't many, trapped underground. All that came to mind was quizzing him or flirting with him. But she didn't feel like flirting—stopping to have sex would delay their progress, and she wanted to get back home. *Maybe there'll be time for that later.*

She learned through cagey interrogation that the first tunnel was built recently for her escape. After about half an hour they entered a larger, rectangular tunnel with strip lighting and an asphalt floor. The second tunnel was one thoroughfare in the city of Leonora's Bottom.

A consortium of aboriginal tribes had created the city from a network of tunnels in Western Australia. The first had been dug by an organization called Aum Shinri Kyo (then Aleph, then Dahaha-Tay just before they were eradicated in the Unification War.) The tunnels had been extended when robotic labor became cheap, and after the excavated tailings became valuable for their traces of uranium. Gold used to be mined here, but by the time molecular separators were developed to easily refine the ore, the element had lost its value.

Maggie occasionally saw someone watching from a cross-passage, and once they passed a sleek vehicle towing a wagon of live chickens. But Oswald explained that they were skirting around the edges of Leonora's Bottom. "Get too close to the Bottom and we'd have to avoid too many people," he said. "And if we try to go under it...well, those are the Momma's tunnels." Then he was quiet for several minutes, as if afraid to let anything else slip.

They left the underground city through another rough-hewn tunnel. After a short distance they emerged from a stone outcropping next to a paved road. The vehicle waiting on the shoulder of the road was a spotless white limousine, of a type Maggie had seen in news reports used by heads of state. Its six wheels were bracketed by ground-effect pads, and its windows and roof solar panels were an inky black-blue.

Oswald pulled up next to the limo, smiled at her, and got out of the truck. Maggie waited a few seconds, trying to decide if she should act impressed. She left the truck when a man climbed out of the limo and answered her question.

He was tall in the way a sapling might be tall, while still looking as if it would bend over in the slightest wind. He was pale everywhere Oswald was dark, which was everywhere, from his powder blue suit to his faded complexion to his wheat-brown hair. Even his eyes were a washed out grey that might have remembered being blue. He turned stiffly to greet her, his face expressionless. "Miss Megaputri. A pleasure to meet you. May I call you Maggie?"

Maggie glanced at Oswald. "This is the guy?" She looked the man up and down. He was a starched suit, an errand boy—she had seen the type before. "This isn't the guy."

Oswald chuckled. "Call her whatever you want, mate. She's your problem now. Princess, meet Simon. God help you both."

Simon cracked a slight smile. "God isn't on our side. He might have been, but, well. Maggie, I hope this scoundrel has treated you...oh, dear." Suddenly the man backed against his vehicle, covering his eyes with one hand. The other hand pointed at the ground and shook like a re-entry fin. "Oswald?" he said, his voice quavering, "Could you?"

The shoulder of the road was packed red clay. It took Maggie a second to see the tiny movement of a little red spider, no larger than an eyeline bead, crawling in Simon's general direction. Oswald stomped on the beast, ground it into the dirt, then stepped back as though nothing had happened.

Maggie watched as Simon peeked under his hand, then stood straight again with a cautious sigh of relief. "Was that dangerous?" she asked. "Worse than the ones last night?"

"Eh, not really. But it'd kill ya."

"I...have trouble with spiders. I apologize." Simon smiled again, his hands trembling only a little as he straightened his jacket. "Maggie, let's get you to civilization," he said. The door behind him opened.

She glanced back at Oswald. His grin was so wide, she couldn't tell if they were playing a joke or not. But the pale suit seemed genuine, if scared out of his mind. "Civilization sounds nice," she said. "Come on, Oswald, I'll buy you real food. Set us up in a hotel room with a real bed."

Oswald snorted. "I'm not coming with you."

"He's also not invited," said Simon. When a glare from Maggie struck him he added, "He understands why."

"I've got my own legal problems. Best if I stay on tribal land."

Maggie crossed her arms, hoping it would enhance her cleavage in the t-shirt she was wearing. "I can get you a lawyer."

"I've got a lawyer. Him."

Simon stood motionless. "He won't find better, I assure you."

"A lawyer. I should have fucking guessed." Walking up to Oswald, she flashed him her best smile. "Come on. Tag along with me for a while. We'll go back to Megasat, I'll show you all kinds of things. It'll be fun."

Oswald hesitated, his eyes widening. Then his teeth flashed in a crooked snarl. "No way in hell am I following you anywhere. You're three pints of crazy in a two pint skirt, you know that? Whatever you two got planned, leave me out of it. I'm not privy to many of the big donkey secrets but I know one lulu, and the thought that you might get involved scares the bloody shit out of me. I've done my job, I've gotten paid, and now I'm off and hooroo." The aboriginal walked back to his truck, still mumbling curses.

For a few seconds, all Maggie could do was stare. After another second she found herself scanning the red dirt for something solid. She found a rock—while a voice inside her screamed, *No, no! That isn't sharp enough!*—and threw it after the man. It missed by a wide margin. "Fine!", she yelled. "I didn't need you anyway. Psycho!"

When she turned back around, Simon was getting into a front door of the limo; her door remained open. The bush truck drove away. Maggie raised a middle finger at it before climbing into the limousine.

The interior sported expensive leather and laserline strips, both in varying glosses of black. She ignored the accents; the minibar magnetized her attention, and she advanced upon it like a predator. Sinking into the plush seat, she poured herself a gin before noticing the other passenger. In the middle of the limo sat an android, an expensive model, with suggestive feminine proportions and wearing a charcoal pantsuit. Simon sat beyond it, facing Maggie, with a rigid wide-eyed expression.

As the doors closed and the limo began to move, Simon cracked another forced smile. "Please, help yourself to the bar. The fabber can also make some food if you like." With a slight shake in his hand, he gestured toward the android. "This is my legal assistant Fianna. Fianna, be nice to Maggie Megaputri."

"Miss Megaputri, I'm pleased to meet you." The android's voice managed to be girly and professional at the same time.

"Terrific," Maggie said. She filled a glass with some amber-colored alcohol. "Legal assistant, huh? Is that another term for fucktoy?"

Simon's reaction was a minor tremble. "I assure you, she has none of those kind of accessories. Only processing and communication upgrades. Maggie, have I angered you in some way?"

"I know your type. Guy just out of law school, working for some big shot. Trying to kiss up to the star any way you can." She leaned forward (*Damn this t-shirt for not being more revealing!*) and smiled. "Do you dream about me, honey?"

"I'm used to making poor first impressions. I hope that eventually, you'll realize your mistake."

"Oh, will I?" She snorted as she sipped; the gin stung the back of her nose.

"I hope so," said Simon, his voice level and firm. "I'm not fresh out of school, Maggie. The first time I passed the bar, I was twelve years old."

"The first time? Didn't it take?"

"That was in North America. I've since become a legal counsel in thirty-five territories, with UN sponsorship as a borderless jurist with additional perks. My legal status is unique; I've leveraged that into influence with more corporate and government entities than I can name."

"Stop trying to impress me. You're a fucking chauffeur. In fact, this car drives itself—what the hell do I need you for? I can get home without you."

"We're not taking you home."

"What?"

"You can't go back to Megasat. Not now. You'll never make it up the elevator. In fact, I might be the only thing keeping you out of Globalpol's custody."

She stared at him, looking for some recognition of the bald-faced lie he had just told. After what Oswald went through...

The glass in her hand felt electrified as a voice spoke: *Make it sharp.* She rammed it against the minibar but it bounced, spilling gin but not breaking at all. She tried smashing it again, then with a scream she threw the glass across the limo. It never reached Simon—the android reached out and caught it without apparent effort.

The lawyer shivered a bit, but his voice remained steady. "Fianna is also my personal bodyguard. I apologize for having to keep her on alert, but you are wanted for questioning in the death of Emile Lambert. I would like to be your counsel, and for all your considerable wealth you will not find a better representative. Before I take your case, however, I need to know whether you really killed him or not." He held up a hand. "Don't answer that. Not until you're certain you want me as your counsel."

At the mention of Lambert's name, Maggie's rage evaporated. She shrank into her seat, nodding. "Okay."

"Maybe it will help if I show you what's in your path if you try to go home. I have several news reports cached. You can also surf any network you like, but I would advise against any uploads, even text. Would you like to use the laserline display here in the vehicle? I can fab spectacles for you, if you prefer."

Maggie shrugged. "The laserline's fine."

While Simon instructed his android to activate the display, Maggie tried to stay calm and keep her head upright. *He knows. Of course he knows. Probably everybody does.*

Two yellow dots appeared, bracketing the edges of her peripheral vision. They grew into lines, arcing upward. Maggie rebelled a little by rolling her eyes during the calibration sequence, but the system was smart enough to compensate. When the arcs met at the top of her vision, the calibration lines faded away and the system menu came up.

The laserline display strips in the limo were more sophisticated eyeline controls that projected images into the human eye at a greater distance. Compensating for eye and head movements, the system surrounded her with a three-dimensional display. It had flaws. Quick movements caused the projections around her to shake. Even more annoying was the transparency the images had—she could still see Simon and Fianna through the system menu, although the black interior of the limo faded away rather well. To project opaque images the display needed to obscure her vision. Spectacle displays could do that, but Maggie didn't like wearing them. There were contact lenses available that could render images with opacity, but the tiny devices were powered by microwave transmission. Users were advised to replace their corneas every few months.

Maggie found the icon of saved news reports and gestured toward it. It opened into a media menu with statistics on the contents. She scanned them with a practiced eye, having dealt with news feeds before. Eighteen licensed news organizations had reports about her, indexed by reporter, presentation theme and time of dispatch. Over three million amateur reports were also available, many of them with higher ratings than the licensed orgs. She pulled up some of the best rated amateur vids and began paging through them with flicks of her fingers.

flick

A wiry, red haired man with a guitar, sitting nude on what looked like a real beach, faded into view. Before he began singing Maggie closed the video. She recognized the guy as a stalker who constantly professed his love for her. A brief check confirmed it—the video's ratings were inflated because of embarrassment value.

flick

The next was a slickly presented collage of images from Megasat, then images of her and Lambert, then the two of them naked and having sex with their hands around each other's throat. Beside the wrestling couple stood a haloed Jesus wearing a butler's uniform and holding a bottle of Orga-ade, the sexual replenishment beverage... Oh, fuck, it was an advertisement.

flick

A log cabin appeared, with subtle misregistrations where the walls met the ceiling, hinting that it was a simulation. The hooded woman sitting cross legged on a tiger rug seemed real, however. She delivered a news report in half-prose, half-alliterative rambles. "Maggie 'Mags' Mega, multimedia magnate...and murderess? Maybe!", the woman began. Maggie listened for a few minutes. As art the performance made no coherent sense, but as a news report it had many informative bits, down to a description of Oswald's truck. *They know everything*, she thought. When the woman began undressing while relating background on Lambert, Maggie flicked it away. Returning to the media menu, Maggie chose one of the better licensed news orgs and brought up its video.

The scene zoomed in from orbit fast enough to give Maggie vertigo, zooming in to fly over the beach of Kajoa. The island's twin volcanoes—Jojaru and Bungali—loomed over Media Bay, the Megasat-owned city that served as a port for all space travel. From the peak of Bungali rose a slender black thread. A second thread sprouted from Jojaru and climbed at an angle, joining the first almost as high as the simulation allowed her to see. Oblong silver containers slid up the dual cables and negotiated their order of passage in a choreographed dance. They faded away into the blue sky, though she knew the cable continued forever. *To home.*

But while Maggie's eyes were drawn upward, the news report tried to pull attention downward. A simulated reporter stood in mid-air, indicating the masses of people on Media Bay beach.

"And returning to our story of the day, fans of Maggie Megaputri are still crowding onto the beach in Kajoa. The variety show star and heir to the Bayuputra fortune went on an unannounced vacation two days ago, jettisoning herself in an escape capsule into the Australian outback. The Megasat corporation insists that Mags is unharmed and enjoying herself, and she will return to her show—and this is a quote from her—'When I sober the fuck up'. This is the first time Mags has come down to Earth since her meteoric rise to celebrity, and her fans are seizing this opportunity to see her in person. They may not know where she is, but they know one thing: To get back to Megasat, she has to come through Media Bay."

A carpet of humanity covered the golden beach. In places, new buildings were being erected, and the news report lingered over shots of portable fabbers being used to produce food, tools, and construction materials. A handful of police were sprinkled throughout the crowd, keeping the squatters in orderly lines for bathrooms and directing them away from the luxury villas and soaring condominiums of Kajoa's residents. A few fans had banners with catch lines from the Megasat Hour. One was shown directing his robots to carve a four-meter likeness of Maggie's face in the sand.

The reporter droned on for a bit longer with useless bits about her fans' dedication. Then the segment ended, and the scene behind him faded out. But the video continued. "In other news," he said, adopting a sad expression, "The Vatican has announced a memorial service for Cardinal Emile Lambert will be held this Sunday..."

Maggie watched until that segment ended, then flicked through some more videos. None provided any additional interest. After a while she began to be conscious of Simon's face, watching her impassively through the transparent display.

Finally she closed down the laserline system and folded her hands in her lap. She met his gaze. "I did kill him," she said.

Simon nodded. "All right. Now, my employer wants to offer you sanctuary—"

"Wait. Your employer—who is this guy?"

"I'm not at liberty to say."

"Uh huh. And he's the leader of the Platinum Donkeys?"

"It's difficult to say that anyone can *lead* a conspiracy of mad geniuses. But if I had to point to someone as their leader, then no, it would not be him. He's merely well-positioned."

"Whatever." Maggie pinched the bridge of her nose to alleviate her eyestrain. Another drawback of shooting lasers into one's retinas. "I don't want to wind up as a trophy at some rich guy's dinner party."

"Do you have any other options?"

"Oh, I don't know." Maggie bluffed a nonchalant smile. "You can drop me off here, I'll wander a bit. It'll be fun."

"You're joking."

"No. Oswald will pick me up. Wait—the news had a shot of Oswald's truck. Is he in danger?"

"Of a sort. Nobody's going to buy the faked death footage. I've kept the media from hounding you by contesting their environmental contracts. I've claimed that landing camera crews on reservation land would cause too much damage for them to compensate by planting trees elsewhere. So only Globalpol is chasing him at the moment." He shrugged. "Oswald's always in trouble. I'll take care of it for him."

She thought for a moment, then flashed a lopsided smile. "You know, the licensed news never brought up Lambert's murder. But my fans did. They assume I did it, and they love me anyway."

"Of course they do."

"And that's why I don't need you." She tapped in a quick search. "I've got six thousand public offers of sanctuary. That's without even asking. Why should I follow a shady lawyer home?"

Simon began to stammer. "I...I mean, we can keep you hidden. I've proven that, haven't I? Besides the police, there are millions of rabid fans lying in wait for you everywhere. Doesn't that frighten you? It terrifies me."

"Nonsense. They're my fans. If I asked them to grab hold of the space elevator and pull Megasat down for me, they'd do it. And they can handle the police, if it came to that."

"You're not being reasonable."

"You don't live my life."

By now, Simon's eyes had widened even more, while the rest of his face was rigid and strained. Maggie blinked twice to get a fresh look at him, and realized what she was seeing. He was terrified. Simon was not stiff because he was a protocol-worshipping suit. He was petrified, and had been from the moment they had met.

Maggie leaned forward with a dangerous grin. "What are you afraid of?" she said with a sultry voice.

"Everything, and that isn't hyperbole," he said, his lip quivering. He swallowed once, hard, then continued. "But I can keep you safe, and I don't think anyone else in the world can say that. Please, Maggie. You need us as much as we need you."

She left the silence drag out for as long as she thought he could stand it. Then she let him off the hook. "Okay, fine. So where are we going?"

"First to an airstrip outside of Perth. Then to San Francisco. I've arranged a false identity for you. We'll have to make you a disguise of some sort. I have a burqa pattern loaded in the fabber—"

"I'm not wearing a fucking burqa." She accessed the laserline system and brought up the fabber controls. "You want me in costume? That's something I know how to do. I'll need to buy patterns."

"I'd rather not risk putting you in powered clothing. They track your vitals, and the authorities can identify you by biotelemetry."

"Nothing powered. Just stage tricks."

Simon nodded, looking slightly relieved. "Fianna, allow Maggie to access my spending account. Make all purchases in my name."

"Yes, sir. It's done."

Maggie dived into the network and found what she wanted, then downloaded them into the vehicle's fabber. The only limit on the fabber's abilities were the patterns it held and its reserves of elemental materials. Some of those reserves were scarce—this fabber was short on silicon, she noted, from creating the minibar's crystal decanters—but the items she wanted were not very exotic.

When she had finished, Simon looked into the fabber's memory to see her ideas. "I don't know if we need all that."

"Better to have it and not need it, right?" She activated the fabber, and it began work. "How long until we get there?"

"Another hour, at this speed. Plenty of time for the fabber."

"How fast are we going?" The ride felt smooth, but now that she listened for it she could hear a high-pitched whistling of air. Maggie tapped the window, but it remained opaque. "Can we turn the windows back on?'

"Oh, I can't handle speed. I'd..." Simon trembled, then reached into a jacket pocket and pulled out a pair of black spectacles. After he put on the electronic blinders he relaxed some more. "I'll tell you what, I can get some work done while you enjoy the scenery. Fianna, unlock the window controls for Maggie, please."

Maggie rolled her eyes, then tapped the window again.

The scenery outside was less than a desert but barely more than an orange haze. Shapes that could have been vegetation zoomed by. Looking ahead, she could focus on things for a moment before they rocketed past. The limo's ground effect pads were visible, lifting the vehicle's tires off the asphalt and producing streams of whirling dust.

Accessing the laserline, Maggie brought up vehicle info. They were moving at 260 kilometers per hour. The vehicle had its own pair of scarecrows to detect and frighten away wildlife, to keep the road ahead clear. She searched for them through the window, and saw dark streaks near the forward horizon. There were no other features in the landscape, nothing recognizable or motionless enough to be appreciated.

This is nothing like orbital speed, Maggie told herself. She had been living at eleven thousand kilometers per hour for most of her life. *I can handle this.*

But after a couple minutes of watching the landscape fly by, Maggie began to feel queasy, and she once again turned off her view.

Chapter 7—Scenery Change

The landscaping at the airport was much more welcoming. Stands of trees surrounded the squat white terminal buildings, and above them all stood a control tower studded with communication arrays. The limo let them out at a VIP entrance with minimal security. After Simon produced the necessary documents (forged under the name Phyllis O'Grady, in Maggie's case) they were let into the glass-walled concourse with no questions.

Maggie changed clothes in the limousine while Simon was still wearing his vision-obscuring spectacles. Her new clothes were miracles of stagecraft. Her shirt was reversible; her skirt unwound and could become a shawl or two other different skirts. The wig was made of memory fibers that were burnished copper-red when coiled, but if she pulled them straight they would change to silky black tresses. Given twenty seconds, Maggie could change herself into a completely different disguise.

She wondered when she would get those twenty seconds away from Simon. Slipping away from him here in Australia seemed foolish; the country was too dangerous, and this was where everyone expected her to be. Maybe she'd ditch him in San Francisco. Maggie tried to remember what she knew of that city. On her show, there had been a skit based in San Fran about a zombie apocalypse—a perennial source of comedy. It involved homosexual zombies that wore tie-dye clothing and had a penchant for raping tourists' brains.

The city probably isn't much like that, she thought to herself as they walked down the concourse; Simon stiff as a board, Fianna holding his arm. *But maybe I should lose the suit now. Maybe I can find Oswald's phone number, or a flight to Kajoa.*

At the window of their gate, Maggie saw something that gave her a shock. "I know what those are", she said, "Those are gelships!"

The craft outside looked like a cloud parodying the shape of a jet plane. It had fat wings that spanned three runways, and a massive, bulbous torso that could have been half a kilometer long. The skin of the gelship was white with red decorations, and with long, black solar panels striped across the top. Except for a band of glass above the fat wings, the ship was windowless. Three more of the giant craft sat further away, occupying most of the airport's available space.

"I've seen where—" Maggie caught herself, and lowered her voice to a whisper. "I've seen where they make those. There's a factory in orbit that pops them out and transfers them to Megasat so they can be towed down the elevator. They glow when they hit the atmosphere. You can watch them almost all the way down."

Simon nodded. "Yes. The hulls are made of aerogel—it's like a sponge with only vacuum inside—and they can only be made in space. The gelships' engines are magnetoprops, and they use the gel hull for electrical storage, so they're environmentally neutral. We won't have to negotiate pollution compensation contracts. It's the safest form of air travel. I won't cross the ocean any other way."

"But they've used up the entire airport. They don't have room to take off."

"They take off straight up. The hulls are lighter than air."

Maggie watched as one gelship disgorged passengers through long, extensible bridge tunnels that led back to the terminal. Hundreds of people, and thousands more in the terminal around her, and millions in airports around the world...it gave her a feeling of pride. Her daddy made these things possible.

When she turned away from the window, Maggie noticed that Simon had gone a few steps closer to the gate, and some of the airport crowd had filled the intervening space. *Now could be my chance*, she thought. But she hesitated. *Do I want to ditch the suit now, or wait?*

As she tried to decide, a hand took a firm grip on her shoulder. "Excuse me, ma'am," the tall man said. "Airport security. Would you mind stepping this way?"

Maggie froze. The man had a white shirt that, as she watched, changed its display to show badges on his shoulders and on his chest pocket. *W. Radicker—Globalpol.*

"I...I...", Maggie began, but the man pulled her through the crowd to the nearest wall. A blinking sign scrolled up the wall's display—'Security: Please Stand Clear'. Then the wall itself wavered and rolled up like a curtain, exposing an alcove with two more security officers and one uncomfortable-looking chair. The tall man steered her toward the chair. But he stopped short, turning back, and Maggie looked back as well.

A silver hand clad in a charcoal sleeve kept the wall from unrolling again and closing behind them. As Fianna held the wall up, Simon ducked underneath. The android followed, allowing the wall to fall back to the floor and become solid again.

The officers pointed at Simon, their hands on their shirt sleeves, ready to activate some device. "Sir," one of them said, "This is a security area."

"And that is my client! Did you think you could talk to her without my consent?" Simon's voice was strong, his teeth bared. He seemed like a totally different person, although Maggie noticed a slight tremble in his hands.

The security officers paused for a second, glancing at each other. Finally they dropped their hands. Officer Radicker, the tall one with the square jaw, inhaled and turned toward Maggie. "Ma'am, are you Magnolia Peaches Megaputri?"

5

"It's all right, Maggie. Yes, she is." At Simon's permission, Maggie nodded.

"Mr. Brovall, isn't it?"

"Yes. Good guess."

"Wasn't difficult," the officer said, rubbing his temple. "My superior is already receiving complaints from your office. I'm sure you're aware that miss Megaputri is wanted for questioning about an incident on Megasat."

"But you haven't brought any charges. She's already answered questions *ex custodia* through my office. Unless you have charges to bring and evidence to back them up, you have no right to accost her."

Radicker ground his teeth. "She entered this airport under a forged identity."

"That was a legal identity registered under the Incognito Act. Celebrities and politicians have a right to travel without being mobbed."

"We have no record of this identity being registered."

"Really? Fianna, when did you complete the O'Grady registration process?"

"At 13:22, sir. Twenty minutes ago."

"There you go," said Simon. "It's registered. I can't help it if your records aren't up to date."

The men stared blankly back at them. They weren't staring at Simon, Maggie realized, nor at her, but past them both. She looked back and saw only the magic wall.

Simon bared his teeth again, this time in a feigned smile. "I know it takes time to access your network implants, but please be polite. You're curious about why the watch you put on Maggie's information didn't alert you to her identity registration. Why don't you let us go now, and check that later?"

"You stopped it." One of the officers broke out of his net access daze and glared at Simon. "Your office put a restraint on all alerts attached to her data."

"I did. Miss Megaputri has privileged knowledge in several lawsuits between the Megasat corporation and competing companies. Active alerts on her status could be used for corporate espionage."

"You can't do that."

"I already have. You'll also note a series of petitions lined up to keep her movements unrestricted and out of the media, for the same reasons. Now, are you going to present a good excuse to hold my client, or do I start filing wrongful arrest suits?"

As they continued to argue, Maggie stepped back behind Simon and his android. With the pair between her and the police she began to breathe easier. She didn't understand all the legal terms they were fighting over, but it was clear that Simon was winning, and Officer Radicker clenched his jaw ever more tightly as Simon spoke.

A flicker of movement caught her eye. Maggie turned around, and with a shock of horror saw that the security wall had disappeared. People were walking through the terminal and sitting at the gates, easily able to hear all about Maggie's legal chaos... A second later, she noticed flickering icons next to each person and a menu system in one corner of the wall. The magic wall had turned into a display, a one-way view back into the airport, with status icons following every traveler She exhaled.

But then an odd thing appeared. It drifted into the field of view just on the other side of the wall, hovering on frantically beating wings. Like a hummingbird, the minicamera spun around in jerky, half-way motions to face into the wall where Maggie stood. She could see the lens of its camera spin and focus upon her.

No. It's a display. It can't be watching me through the wall, it can't be...

"Maggie?"

She turned around to see Simon and the officers looking at her. Simon had his arms crossed, his hand shaking just a bit. "I think we've come to an accord," he said.

"Not quite," Radicker said. The other two glared at him in silent communication, and he shot a defiant look back. "Yes, this will do. I'll take responsibility."

"For what, officer?", asked Simon.

Radicker fished something out of his pocket. "Miss Megaputri, we can't detain you," he said with a growl. "You're free to go with one stipulation. You're to wear a governor at all times."

"Governance is optional after the age of twenty-one. She's chosen not to comply."

"She's been *non compus mentis* for five years, making compliance mandatory."

"*That* is a tax dodge by the Megasat corporation and is under appeal."

"Okay. But while it's under appeal, she wears a governor." He held out a golden band. "I'm not letting her back into the airport, let alone out of it, without one."

It was Simon's turn to clench his jaw in frustration, but he looked at Maggie and nodded his assent. She stepped forward and took the governor. A solid band of metal, the bracelet was ornately engraved to appear as if it were a chain, with eyeline beads hidden in the crevices. She avoided looking at the control beads as she turned it over, then she shook her head and offered it back. "I'm sorry," she said, "It doesn't go with the dress."

Radicker's teeth seemed like they were about to break. "It's mimic-metal. Accessorize it yourself. Mr. Brovall, I think we're done here," he said, and with a look at the security wall it rolled up into the ceiling again.

Maggie followed Simon and Fianna back into the terminal. A horde of people watched them with suspicion as they escaped the security cordon. But Maggie couldn't see where the flying camera had gone. She was trying to peer over the crowd to search for it when Fianna tapped her on the shoulder. The gelship was boarding. Time to go.

———●———

The massive gelship gave its passengers something that older forms of air travel could not: Room. The passenger deck was a three-story oblate ring around the lower part of the aircraft, with comfortable chairs placed around dining tables with net displays and android call buttons. The table display counted the time to arrival (19 hours, 23 minutes) and advertised a couples dance in the fore deck later that evening. Food concessions and sleeping berths ringed the interior, while the exterior displays gave a magnificent window view as they lifted off. Maggie watched the liftoff from a seat near the window, then joined Simon at a table far from the edge.

"I apologize for not sitting closer to the window," he said as she buckled herself in. Fianna sat at the table also, looking like the mannequin figures in the pre-flight safety briefing. "I'm afraid that I really can't stand heights."

"Don't bullshit me, Simon. You did fine back there with the police."

"Oh. No, I'm not afraid of policemen. There's no sense being afraid of government authority, it's too omnipresent. Might as well fear the air."

"Uh, huh. But you're afraid of everything else."

"Not everything. Multiphobic though, I assure you. And I have a congenital heart condition, so it doesn't pay to take risks." He nodded at the governor, which Maggie had looped around her wrist. "Speaking of which, there's a risk I wish we didn't have to take."

Maggie looked at the bracelet. Its eyeline control blinked an icon into her eye, requesting activation. "I thought governors were just personal network devices. Why does it bother you?"

"They're much more than that. The governor is meant to be a child's best friend and worst confidant. It records your life, tracks your movements, gets into your head and..." He paused, and with a shaking hand tapped the table display to order a drink. "We'll deal with it when we land. For now, we don't have a choice but to keep it around. But don't talk to it, and don't listen to anything it says."

The governor was still blinking for attention, writing an icon in the center of her vision if it was anywhere in her field of view. "The policeman said that can I make it match my dress?"

"Hmph. Yes. Go ahead and do that."

She reached out and tapped the air where the icon appeared to be, and the eyeline menu system unfolded in front of her. The controls were simple—the top level menus were 'Conversation', 'Network', and 'Settings'. She rummaged through the settings menu and found the mimic-metal controls.

There were several metal selections, and a vast number of shapes. She chose one and watched as the governor turned silver and grew into a long, thin pendant. Another option made it a lozenge fit for a shirt pocket. "I never had anything made of mimic-metal," she said, paging through the options. "It's kinda cool."

"Why would you? It's common, a cheap trick for consumer devices. You can afford real jewelry. But you probably have a lot of things with mimic-metal inside them. That stuff saved the world."

"Oh? I missed that in history class." History had always bored her, and she couldn't think of anyone on Megasat who considered it important. "Were there riots over costume jewelry, then?"

"Electronics, and yes, nearly. See, that gadget is plastic, with just a little bit of common metals on the surface. Nanoscale machinery permits the metals to be rearranged, forming various compounds.

But it's not just for show. The rearrangement of compounds allows it to change its chemical properties to resemble other metals, at least on the surface. Mimic metal is used as a substitute for other metals that we used to have in abundance but have mined dry—gallium, chromium, cobalt, gold, and so on. Without that stuff, we'd have run out of raw materials almost a century ago."

She paged through the menu some more. "There's no selection for platinum."

"Platinum has properties that mimic-metal can't duplicate. That's why it's so valuable. Look for a silver alloy that resembles it, one should be in there."

Maggie found the alloy and set the governor into a slender, smooth bracelet with a silver-blue finish. Closing the menus, she lifted her wrist to appreciate the device. It flashed another icon into her vision. "Damn. It still wants my attention. Can I shut that off?"

"No, and that's the problem. Better if you put it in your pockets."

"I like it as a bracelet. I'm going to see what it wants."

"All right." Simon's voice was quiet. "I did warn you."

Maggie activated the icon and followed the alert into the 'Conversation' menu. The eyeline control abruptly shut down. But a voice sounded in her head.

"Hello, Maggie." The voice was male, calm, and almost monotonic. "How are you feeling?"

Her face must have reacted. Simon nodded sagely. "What you're hearing are directed acoustics centered on your ears. Would you like to tell me what it's saying?"

"It's just saying hello. Do I...talk to it?"

"I'd rather you didn't, but my advice doesn't make much impression on you, does it?"

"Of course you can talk to me, Maggie," the governor said. "Would you like to talk about what happened on Megasat?"

A chill ran down Maggie's spine. "No. I mean, I pressed the wrong button and ended up here. Why?"

"What did you do before that?"

An android placed a napkin and a martini in front of Simon. He sipped it while shaking a finger at her. "They are recording everything you say, you know. As your lawyer I'd advise you to...oh, never mind."

"Before that? I did my fucking show, that's what I did. Why the hell are you asking?"

"I'm sorry. I don't mean to upset you." The voice managed to sound apologetic. "I just want to know more about you. Maybe we should start at the beginning. Would you like to talk about what your mother did to your fa—"

In one smooth motion Maggie pulled the governor off her wrist and flung it away. It skittered across the floor, coming to a rest at the railing in front of the window.

Maggie crossed her hands on her lap and looked at Simon innocently. "Oops. It slipped."

Simon chuckled. He called an android waiter, and directed it to retrieve the device. "I told you, it'll get into your head. It has every piece of data that's ever been filed about you. It adapts, so the more you talk to it the better it'll be at reading and manipulating you. Anything you confide to it can be forwarded to the authorities. But its primary purpose is to eliminate illegal acts before they begin, by conditioning, persuasion, and punishment, if necessary."

"Who the hell would own such a thing?"

"Everybody, by law, from age three to twenty-one. Save for some native peoples on reservation lands, and they often wear governors voluntarily for their other useful abilities. It's all in the service of making good citizens; driving every child inexorably toward sanity, as defined by the powers that be."

The android dropped the bracelet on the table. An icon flashed in Maggie's vision; she took Simon's napkin and draped it over the thing. "I never had one of these. Should I have had one of these?"

"You did, it's in your medical history. You just don't remember. Mega took it away when he adopted you, when you were six. He never gave it back." Simon dunked the olive in his drink with one finger, not meeting her stare. "I'm sorry, Maggie. Maybe he should have, but...he didn't. And so, we are what we are."

I am insane, she thought. *I could have been normal. But I'm...*

"And you?" she asked.

"My father was a programmer, enhancing and testing new software for the governors. He hacked mine to be ruthlessly overprotective. I remember one day I lit a leaf on fire with a magnifying glass. That night the governor refused to let me sleep until I had watched a documentary about the Dresden firebombing. I was four years old."

He said it so calmly, and his grey eyes were so wistful and sad, that she almost didn't notice he wore a slight smile. "But I've made the best of it," he said. "Because my mental problems were caused by the governor program, I have a unique legal status. You could say that I'm licensed to be crazy. And being a multiphobe with a heart condition, the government takes a great risk whenever they try to intimidate me. I have summary judgments that I've never seized because they would nearly bankrupt the departments responsible. I'd rather hang it over their heads."

"So that's why you work for the Platinum Donkeys."

"Let's not talk about them right now," he said, nodding toward the governor. "Wrap it in that napkin and put it away somewhere. We should have fabbed you a handbag. Still can, if you like."

"No, there's a pocket in this dress." She tucked the governor away. Her feelings for Simon were confusing. He was so frail, yet possessed some magnetic hidden strength. "Did you...grow up to be much like your father?"

"In some ways. Programmers hack computer systems. I hack legal systems. Ultimately, I think he worked with a better class of people."

They changed the subject, by mutual unspoken agreement. For hours they talked about their business experiences. Maggie regaled him with vivid descriptions of Megasat and the people living there. Drinks came and went, and a supper of fabbed clams whose shells were shaped like little gelships, complete with the airline's logo. Throughout it all Simon remained witty and knowledgeable as long as they skirted around topics that unnerved him. Maggie held back her interview skills, not wanting to push him into a panic, but part of her was curious to see the man's full capabilities.

When she mentioned that she would like to look out the window, Simon began to shake, pleading vertigo. So of course Maggie had to check out the view on her own.

But from the huge bay window there wasn't much to see. They were over the ocean, and the vast expanse of water shimmered in the midday sunlight. Puffy white clouds clustered on the horizon. Far below Maggie saw a ship wake, and an icon on the window brought up information about it. It was a trawler bot, a huge, squarish ship that skimmed the Pacific for floating waste, part of the worldwide ecological retrieval program. Through telescopes on Megasat, Maggie had seen orbital trawlbots cleaning debris out of low Earth orbit, their cylindrical hulls bulging with ablative capture gels. She was amazed how different the designs were for essentially the same task.

When she returned to the table, Simon was talking with Fianna, but he stopped as she approached. Maggie winked at him. "Already switching to another dinner companion?"

"Just checking on business. I couldn't replace you with an android, Maggie."

She frowned, and rubbed the fabric over the wounds on her arm. They had just begun to itch. "I don't know," she said. "Sometimes I wonder how much difference there is. I bet there are some people you could replace with an android and not know the difference."

"Ask them to write a poem."

"Excuse me?"

"Tell them to write a poem. Any poem. Unless someone has loaded automatic writing software into the android, it won't be able to do it. Here. Fianna," he said, "Write me a poem."

The android turned her featureless face toward him. "Sorry, sir. I don't understand."

"Look up the definition of poems and poetry. Then compose a poem for me."

"I have access to network databases of poetry. Please state search terms."

"No, I do not want you to search for an existing poem. I want an original poem. I want you to make one for me."

The android sat for a few seconds. Then: "I'm sorry, sir. I don't know what to do."

"That's okay, Fianna. Good work. Go back to standby mode." He flung his hands up and smiled. "You see? Even if she had writing software, you'd probably be able to tell. It would feel mechanical. Algorithmically-generated poems are lifeless, rote. Or they're a mish-mash of famous poems that you'd recognize. Either way, there's no creativity."

"What if someone built a really smart android?"

"Fianna here is about as advanced as androids come, but she's no smarter than a dog. Don't get me wrong—a dog that can speak and use the internet is a wonderful tool. But even if she were more advanced, I don't believe she could compose a poem. Raw computing power does not translate into creativity. Creativity is...something else, something rarer."

Maggie nodded, then leaned forward and grinned. "Okay. So write me a poem."

"Me?"

"Hey, I've got to be sure."

"You..." He gasped, then chuckled. "All right. I walked into that one. Um. Poetry really isn't in my bag of tricks."

"Give it a shot. Or can't you?"

"Ah-hah. Hmn." Focusing on the ceiling, Simon sipped his drink in a blatant attempt to stall. After a few seconds he put the glass down.

"There once was a maiden made mad,

who made those around her quite glad.

She was a lovely view,

with behind of blue—"

"Hey!"

"I'm sorry!" he said, drawing his arms inward and shaking. "I—I meant the sky behind you. At the window." When she laughed, he became calmer. "I told you, I'm no good at this sort of thing."

"That's okay. At least you're human."

"Yes." Simon's gaze remained fixed on Maggie, and his smile could almost be called dangerous. After a long pause in the conversation he tilted his head. "I believe it's your turn."

"Me? I do it all the time. The poetry thrash is a repeat segment on my show."

"I thought that was a guitar competition."

"Well, that's part of it."

"So write me a poem now," he said. "After all, I have to be sure."

Maggie gave him a look that made him tremble, but she tried to mellow it with a smile. *Challenging me, little man?* Her mind began to piece together elements for a quick composition. *He wrote about me, I'll write about him. And donkeys. And 'behind'...hmmn.*

In less than a minute, Maggie was counting the cadence on her fingers, a luxury she never allowed herself on camera. When she made it fall into place, she smiled and began, with extra care to enunciate the important pauses:

"Behold the man behind gray eyes.

No beast of burden stops the world.

From pasture, hill and farm they rise,

Behold the man. Behind gray eyes—

Not muscle lean nor hardened guise—

Hides quiet skill, adept, unfurled.

Behold the man! Behind gray eyes,

No beast of burden. Stops, the world."

Simon's jaw went slack. "That's magnificent."

"Thank you." She swallowed a gulp of gin. "I did cheat, though. I made it into a triolet; that let me reuse lines."

"Nonsense. It's marvelous. Fianna, save the last two minutes of conversation."

"Yes, sir."

"I do better on my show. If I had a backbeat or a guitar track..."

"Stop being modest. It's the only thing that wears badly on you." His chiding tone stopped her in mid-sentence. "You should know, Maggie, there's talk in the North American territories about making you poet laureate."

She snorted. "Bullshit." Simon held a level, confident stare. "You can't be serious," she said. "My poetry is shit, it's doggerel. I compose to guitar thrash, for christ's sake."

"Yes, well, supporters of the idea say that you're bringing poetry back to the masses. And you were born in America; they'd love to claim you as their own again. But most importantly," he said, his voice dropping to a harsh whisper, "There is no one better. The entire world has been driven toward a bland average. What used to be a bell curve has been hammered into a thin spike, centered on the boring intellect of the median. People such as you and I are rarer now than at any point in human history. We may even be going extinct."

At that last, Simon sat back in his chair and bit the knuckle on his trembling hand. After a deep breath he continued. "I'm sorry. I can't blame them, and I hope they don't blame us for being unique. Or for how this all ends. The future belongs to the creative; if that means the future belongs to the insane, then normal people will have to learn to accept that. But we should discuss lighter subjects." He began sliding his finger across the table display, bringing up pictures from the menu. "I believe that I'll have some dessert. Would you like anything?"

Maggie activated the table and flipped through the options. But she was distracted by a blinking icon that indicated an announcement. When tapped, the icon unfolded into a colorful flier with a map of the gelship. "Hey. The dance is beginning in the forward lounge." She gave Simon a grin. "I want to dance. Let's go."

The lawyer almost choked. "W-What? Oh, no. No, I don't dance. Neither should you—we're trying to keep you incognito, remember."

"The wig's clasped to my scalp, it's not going anywhere. Come on, it'll be fun."

"Absolutely not. All those people. And from the forward lounge, you can see the horizon, the water... I, I couldn't."

"Fine. Whatever," she said, unbuckling and getting up from the table.

Simon mumbled something about "...as your lawyer...oh, never mind," as she headed toward the nearest stairwell. One level up was the entertainment deck, where seats were arranged around banked laserline tables where people sat watching videos or playing in shared games. Forward from there, at the front of the gelship, a crowd gathered in a bow-shaped room whose tables had retracted into the floor. The captain was there, announcing the rules in his white uniform and cap.

There was to be an hour of casual dancing first, so that singles could pair off before the dance competition began. Maggie scanned the room, measuring the quality of the men around her. As the music began, she lured a handsome specimen to her with a smile.

The dance started with algorithmic country music, the twangs and brush beats composed on the fly, the melody always new but the repetitive pattern easily found. The algo was adaptive; it tried to match the complexity of its music to the average skill level of the dancers on the floor.

Maggie blew away the curve. Her handsome boy stumbled on a sashay and she abandoned him, capturing another partner with a bat of her lashes and a craned-neck view of her breasts. The next song was ballroom punk, and the adaptive algo bifurcated the tune into a droning backbeat with a heady, anxious guitar line just for her. Her partner put his hand on her hip and tried to lead, but Maggie snorted and pushed him into the submissive role. Forcing him to follow the shrieking guitar, Maggie wore the boy like a halter, and showed him what couples moshing was all about. When the song changed he backed off, panting, his erection trying to force its way through his slacks.

Some eager stud stepped up and took the last one's place, but Maggie couldn't get more out of him than a two-step and a pelvic thrust. Laughing, she snared another young man by a subtle puff of air on the back of his neck. He lasted through two songs before Maggie's expert movements, following the complex part of the music, drove him to the bar in search of a drink. He didn't offer her one, so she forgot him. She found another partner, then another for the next song, pushing each to his limit then discarding them.

The casual dance ended with a crescendo of thrash guitar. As the lights came up Maggie realized there was a ring of dancers at a respectful distance around her. She chuckled and scanned over the crowd, trying to decide who she should use for the competition.

Let them come to me, said a part of her mind. *Let's see who's the fastest at swimming upstream.*

But as she stood on the dance floor the crowd retracted from her, pairing off at the bar and in the corners of the room. The men she had danced with glanced her way and shrunk back; her mosh partner couldn't even meet her eye.

They're scared of me. They know.

They don't know anything. Except that I'm better than they are.

They were malleable, she knew. She could walk over and pluck one from his partner's arms and he would have no choice but to follow her back onto the floor. She could write the scripts, have them stand on cue, pull their strings and puppet them through the dance. But she couldn't make them keep up with her.

It's not my fault if they can't handle me.

But it was. Her obsession had led her to this. Gymnastic classes since the age of eight, both in full gravity and zero gee; acting lessons at ten; writing, choreography, singing and dancing tutors all through her life. She had obsessively pushed herself toward perfection. A goal she had reached for so that...maybe Mega wouldn't throw her away.

The futility of Maggie's teenage years were reflected back to her in the eyes of her frightened suitors. Years of driving herself to be useful, to be valuable, so that no one would remember that she was a stray existing on their goodwill. She had spent her life bartering for Mega's attention with a series of ever greater antics driven by her ever-increasing skills. Now she was on top, able to fluster and conquer at need—but unable to view lesser men as anything but prey. They couldn't handle her, and she didn't know how to use a light touch. She needed the most capable of men, those able to put aside their fear.

Maggie stormed out of the ballroom.

She found Simon in the same place as she had left. He watched her approach with one hand on his drink as if it were an anchor. Maggie gave him a dangerous smile, and leaned on the table to accentuate her neckline.

"I'm going to bed," she said in a low, sultry tone. "You should come with me."

"Oh. Um, no, I'll be sleeping here," he said, with a slight tremble of his hand. "The berths in these ships are like Japanese coffin hotels; much too claustrophobic for me. They don't mind if you sleep at the tables, as long as you stay buckled in."

"I don't think you understand. I want you to come to bed. With me. Right now."

His eyes went wide; his entire body tensed as he fought his shivers down. "I—I don't think *you* understand, Maggie. I have a deathly fear of enclosed spaces. And the dark. And, to be honest, femme fatales." He swallowed hard, then continued in a more level voice. "I shall be sleeping right here."

Maggie stared at him, her own body tensing, her mind wheeling with spurned rage. But after a few seconds she spun around and stomped off to sleep alone.

Chapter 8—Spotlight Downstage Interstitial

———◈———

Niklaus Gorjanu thought he had his career figured out. While all the other students in college were desperate to find a field where they could be employed and productive, Niklaus discovered an academic niche that would never become outdated or obsolete. He wanted to be a historian.

The science of reconstructive historical simulation fit him like a glove. More than anything else, Niklaus loved to create things. He had programmed his family's fabber by the age of six. (His tu'ro' candy ice cream was even a moderate success—the cheese curds did not congeal well, but if you dug around them the chocolate and quince bits were fine.) The field excited him; he poured his fabber talents into replicating historical objects to study their workings.

Soon he realized how boring historians were.

They would replicate puzzleboxes or racing cars, poke around in the duplicates as carefully as if they were originals, then recycle the artifacts and recreate them with tiny improvements. Occasionally a historian might create stone age pottery or a copper age adze, but these were thought to be too simple to waste time studying. Reconstructive simulation excelled at uncovering the mysteries of complex machinery, not crude ancient objects.

But Niklaus knew how to revolutionize his chosen field, even before he had completed his degree in it. Niklaus set out to fab a dinosaur.

Paleontology was not history, but with the modern tools available he was sure that was only a failure of imagination on the part of whomever made up the categories of study. What a dreadful job THAT must be. Fabbing a dinosaur should be possible, with the reams of information known about the beasts from fossil research and from comparison to modern species. Niklaus intended to make a dwarf therapod, like *Elopteryx nopcsai*, because Franz Nopcsa was a local hero and the thesis committees liked dissertations with local flavor. Also, it would be the closest thing to a Tyrannosaurus that would fit in his fabber, and Tyrannosaurs were cool.

Niklaus built a skeleton and planned for organs and musculature, but nerve tissue eluded him. His fabber refused to create a living brain.

Niklaus had been designing fabber patterns since childhood and he knew the machines' capabilities. Fabbers were invented by someone who imagined protein synthesis on the large scale conjoined with deposition manufacturing techniques made small. Between those technologies lay nothing—from a water molecule to a wardrobe—that could not be created. Cell clusters could be engineered with specified DNA sequences, stacked together with nanometer accuracy, and connected with tissues made from procedurally generated protein and cellulose. There was nothing unique about neurons that should have made them unfabbable

He looked for help from hobbyist sites on the CenNet that brokered in bizarre and speculative fabber patterns. There he found a strange person named Burro, who communicated only in plaintext, and who claimed to be a mediator between Niklaus and a reclusive, eccentric expert in fabber pattern design.

"My contact," Burro said, "Sends the following note: 'Sorry, pal, you're screwed. Fabbers are locked out of making almost anything interesting. No weapons, no dangerous narcotics, no gray matter.' Would you like me to help you design a robotic dinosaur instead?"

For Niklaus, this revelation took all of the momentum out of his Elopteryx project. No wonder historians were boring. Modern civilization forbade playing with the interesting parts of history. Without direction, Niklaus began fiddling with the patterns, trying to decide what next to plan for his career.

Once a week or so Niklaus fabbed a beautiful, brainless Elopteryx. Then he would masturbate, running his hands over its stubbled scales and fine protoquills, dumping the dead thing into the recycler when he was done with a weighty and growing sense of shame.

———◉———

Maggie missed the approach into San Francisco. She was busy enjoying the gelship's full shower facilities; an extravagant expense that she charged to Simon's account. By the time they turned off the water and ordered the passengers into their seats, she felt better and had a new theory about the night before. The men at the dance had probably smelled a day and half of the Australian outback on her. Enough to repulse anyone, she told herself.

The terminal was much larger than in Perth, with a thicker crowd that made Simon jumpy and distracted. Maggie considered ditching him, but before she made up her mind he offered breakfast. The bistro was passable, with an expansive selection of fabber-made pastries and coffees. Maggie got an omelet sculpture of the Golden Gate Bridge. After it arrived she realized it had the texture of foam rubber. Fabbers tended to sacrifice flavor for exotica, she knew, but she had been hoping the restaurant's pattern designers were superior to the ones Megasat licensed.

While she was picking at her eggs, an android arrived and handed Simon an oblong copper box. He examined it then passed it to Maggie. The lid had a thumb print latch; she opened it and found nothing inside.

"I ordered that from the airport's public fabber," he said. "It's for your jewelry."

"You know, when you give someone a gift, you're supposed to give the jewelry, not just the box."

"It's radio-proof—put the governor inside. We need to block its transmissions or it'll report our location at every step."

Maggie fished the governor out of her pocket. It blinked icons into her vision, and she felt a sadistic thrill as she clapped the case shut on the demonic thing. "So does this mean we're hidden?"

"Nearly. Fianna, after we pay for our food go into alias mode. Select an alias at random from those tagged 'never used.'"

"Yes, sir," the android replied. "Your alias will be Howard Divanni."

"That's fine. Maggie, are you ready?"

"Wait. Another registered alias isn't going to help. Not after the trick you pulled with mine. They're going to be watching."

"Very good," he said, nodding. "But this isn't a registered alias. Howard is a real person—someone for whom I've done pro bono work in the past. In return, he signed a contract allowing me use of his identity at some unspecified date. It's quite legal, merely an altered power of attorney contract. For the next twenty four hours I'll use Howard's accounts and Fianna will spoof his hardware idents. When I've run out of time, I can choose someone else. I've made many such arrangements."

Maggie frowned and ran her fingers over the smooth copper case. "You said this thing would give away my location?"

"Yes, and record all the conversations you have. I think they gave it to you hoping that you'd lead them to the Platinum Donkeys. They have a hard time following me." Simon drummed his fingers on his coffee cup. "Although to be honest, we're taking a risk in any archology. Cameras are everywhere. I'm not sure we can really avoid being tracked. But might as well make it a challenge for them."

"Yeah. Okay." She put the governor case in her pocket with a sense that she had narrowly missed a pitfall. Ditching Simon meant losing his bag of tricks. She had no idea how to hide from the authorities; they'd find her easily. She didn't even know how to access her financial accounts. On Megasat, she never paid for anything. Probably someone else did. She wasn't sure.

Simon pushed his chair back and took a deep breath. "So. Now for something that I have been dreading. Unavoidable, really..."

"What?"

"To get anywhere in San Francisco," he said, with a stammering lip, "we have to take the trolley."

———————◦———————

The 'trolley' was a boxy vehicle, large enough to seat twenty people, with 19th century style wood furniture and no wheels. It sat, painted in festive reds and yellows, suspended from a series of matching arched columns. Simon offered Maggie the window seat, then he put on his spectacles, sat nearby, and clutched Fianna as if the android were a life preserver. Maggie looked around for the source of his nervousness. The trolley was full of people, but with the open seating arrangements it didn't feel crowded. The voice that asked people to stand clear of the doors was bright and cheerful. The windows were large enough that claustrophobia was unlikely—

As she turned to look out the window, the pavement below dropped away.

When the columns tilted and moved, their ends picking up from the pavement below, Maggie put it together. The trolley walked on six giant legs that arced over the top of the vehicle like a spider's. It rose from its sitting position and picked up speed, heading for the wall of the airport. A thrill of danger went through Maggie as the trolley scuttled up the building, planting its legs in concealed crevices in the concrete wall. Handholds for a giant trolley-bot as she looked ahead, Maggie could spot more of them marking a path.

"Oh, Simon, this is cool. Come on, you've got to see this!"

"No, I don't," he squeaked, hugging his android tighter.

The passenger cabin swayed a little as the trolley climbed on to the airport rooftop, but the many-legged vehicle compensated for its motions well. It scurried across the top of the terminal building, using handholds on the ribs of the glass roof. Then it stepped across to an adjacent building, some sort of warehouse, without breaking stride. Maggie could see other trolleys ahead of them, as a constant stream of arachnoid transports walked to and from the airport.

"This is great," she said, poking at her terrified host. "But why not just use the road?"

"There are no roads in the arcology," he moaned.

The front of the trolley looked out over an expanse of metal and glass. Maggie got up, ignoring the disapproving tone of the robot as it asked her to remain seated. She walked to the front of the cabin for a better view. Some of the other passengers smiled at her, but she ignored them as well, until someone tapped her on the shoulder.

He was an older man in rumpled clothing; the type of seat filler that Maggie tended to forget ten seconds after meeting them. "First time in San Fran?"

She nodded and walked past.

The spider-trolley moved quickly, pulling itself over roofs and up walls using the indented steel handholds that seemed to be everywhere. The roofs themselves were covered with solar panels, or paved with thin pedestrian walkways, or lined with dirt beds in which grew an impressive variety of flowers and shrubs. In the distance Maggie could see a hill rising over the rooftops, but it also was crusted with shiny black buildings and twisting walkways. There seemed to be no break in the architecture. The trolleys had full freedom to roam the city by the simple strategy of walking on top of it.

"Oyster Point Boulevard, next stop. Please take your seat."

Maggie held onto a wooden fixture as the trolley slowed to a stop, then spun around with quick steps until it was aligned with a pedestrian walkway. It lowered itself and one person got off. Maggie took their seat, and the walking trolley rose up and scampered off again.

Looking to the horizon, Maggie saw water in one direction but nothing but buildings everywhere else. She was used to packed habitats, but this was Megasat writ large. The San Fran Arcology was an artificial hab with no limits on its resources. Fabbers converted waste into food and electronics. The ocean could be filtered to provide water; power came from the sun and from power farms across the continent. Recreation areas were indoors, or more likely virtual. With nothing to limit their growth, humanity had packed themselves into warrens, taking advantage of the efficiencies of concentrated population. They had used every square meter, to the point where even having roads was considered a waste of space.

Still, the housing units looked spacious enough, and the residents she saw on the walkways seemed happy. Perhaps they weren't packed as tightly as it appeared. It was either utopia or dystopia, Maggie was sure, but certainly nothing in between.

The trolley's stops seemed to be silently dictated by the passengers. Maggie sat through three more, watching as they moved nearer a group of tall skyscrapers in the distance. Then Fianna spoke, announcing that the next stop was theirs.

Their stop was a walkway on the side of a tall building. The spider-trolley hung off the edge, touching the side of its passenger cabin to the top of the railing. Maggie walked down a few semi-circular steps to the pedestrian area. Once Fianna led Simon down, the steps retreated back into the walkway surface. The trolley stepped past them, its legs swiveling over the top of the cabin to catch handholds higher up.

Maggie ran back to the railing to look. The trolley was already crossing the threshold of the roof, hidden in part by hanging foliage from planters on the building's side. She looked down and saw more greenery, down to the next rooftop below. When they were approaching the building the gardens had looked spotty and thin. Cunning placement made them appear as thick as a forest when seen from her vantage.

"The grass is greener on this side," she muttered.

"Hmmn?" Simon had backed against the wall, as far from the railing as possible, and was trying to compose himself. "Yes, well, it keeps the herd from straying, I suppose. Can we continue, please?"

"Sure." Maggie spun around and smiled. "I was just letting you catch your breath. Wasn't that wild?"

"Yes. 'Wild.' Fianna, please lead."

"I've got to do a skit with those things when I get back to my show! We can make scale mockups of the trolleys. Have two of them get into a fight, then crash through a skylight into a celebrity ball...no, no, wait! We'll have a trolley meet a car on the street. And it can't figure out what the car is, right? But the car can't get around it. So the spider-trolley catches the car and starts fucking it—"

"The two almost never meet, Maggie. There are no roads here."

"My show is entertainment, not a travelogue. Speaking of which, where are we?"

"An apartment building. We're meeting a client of mine."

The android took them on a short walk along the path and into a corridor. Although the outside path was plastic and tile in neutral colors, the interior walls were expressive and gaudy. Every twenty meters or so the colors and textures changed. A length of purple siding with an interior neon glow gave way to a cobblestone facade which abutted a faux tree-bark exterior with tiny robot squirrels scampering across it. In the center of each customized length of corridor was a matching door, and next to that a standardized black rectangle that displayed the residence's address. The three of them walked past a dozen apartments before Fianna stopped at a double unit. Its facade was blank, the same gray plastic as the exterior walkway, although it had a large wooden sign straddling the two units that read 'MADAME SUIZ'. Smaller signs were perched on top of the gray doorways; one said 'Antiques', and the other 'No Entry'.

Simon motioned Fianna toward the Antiques entrance. The android held the door open with a mock curtsy.

The air inside caught in Maggie's throat. It was thick with incense and ten degrees hotter than the air outside. The dim lighting was enhanced by the thin passageways between racks of shelving that held an astounding array of junk. Glassware was piled next to strings of toy trains, over a shelf with moldy tomes covered in what looked like real leather, while across the aisle porcelain dolls sat propped against faded metal signs beneath a stack of amber-encased insects and jagged lumps of quartz. As Maggie stepped deeper in she saw movement on another shelf. There a tiny robot—like a miniature peacock without a head—was dusting a set of metal hand tools whose blades were painted with wildlife scenes. She took another step and realized that Simon was not with her. He was still standing in the doorway, his body shaking, his eyes wide and looking past her.

"Leah," he said, in a voice that sounded too strong for his jittery frame. "It's a bit stuffy in here. Any chance you could let us in the other entrance?"

In front of Maggie something moved, something that she had thought was another pile of faded throw pillows, or perhaps a sofa in bad need of repair. It lifted its head and a hood fell back on its shoulders, exposing a round, splotchy face with a long splash of greasy black hair. The robed woman glanced at Simon, then looked at Maggie. Her smile got wide enough to show jagged, yellow teeth, and the woman cackled in a way that was either well practiced or completely natural.

"Nah. I have things piled back there," she said. "If you can make it through the store, it opens up in back."

Then she turned and shambled off, through a bead curtain that promised a well-lit area beyond.

Before Maggie reached that curtain, Simon dashed by her at a full run, pushing her into a rack of bead jewelry that clattered as she fell against it. Fianna was more polite but just as swift, stepping past Maggie in graceful strides. Maggie paused a moment, wondering how sharp the painted saw blades were, before she joined the others in the back room.

The back room was more open by the virtue of its junk being in piles on the floor instead of closely arrayed shelves. Leah chuckled and waved them through another doorway. "Come on. Trust in the lord, he'll see you through."

"Stop *that*, please," Simon growled.

The next room was clearly part of Leah's living space, though no less cluttered, with furniture arranged around a video display. Stacks of thin books overlay everything, and on the wall was a sconce with a single fat candle. Leah tapped the candle—its tip blared alight—and excavated a chair to sit on. Maggie waited for her to clean a second or third chair, but the lumpy woman only smiled.

Maggie looked around for a moment. The chairs were smart foam, formless blocks that adapted to whoever sat on them. She kicked one over, spilling books across the room, and sat down. The chair yielded and wrapped itself around her, adapting just as well on its side as standing up.

Leah cackled. "So you're the legendary Mags. Simon, you led me to expect a frightened little girl!"

"No," Maggie said, "That would be him."

Simon crossed his arms, standing with Fianna in the least cluttered part of the carpet. "You haven't changed, Leah. Wasn't it a violation of the fire codes that got you kicked out of Austin?"

"Cleanliness is next to godliness," Leah said. "Besides, I can't afford to put all my stock in storage. The prices are exorbitant; nobody cares whether real artifacts survive, only whether they've been digitized or not."

Maggie picked up a book and thumbed to the beginning. A copyright notice said 1936. "These are all real?"

"Real as the day they were printed. Ever hold something that wasn't made in a fabber before?"

The book had a faded yellow jacket with a short tear. Maggie placed it back on the ground carefully, afraid it would crumble into dust. "I didn't know people kept junk this old. Is it illegal?"

"No," said Simon, "just ridiculous."

"Fuck you. You ask for my help then insult my livelihood? I've got a good mind to turn you over to Globalpol, see if there's a reward."

"There isn't any. And you'd have a lot more to lose than we would if the police came here. Especially since you would no longer have an attorney."

Leah mumbled. "Show respect when in another's lair, is all I'm saying."

"Madame Suiz, if I didn't respect you, we would not be here. Now can you run the tests or not?"

"Of course I can," she said, looking sideways at Maggie. "How long has it been since you've eaten?"

"About...an hour."

"Is that a problem, Leah?"

"Nah. I just have to calibrate for it." She stared at Maggie for a few seconds, chewing on her bloated lip. "All right, let's do this. Come on, the lab's this way."

"Wait," Maggie said. 'Do what?" But Leah had hefted herself up and left the room. Simon motioned for Maggie to follow.

"We're here to do a blood test, Maggie," he said. "I'm sorry, but it's important."

"What?"

"I'll explain afterward. If I'm right, this will help our legal position immensely. Please."

She frowned at him, but followed.

Their host led them through a short corridor into a bedroom, where she pulled up a corner of an antique rug to expose a set of large square tiles in the floor. She tapped a sequence on the tiles and they swung down, creating a hole through which a ladder extended. Leah skipped rungs as she climbed down the ladder, and to Maggie she looked almost like a chimpanzee. Trembling from the height of the climb (though it was only three meters, if that), Simon sent Fianna down first to spot him. He clung to the ladder, moving both feet to a rung and pausing before attempting the next.

The room below was so different from above that for a moment Maggie thought they had mistakenly dropped into an adjacent showroom. On the spotless white floors stood rows of squat appliances, their hulls polished and pristine. A long table held an assemblage of glass tubes and beakers that, while complicated, appeared to have a purposeful design. More glassware and equipment sat in a pair of glass-paneled cabinets. A rack on the wall held a pressed, gleaming white lab coat. The only haphazard thing in the lab was another candle in a wall sconce, which Leah tapped to turn on.

Muttering under her breath, Leah shrugged off her faded robe and dropped it into a bin. Maggie gasped at the sight of the woman's body, clad only in a slip and panties. Her torso was as fat and shapeless as it had seemed beneath the robe, but her limbs were shocking, sculpted perfection. A closer look made her realize that 'sculpted' was the operative word—there were Megasat corporate logos on each forearm, and thin strips of slightly darker skin around each joint.

Leah saw her looking and grinned. "Nice work, these," she said, tapping on her elbow. Then she pulled a coat off the rack and slipped into it. "They designed them in that big retirement home for rich people you've got up there. Should thank you for that."

"We've got...some retirees, I guess." There were a few dozen permanent residents of Megasat, old people who thought zero gee would stretch their final years out longer. She had avoided them all her life, except for those occasions where Mega forced her to socialize. "They mostly have their own limbs, though."

"Limbs, maybe. Organs? Don't be too sure. All kinds of life-extension research going on up there. I've bartered what I could—limbs, new pancreas, a couple other supporting organs. My immune system's pure phagotech. Thank the dark lord we have artificial white cells to make smart decisions about what's a disease and what's an upgrade." With her coat buttoned, she shambled toward the table. "Now let's see how they've upgraded you."

"I don't have anything like that inside me!"

"No, nothing like that," Simon said. "But please, humor us."

As Leah came toward her with a blood kit and a folding chair, Maggie gave her a suspicious frown. "So you're a total slob upstairs, but I'm supposed to believe this room is clean? What century is that needle from, anyway?"

"The needle was fabbed this morning. Sterile as a nun's ovaries. Now come on, sit down," she said. Maggie obliged, feeling nervous, but Leah's movements were skillful and meticulous. "Trust me, kid. Having a cluttered laboratory is stupid, and stupidity's a sin. I live an effective life, dear, and that means being clean where I have to be.'

The needle was painless. Leah filled two small ampules with blood, then pressed a ball of fluff against the wound. Maggie waited until she walked away before saying, "I didn't know stupidity was a sin."

Simon looked on, sighing. "Not one of God's sins. You're lucky the unification guaranteed freedom of religion, Leah. If Satanism were illegal, I'd have never gotten you out of that jail cell in Austin."

"Now, now, nobody actually worships Satan. But I do take a left-handed path." Leah used a thin glass rod to take blood from the ampules. Then she squeezed out two precise drops into each of several test tubes filled with a variety of colored liquids. "This is going to be a minute or two, kids."

Maggie checked the needle mark for blood, then tossed the bit of fluff onto the floor. Stepping closer to Simon, she hissed at him. "I want some answers, suit boy. What kind of tests are these?"

"They're nothing serious. We just want to know what kind of drugs are in your system."

"I don't do drugs. I mean, I wanted to, but I couldn't get any. Smuggling narcotics up a space elevator is impossible. I quit trying when I was fourteen."

"We're not testing for narcotics, Maggie. Please, patience."

"And why come here? You could forge me an identity and check me into a hospital. Or do you get a kickback for every patient you refer to Madam Creepy?"

"A hospital wouldn't perform most of the tests we're doing. Leah's the only hobbyist I know who can. Thanks to those," he said, nodding toward the row of machines on the floor.

Maggie inspected the nearest. It looked like a kitchen appliance, with a hinged lid and a series of complicated displays on its side. There was also a thick pipe leading into it with the word 'FEED' stenciled across it.

"That's just a fabber."

"It's an unlicensed fabber," he said. "Completely unrestricted. Leah cobbled one together and had it make copies of itself. That's how she built this extremely illegal laboratory. They don't allow just anyone to have chemical refineries in their basement, you know."

Maggie walked over and lifted the fabber's lid. The hollow inside was lined with carbon-black plastic. At the bottom of the cabinet sat a neat stack of books, the last batch of items created. Seeing a familiar color, she dug through the pile and pulled one out. The book had a faded yellow jacket with a pre-fabbed tear. "Hey, Leah," she said, holding the book high. "What the fuck?"

Glancing over, Leah cackled. "A girl's got to make a living. Now sit down, I have something here."

"What?" asked Simon, walking over to the table. Maggie joined him. She noticed that some of the test tubes had changed colors. Leah pointed at one of those, while paging through a book of complex symbols and names.

"We've got Levadopa. Amantadine. There's a stew of phenylalanines in here. I think the dosages are subclinical, but together they're going to do something."

"What does that mean?" asked Maggie.

Simon held up his hand, pushing her to be patient. "What else?"

"Let's see." Their host noted another set of colored solutions, and cross-referenced them in her book. "No serotonin precursors, but we have homeotonin and some kind of butyrophenone analogue. And..." She tapped a tube whose solution had turned bright purple, and broke out into laughter. "Heh, I'm seeing traces of BZ. Holy shit, they've got you on one hell of a cocktail, kid."

"This is bullshit. I haven't done any drugs!"

"What's their purpose, Leah?"

"Ah, a little bit of everything. Some of these are dysphrenic, others are anti-psychotic. I think they were trying to get the mix right." She turned and flashed her jagged teeth. "Mags, they *made* you crazy."

"What?"

Simon folded his arms. "You take supplements."

"Everyone takes supplements. On Megasat you can spend half your life at zero-gee. The supplements keep your bones from snapping."

"Your supplements are different from everyone else's."

"I grew up there. They had to give me a special formulation because I was younger."

"Now that you're an adult, why are they still giving you custom supplements?"

"Because I—" Maggie paused. "Those fuckers."

Leah read from her book. "Hallucinations, hyperaggression, increased libido, delusions of grandeur...any of those sound familiar?"

"Those motherfuckers. I'll fucking kill them."

"I'll take that as a yes."

"That fucking Tom. And Percy, too. It's got to be them. I'm going to rip their fucking hearts out!"

"Now, if they were smart about it, the dopamine antagonists are in here to deal with the nausea, dyskinesis, and self-control problems. Well, maybe they didn't care about that last one."

"That ratfucker told me, 'We've been running ads like that for years'. They doped me up to make better television!"

"That may have been part of it," said Simon. He continued to speak, but Maggie didn't hear him. She was pacing around the lab, pulling at her hair and looking for something sharp.

It's all their fault. Everything. Every man that I killed.

Not an excu—

Yes, it's a DAMN good excuse, screamed something inside her as it broke free. She beat her fists on a fabber's hull, turned and kicked at the glass cabinets. The glass cracked into thin, welcoming shards; she kicked again and it disintegrated, crumbling into useless nuggets of safety glass. Reaching inside she grabbed at wires and smooth devices and flung them over her shoulder. Her arm swept across a shelf, dumping half its contents on the floor. Something glittered—a glass bottle had smashed by her feet. She lunged for it, grabbing it by the neck, and then there was someone behind her. She spun, thrusting.

The broken bottle thudded into Fianna's chest. Her grey jacket had blunted the impact; Maggie couldn't tell if her weapon had pierced the plastic skin. The android grabbed her forearm. "Simon wants you to calm down," it said.

"Fuck you, bitch! Get the hell away from me!" Maggie tried to pull her arm back to stab again, but Fianna slapped the weapon away with a force that left her hand numb.

"Simon wants you to calm down," it repeated in the exact tones as before.

"Shut up! Shut up," she screamed, her breath catching in her throat and turning into ragged sobs. She flailed at Fianna's chest with her free hand then collapsed, sinking to her knees, leaning her weight on the android's cool, unmovable frame. Tears blocked her vision and for a time she let them flow. When her breath eased, when the tears stopped and Fianna had released her, she wiped her eyes on the android's jacket and stood up.

"Okay. Okay, lawyer man," she said, tilting her head and showing teeth but not a smile. "What do we do? Where do we go from here?"

Simon's entire body shook, but his voice remained steady. "You want revenge."

"Damn straight I do."

"You'll get it," he said, his voice becoming soft, and sad. "You'll get it."

For a few seconds, the four of them were motionless except for Simon's trembling. Then Leah, sporting a wicked smile, clapped her hands together.

"All right, I think we're done here. Robots will clean up. How about some tea? Caffeine might smooth out any withdrawal symptoms you get, by the way."

"How bad is her withdrawal going to be, Leah?"

"It'll be slow, but not too bad. She's probably in the middle of it now. How about some tea for you, Simon? Cream and sugar, right?"

"He doesn't need tea," Maggie said. "Nobody drugged him."

"Now, girl, when you have a suitor—"

"I'm *not* her—," Simon began.

"—you feed him as often as possible. You know what they say about the quickest way to a man's heart."

"Yes," Maggie said, letting the word end with a hiss. "Go in under the ribcage, stab up toward his shoulder blade with a twist to the left."

Leah froze in mid-stride, and turned to look at her. Simon's eyes went wide. After an uncomfortable second of silence, Maggie added "His left."

Leah's face turned red as she broke into a fit of cackling laughter. Simon, without a sound, buried his face in shaking hands.

———◉———

Chapter 9—Musical Guests

The tea was okay. What Maggie found most soothing, though, was Leah's decor. As they went deeper in, the old woman's home seemed to lose all sense of propriety, so that the kitchen had dioramas on the counters depicting scenes from Hieronymus Bosch's paintings of hell. Scores of little plastic robots were torturing each other or cut into twisted pieces or smiling serenely or all of the above, and when Maggie glanced away they shifted positions into a new tableau. So she sipped her tea and kept her eyes on them, daring them to move while she could see them. Being able to control even this tiny world made her feel better. Picturing Tom and Percy's faces on the more miserable victims helped, too.

She did, however, make a note never to look into Leah's bedroom.

For a long while, Simon and Leah left her alone as they argued in the living room. Maggie caught snippets of their conversation but didn't make any attempt to pay attention. She didn't feel like listening. She felt numb. Yet coiled also, like a crouching predator that had waited to pounce for too long.

After the argument went silent, Leah shambled back into the kitchen, chuckling. "That boy can be stubborn. Oh, did that light go out?"

The candle on the wall sconce had been lit, but Maggie had touched it out of curiosity. It felt like wax, and some came free on her fingernails, but as soon as she had touched it the light had turned off. Maggie had left it alone after that. The red lighting from the diorama better suited her mood.

"Sorry, that was me," she said. "I wanted to see what it was made of."

Leah smiled and tapped the candle to light it again. "It's piezoelectric wax. One of my few profitable fabber patterns. My fabber feed is so expensive, I'm lucky that I have some royalties coming in. I don't know how normal people manage."

"I think they," Maggie began, then paused. She had no idea how normal people managed their money, how they made or spent anything. She asked people for things, they bought them for her. "Never mind. I really don't know much about money."

Sitting down at the table, Leah instructed the adjoining kitchen fabber to make her a cup of tea. "Rhetorical question, kid. Normal people make patterns, or programs, or entertainments, or they get by on their regional stipends. All they spend money on is fabber feed and entertainment, after all. It's dead easy to live a quiet, happy life, for those who want that kind of thing."

Her order was done; the fabber unit opened and she picked up her new cup, new saucer, new spoon, new tea. A minute ago they were all unformed feed. Maggie scratched her nails against the tabletop.

"Leah? What will the new me be like?"

"Hmmn" Leah sipped through a wisp of steam. "What 'new you'?"

"I mean...when the drugs wear off."

"Oh, you might not notice a difference. You probably started out unbalanced, and they just kept you on edge to keep you from getting well. Insanity fades with time. The pain that caused it becomes a memory. You learn coping mechanisms that let you approach the world on more reasonable terms. You mellow out." The old woman perhaps meant to be comforting, but her yellow-toothed smile was grotesque. Maggie felt as though a grub was fantasizing to her about the turn of the seasons. "They didn't want you to mellow, so they kept your system off balance. Given time you'll calm down. I was a firecracker at your age, hoo-boy. But by the time I hit my sixties or so I don't think I was crazy anymore. An odd bird, yes. But not crazy, just mellow."

"How can I tell when I'm mellowing out?"

Leah shrugged. "You'll act the same, until one day when you realize you're making no sense. You'll recognize when the things you do and say seem random. They're never random, though, not ever. They come from deep inside, from that hurt place, from that ragged scar in your brain stem. Someday you'll learn how different those thoughts are, how the crazy thoughts taste different than the sane ones. That's when you'll have a decision to make."

"What decision?"

"You'll need to decide if those hurt, crazy thoughts are valid or not. Has your entire life been a lie, based around the delusions of a malfunctioning hindbrain? If so, then discipline yourself back into sanity. Become one of the norms, one of the *sheep*." She sipped her tea and waved a hand in the air, dismissing the entire world with a gesture. "Or...you can embrace the crazy. Let your subconscious tell you what to do, because it generally knows best anyway. You'll have the discipline to restrain your impulses, but the power to let them run wild when needed. You can have the best of both worlds. There's nothing more dangerous than a psychopath who has learned how to act normal."

Maggie felt bile at the back of her throat as Leah gave a twisted, conspiratorial grin. *Is it her face or her message that's so repulsive? Or is it neither—is it something inside me, refusing to listen?*

"So you stuck to your guns, huh?" she blurted out, her voice rising. "You figured it all out, and that got you—what? A shitty little house that's safe as long as the cops aren't looking? So you found yourself and you're a fucking freak, and that's all you want out of life?"

The smile disappeared, but Leah seemed blasé, not offended at all. "No. This is enough for me, I guess, but I've been waiting for other opportunities. What I want is power. That's why I'm coming with you."

"With us? To where?"

"To wherever you're going. It's my payment for services rendered. The big bad Donkeys are up to something and I want in. I hope it's Armageddon, I really do. As for what I want, I want to be Empress of the world. I want to see every Christian, every hypocrite and every conformist gutted. I want to see their entrails rotting in the sun. And I want a throne made of their children's skulls. I want to feel it creak every time I scratch my ass." Without taking her eyes off Maggie she took another sip, and Maggie thought she was going to continue after that. But instead she put her cup down, folded her hands, and gave another repulsive smile.

"Huh," Maggie said. "Well, I'm glad you mellowed out."

Leah cackled and pushed her chair away from the table. "You ain't the only one, kid," she said, standing up. "Now I've got to pack. Use the shower, the fabber, whatever you want. I'm thinking of torching this place when we leave, anyway."

She shambled out of the kitchen. Maggie dumped both teacups into the fabber's recycling bin, and told the machine to give her a double-shot of scotch.

Simon came into the kitchen just as that order was ready. "Hey. How are you feeling?"

"Fine," she lied, downing the scotch in one gulp. Then she tossed that glass in the recycler and gave him her best stage smile. "Where to next?"

He looked at her with an uncertain frown, and sat at the table. "If you need some time... I mean, if things are going too fast for you, we can stay here for a day or two before we go on."

"No! No, I'm ready. Whenever you are. Let's go. Yeah."

Slowly, Simon nodded, his hand beginning to twitch. "All right. Um. Because the next leg of our journey is going to be difficult, and I'm going to need your help."

"Really? For what?"

"Maggie. It's not easy to travel around without being seen by the authorities. There are cameras in every public space, and they can identify you by the way you walk if nothing else. Any travel arrangements I make, no matter what identity, will go through databases designed to distinguish us from everyone else. I do have a plan, though. But I need you to do two things for me. The first and most important is, I need you to *try* to behave."

He paused, watching her face, but she stayed frozen. *I'm a freak. We're going to be caught because I'm a freak.*

"I know it's not always your fault. But we need to pretend to be normal people. That means no tantrums, no fights, no...flirting with helpless young men. Do you understand? We need to put on an act. You can do that, can't you? You can act normal?"

"Yes, I can," she said with a small voice. Then she sniffed and the rest came blurting out. "I never meant to kill anyone, Simon, and I didn't mean to break anything downstairs and I'm sorry I hurt Fianna—"

"Fianna's fine. She's my bodyguard, she's well-armored."

"And I really can act normal, I used to do it every day. Not on my show, I mean..." Taking a deep breath, she rubbed her eyes. "I can. You haven't seen me really act, Simon. I can do it."

"Good. I know you can." He smiled. Maggie smiled back, though she wasn't sure that she could live up to her promise. "As for me, I'm going to have to be heavily medicated. No real option there. But maybe that can be part of my disguise. That's the other thing I need your help with."

"What?"

"We all need disguises to fit our cover story, and you know more than I do about costuming. Do you think you can fab some disguises for us?"

"What's our cover story?"

Simon almost winced, as if he had bitten something sour. "Well, I wish I could have found another way, but... We're going to be groupies for a band."

For a second Maggie thought he was joking. Then she cracked a smile. "Oh, yeah. Yeah, I can work with that."

———◦———

The band's name was the Solar Lumberjacks, and Maggie had never had them on her program because they sucked. That may have been unfair—her standards were high, and 'Sol Lum' (as they were called) had never made it above a regional novelty act. Their gimmick was using chainsaws in their music, along with precisely fabbed, resonant cylinders of wood. The effect was akin to wood chimes being fed into a garbage disposal, with a reverb filter, and then amplified with the pure sonic fidelity of a 19th century gramophone.

But they had fans, and they toured quite a bit, having nothing better to do. Like most entertainers their income depended on giving performances. Sol Lum liked to roam all over the American west and northwest. Maggie had a theory about that: She guessed that if they ever gave a concert in the same place twice, they'd be arrested for lack of talent.

Stop that, she thought to herself while boarding the tour bus. *You have to pretend to like this band.*

The 'tour bus' was a double hotel suite on wheels, a massive recreational vehicle that took up two lanes on the Golden Gate bridge. They had boarded at the Fort Point transfer facility, where spider trolleys mingled with ground vehicles headed outside of the city, and where Maggie got a few new ideas for her trolley-car rape skit.

The fans allowed on the bus were winners of a raffle. It didn't surprise Maggie at all that her, Simon and Leah's new identities were already listed as winners. In fact, she caught hints that the band's entire tour was arranged by either Simon or his network of contacts. She meant to ask him about that later. On this trip Simon's cover was that of a doddering old grandpa, and he was layered in old age makeup and drowned in antipsychotic medications. The poor bastard almost didn't know where he was. Fianna, in a skimpy nurse's uniform, served as a wonderful accessory and distraction for his disguise.

Leah, as the member of their trio for whom the police were not yet searching, wore the least amount of makeup. She only had a change of hair color and padding for her limbs to make them as fat as the rest of her body. Blue jeans and a jacket with the band's chainsaw/ guitar logo on the back finished her disguise. She was 'mom', the biggest fan of the three, dragging her family on tour with her favorite band.

Maggie saved the most clever disguise for herself. From the fabber she made a substance that turned her hair brown and gunked it up into rastafarian dreads. Another cream she had worked with in the past self-assembled into short strands, and gave her an instant five o'clock shadow. She bound up her breasts (which was as uncomfortable as she had remembered) and wore loose fitting slacks and an oversized t-shirt from the band's last tour. The last time she had played a seventeen year-old boy it had surprised the hell out of the audience when she had washed away the disguise. Although that did involve an on-stage shower and a self-releasing breast strap. The skit had progressed into a wet t-shirt contest, and then into a no t-shirt contest. But she knew that she could play the part.

Even better, while immersed in the role of a hetero boy she'd have no urge to flirt with any attractive (or talented) band members. She was determined to behave, to show Simon that she could take her situation seriously. Her recent revelation had convinced her that she needed him. If for nothing else, she would need a lawyer's help to regain control of the Megasat hour and fire Tom and Percy. Or to get her off death row after she dealt with them herself...

She needn't have worried about the Solar Lumberjacks. After drunkenly welcoming their fans onto the bus, they cocooned themselves into the forward suite with a handful of miniskirt-wearing tramps. The remaining dozen fans were left in the rear suite with couches, a snack fabber and a rear wall display playing what was either a concert video or a logger documentary—Maggie wasn't sure which. She helped Fianna lead Simon to a plush chair somewhat removed from the noise.

As she turned around, a familiar shape made her freeze. The minicamera hovered in the air an arm's length away, panning around the room with a lazy spinning motion. Two more floated in the corners of the suite focusing on individual guests. Their buzzing wings were drowned out by the concert soundtrack, but Maggie thought she could hear them, thought she could feel the noise raising the hairs on the back of her neck.

She stepped backward and bumped into the android. "Fianna?" she said, spinning around, not looking. "Tell me, are there minicameras in this room?"

The android straightened her nurses' cap (*Did he program that into her?*) and scanned the room with her blank face. She turned back to Maggie. "There are three robotic cameras in the room."

"Really? They're really there?"

"They are there, there, and over there," Fianna said, pointing with quick fluid motions.

Exhaling a sigh of relief, Maggie turned around. The cameras were watching the entire crowd, not just her. One woman seemed to be directing them with motions of her hand—she had a ring that could be an eyeline control. Maggie went up to her, keeping her voice gruff and low like she had practiced. "Those your cameras?"

"Yeah," the woman said. "I'm doing a documentary on the tour. I'll have it on the net right after we get to Portland."

She seemed friendly, even though she only looked at Maggie with quick glances, as if the cameras were giving her trouble. "Why don't you just stream them live?", Maggie asked.

"Are you kidding? I'm not Maggie Mags, I'm going to want to clean the footage up afterward. Besides, I'm having a hard time keeping them from bumping into things."

"They should have auto-avoidance. What studio package are you using?"

"Oh," the woman said with a disappointed tone. "I just fabbed the cameras, I didn't buy any software for them. You know about cameras?"

"Uh, a little."

"Want to help? I can use a hand."

It took Maggie a second to consider the offer. Having control of the cameras would let her keep track of where they were, and more importantly, which ones were real. But she couldn't. "Sorry. I'm not connected. Just dumb clothing."

"What? Like, no net access at all?"

"Yeah." Maggie backed off, shrugging, and the filmmaker turned back to her invisible controls. Wishing that they had given more thought to their cover story, she sat with Leah and avoided eye contact with everyone. The crowd settled in and ordered drinks as the bus began to roll.

Leah grinned at her and pulled out white gloves and a small wooden box from her small duffel bag. "What's the matter? Fans make you nervous?"

"No. Those cameras do."

"Cameras? You??"

"It's complicated," Maggie growled. Leah cackled.

"Well," she said, putting on her white gloves, "I know how we can pass the time. Want a tarot reading?" She opened the lid of the box. Inside was a deck of cards, the top one showing a demonic figure carrying a bindle, with ragged pants down around his goat-like feet and a prominent erection.

Maggie rolled her eyes. "Not everyone gets off on the death imagery, grandma." While the old lady cackled some more, Maggie got back up to grab a drink.

An hour later, after several watered-down gins, Maggie concluded that Sol Lum treated their fans like trash. The band had kept to their suite, and the door was guarded by a butch-looking roadie with obscene words tattooed on her knuckles. The fans in the back didn't seem to mind; they had an insatiable appetite for the concert footage, and sing-alongs broke out every third song, although Maggie couldn't swear that they were getting the lyrics right under the chainsaw noises. *If I had organized this, there'd be a spectacle. That's what fans want to see.* The events she threw for fans included meetings with the producer, memorabilia and stories, and face time with her. She had always tried to interact with her fans when they came to visit Megasat. *Of course, I've hurt a few,* she thought, remembering the man who broke his wrist during her last show. *But I gave them events to remember. And seriously, who loads cheap drinks into their fabber? Are the watered-down patterns cheaper?*

The cameras were bothering her also; flying in close, hovering over people's heads, and always that buzzing sound that she somehow could hear through the chainsaw's roar. At first she avoided them by getting another drink whenever one approached her. But soon she found herself with a drink in each hand and no way to carry a third. After some of the fans gave her strange looks when she downed two glasses of watery gin in two gulps, Maggie began scheming of ways to stay moving while being inconspicuous.

She decided to alter her role from wallflower to host. At first she sat near the fabber, playing with its menus and offering to dial up anything other people wanted to order. Soon she was delivering orders across the room, picking up glasses and plates for the recycler, and was the first on the scene with sponges when one of the fans got tipsy enough to spill their beer. It felt good, making the craptastic tour a little better for everyone. But she had hoped that by hosting she would become invisible to the cameras, who should be focused on those who were doing more interesting things. No such luck. The filmmaker kept trying to include her in conversations, and made sure to linger the cameras on her whenever panning the crowd. Maggie got the impression that the girl was attracted to her, and mentally kicked herself for talking to the girl earlier.

A break came when a red-headed teen checked her handbag display and asked them to mute the concert footage. "Guys, guys!", she shouted, despite that fact that most of Sol Lum's fans were young girls. "We're almost at my family's park! Let's turn on a window!" After a group agreement, one of the walls of the room was turned into a virtual window looking out of the bus. Curious, Maggie pushed her way to a better view.

They were traveling almost as fast as the limo in Australia had been, but the scenery outside could not have been more different. The highway cut through hills that began with a gentle slope but turned up at a sharp angle. On the side of the hills and in the valleys between them, the ground was covered with buildings, lesser roadways, and life. Cultivated trees, flower gardens, and the indistinct forms of people on walkways blurred past the window.

To Maggie, this was a dense urban city, like the nicer suburbs of Osaka where her show's correspondent filmed. They had just left an actual urban arcology, where people spent most of their time indoors and never used a road. But this small outlying town looked more populated and vibrant than San Fran. The metropolis seemed stagnant; the suburb was overcrowded and pulsing with energy. How it came to be like this, Maggie couldn't imagine.

"It's the next valley," the girl said, watching a display on her shirt sleeve.

A few seconds later the bus zoomed past another foothill. By some standards the other side was bare. The buildings abruptly ended, and trees were scattered on the slope of the hill. The valley beyond was covered in dense foliage of every shade of green, and in some spots there were sprinkles of yellow and blue. It took them a minute to zoom past the overgrown field—the valley was maybe five kilometers wide—before another foothill flew by and the city reasserted itself.

"That was cool," said the filmmaker, who had steered her cameras to hover by the window. "Your family owns all that?"

"Yeah." The landowner smiled with pride. "It used to be my grandfather's farm. He just never sold it to Farmland Reclamation. We want to get it added to Mendocino forest, but we need to buy robots, first."

"For what?"

"It needs a lot of work. It's not 'natural' enough. Too many...um, invaders, I think they call them..."

"Invasive species," Leah said, leaning into the conversation. "That plot's choked with weeds and volunteer crops, kid. If I were you, I'd sell it."

"No way! We already bought the robot patterns. It's the software that's expensive."

Leah chuckled. "I'm just saying, they'll take that land from you before long. Thirty million immigrants a year to North America; they've got to put them someplace. They'll invoke eminent domain and turn the whole plot into another strip mall overnight."

"Well, I like it," said another girl. "We ought to turn all the strip malls back into forests."

The filmmaker looked up from her controls with a sour face. "I don't know about that. I like going to Santa Rosa to shop, sometimes."

"Shop on the net! That's what the fabber's for!"

"You can't make everything in a fabber. When my dad bought a car, we had to go to a showroom."

"Showrooms just have big, car-sized fabbers."

"Well, we didn't have one of those in our house. Besides, sometimes I just like to shop, you know?"

The girls giggled in agreement. Leah went back to her seat, shaking her head. Someone turned up the concert footage, and the tour went back to normal. Maggie sat looking out the window at the landscape flying by. After a while, though, she noticed Simon was awake, staring out the window, and whimpering softly, so she turned off the window and went back to hosting the party.

Another girl, a slender brunette, approached her with an intent stare. "Like, hi," she said. "Could you fab me a data pad?"

"Uh, let me check." The fabber had such a design, suitable for taking autographs and uploading them to the CenNet. "Will this do?"

She checked the design. "Yeah, that's great! I'm starting up the petition. You want to be the first to sign?"

"What kind of petition?"

"Like, you haven't been listening at all, have you?" In truth Maggie had not been. The fan's chatter was background noise to her, more pleasant than the chainsaw music if only because it was produced at lower volume. She had been listening for the buzz of the minicameras, so that she could tell when they were moving toward her. "We've been talking about getting Sol Lum on the Megasat Hour!" the girl said.

Maggie blinked. ' You think a petition is going to do that?"

"Well, Mags is down here on Earth looking for ideas for her show, right? It's, like, got to get her attention. Imagine, the best band in North Am on the best show in the world!"

Maggie focused on breathing. Smooth air in, soft air out. She thought about sad things, scary things, all the acting tricks she knew. Anything to keep from laughing in this poor girl's face.

She was saved by a 'ding!' from the fabber as it produced the tablet. The girl pulled it out of the bin, and worked for a minute as Maggie handled another drink order. When Maggie turned around again, she found the pad thrust in her face.

"I, ah, I can't sign it. I'm wearing dumb clothing."

"Oh. Well, give me your public ident key."

I don't even know what that means. Everything Maggie purchased, every paper she signed, was handled by someone else in her name. If there was a key that verified her identity, she didn't know what it was. She certainly didn't have one for her cover identity. "I can't," she said, thinking fast. "My old man has locked it."

"What?"

"He locked my identity. I hacked some of his systems," she said, putting a swagger into the performance, trying to sound proud of the confession. "I'm kinda net-grounded until I'm eighteen. Then I'm cool."

The girl looked at her like she had grown a second head. "He can do that?"

"Yeah. Sorry." The explanation, weak as it was, seemed enough. Maggie stalked off after some discarded utensils, and the girl rejoined the crowd to circulate her petition.

On her way back to the recycler, the butch roadie that guarded the other suite waved at her. Maggie had to dodge two of the damned cameras as she made her approach.

"Hey." The roadie's voice was low, close enough to a whisper that Maggie had to lean closer to hear over the music. "Can you get me some whiskey?"

"Sure." Before Maggie could turn around, the girl put a hand on her shoulder.

"Make it a bottle, and I'll get you in to see the band."

Maggie nodded and backed away—and the wings of a minicamera clipped her hair. For an instant she looked around the room for something to smash against the annoying thing. But she saw Simon watching her, and Leah showing her cards to the girl with the petition, and something inside her relaxed. *They're just amateurs. Give them some slack.*

But an idea occured to her.

Maggie dialed the fabber for a bottle of whiskey, then went to see the filmmaker. She was engrossed in watching through a camera as it watched Leah and the girl and the petition. Leah had her deck of cards out, and was giving the girl instructions on how to deal them.

"Listen," Maggie told the filmmaker, "You want to get some footage of the band?" The girl looked up, surprised and hopeful. "I can get you in."

"Really?"

Maggie nodded, and lured her back to the fabber to explain. The girl took the bottle of whiskey with a skeptical frown. When she brought it to the door, the roadie glared from across the room, but she took the bottle and punched a code into the door. The filmmaker almost jumped for joy, and she hurried to program two of her cameras to fly in formation with her as she left the room.

The third camera was stationed in a corner, overlooking the fans and video display. Maggie fabbed a dish towel and threw it over the buzzing thing. The minicamera dropped to the floor with a clunk. She waited to see if it could work its way free, but after a few seconds of fitful flapping underneath the towel the camera seemed to give up and shut down.

Smiling, Maggie felt the tension in her shoulders drain away. Even the chainsaw music sounded relaxing. A bottle of whiskey of her own began to sound like a good idea...

The scream was loud but strangled, and almost next to Maggie's ear, so that she jumped and grabbed the nearest thing—a sofa cushion—to use as a weapon.

The girl, the one who was playing cards with Leah, had stood up suddenly and flailed at herself. She beat at her shirt and jeans again with another terrified scream, then tripped and fell, thrashing her arms around as if to protect from something invisible. As Maggie watched, the girl's thrashing turned into convulsions, her entire body arcing, blood spraying from her mouth.

"What the hell?"

Maggie and the roadie got to the girl's side at the same time. The other fans stood up to see what was going on, and crowded in around them. The roadie held the girl's shoulders. Maggie patted her cheek, trying to get a reaction. Her eyes were staring, unfocused. The blood was from her tongue; she was biting it, breathing through her teeth.

"Get a medical kit!", yelled the roadie.

"From where?"

"The fabber, you idiot!"

Oh. That's what that menu is! Maggie ran to the fabber and found the menu item she had ignored before, with the icon of a pulsing red cross. It gave a short list of options; she chose 'seizure'. The fabber dinged in seconds, and Maggie brought the lumpy device it created over to the patient. The device unfolded itself, took a step closer, then plunged a short, steel needle into the girl's arm. As the girl convulsed, the needle pulled free from the robot, connected by a slender, flexible tube. Text scrolled up on the robot's tiny screen, some of it flashing and red.

In seconds the girl's eyes, which were open wide but focused on nothing, relaxed and closed. She stopped thrashing. She sighed as she exhaled, and Maggie realized that she had been holding her own breath in.

When Maggie stood up the roadie took her place and kneeled to read the robot's display. Everyone in the room was watching the scene. Everyone, Maggie noted, except the one person picking up her cards from where they had been scattered.

Maggie stepped close to Leah and whispered. "What the fuck did you do?"

"Nothing. Just gave her a tarot reading," she said, grinning.

Leah bent down to pick up another card but Maggie stopped her, intending to wring a confession out of the old woman. Then she noticed the card had oily droplets on it, shining with the light from the concert screen. Leah was wearing gloves.

"What's on the cards, Leah?"

A soft cackle, just above a whisper. "Oh, it depends on the card. Every fortune's different. That one has a bit of mescaline. I seem to recall she drew the six of wands, that's alpha-thujone, and the Angel; there's quite a bit of LSD on that one..."

Maggie punched her—the arm she hit felt hollow—and swore under her breath. Walking over to the minicamera, she retrieved the towel and used it to pick up the cards, careful not to touch them with her hands. When she had them all, Maggie wrestled the remainder of the deck from Leah's grasp with a savagery that made the fat lady blanch. By then the roadie was making a call on her shirt sleeve. Maggie walked around the crowd and dumped the bundle into the fabber's recycler just as the roadie looked up from her call.

"You—what happened?"

"I don't know. When she freaked out, she almost ran into me." By habit, Maggie reached up to fix her hair, then decided to turn the motion into a more manly ear scratch "What does the medic thing say?"

"Some kind of drug interaction. Don't understand it. Was she doing drugs? Anyone know?" A few of the fans shook their heads; one claimed that she wasn't that type of person. The roadie turned to Leah. "She was with you. What happened?"

Leah took a deep breath, her eyes shifting from one side to another. *Bitch*, thought Maggie. *Even I can tell you're stalling. I'm going to have to think of—*

"My fault!", came a throaty bark from across the room.

The crowd turned to look at Simon, who was sitting, wobbly but upright, with one hand raised. "It was my fault. I have...pills," he croaked.

Maggie took the opportunity. "Grandpa. Did you ask her to fab your pills for you?"

Simon nodded and spun his hand, encouraging her to roll with that. With the old age makeup and the hoarse voice, he looked like a jittering corpse. *If the drugs are doing that to him, I owe him one for this. But if he's acting, I want him on my show.*

"His fucking pills," she said, turning to the roadie. "They're nasty stuff. The doctors are trying to regrow his brain, see, and... Well, if she crushed one and got it on her fingers, then licked them, that would be bad."

"How bad? Is she going to be okay?"

You're the one standing in front of the medbot, asshole. "I think so. Mom? Wouldn't you agree? She'll be okay in a few hours, right?"

Leah arced her eyebrows and crossed her arms. "Oh, sure. Better than ever. Just let the poor thing rest a few hours."

Almost in unison, the crowd breathed sighs of relief. A few carried her to the sofas in the back of the room. Maggie went and sat next to Leah, and as the conversation started again and the volume of the music went up, she leaned over and whispered.

"Pull any shit like that again, Leah, and I will cut you open to see what organs are still original."

"Fuck you," the old lady said with a crooked grin. "I gave that girl an experience she'll never forget."

"You almost killed her."

"That's why it'll be unforgettable. These kids are mindless sheep. I was trying to give them a little enlightenment."

"Yeah? So you were just trying to enlighten me, too?"

"You're famous. I'd love to fuck with you a little."

"Okay. I'll be on my toes from now on. But that wasn't just a stupid kid. That was one of my fans. You do not fuck with *my* fans. Understand me?"

Leah snorted. "Lucifer on a stick, girl. You really think you're better than everyone else. The only difference between you and those kids is that something happened. Some kind of trauma screwed you up, in all kinds of interesting ways. Now you want to hog all the enlightenment to yourself. Me, I want to share. Everyone gets a little trauma, everyone gets a little closer to God. You got a problem with that, tough. I'm not scared of you."

Maggie was taken aback for a second. But only a second.

"You should be," she whispered through a wide grin. "Because I have four billion people who'll do anything for me, and I'll do anything for them. So you be careful who you share with."

Before Leah could respond, Maggie got up and walked away to get herself that bottle of whiskey.

———◉———

The rest of the trip to Portland was subdued. The bus stopped at
the next big city, Medford, Oregon, to give the unconscious girl to
an ambulance. A uniformed android got on the bus and, relaying a
bored man's voice, asked questions for about a minute before wishing
them a good day. Maggie was startled by how little fuss there
was—she had been expecting policemen, and hoping to see Leah
taken away in chains. But after thinking about it she realized that
the authorities already knew everything. The medbot had relayed
its test results to them. If there were cameras on the bus (besides
the filmmaker's minicamera, which Maggie buried under the sofa
cushions) then the police had that, too. There was no curiosity about
the event because the authorities already knew, or thought they
knew, everything.

She spent the last hour brooding, drinking whiskey, and
wondering if their cover had been blown.

But when they reached Portland everything was arranged. While
the fans were unloaded into the backstage of the concert hall,
Maggie, Leah, Simon and Fianna were met by a car that whisked
them to a nearby industrial complex. The grounds were covered by
large, slow-moving machines and robots that tended them, made
visible by their running lights in the evening dusk. They reminded
Maggie of orbital shuttles, ferrying supplies from Megasat to
factories and research stations. When the shuttles docked they were
swarmed by maintenance robots, and on the dark side of the station
the swarm appeared as flocks of crawling lights. She used to pretend
the lights were space fairies trying to steal precious cargo.

In fact, the large machines in the train yard turned out to be
cargo haulers. But Maggie was surprised when the cargo turned out
to be herself.

Fianna led each of them to their own cargo car, and showed them
a secret compartment in the back that held a seat and a sleeping
bag. The interior of the machine smelled like metal shavings and

alcohol. The walls were caked with grimy dust. But by then Maggie was drunk, and she was happy to not be sharing a ride with Leah anymore, so she didn't complain.

The sleeping bag was powered, and although it didn't allow outside connections it had voluminous information about the hauler's current status and the area it was traveling through. Maggie checked their route from Portland to the east. Large regions of Oregon were marked in green, while blue dominated the state to the west and north. She brought up more information. The green areas were rejuvenated wilderness; the blue were cities. She watched a video of urban sprawl as dense as the shopping districts north of San Francisco, ending suddenly in an expanse of untouched greenery. There were no lightly populated areas, no wilderness showing damage from man. Their entire journey would pass, alternately, through either Metropolis or Eden.

Their route ended in Idaho, in the wilderness.

She watched a few more videos and fell asleep to one that she enjoyed enough to loop play. It showed a simulation of a nearby wilderness area, where a mountain had exploded over a century before. In the simulation, ash blew across the landscape like a rocket exhaust, and in her dreams the mountain was Megasat. The thunder of the explosion became the wails of her production crew and she—fat and old and watching from her mother's home in Carolina—would laugh and laugh and laugh.

———◦———

Interstitial

Rashmigopalan Saptenshu believed that three things were essential to a true british pub. It had to have fabbers at each table, with licensed patterns covering the gamut from Bushmill's to chai. It had to have plenty of broad screens so the crowds could watch cricket. And it had to have both open areas with close-set tables—people went to pubs for the company—and quiet booths where a man could have private drinks with his mates. Gentry's Pub had all those things, but Saptenshu marked them down a point for the awful African trance music. Still, after his fifth pint even that wasn't bad.

His friend Mick came in, made a beeline for his booth, and scowled when he saw the four empty glasses. "You've started without me."

"Yeah," said Saptenshu. "Hard day."

"Mine's worse. But you first. I've got to catch up."

Mick sat down and fiddled with the table menus. Saptenshu blinked to clear his vision, then decided to drown the fuzziness with another swig of ale.

"My fucking job's gone," he said, slamming the glass down.

"You're kidding me."

"Do I look like a man who's kidding?"

"You told me you were the only fussing researcher—"

"—fusion."

"Fusion, right, the only one of those in the isles. How could you lose your job?"

"I didn't lose it. It's fucking gone. All research cancelled, not worth doing anymore, is the official line." Saptenshu drained the rest of his pint, and looked around for a chaser. He had forgotten to fab one. "A hundred years it took, to make fusion work. Another hundred to make it 'environmentally friendly'. Then they ordered us to make it 'non-weaponizable'. I've got a fucking miniature sun in my laboratory. How am I going to make that impossible to misuse? They want to idiot proof the whole fucking world."

"I'm being relocated," said Mick.

For a moment, Saptenshu wondered how that was relevant. Mick had already retrieved a pint from the fabber and gotten it to his lips by the time Saptenshu realized the topic had changed. "To where?"

"Chile."

"The country?"

"No, Sapt, the stew. I'm cutting you off. Least until I catch up."

Saptenshu nodded. "Well, you did sign up for the relocation program."

"Yeah, but I thought they'd send me to Cornwall, or maybe New York, I could do with that. But bloody South America? I don't know why they'd send anyone there."

"Evening out the population," muttered Saptenshu. "Balancing demographics. Every region needs to have the same density, the same mix of ethnicities. Idiot-proofing the regional planners."

"Whatever. I'm going to appeal. 'Course, Sinead and the kids are mad for the idea. Want to live on the beach."

The crowd in the pub cheered as someone on teevee hit a wild slog. Glasses were raised in celebration. Everyone was having a grand time.

"So what are you going to do, Sapt?"

"Eh? I'll do what's expected. I'll get a stipend, and I'll spend it all here drinking every night. What else can I do? Maybe join the damn donkeys, I suppose."

"Come again?"

Saptenshu found a new eisbock in the fabber menu, a strong brew, and he ordered a pint. "Weirdest thing, Mick. My teevee sent me an invitation to a club called the Platinum Donkeys. Some bloke that calls himself Burro has hacked into the Megasat network. He's buried a stream cipher in the broadcast, and he's tailored it to match individual public keys—"

"Wait, Sapt. I'm not following you."

"No," Saptenshu said. "Nobody does. It's just a club, Mick."

"So you going to join?"

"Fuck, no. A bunch of old scientists, sitting in some virtual space and whingeing about their lot? No, I'd rather be a drunk. It's a fine profession, older than science itself."

The fabber door rolled back; he reached in and grabbed the frosted mug. Mick tapped his glass with a fingernail.

"Sure about that? I would think the scientist came first. Someone had to make the booze."

"The first alcohol was probably in rotting fruits. But the person who discovered that, he might have been the first scientist. Science and drunkenness were probably born together."

"Well then you're in good company."

"Yeah."

The tribal music made Saptenshu's head nod, and it made the eisbock taste a little less bitter. The carousing cricket fans lifted their glasses in the air in an infectious celebration. Sapt wondered what the score was.

"Well," said Mick, raising his own glass, "Could be a worse life, eh? To Utopia, mate."

Saptenshu shrugged and lifted his mug. "To Utopia."

They clinked their toast and they drank.

———— ◉ ————

Chapter 10—Casting Call

Gentle as they were, whoever knocked on the walls of her metal transport would have died if Maggie had been able to reach them. She woke strangling the leg of her chair, with pain flashing through her temples and her head ringing like a bell. A polite voice called her name and knocked again. Maggie stumbled upright and threw open the hatch.

Outside, on a field of grass, stood a slender man in a smoking jacket, bow tie, and white gloves. "Miss Megaputri?" he asked, glancing over her, wrinkling his thin mustache in displeasure. "Oh, my. They told me how you were traveling, but I couldn't really picture it."

She blinked in the bright sunshine. "Who the fuck are you? And where the hell—"

Having lived most of her life in outer space, Maggie didn't expect that any scenery, no matter how beautiful, could cure a hangover. But the landscape she saw almost did the trick.

To her right lay open air and clumps of steep, green mountains cascading down into a lake that seemed a perfect mirror. Her transport sat on a winding road that descended past thick stands of evergreens and tall outcroppings of gray and pink granite. Above the road, to her left, stood a mansion of rich orange wood and dark, glistening stone. Its steep rooftop was a deeper red, accented by pockets of snow that matched the windows' white shutters and the ornate, filigree-topped columns around the entrance. The clearing around the building was spotted with grass and evergreen hedges, which a bright green android was trimming into perfect bullet shapes. Above, the cloudless sky was such a deep blue that she almost thought she could see stars within it. For a moment she forgot her headache...until she accidentally glanced at the sun and winced in pain.

"Welcome to the Van Hoogen chalet." the man said, offering his hand. She took it and accepted his help down from the transport. "I'm Ted, but Delano insists that guests call me Bailey. It's tradition to belittle the butler, I suppose. Mister Brovall has retired to his room; this kind of travel is hard on him. But he thought ahead, and warned me not to let you meet the other guests looking like *that*."

Scratching at her chin, Maggie realized she was still dressed as a boy. "Oh god, yes. I'd kill for a hot shower."

Bailey smiled. "Well, I think we can provide that without bloodshed. This way, please."

He led her through the hedges to the back of the chalet, which faced a thick stand of tall pine trees, with specks of snow cradled high in their needles. Maggie felt the wind hit her and shivered. It was late March, and had been balmy in San Francisco. She tried to remember her geography—wasn't all of America in a temperate region?

"In here, mum," Bailey said, holding open a door that blended in with the base of the chalet. She walked in to find a room from a demented dollhouse. Velvet curtains trimmed with lace hung on the walls. There was no furniture, but on the fur rugs that covered every square meter of the floor stood wheeled racks carrying dozens of extravagant evening gowns. One curtain, drawn back, exposed carved wooden shelves holding a jumble of curiosities, including a row of chalet-shaped sconces that bracketed a silver tea service.

Maggie expected to see an android playing dress-up and housewife, until she realized that the dresses were intended for her.

"They're servant's quarters, but they have all the amenities. You can clean up here, then I'll set your things in the guest suite on the third floor. The shower is through that door there. All of the clothes should be in your size; wear whichever pleases you. Dinner will be semi-formal. Lunch is casual, but it's going on now, don't feel the need to rush to it."

Maggie fought the urge to run and see the shower. "Servant's quarters? Do people own servants these days?"

"The word is 'hire', mum, and Delano does. When you're ready I'll come introduce you to him and his guests. There's makeup and hair supplies on this shelf," he said, drawing aside another curtain. "I ain't no hairdresser, but I can get an android programmed to help you, if'n you need one."

"No, I'll be fine," Maggie said, narrowing your eyes. "Why did your accent just change?"

"Oh? Damn." Bailey cleared his throat, then dropped his arms to his sides, affecting a stiff servant's pose. "My apologies, mum. I'm actually from Montana. Delano insists on certain...affectations. He refuses to talk to me as a psychologist, but as long as I wear a uniform and talk like a Brit he trusts me absolutely. It'll be worth it when I publish; he's a rare case study, not to mention the papers I might get out of all of you."

"You're a psychologist? What the hell are you doing here?"

"Perhaps you've heard the saying that bank robbers rob banks because that's where the money is? Well, this is a gathering of the most psychotic people on Earth, with Delano and yourself as the prize cases. Where else would a good clinician be?" He reached up and took a mahogany box off a high shelf, opened it and showed her the inside. "Now if I may ask, mum, would you be needing any of these?"

Strapped to the floor of the box was a collection of knives. Their handles were silver or gold or leather-wrapped, or decorated with tassels or gems. Their blades differed also, in shape or in size, but they were all gleaming, spotless, and sharp.

Maggie backed away. "No. No, I don't need anything like that."

Quickly, he closed the box and tucked it under his arm. "Excellent. Just a little test, I hope you understand." Then he pulled aside another curtain to reveal a door. He opened it and stepped through, making little notes with his finger in the air. "Very interesting," Maggie heard him say as the curtain drew itself closed again.

She took three seconds to contemplate the weirdness before charging for the shower.

It was everything she had fantasized it to be, and more. Limitless water, viciously hot. After her first scrub with soap and sponge, she pretended to be a comet, and that the water was unfiltered sunlight, blasting away the ancient ice that trapped her. The tiles in the bath were speckled marble, and if she squinted they looked like a starscape, until the clouds of steam grew so thick she could hardly see at all.

After an hour getting clean, she spent another hour sorting through the dresses. Finding a suitable outfit meant mixing a dress with the blouse from another dress, the accessories from a third, an entirely different set of shoes, and so on—when she was satisfied, she laid the clothes aside and worked on her hair for most of another hour. In the middle of combing and spraying there came a knock at the door.

"You said she's in here, Bailey? No one is answering!" The deep voice grunted as whoever it was pounded harder.

Maggie was still wearing a folded towel. She swore under her breath and leapt toward one of the wheeled dress racks. The curtains parted by themselves, and she saw the door opening just as she rammed the dress rack into it. The gruff voice cried out in pain. Maggie grinned. "I'm not ready yet!", she yelled. "And I'm not decent. Go away!"

The intruder muttered for a second before raising his voice. "Yes, yes. Beauty cannot be rushed and all that. Fine. But do make it to dinner, at least."

"I'm almost done," she said.

After the footsteps of the intruder had faded, she knocked the dress rack onto its side, making sure the now immobile cart was wedged against the door.

But her stomach rumbled at the thought of dinner. Although she had eaten the scones and drained the tea service, real food sounded appealing. She had already picked out her clothing—a white sun dress made from sequins shaped like shark's teeth, with an underlying satin chemise that covered her arms and matched the mimic-silver pumps. With only a touch of makeup to do, she could have been finished in another ten minutes.

Maggie dawdled over every remaining preparation, and didn't emerge for another hour.

———◦———

Bailey leaned and whispered in her ear as Maggie entered the Victorian drawing room. "This is Pierre Martineau. Disassociative with blunted affect. Don't be offended if he doesn't speak, he only communicates electronically. Again, I apologize that we can't risk giving you powered clothing."

Pierre smiled, showing small display screens on each of his teeth, all of which had a yellow, animated smiley face. Maggie smiled and nodded her head as they passed.

There were about a dozen people milling about in a room that, except for the eclectic furniture scattered about, could have comfortably held twice as many. But the space felt cramped. Everyone seemed to be trying to avoid each other by staring out the vast bay window, reading one of several thick tomes littered about, or (in one fellow's case) huddling in the corner and talking to a glass container. Bailey noticed her glancing at him and whispered again.

"That's Doctor Warren Poltrasky. Brilliant physicist. But a paranoid delusional, I'm afraid. High functioning—oh, of course everyone's high functioning."

At an elegant cherry bookcase stood Leah Suiz, in a purple ballroom gown that made her look like an overdecorated plum. She was turning through a book at rapid speed, lifting a puff of dust into the air with each page. She spared the newcomers only a glance, and Bailey said nothing as he pulled Maggie past.

They walked by a satin lounger draped with pillows shaped like African tribal masks. A bronze-skinned bald man was admiring one of the masks, but he dropped it and bowed as Maggie passed. On his back, in a scabbard cunningly woven into his smoking jacket, was a sword with a fat, curved blade. He stepped forward, about to speak, but Maggie waved him off as Bailey pulled her deeper into the room.

"Fascinating case, that one. Prince Hasan ibn Maveth, the son of an Arabic sheikh and a hasidic Jewess. I don't know if that contributed to his rapid cycling bipolar disorder, but it certainly couldn't have helped."

This is an asylum, Maggie thought. *They're all freaks here.*

One man was at a writing desk, with detached tufts of his own gray hair in both hands. Some of the hair had been stuffed into the desk's inkwell, and with one clump he was drawing on the leather writing surface one of the most intricate and beautiful pictures of rutting llamas that Maggie had ever seen.

"Augusto Fros," said Bailey, steering her past the man and his frenetic, driven strokes. "Another delusional, and a bit histrionic besides. Don't ask him about the llamas, he'll go on forever."

They're all like me. So why do I want to run away?

Two people were standing together and holding the only conversation in the room. One was an Asian man in a crisp green suit and fiber optic hair that shone yellow at the tips. The other, with his back to Maggie, was a portly man with woolly brown hair who was boasting about some sexual conquest.

Bailey stopped Maggie before they interrupted the men's conversation. "That is Bartholomew Hwong. Obsessive-compulsive. And narcissist, also, I think. That's a common trait in high functioning savants who grow up without governors. But he's a bit of a cipher, this one—can't quite figure out how he works, yet."

"Have you diagnosed everyone here?", Maggie whispered back.

The butler's smile was one of pride and reassurance at the same time. "Well, not you, mum. We just met."

"You're lying. Keep doing it." She gave him a knowing glare. "So who's the troglodyte?"

"Ahem." His smile fell, and he leaned closer. "That would be Delano. Histrionic, narcissist—surely. Megalomaniac, to be certain. Also, he possesses one of the most fascinating neural disorders I've ever seen."

The Asian man was staring at Maggie over Delano's shoulder, and after a few seconds the shorter man took the hint. He turned, sloshing liquid out of the drink in his hand, and gaped, open-mouthed, at her.

His ruddy skin, high cheekbones, and flat nose defied any attempt to guess his lineage. Any race on Earth, or all of them, could have claimed a portion of the man's genes. But it was Delano's eyes that drew attention. They were piercing, predatory, and wandered independently; as he stared at her, one eye stayed fixated on something that the other roamed about to find. Finding it, he smiled, and Maggie felt as if he were salivating over an unexpected buffet.

"Ravishing," he said. Then he turned to the butler. "Bailey! I demand that you introduce this creature to us at once!"

"Sirs, please welcome Maggie Megaputri. Maggie, this is Delano Mboza Van Hoo—"

"Delano. First name basis, I insist." He took her hand before she could react. "You kept us waiting but I forgive you. Now we must talk. In private." Still holding her hand, he turned and roared. "Bailey! Herd everyone out of here. Put them in the—the dining room, that will do."

"Yes, sir."

"Now wait a minute," said the man with the sword and rifle on his back. "You've been shuffling us about since we got here. Now our hostess arrives, and we should be sent off again?"

"Hasan, I need just a few minutes—"

"Wait," said Maggie, pulling her hand free from Delano's grasp. "Hostess? What the hell does that mean?"

Hwong raised his hand politely. "I, too, would like to speak with Maggie Mags."

"You will all get your chance."

"When?", said Hasan. "We all have questions. Why should you monopolize her time?"

"Because this is my house. This is my meeting! That is, as much as it is hers."

"What? Hold on." She took a step away from Delano, whirled and pointed a finger. "If you're the guy answering questions, then I've got a few of my own."

Delano grin was so tight, his teeth almost squeaked. "It would save you some embarrassment if you asked them in private."

"Embarrass? Me? Hah, I don't think so."

Hasan folded his arms in a smug pose. "I imagine that she has instructions for all of us."

"Yeah, sure I do: Shut up and let me talk. You—what you do mean, this is my meeting?"

For a moment, it seemed that the aristocrat's red face was going to boil over and burst. He looked around the room. "All of you leave this room or I will have you killed."

Maggie laughed. She couldn't help it—while this pudgy troll pretended to be dangerous, she had been wondering about the sharpness of the decorative blades on the wall. "Are you kidding? Who do you think they're more afraid of? You, or me?"

Delano's back stiffened, and he got a queer look, with one eye glazing into a distant stare while the other rolled about in turmoil. Finally he relaxed, with a confident smile. "You're right, milady. They fear you, of course. And only you can ask them to give us a minute's privacy, and expect to be heeded. I would ask you to do this, for both our sakes, and in return I promise all your curiosities will be settled."

The room was silent as Maggie looked around. Leah wore a wicked grin, while most of the others seemed puzzled or angry. The only motion was the balding scientist with the glass jar who tiptoed toward the door. As he passed Bartholomew Hwong, he leaned and stage-whispered, "...they're plotting something."

Shaking her head, Maggie sighed. "All right. All of you, give me five minutes."

The donkeys filed out through the Victorian double doors, some murmuring to themselves. Hasan was the last. As Bailey touched his shoulder to usher him out, the man flinched as if struck, and gave the butler a deadly glare. But he followed. As the doors clicked shut, Maggie turned to Delano with a glare of her own.

"Okay, what the hell are you talking about?"

Delano's chuckle was slow and deep. "I remember meeting you as a tiny orphan, by Mega's side. Such a shy child."

"I don't remember you."

"Why would you? A single meeting, as you voyaged toward the stars? Mega was an associate of mine—I mined the material that built his elevator. But we were never close, and you went to live in orbit where I could not follow. I thought you were still that shy girl, despite your exhibitionist stage persona. I was wrong. You are no Esther, and I do not wish to be your Vautrin."

"Whatever. I don't care. Why did you bring me here? Who are all those people, and what do you mean it's my meeting?"

"Those are the Platinum Donkeys. The most competent, damaged, graced and demonized people on Earth. And you, my dear, are their queen. I invited them here on your behalf."

"What?"

He smiled, and there was something off about that, too, a crookedness that made even friendly gestures seem odd. "Do you want to know how we find insane geniuses? Simon Brovall looks for madmen who have run afoul of the law. Whereas I—I read your fan mail."

Maggie clenched and unclenched her fists. She felt as if her chest were squeezing in time, and with as much fury. "You...*what*?"

"An employee of mine, whom I call Burro, copies it for me. And a rich vein of insanity it is."

Before she registered the motion, Maggie had reached toward the nearest object, picked it up and hurled it. It was a brass statue; it arced inches from Delano's head and thudded against the wall. Grinning, he ducked a full second later. "Hah! Yes, I know your kind. Shyness transforms into rage!"

"Fuck you!" She ran to a curio cabinet, ripped it open. The first china platter sailed wide, smashing against the bookshelf. The second was short, and bounced off the couch he stepped behind.

"This is how you play, isn't it? I know this joust. Every action a flirt and a threat. Escalate the aggression, outdo the crazy, and to the loser goes the shame!"

"What shame? I don't need any shame!" She threw a decanter, and a crystal figurine. Her aim was awful; they shattered against the wall.

"That's it. What use is shame! But how far will you go? How long until you realize your opponent is just as unfettered—and just as unbalanced!"

He grabbed a book from an end table and flung it at her. His aim was better, but Maggie ducked, and the hardcover crashed into the curio. The cabinet's back mirror cracked. At first instinct made her look for shards of the glass to use as a weapon, but none had fallen. And a voice in the back of her mind made her stop.

He's right. You can't win this with a tantrum.

She inhaled, paused for a second to savor the cool air in her chest, then let the breath out. *This is just another interview, just like on the show. Another pompous twit to be pumped for information.*

"Okay," she said with the last of her long breath. "So why me? Why spy on me and why bring me here? You must have a reason."

"Insanity is its own reason and reward," he growled. Standing straight he fixed his jacket, while one eye surveyed the room and its debris. "But yes, I do. My Burro controls Megasat. When we find a likely candidate, we send encryption keys through your broadcasts. You, and the communications network that you command, have been recruiting donkeys and linking them together."

That's why Oswald said... "They all think that I'm in charge."

"Exactly. Only Simon and Bailey know the truth—that I am the link that ties us all together. They bow to you, but you must make them listen to me."

"Why? What do you have in mind?"

"Disaster and retribution." His grin held a jagged malice. "Have you read Steinbeck? Early 20th century—I have a copy of *Grapes of Wrath* over there," he said, pointing at the bookshelf while literally keeping one eye toward her. "'Man reaches, stumbles forward. He may slip back, but never a full step. But if the step were not being taken, if the stumbling-forward ache were not alive, the bombs would not fall, the throats would not be cut.' That world he feared has come to pass. There is only stagnation, no forward steps. The ache to stumble has vanished, the bombs never fall, the throats *are not cut*. The spirit of progress is dead, and man will follow. For the world to have progress, there must, *must* be ruin."

When he stopped speaking, she could only stare. He frowned then, seeming suddenly self-conscious. Smoothing his jacket, he cleared his throat and continued in a calmer voice. "I intend for us to bring that ruin."

Maggie stared for another second as chills worked their way up her back. *Okay. Fuck the interview.*

She grabbed more china and threw it, smashing cups and saucers against walls and furniture. He tossed a pillow, then reached for more books. Maggie picked up a crystal bowl that glittered in the light, and paused. "Wait, wait." He stopped, book held to his ear. "Are these real antiques?"

"Some are. Some are patterns that I bought because they were more expensive than the originals."

"Oh."

She hurled the bowl at him; it landed at his feet and fractured in a crescendo of ringing notes. The book he threw went wide, crashing through the bay window. Maggie pushed the empty curio over and reached for jewel-encrusted eggs on an end table But when she turned back to Delano he was holding his cheek. It was bruised, with specks of blood.

"Good throw," he said, with one jittery eye.

"Did I hit you?"

"You will." He examined the blood on his fingers, and laughed. "Autonomic precognition. My body reacts to stimuli from minutes or hours in the future. It's an ability that my family has treasured for generations. Kept their children from governors, who would convince us we were delusional. My father taught me to use it for my advantage, as his father did for him. The thrill of a closed deal, the disappointment of a failed gamble, or just knowing injuries before they happen—"

"Yeah, it's great," she said, winging the egg at him. It hit square on his cheek, jewels popping from the impact, but Delano barely flinched. The bruise and scrapes looked exactly the same as they had a minute ago.

"—and thus, knowing when to end a game. Bailey!"

The arched Victorian doors opened. Bailey leaned into the room, with a row of curious heads peeking from behind him. "Sir, the guests wish me to inform you that your time is up."

"Yes, yes. That's fine. We're out of china anyway." Delano strode past Maggie as if she were no longer there, raising his arms in a grand pose. "Assemble everyone in the dining room. Bring styptic, wine and cheese. Let us convene this council of war!"

———◉———

Chapter 11—Props and Costumes

The Van Hoogan dining room consisted of a long mahogany table in an otherwise barren, oval room. The walls were matte black and curved smoothly into the ceiling. On the black carpet stood a row of androids in livery, each holding a platter of cheese, fruit, or glasses of wine. The guests picked at the food and milled around the room, avoiding each other, although a few surrounded Maggie as she entered.

A pair of medical robots met Delano, extending their stilt-like legs to examine and treat his bruised cheek. Maggie headed toward him, intending to use one of the slender robots as a club, but Bailey took her arm and pulled her away.

"Please sit over here, mum," he said over her sputtering profanities. "I'll serve you myself."

"Get your hands off of me. I don't want any cheese. I want a long knife."

"You should get the lady what she wants," said Hasan, standing at her shoulder. "Or perhaps I will."

Hwong folded his hands. "I don't feel comfortable with weapons. Perhaps, if miss Megaputri would tell us what made her so angry..."

A voice at the table interrupted him. "Maggie is a passionate woman. But I'm sure she's only kidding about the knife. Aren't you, Maggie?"

They all turned. The speaker was Simon, sitting at the table with a wineglass in his hand, Fianna standing by his side. As Maggie yanked her arm away from the butler and stepped toward him, the android moved to intercept, but Simon waved her away.

"Simon," Maggie said, not sure of what to say next. Delano and his pet manservant were in earshot, and the psychos surrounding her made her skin crawl. She inhaled to compose herself, pretended she had heard a stage cue, and gave him a practiced smile. "You look like hell."

The lawyer had new, dark bags under his gray eyes, and his hand trembled enough to slosh wine almost to the rim of his glass. "Yes, well, I only managed our little trek under a lot of medication. Spent that last leg completely sedated. It does take its toll, I suppose."

Maggie nodded. She had gotten used to seeing a look of terror on Simon's face, but now the man seemed haunted and drained. His jacket hung on him like an oversized shell. But he maintained a thin, brave smile, and before she could speak he interrupted again.

"So you and Delano are fighting? You know, he's a very dangerous man."

"Yeah. Well, I'm dangerous, too."

"Quite. Perhaps we'll compare later. But for now, as your lawyer, may I suggest that you not make him angry? Unless, of course, you feel that you—"

"Everyone! To the table!" Delano bellowed. He marched to the end seat, his cheek covered with a passable layer of makeup. Maggie sat down in the chair that Bailey offered, to Delano's left, across from Simon. The balding physicist sat next to her. The man placed his jar of undulating clay on the table, then possessively hugged it to his chest when he caught Maggie staring at the thing.

"Now then. I—or *we*, invited you all here with only two instructions. One was to be as covert as possible. The other, to bring with you some means, some plans, some weapon that will cause global disaster." The red-faced man stared ahead with one stern eye, while the other eye glanced at each of the assembled in turn. "Let's see what you've got."

For a second there was silence. Then Bartholomew Hwong raised his hand. "Excuse me. You weren't really clear about that part. Could you please explain?"

"Not clear? Disaster! Cataclysm! You're all freaking geniuses, you're supposed to use your imagination! What part of 'destroying the world' is not—AAAARGH!" Delano suddenly pitched forward, his eyes bugged out, his hands plunging into his crotch. Bailey was at his side in a second. He waved the medical robots closer.

"I'm fine, I'm fine," Delano said in a strained voice. "I think...an ice pack." Nodding, Bailey ran out of the room.

Maggie heard a tittering laugh from the far end of the table. Most of the donkeys were either amused or impatient. Simon was smiling. She almost laughed herself when Bailey returned with a pink rubber bag that Delano took and kneaded into his groin.

"These things happen." He gave a crooked shrug, and his wandering eye darted back and forth in search for something. "Just a forewarning that my evening may not go as planned," he said, glaring at Maggie with his steady eye. She forced herself to choke back a snort. "Anyway...cataclysm. Simon, you begin."

"Me?" Simon ducked his head and glanced around. Then he put his drink down, as the tremors in his hand grew stronger. "I, er, well, many of you know me. Some of you know I keep a stock of false identities and strong ties into the global legal system. I, um, I've..."

"Just out with it, man!"

"Yes. Well, I've arranged a storm of legal filings. Individually they're little more than nuisance suits. But taken together—under dozens of identities, some of them respected legislators and judges—they might possibly clog the legal system. I've also identified contradictory clauses in international treaties, all the way from Bretton-Woods to the Unification Charter, and by petitioning for *ab initio* voidance of international law we might be able to force judicial and executive bodies into a lengthy arbitration process—"

"This humble weakling," Delano interjected, "has positioned himself to shut down the legal system. Police without the authority to arrest, courts without the authority to pass judgment. Legal chaos, across the globe, for, what did you say, Simon? Days?"

"A few days, at most." He seemed to be shrinking back into his ill-fitting suit. "If it works. Nothing on this scale has ever been tried before."

"I have confidence in you. Now, who else brought me something? Eh? Bartholomew, we discussed possibilities earlier."

The thin Asian folded his hands together. "Ah. Yes. I have subverted the compilers for many popular android skillsets. With a command, I can shut down perhaps as many as ten percent of all androids."

"Only ten percent? That's barely enough to make the news. Wait—can you send them into a murderous frenzy? If we could cause havoc, rather than a spate of service calls..."

Hwong paused, open-mouthed. Then he bobbed his head. "I will work on it."

"Fine. Fine. Anyone else?" When nobody answered, he banged his fist on the table. "You mean you all came to me *empty handed*?"

Near the far end of the table, a shrill voice piped up. "I have something."

Delano squinted. "Eh? Miss Suiz, isn't it? As I recall, you weren't even invited. What did you bring me?"

Leah stood up. Her purple dress was already stained with wine; a man next to her in an immaculate white suit was desperately using a towel to blot at the table. "I have a broken fabber," the old woman shouted.

"Call a repairman and stop wasting my time."

"No—I mean I have broken the fabber safeguards. I can make anything. Including an upgrade unit that will break other fabbers."

"Hmn? Show me."

In unison, Delano slid his fingers over the table surface as Leah tapped at the sleeve of her gown. The top of the table faded to black. Then a pattern appeared, a wireframe of a clunky, lizard-like robot and a list of specifications and abilities. Delano moved his hand, and the image in the table rotated to match. He smiled.

"Now, this is a fine gift. With unlimited fabbers we can create weapons, build an army if we had the time."

"It can carry and install a pattern library," Leah said, and her grin seemed directed at Maggie. "We'll be able to add psychoactive drugs to food patterns, turn weapon requests into guns and knives. Get everyone high, then let them make their own weapons. Arcologies will become living Hells."

Delano waved his hand in dismissal. "No, no. Our ultimate goal is to rule the world, or what's left of it. Give everyone unlimited fabbers and they'll put up resistance. You're talking about arming the peasantry. But we can use this ourselves. Thank you."

He shut down the display and the table went back to simulated mahogany. Leah frowned, and sat down with her arms crossed, spilling another glass of wine and eliciting a shriek from her neighbor.

Before Delano could speak again, the gray haired artist leapt to his feet. "What I want to know, is what *she* is planning for all of us!" With an angry flourish, he jammed his finger toward Maggie.

Maggie blinked. She looked at Simon, who rolled his eyes.

Delano sighed. "Senor Fros, she is the one whose communication network binds us all together. And she will be funding our revolution with her limitless wealth."

Maggie's jaw dropped open, but a gesture from Simon kept her silent. *I will?*

"That's not what I meant," said Augusto Fros, smoothing back his thinning hair. "I mean the phagotech research aboard Megasat. Artificial immune systems are based on heavy chain antibodies that are found only in camelids. She's searching for the secret of immortality, but at what cost?" As everyone stared at him, he pointed an accusing finger at Maggie again. "Don't you people see? That woman's satellite is packed full of alien llamas!"

Maggie couldn't help it anymore; she broke into uncontrollable laughter.

The rest of the donkeys laughed, or argued, or tried to outshout each other, with Delano and Fros leading the rest. As the meeting fell into anarchy, the scientist next to Maggie tugged on her sleeve. "Um," he said when she looked his way, "I really like your show."

With a couple quick inhalations, Maggie got her breathing under control. "Thanks," she said, still chuckling. "Professor...?"

"Poltrasky. But, Warren. Warren is fine."

"Thanks, Warren. I, ah, I like your thing there."

He put the jar back on the table. It was a closed glass cylinder without any seam or lid, and inside was a translucent lump of clay. As he moved his hand in front of it, psuedopods formed in the lump to follow his motions. "It's a room temperature superfluid. Frictionless, more sensitive than a SQUID to electromagnetics, but unstable in an atmosphere. I created it, but nobody will fund me. They've tried to ruin me..."

"I'd fund you," said Maggie. The thing poured itself taller as she leaned toward it. "What's it good for?"

"Oh, its applications are limitless. It's, I mean... Well, you can't expect me to list limitless applications! Obviously, they're infinite!"

"Okay, okay."

Wild-eyed, he pulled the jar back to his chest, glancing about at the squabbling mob. "Still, if you'll fund me, I'll come up a with a list. But can I tell you something?" he asked, his voice just audible over the yelling. "I'm not the only one they're trying to ruin. You're not really in charge here, are you?"

Maggie almost answered him. But she paused. Something told her the truth would be dangerous. Warren was a timid man, but she could see his fierce intelligence just beneath the surface. Yet he was in awe of her. All of them were, in some way. If she dispelled that...what would they do to her?

Besides...I kind of like being in charge.

But she was saved from answering by Delano's victory, as he outbellowed everyone else in the room.

"...and I will hear no more of it!", he shouted, and in the seconds after his fist hit the table there was silence. Augusto Fros sat, hunched over, with a rubbery-mouthed frown. Delano glared at the man for a moment, then he rolled one eye toward the other guests. "Now then. Does anyone else have anything truly destructive to offer?"

Hasan ibn Maveth cleared his throat. "You wanted I should bring something, so I mustered an army. A hundred trained troops, almost my equal."

Delano sighed. "A hundred? Pitiful."

"Oy, you don't know the half of it. Our weapons are obsolete, and we're stuck on a reservation with guarded borders. But that's the best I can do." Hasan gestured to encompass the rest of the donkeys. "And I should think that's the best any of us can do. You wanted secrecy *and* criminal conspiracy—those two things are incompatible in this modern age."

"It is possible to evade the authorities, sir."

"I'm sure it is. Absolutely sure. Because you would not be insisting it of us unless you had done it yourself. Isn't that right? Tell us, Delano, what are *you* planning? Why should any of us show you our hand, unless we know what you're holding?"

Delano drew himself up, smiling. "All right. Very astute. I had planned more pomp and ceremony for later this evening, but perhaps, yes. I should give you the tour."

"I think that's an excellent idea," said Simon, his eyes fixed on Maggie. "Everyone should know what they're getting into."

"It's settled, then. Bailey! Prepare the rail car!"

With a backhand throw, Delano flung his icepack across the room. It struck an android in the chest, and the mechanical servant toppled over. People laughed. Maggie paid it no attention; she was caught between Simon's warning look and Delano's lopsided grin.

⎯⎯⎯⎯⎯⎯◉⎯⎯⎯⎯⎯⎯

If any of the donkeys were surprised to find a rail car in the basement of the chalet, they made no mention of it. A monorail as wide as a man's shoulders sprouted out of the tile floor, turned horizontal, and led out through a gigantic hole in the wall. Sitting on the rail was a bullet-shaped vehicle, tucked between racks of authentic wine bottles and the gleaming machinery that recycled garbage into fabber feed. Maggie thought that it all seemed like perfectly natural equipment to have in a madman's basement. A Jacob's ladder and a mechanical fortune teller would have been right at home.

Delano selected Maggie and half of the others to take the first tour. Hwong and Hasan insisted to be in the first group, although Hasan seemed more interested in shadowing Maggie. She made sure Warren joined as well. Simon refused to go as far as the basement, pleading claustrophobia, and hinting that Delano had no secrets from him.

Unlike the rest of the chalet, the interior of the rail car offered no luxuries. The seats were metal grates. A fine layer of dust covered the floor and caked around the edges of the windows. There was a large space with hooks and straps for some kind of equipment, but it was empty. Delano started the vehicle by placing his hand on a control pad, and thereafter controlled it by tapping controls on his jacket's sleeve.

"My mining concerns are all very high security. None of them can be accessed without a DNA scan from a foreman. This car, only by me."

The car entered the dark tunnel and canted downward at a steep angle. "The mine is currently about forty miles away. Once we get to speed it'll only take a few minutes to get there."

From a seat in back, someone leaned into the aisle. "What do you mean, 'currently'?"

"It's a filter mine. We tear natural rock out, use molecular filters to extract the useful elements, then replace the hole with a synthesized granite made from whatever remains, the elements we have in abundance. Then the mine moves on. In this way, we're moving through the Rocky Mountains, hollowing them out as we go. I should take you to our Himalayan site—not as commercially successful, but far grander."

With a lurch, the car accelerated enough to press Maggie against her chair's steel back. Next to her, Warren bobbled his jar before catching it in his arms. "Shhh! Shhh!", he whispered to it as the translucent blob rolled around the inside of its container. He shook it a little, and the thing splatted across the interior, hugging every surface. Over several seconds, it flowed to the lowest point and reformed into a lump.

"I'm sorry, I'm sorry," he said, petting the glass. Then, seeing Maggie watching, he hugged the jar to his chest.

Several minutes worth of brown, gray, and pinkish stone streaked past the windows. The view ahead was black, with only the slight curve of the roof visible in the car's headlights. Maggie began to plot a comedy skit, in which she could wear a dress printed to resemble the Rocky Mountains. She would spread her legs, and a bullet train would dive down...

Bright yellow signs leapt out of the darkness and flew past, and soon they were followed by a side tunnel with an offshoot of the main rail. Warren bolted upright. "Were those were nuclear warning signs?"

"Yes," said Delano, with a casual wave of his hand. "One of the mine's products is uranium. Rather than stress the continental grid with our power demands, these filter mines are licensed to operate fission power plants."

In the row behind Maggie, she heard Hasan grumble. "Yet they won't license fission for reservation use. Any chance you'd like to set up a mine in Israel?"

"If all goes as planned, your people won't be trapped on a reservation anymore."

Bartholomew Hwong raised his hand. "But power from the grid is free. The supply is nearly infinite. Why would you—"

"*Not* infinite." Delano grinned. "I'll show you infinite."

They sat in silence a few more seconds. Then the mountain opened up.

The monorail entered an enormous cavern, hundreds of meters long, with a ceiling five meters above the car. The stone walls were perfectly straight and at right angles to the floor, and they were layered with speckled colors that ran past like wavy ribbons. The light in the chamber came from the headlights of machines, the largest of which looked like floor buffers crossed with some giant, spidery vacuum cleaner. Their circular steel heads were crammed with grooved teeth, and in back of their six legs sprouted two-meter thick hoses. A few of the massive robots were pressed against the wall, their heads spinning, the teeth tearing at the rock. Smaller, insect-like robots tended the digger machines, repositioning hoses and making spot repairs.

In the midst of the diggers stood massive support columns, of some pinkish plastic substance, that flared as they met the floor and ceiling. Maggie bent down to get a better look at the ceiling, and saw that it was composed of interlocking tiles of gray stone. From the supports flowed a pink web of material that criss-crossed the ceiling, touching every tile.

Delano nodded at her and pointed. "You can see that we dig down into this chamber. Those supports are ooze fabbers. Feed them at the bottom, and they extrude the ceiling downward a centimeter at a time. The ceiling is made of artificial granite fill—silicates mostly, dead cheap stuff—and it goes on upward for another quarter kilometer. We'll replace the entire mountain range eventually. But from outside, you won't be able to tell."

He then stood up and pointed out the window. "See where the tailing pipes lead? That's the molecular filter refinery. It pulls out elements and separates them, just like the recycler in your kitchens, but on a larger scale. The valuable elements we sell. The worthless ones we make into fill granite. But some of the useful elements, ah, those we make into more robots. Robots dig the material, process it and reproduce themselves."

"Self-replicating robots are highly illegal," said Hwong.

"But licensed for operations of this scale. You haven't seen anything illegal. I doubt you will. The laws don't handle people like us." He turned and smiled at Maggie. "You know, I'm the one who named us the Platinum Donkeys. Would you like to know my inspiration?"

"I've heard it," she said. "Cardinal Lambert told me it was based on an old book, the *Golden Ass.*"

"Lambert. Hmph." In the window Maggie could see Delano smiling, but she also noticed how he clenched his fists. "That idealist. He tried to put his own retroactive stamp on my creation. I admit that I encouraged such embellishment—it's important for a revolutionary group to have its own mythology. But no, my inspiration is here. Come to the window, all of you, we'll be at low speed for a while and it's quite safe."

The others in the car stood up and joined Delano at the window. Maggie was again reminded of the swarming dock robots on Megasat, except that the headlights of these robots cut visible cones in the dusty air. Delano was searching for something, his eyes working independently. Soon he found it and pointed. "There! That line over there, the four-legged ones, do you see them?"

The robots he pointed to were only a few meters long. They looked like rectangular boxes with four thick legs, and had some kind of metallic skirt girdling their bellies. They traveled in a line that broke into apparent chaos in one corner of the cavern. There, the quadrupedal robots stopped, retracting their legs until their bellies touched the ground. Every few seconds they shook as if they were being hammered on from below. As Maggie watched, one stood back up and walked to a new patch of ground before hunching over again.

"Those are assayer robots. Officially they are 'Autonomous telegeodynamic charged-phonon resonance assayers', with no useful acronym. Colloquially, the mining industry calls them donkeys. Because they kick at the ground, you see. They send a concussive force and a powerful electrical jolt downward, detect any return signal, and thereby build a map of the ores beneath them. Those are ytterbium donkeys; they're tuned to assay rare earth elements in gneissic ore."

"I get it," Maggie said, "So are there also platinum donkeys?"

Delano flashed a wide smile. "Very good. Yes, there are, although not in this mine. A fine mascot, hmmn? Smart devices that can sense what's of value, and who spend their entire existence kicking at the world?"

"Truly you have a sense of the mythic," said Hwong.

"Well, at least you weren't calling us asses," said Hasan.

"I don't know." Maggie shrugged. "I like the other explanation better."

Delano grunted and frowned. Then he waved everyone back into their seats, and lit up a control on his jacket sleeve. When he slid it forward, the car accelerated with a lurch.

Following the laser-straight mineshaft, the monorail pitched into a shallow slope and built up speed. Maggie saw the rail fork ahead, one track leading into a tunnel on the far wall. Their car took that turn, and at enough speed to cause the seats to tilt and the undercarriage to squeal. Some of the donkeys grumbled; Maggie laughed. They traveled a short distance into the dark tunnel before the car's headlights revealed a bright orange bumper and the end of the track. With impressive skill, Delano braked hard and slid to within a meter of the end.

He grinned at Maggie. "Now, this is what I brought you here to see." With a tap on his sleeve, the entire car shook. At first Maggie couldn't tell what was happening. Then she noticed the orange bumper rising in front of the car. The section of track they were on was elevated above the tunnel's floor, and they were descending into a shaft.

A deep shaft. After a minute, when she had gotten tired of watching the ribbons of gray, pink and green stone roll by, she caught Delano's attention. "At this point I'm guessing you dug deep enough to find mole men. Maybe a dragon. Or the devil himself?"

"No," he said, chuckling. "But tell me. Did Lambert warn you about the T.E.M.?"

"No."

"Perhaps, the 'Terrible Emotional Momma'?"

"I've...heard the name."

Hwong raised his hand. "As have I."

"Yes. Another trifle, more mythology. But in good service, this time, as the T.E.M. is my greatest secret. Our secret, I should say, for we will use it together." Delano grinned at Maggie, his one eye spinning lazily. "Even with all my family's resources, I could not find access to any of the great weapons of recent history. The last two centuries are too well policed, and the doomsday weapons of the 20th century have long been dismantled or neutralized. It was not until I researched the great men of the 19th century that I found my answer, and then I applied my resources into enhancing that into a threat that could not be anticipated. In the end, it was simple. We build great structures so casually, magnifying steam age works into great threats posed no difficulties, not for someone of my talents. But the acronym—the original form—holds no romantic notions. T.E.M stands for nothing more complicated than 'Tesla's Earthquake Machine."

As he spoke, Maggie saw the end of the shaft wall scroll past the car's headlights. They descended into an unlit space and came to a gentle stop. With a touch on his jacket Delano caused the cavern to erupt with light.

For what seemed like kilometers, the headlights of robots shone out of the darkness. The squat cavern seemed to go on forever, in every direction, with a few support beams the only shadows in a sea of light, granite, and chrome.

"Over two hundred thousand donkeys," said Delano. He stood and went to the window, and the others in the car did the same. "Made from the material of the mountain itself. But these have a difference. Instead of assaying ore, these are programmed to build up resonance waves in the Earth's mantle. By steering these waves to the crust we can cause devastation on a massive scale. This is our path to greatness, my friends. This is the sword that will make us emperors and bury our enemies in rubble."

"No," said Warren, his face plastered to the window. "No, you don't have enough energy input. Not for global range."

"Are you sure? I haven't tested it yet; it would reveal our hand. But my calculations are sound. Remember that resonance effects depend on the square of the input. And I have seven other installations like this, scattered in mines around the world. They're linked together, using ultra-low frequency waves in the Earth's mantle, a subterranean network of whispers."

"The square? Oh, god, you're right. The square." The little man shrank back from the window and returned to his seat, counting on his fingers.

Delano smiled at Maggie. In the glare from outside the monorail car, his skin took on the appearance of burnished bronze.

"So what should we destroy first? London? Beijing? New York—oh, don't choose. We can hit them all at once. But we'll need more surprises than this. We need each of you to sow chaos, by whatever means you think best. It is not my intention to start a war. We will murder our enemies before it dawns on them that they should fight us."

His roving eye flailed as he turned back to Maggie. "And then we shall build a better world, a world where our great attributes are encouraged rather than stifled."

Maggie crossed her arms. The air was stuffy and warm. She shivered.

"Eight point seven," Warren said. "Your maximum magnitude is eight point seven Richter, I think."

Delano beamed. "Thank you, Warren. Well done. I designed it to be strong enough to obliterate modern arcologies, but it took me years to work through the calculations. We'll need sharp minds like yours in our new world."

The scientist flashed a twitchy smile, then backed into the corner and began muttering to his jar of clay.

Chapter 12—Exit, stage left.

The trip back was dour. Hwong asked a stream of questions about the Momma and its construction, and Delano evaded them one by one. The other passengers were silent; they looked like corpses in the gloomy lighting, and spooked Maggie whenever one of them shifted, mumbled, or yawned.

But strangest of all was Prince Hasan. When they started back, he pulled his scimitar out and placed it on his seat. Then he went to the back of the car and sat in the shadows on the floor. After a while, Maggie could hear him sobbing.

When they reached the chalet there was a moment of confusion as the passengers staggered out while the other half of the guests tried to barge their way into the monorail car. Maggie ignored them all, and she burst out from the cellar looking for fresh air and sharp objects. She allowed Bailey to herd her toward a guest room at the top of the chalet, with a magnificent carved balcony that looked out into the pine forests. The cool air felt marvelous. The steep upward slope of the mountain was covered with tall pines in lustrous shades of green. The closest trees were near enough that she could smell their scent and almost touch their needles. Above shone a warm sun in a majestic blue sky. The beautiful surroundings, so like her distant memories of a childhood on Earth, made it impossible to feel troubled.

After a while relaxing in the sun, she decided that if she wanted to feel troubled, she had every right.

The guest room had been reserved for her; her 'boy' disguise, clothes that she would never wear again, were draped on a love seat in one corner. The bed was a grand four-poster, draped in lace. On

168

the brass-studded hope chest at the foot of the bed lay a smooth copper box and a coiled length of leather. As she approached, the box buzzed and moved as the governor inside tried to get her attention. She stared at it for a second, then picked up the other object. It was a bullwhip, with a soft, rubbery handle shaped like a penis.

She tossed it into the woods, then stomped out of her room looking for Simon.

She started on the first level—knowing Simon's fear of heights—and checked every closed door. Soon she found him in an elaborate bedroom/office decorated with mahogany furniture. Bailey stood in a corner near the doorway, almost as a lookout, and he gave Maggie a nod and a smile when she entered. Prince Hasan was there also, curled up on the curtained bed. When he saw Maggie he got up, wiping his eyes with his jacket sleeve.

Maggie glanced over the man's muscles, his giant sword, and the stream of tears on his face before turning to Simon. "Yeah. Um, do you have time to talk?"

"Hasan and I were almost—"

"No, please," said Hasan, getting to his feet with exaggerated effort. "My concerns are not important."

Simon reached to grab the man's arm, but caught himself. "Please, Hasan, stay. All of us should have a talk."

"I can't. Excuse me."

He swerved past Fianna and Maggie with a catlike grace. By the time he left the room, he was running, and sobbing again.

"What was that about?"

Bailey stepped forward. "Ma'am, Hasan is depressed."

"Oh? He's the most heavily armed crybaby I've ever seen."

Simon motioned to Fianna. "Yes, and that's a little worrisome," he said, as the android walked to the door and closed it. "But he'll be all right. I have faith in the man. He won't fall apart or become violent."

"It only takes a few hours for Hasan to swing between extremes. I'll talk to him later," said Bailey.

Once Fianna had returned to his side, at the day seat by the window, Simon nodded to Maggie. "So what can I do for you?"

She clenched at the fabric of her gown with both hands. "Why did you bring me here?"

"Partially, at Delano's request."

"Okay. So why does he need me? Or, or anyone else? He's got—do you know what he's got down there?"

"Yes. But his plans are too big. The Momma isn't going to be enough. To reach his goals, he needs help from others like us."

"It's more than that. Delano grew up in a small mining town in Namibia, as far from civilization as it's possible to get. His abilities set him further apart from society. I think he needs other exceptional people around simply because he's lonely."

"Your diagnoses are a little too pat, Bailey."

"What goals? I mean, what does he really think he'll get from all this?"

Simon inhaled deeply. In his fist was a strand of beads in an odd variety of shapes, and Maggie saw him rub them between his fingers until the knuckles turned white. "If all goes as planned, the donkeys will go home and cook up trouble. Delano's Momma will destroy several major cities. In the chaos, we'll retain communications through Megasat, making Delano the only one able to direct troops or weapons on a global scale. Using whichever invention works best—or the Momma, if nothing else—he'll kill all the world leaders and armed forces, then announce himself as new emperor." Shaking his head, he sighed. "I think he wanted you as empress, you know."

"Well, fuck that. If that's the only reason he wants me around—"

"Pardon, mum, but it's not the only reason. The Platinum Donkeys are antisocial and they distrust authority. There are only three people on the planet they might have followed into a war, and Delano isn't one of them. You are. So is Simon."

Simon jabbed a finger at Bailey. "Don't count me. I've only ever offered legal advice."

"I am counting you, sir. You underestimate the respect they have for you."

"Okay," said Maggie, "So who's the third person?"

They fell into silence for several seconds. Maggie glanced between the men—they seemed to be holding their breath. Finally she threw her hands wide and shook them. "Who is it?"

"Emile Lambert," said Simon.

Maggie felt her arms fall limp at her sides, and for a moment she couldn't breathe. Simon shook his head again and continued.

"Emile had a different plan for the Platinum Donkeys. He thought that we could integrate into society, prove to them the worth of our creativity and genius. Change the world by setting an example, making it so the world powers would no longer fear us. But Delano wants the old order destroyed, and for his kind to come to power. I understand his hatred. But I just..." Maggie could see a tremor building in the man's shoulders, and his hands shook. "I just don't want to hate the world. Even when they give us reason, I don't think we should hate it."

She looked at Bailey: the butler was standing, arms crossed behind his back, in quiet witness. After Simon had a moment to compose himself, she spoke to him softly. "But...how can he hate the world? All those people he's going to kill..."

"Most of the world are bystanders. But the systems that drive this world, they might deserve hatred."

"But things don't seem that bad. I mean, don't people seem happy? I've seen them in vids and they—"

"Vids? You've experienced the world through vids?" Simon leaned forward, shaking his bead-wrapped fist and shouting. "Then you're not even acquainted with the real world, Maggie. The world you see in those vids is gone, it's ancient, it was dead before our fathers or grandfathers were born. The world *now* is one interconnected city, concrete and hard plastic, with a few remade wildernesses where people are forbidden to go. The world is a *machine*. And if you don't fit as a part of that machine, if accommodating you causes a loss of efficiency or the tiniest threat to its function, then you're discarded, you're surplus, you're nothing. And it's perfectly valid to hate *that*. I do. It terrifies me, it just..." He choked back the last bit, and pressed his trembling hand to his mouth to compose himself.

After a few seconds and a deep breath, he continued. "Maybe if we had children. Maybe if we had something that biology forced us to love, we'd feel the need to keep the world intact for their inheritance. But we're too broken and clear-eyed for that."

"No," said Maggie, almost as a whisper. "No, if I had something to love, I think I'd hate the world more. It would be threatening."

"Well, that's my point from another view. We fear the world because it is not like us. They fear us because we are not like them. Emile wanted us to claim a stake in the world, and teach them not to fear us; Delano just wants to push it aside. I think in the end, Maggie, it's going to come down to you."

"No, no." She backed away, pressed up against a smooth wardrobe, waved her hands in front of her. "I'm, I'm not right. Don't ask me. You, Simon, what do you want?"

"I was torn." Calmer but still shaking, he held out his string of beads. "Emile helped me decide. He made me this rosary."

Maggie stepped forward and took it. She hadn't seen the ivory cross when it was hidden in Simon's fist. At first she thought it plain, but then she noticed the small symbols etched across its face, symbols that seemed not at all religious. The beads were odd also, flat circles, diamonds and other geometric shapes with words etched onto their faces. Strings branched off the corners of the beads seemingly at random, and they connected to others anywhere on the chain. This rosary was no amulet; it could never be worn. The interconnected beads formed something like a mesh, or a circuit.

"It's a pretty simple program. It more or less absolves hatred and fear. Those aren't sins. The one pathway to sin in that flowchart is through wrath. See the end strand, the diamond connected to the circle?"

She found the beads. One said, 'IFF (wrath) y/n', and the next read, 'Grace=FALSE; Sin=TRUE'.

"Cowardice isn't a sin. Hatred isn't a sin. When the world hates you, hating them back is clear-eyed and rational."

"Oh, yes," said Bailey. "Sounds perfectly rational to me."

"My sin, if I were to commit it, is wrath. And I don't want to commit it. No matter how alien and cruel the world is. Do you understand, Maggie?"

"Yeah, you found religion. I'm not a religious person." She tossed the rosary back to him.

Bailey nodded. "A good thing, too. Modern psychological literature lists religion as a subclinical delusion. We don't need any more of those around here."

"Yes, yes, Emile had an agenda. I'm not stupid, I recognize that." Simon stuffed the rosary into his pocket. "But as a solution to a complex problem it was helpful. His basic lesson was that we can't avoid being what we are. But we are not monsters. Find that which will make you into a monster, and avoid doing *that*. Delano's plan, should he succeed, will make monsters of us all."

"To be honest, sir, I think it's doubtful that he'll succeed."

"I agree." Delano is an intuitive planner. His intuition is very good, but he has no talent for Machiavellian plots, and that's what it takes to maintain a conspiracy like this. If not for the legal labyrinths I've set up, we'd all be in jail. Even so, I think the police have infiltrated the group."

"I've suspected the same thing," said Bailey.

"I know who I can trust."

"I have my eye on one in particular."

As they spoke, Maggie began to hear a faraway buzzing sound, just loud enough to distract her from their conversation. She stomped her foot to clear her head and to get their attention.

"Look—I don't care! Throw them all in prison, Delano first. Everyone here is long overdue for a straitjacket. Give it to them. I just want to get back home and spend five minutes in a locked room with my producer, my director, and a sharp knife. Simon, you promised that you could get me back to Megasat. How does mingling with these lunatics help me do that?"

With a sigh, Simon rubbed his temple with a trembling hand. "With your proxy, Delano will be poised to acquire the Megasat corporation."

"What?"

"That's why he—"

The door crashed open, rattling vases and lamps throughout the room. Through the doorway strode Delano, with a small cluster of guests in his wake. "Bailey, there you are," he boomed. "You should be attending to dinner—"

Maggie cut him off. "Hey! What is this about you trying to take over Megasat?"

Delano looked at her, then at Simon, then his eyes split to point at them both. "Simon, I insist on being present when you discuss financial matters."

"She has questions, Delano. Apparently you didn't sate her curiosity."

"Ah. Hmn." He smiled at Maggie, throwing his arms wide. "I'm merely representing your interests, my dear. You've been a ward of the corporation for so long, I wanted to become your new guardian."

"What bullshit are you talking about? I don't need a guardian."

Simon raised his hand, as if to try and calm her. "You're *non compus mentis*. Legally, you need a guardian."

"And let's be honest," said Bailey, stroking his mustache with one finger, "You fall somewhere between a 'public hazard' and a 'natural catastrophe.'"

Maggie turned on him. "Aren't you supposed to be helping?"

"Oh, no. I'm just an observer."

"We've been contesting the Megasat corporation's custody agreement. I've tried arguing your status should be normalized...but considering the recent killings, I think that approach will fail. Best we can do is make Van Hoogan industries your new guardian."

"One corporation, the other corporation, what does it matter?" said Delano. He tried to put his hands on Maggie's shoulders, but she backed away. "Nothing will change for you, dear lady. We're just shifting numbers on a balance sheet."

"Yeah, right. Do you really think Mega will stand for this?"

All the men who were readying for their chance to speak—which apparently included all of them—caught their breath. The pause lasted long enough for Simon to blink, rattle his head, and say, "Pardon?"

The buzzing sound behind Maggie's head grew louder. "Mega owns Megasat. I get an allowance. I don't own anything. He's not going to let you take the satellite, or me, without a fight."

There was another second's pause, while Bailey and Simon looked at each other, and Delano's cross eyes shifted between them both. "Maggie," said Simon in slow, soft tones, "Mega is dead."

It was her turn to stop breathing. She put her hands on her ears, to stop the buzzing from pounding into her skull. "No. That's not true."

"He died five years ago. That's when they declared you not of sound mind."

Bailey coughed into his glove. "With cause, I think."

"Oh, god. I should have known she would do this. I should have noticed—"

"No. No, no no..."

———◉———

—when the police at the airport were arguing, and she tuned them out, they were saying, "Her legal guardian was Mega, and he's dead. If you're not a representative of the Megasat corporation, why should you be allowed to act as custodian?"

But Simon had an answer for that, he always did—

———◉———

Fucking Delano beamed at her. "But don't you see? You were Mega's heir—"

"No!" she screamed, "Shut up! No!"

———◉———

—"That may have been part of it," said Simon, but Maggie stopped listening. She paced around Leah's lab, looking for something sharp, as he continued. "They might also have used the drugs to prevent you from taking control of the corporation when Mega died..."

———◉———

"—you own everything. Megasat, the corporation, it's all in your name."

She backed up against the corner of the bed, shaking her head with her hands clapped around her ears. But even through that, even through her sobbing, she could hear them and she could hear the damned buzzing. "No! I don't want it, I don't..."

"What do you want, Maggie?"

"I wa—I wa—", she said, unable to keep a breath. "*I want my DADDY!*"

And with that painful cry, she collapsed onto the floor, curling up and rocking on her knees. Simon was at her side in an instant. She shrank away, shivering, wailing—

—and then something snapped.

In one fluid motion she stood back up, into a balanced pose. Simon was knocked back by the sudden movement.

Her need to cry was gone. She raised her head, threw her shoulders back. She felt powerful. Statuesque. Her skin seemed radiant, as if spotlit, as if a studio of cameras were on her and the ratings were scrolling up. With a smooth, predatory stare she surveyed the room. The men that surrounded her had changed. They were an audience to tame, they were eyeballs to enslave. They were meat.

Simon crawled backwards to Fianna's side. "Bailey?"

"Something odd there," the butler said. "Not a schizoid break, I don't think. Dissociative in some way, though."

She glared at him. 'Shut up, Montana." He withered, stepping back against the wall.

With a step and a turn, she faced Simon, who had put his plastic tart between them. "You want to fuck Megasat? I'll give you names and embarrassing details. Do you know how many parties I've attended with corporate suits? I know what kind of blackmail to cram between their cheeks." She pointed and scowled, and the poor man clutched at his chest. "But you work to get me free, you understand? No criminal charges, no guardians, none of this proxy bullshit. You got me?"

"Y-yes. I'll do what I can."

"Good." Movement in the doorway caught her eye. Some of the guests were sidling out of the room, while other, hardier donkeys shoved their way in to see the show. Delano had a hand raised as if to stop them, while one eye stayed on her. She advanced on him.

"As for you, you cocksucking Cassandra," she said, jabbing her finger into his chest, inching him backward. "Keep your goddamn, shitgrubbing badger paws off me and mine. You don't touch my company, you don't touch my satellite, and you don't touch me. And if your Twat-Eating Momma hurts one of my fans—" Stepping close enough to press against him, Maggie reached for Delano's crotch. She found the bulges there and squeezed them with all her might. "Just *one* out of four billion, I will bury you deeper than you've ever been. No, I won't leave enough of you to bury. Got it?"

Delano focused two eyes on her with a placid stare, despite the vice grip she had on his testicles. "Certainly," he said.

She gave another crushing squeeze—getting no reaction—and then pushed him aside. The audience at the door suddenly decided to leave the show. She walked out through them, as they stood with their backs pressed against the walls of the corridor.

One in a purple dress, furthest from the doorway, cackled as she passed. "Feeling good, psycho?", asked Leah.

"Fuck off, bitch," Maggie said, stalking past. She mounted the stairs as if it were a coronation, and gouged her fingernails into the cherry banister as she climbed.

After she had gone up a floor, she felt the audience drop away. Nobody was left to carve a path through. No reason for the cameras to be on. But she maintained her poised thespian walk and her practiced, feral grin.

Pretend they're still watching. Pretend that you're in control.

As she reached the third floor, as she headed toward her room, the buzzing began again. She tried to ignore it. Just a technical glitch, a stagehand fucking around on the job. She pretended not to hear it.

It's easy to pretend. Pretend the cameras are on. Pretend they're all following your script. Pretend that you're in charge, that you've always been in charge.

She got to her room, slammed shut the door. Walked to the balcony door and slammed that shut too.

Pretend your Daddy's still alive.

She felt the collapse before it took hold. She leaned against the wall, clutching the curtains, as strength drained from her limbs. Her body began to shake, on cue with her ragged sobs, as the buzzing grew louder.

Maggie turned around and watched the door not open.

A pretend door opened, superimposed on the real bedroom door. She watched, half-lucid, as pretend camera bots flew in through the pretend doorway. Control strips snaked onto her walls, stilt-legged servants carted in trays of liquor and knives, a unicorn pranced in with its foreleg gears grinding, and every single one of them vanished when they were no longer in her immediate vision.

Then he walked in, through the open doorway that wasn't there.

He wore a plain work shirt, a businessman's slacks, and a kind smile. His rounded eyes looked at her with love, but his hands dangled uselessly at his sides. His hair was the same blonde as hers, something she had never noticed before.

With a hoarse whisper, she asked, "You're not Mega, are you?"

He smiled again, yet his face was sad. His eyes were in pain, yet full of love. *I'm pretending all of those expressions. Which of them did I actually see?*

"You're my real father. That's how you looked, just before mom—" She caught herself. His expression didn't change, it never would again. She couldn't imagine it doing anything except stare, and stand, and open its mouth to speak.

"You're a very special girl," the apparition said.

On the last word Maggie blinked, or thought she had, so that for an instant she saw neither the vision nor the reality. When her eyes opened again her father and his entourage was gone. The bedroom door was shut.

Something was still buzzing.

She spun around, looking into the high corners of the room for an errant camera or—she hoped—some insect. It didn't sound like a camerabot. The buzzing modulated, almost like human speech, if through a tinny speaker or from inside a metal box. She started searching the bed, throwing aside the lace-bordered satin sheets, because the noise seemed to be coming from there. A random glance solved the mystery. At the foot of the bed, the copper box containing her governor was vibrating enough that it was jiggling across the hope chest.

Gritting her teeth she grabbed the thing and ran to the balcony door. But she stopped with her hand on the latch. The buzzing was distorted speech, but not the governor's computerized monotone. The voice seemed human, and warm. And it was female.

Maggie opened the case.

"Maggie!" the governor said. It didn't try to shoot lasers into her eyes or otherwise get her attention. In fact, all the eyeline beads were dark. "Thank god you've answered. Please, you've got to listen, you're in terrible danger."

"Who the hell are you?" A chill crawled up Maggie's back. *Is this real? How do I tell, when technology can do anything?*

"My name is Lieutenant Susan Jones of Globalpol. We've been listening through the governor for you. We needed to warn you, you're in danger."

"Simon told me the governor couldn't work through the box."

"Simon doesn't know everything. Are you alone? Is there anyone in the building who you think might be dangerous?"

"Yes," Maggie said. Her shoulders slumped and the words started gushing out. "Every single fucking one of them is dangerous I'm in a house full of wackos and this Delano guy has—"

"Okay. Calm down," it said. "We can protect you. But you have to come under protective custody. You're not under arrest, if we wanted to do that we would have done it in Perth. Are you willing to come with us?"

"Yes," she said again, before she had thought about it. If she wasn't in trouble, the police needed to stop Delano. "But I don't know where I am. I'm in the mountains, somewhere."

"That's okay. Just walk out on your balcony."

Confused, Maggie paused for a moment before pulling the door open.

The sky was as blue as before, and the scenery as gorgeous. The sloping forest floor held small shrubs and exposed rocks, with a sprinkling of needles and leaves. A breeze ruffled across the treetops, making the pines sway. Maggie went to the railing. She began looking about for people, when she noticed the one pine tree that had stopped swaying and had started to fold up.

The lower branches of the tree bent upward, tucking neatly together against the thick trunk. Above that a set of branches twisted themselves together, their needles meshing into a solid weave and transmuting into a dull silver. The trunk flowed upward, leaving a slender, flexible support bracing the center of mass against the ground. The top branches, knitted into two flat silver blades, began to spin. They picked up speed, cutting through the tops of other trees nearby. The folded branches in the central part flowed like water and turned charcoal grey, with another, smaller rotor spinning to one side. The support snapped; the machine bobbled in the air, shifting to drop sled rails, form a doorway, and extrude stubby wings.

I didn't know they made mimic-metal helicopters, Maggie thought. Then she frowned. *No, of course they don't. This isn't happening. I've lost it.*

The copter rose above the treetops and flew closer, creating a new, powerful wind that was harsh with the smell of cut pine. Maggie looked up, trying to force herself to see the sun through the delusion's hull. It descended next to her balcony, buffeting her hair and making the railing quiver. An android of the same material as the hull leaned out of the cargo door, extending its hand.

This is it. If I lean over the balcony, I'll be reaching for an illusion. They'll find my body in the woods, and never know...

Someone shouted behind her. Maggie turned to see Simon, pushing Bailey aside as they charged through her bedroom door. Before they could reach her, before she could warn them away, a gray metal arm hooked around her waist. It lifted her up in a rush of wind that smelled of pine and ozone. The donkeys gathered on the balcony, watching her ascend, as they and the ground fell away.

⸻⸻●⸻⸻

Chapter 13—Ensemble Freeze
Interstitial

Delano rotated his snifter of brandy, staring at it—and also off into the distance, toward the treacherous blue sky.

"What will you do now?" asked Hwong. The man shadowed him so much and asked so many questions, Delano was worried he'd ask to be paid a salary.

"What I will do is never at issue. 'When' can be confusing. But my mind makes itself up, so I've already done what I must do."

Hwong's face was expressionless. Sometimes Delano could detect a slight tilt of his head by the way his fiber optic hair settled. This time he gave nothing but his typical, intent smile.

"I don't understand."

Delano put his snifter down, already knowing how the brandy would taste, and already knowing he would not drink enough to get drunk that afternoon. Maybe later in the evening. He could feel a comfortable buzz enveloping him, but it was yet hours away.

"My dear Bartholomew, did you know that my father owned the last diamond mines in Namibia?" He waited for the hesitant Asian to give a slight shake of his head. "He did, in fact. I remember visiting them as a boy. It was before fabber technology became commercially viable—the end of the diamond market was coming, but we were eking out all the profits we could.

"I remember one time I sat on an overlook above the main shaft, watching the men and those clumsy old machines. The sun was hot and I had a kheffiyeh, but I had taken off my headwrap because I had felt wind in my hair a few minutes earlier. I felt then that, some time later, something struck me on the face. My chin bled, and there were abrasions across my neck... It was unpleasant, of course, but I was accustomed to my foresight by then, and I took the injuries as a clear warning. I had been thinking of climbing down the cliff side to join the workers for lunch. Obviously, if I did that, I would slip and scrape myself on the rocks. So I decided to stay where I was.

"It was almost an hour later that my father's helicopter landed, on the flat overlook where I was sitting. It kicked up gravel from the escarpment, blew it around like a miniature dust storm. I put my hands up to shield my eyes, but bits of rock and sand embedded themselves in the wounds on my chin and neck—and I knew I had been a fool.

"My father got out of the helicopter and quizzed me about my injuries. He was teaching me to use the gift, just as his father taught him. I explained, and immediately afterward I felt his slap on my face, although he would not raise his hand for several minutes. I never have learned how he managed to time his punishments like that..."

He picked up the brandy snifter again, feeling that it was time for him to quaff what he had tasted minutes before. After a leisurely draught, he smiled at Hwong. "What angered my father was my cowardice. If I had wanted to climb down the cliff, that is what I should have done. The gift is not a warning, he told me. It is a verification. There is no logic in trying to evade one's senses. I must always commit to a course of action and engage, and damn the consequences, especially when they have already revealed themselves."

Hwong nodded, but the man's eyes were still puzzled. Delano waved at him to prevent the tedious questioning. "What I am saying is that I already know what I must do, because I felt myself do it hours ago. I felt the rush of excitement, the thrill of success—and, yes, a shadow of guilt. I felt it because it will happen, must happen, and thus I have no decision to make."

"Yes. But what will happen?"

Delano smiled, and with an adamant will he forced both of his eyes to focus on his sniveling companion. Hwong really was a dim bulb, as mad geniuses went. Once he had secured his empire, some program would have to be invented to weed out the low-watt donkeys. But for now he needed them. First he had to deal with traitors, and trollops, and threats to his immediate plans.

"I am trying to tell you, good fellow," he said, swirling his brandy again, already savoring the taste of his next sip. "That the deaths were on my head hours ago. I sent the command minutes ago, when my predestined course of action was clear."

He sipped the liquor, just as the taste left his tongue.

"What will happen now is that we will bask in our future victory."

<hr>

It seeped into Maggie's brain, slowly, that the police helicopter was real. There was no other way to explain the detail: The uncomfortable spongy harness, the vista of the foothills below, and the strange, mimic-metal android that was her only companion. She tried asking it questions, but it shook its head and said nothing. The governor had fallen from her hand during her escape.

Escape? Abduction? She realized that it depended on her intentions, and she was too numb to sort them out.

Through a small window Maggie watched the terrain. They flew across rock-strewn woodlands, until the pine trees broke into gentle, grassy hills. A sparkling blue river twisted through the prairie in almost random loops. The copter flew low enough that Maggie thought she saw a massive herd of animals. They appeared as a wide brown swath, speckled throughout the grassland, that shifted its boundaries like an amoeba.

When they hit civilization, it might as well have been a brick wall.

There was, in fact, a wall—a wooden palisade that would have been old-fashioned if every log had not been a perfect replica of its neighbors. The logs were a veneer, as they joined smoothly into the plastic and metal of buildings that abutted them on the other side. And buildings were everywhere, packed in organized patterns throughout the civilized side of the fence. A square adjacent to the wilderness looked like a shopping mall; another had the look of an industrial plant. Office buildings proliferated, four and five stories high at the edge of the palisade and rising higher as they flew deeper into the city. Except for trees and flowerbeds cultivated along walkways, nature had suddenly vanished whereever man lived.

Soon the city itself changed character. While the outskirts were urban enough, they flew on a path toward architecture that looked dense and strange.

Maggie remembered San Francisco, and how the city had become a solid carpet of tall, glittering buildings covered in solar cells and walkways. Here she saw the beginnings of that kind of transformation. This city—she didn't even know its name—still had roads. But they cut between giant buildings, some of them a kilometer square and dozens of stories tall. In places the structures were advancing on the streets, curving over them in arches that could have been artistic from the ground. From her vantage they looked aggressive, like slow-motion waves arcing over the remaining bits of terrain, ready to drown them. She wondered how long it would take for the architecture to take over, for the city to become one solid arcology, traversable only by spider trolleys above or deep tunnels below.

Outside the city lay nature unspoiled. Suddenly, she understood the world. It was not that different from Megasat. Which reminded her that those in control of Megasat were corrupt, and wanted only to use her.

The copter landed on a rooftop like thousands of others. Four men in Globalpol uniforms were there.

"Where am I?', she asked as they walked her from the copter.

"Boise, Idaho, ma'am." The man was tall and square jawed, and seemed familiar. "You have the right to remain silent, both verbally and electronically. Any communication you make can and will be used against you..."

He kept on but Maggie quit listening, except to nod at any question he asked.

———◦———

For some reason, being left alone in a locked, mint green room made her feel better.

She was sure that the copter ride had not been a delusion. The chair she sat on, the cold metal table in front of here, were real. Maybe she could trust everything that seemed solid, and only things that were transparent were fantasy. But that made her think about Mega, and before she could help herself she began to cry.

Soon after that, the door opened, and Maggie forced herself to breathe deep, dabbing her eyes with the sleeve of her gown.

Officer Radicker—Mr. Square Jaw—and two other men entered. Chairs rose up from the floor on the other side of the table. Only one of them sat down. Radicker stood, looming over Maggie, while the third leaned against the wall near the door.

"All right, Ms. Megaputri. Let me explain to you how much trouble you're in."

She looked up at him, raising her chin defiantly. "I want to speak with Susan Jones."

The weedy man in the chair snickered, although his eyes looked hollow and dead. The one by the door sighed. "Told you she'd form an attachment quickly. Might as well tell her, Bill."

"There is no Lieutenant Jones," said Radicker. "It's a personality the governor loaded."

"It lied to me?"

"It's programmed to get you to interact by any means necessary. Once it was able to contact us, we fed it instructions for you. You're lucky we had an extraction vehicle standing by."

"We know everything that went on in there," said the weedy man. "Your little gang is outclassed, all the way."

"It told me I wasn't under arrest. Did it lie about that, too?"

"It did what it had to do. Yes, you are under arrest. And no, Globalpol is not legally responsible for misinformation fed by governors."

Maggie nodded, still numb, but beginning to appreciate her mistake. "I think I should have my lawyer, then."

"You'll get one in court."

"And not before then. Simon Brovall isn't getting you out this time. We have an entire wing of this building full of lawyers, making sure there are no technicalities, no grounds to spring you."

"Can you hold me without a lawyer?"

"Yes," said Radicker. "Because you've given us just about every legal reason to suspend your rights. Murder, conspiracy to commit terrorism, compromising a fabber, and let's not forget the fact that you're certified insane."

"Be gentle, Bill," said the observer. "You want to make a connection."

Radicker looked over his shoulder. "I'll do this my way, Theo." Then he pulled one of the chairs out and sat down. With his arms crossed on the table, he leaned toward Maggie and lowered his voice.

"See, our psychologist over there thinks you can be reasoned with. That you'll see things our way if we buddy up to you. But I've heard what you do to your buddies," he said, slicing his finger across his throat. "No, I think I know the truth. I think you're at the end of your rope, aren't you, Maggie? I think all you need is a push and you're going to collapse completely. I mean, the first thing you did when you got in here was start to cry, right?"

Maggie stared at him, keeping her expression neutral, careful not to laugh in his face.

"So let me tell you what's going to happen if you don't cooperate with us. We're going to carpet bomb a lot of potential sites that might be housing Delano's Mommas, just to be on the safe side. Then we're going to take everyone in that house by force. They're going to fight back, because they're stupid."

"They're not stupid."

Weedy laughed again. Radicker ground his jaw.

"They're going to fight back," he said. "And there's going to be a lot of bloodshed. I'm going to personally make sure that Simon Brovall is on the casualty list. Then you're going to go to trial. They'll pump you with drugs, carve out pieces of your brain, and finally throw you in the same institution where your mother rotted away. Because that's where girls like you end up, Maggie."

She swallowed. "I'm not like my mother."

"Oh, no. Your mother only ever killed one man."

This time, although she wasn't expecting it, she was ready. Something snapped within her, something that held back a flood of anger and confidence. There were no buzzing sounds, no delusions, only a sudden, seething conviction that no one was here to help her, and no one here could show her up. The stage was all hers.

Maggie shifted position, tensing, sitting straighter, and gave Radicker a slight smile. The observer noticed—his eyes went wide. "Bill..."

"It's okay," she said to him. Then she turned back to Radicker. "I'm okay. But you—Bill—you're wrong about everything. You really should have tried to make a connection." She leaned closer to him and whispered, "See, I really did like the people I killed."

He leaned back. Now she noticed pauses in his motions, little spans of time when his eyes glazed over. The other one at the table went through the same lapses. Theo, in the back, didn't—she guessed he didn't have implants shooting messages into his brain. Maggie posed with an index finger on her chin, and spoke before they recovered from their fugue.

"What I want to know is why you didn't arrest Delano long before this. You said you know everything about what he's doing—why did you let him get this far?"

"We were going to take him in when it was most profitable," said Weedy.

"Profitable? What kind of profit are you looking for?"

"He means 'most efficient,'" said Radicker, clenching his jaw. "When we do it isn't important—"

"Oh, no, I think it is. And I think he meant exactly what he said." Smiling, she glanced between them both. "When you do put Delano in prison, the Unification government is going to take everything he owns, isn't it? You wanted the Momma, didn't you?" Their eyes glazed over again; she kept going. "Or did you want more than that? You wanted to wait until Delano had me, didn't you?"

"We've already got enough to put you away, and seize everything you own."

"But I don't own anything. I'm a ward of the corporation. But you gambled that Delano was going to get custody of me, so that— You wanted Megasat, didn't you? Awww," she said, pouting. "Is the widdle world government scared that the only route to space is in private hands?"

She gave them a second to recover. The weedy one came back first, his slack-faced expression breaking into a wide smile. "She's good."

"Doesn't matter," said Radicker, standing up with force and kicking over his chair. "We're on plan B now, Maggie, and that means destroying the Momma and killing Delano and everyone he's recruited. A lot of people are going to die. Unless you get close to Delano for us."

Maggie laughed. "And do what?"

"Find out where the Momma installations are. Find out if he has a deadman's switch that will activate the device if something happens to him."

"What, your pet shrink can't figure that out by himself?" she said, nodding at Theo, the silent one by the door.

He took a deep breath and stepped closer. Radicker opened his mouth to speak, but deferred to Theo as he approached the table. "Look, Maggie," he said, "I don't think you really want to hurt people. You know Delano does. The government exists to help people and keep them from harm. You want to be on our side."

"Help people, huh?" She smiled. "I know what your government is doing. On Megasat we separate living areas from environmental controls because it's necessary. You're doing it here on Earth. Crowding people into arcologies while making natural spaces forbidden to enter."

"The pro-environmental diaspora is a well-known global agenda."

"But the world you're building isn't healthy. And those who aren't healthy can't live in it. So you force people to wear robot jewelry programmed to brainwash them into liking what they've got."

"What you call brainwashing is widely considered social unification. Only a united, global society could have put an end to pollution, war—"

"—creativity, genius—"

Weedy interrupted them with a laugh. "You don't know what genius is." The sunken-eyed man leaned toward her, tapping his forehead with one finger. "I'm hooked up to more processors than you've probably interacted with in your life. I've replayed this conversation a hundred times, and I've got twenty predictive simulations telling me how it's going to end. This is the future—computational power without the attendant risk of insanity. Creativity is inextricably linked with mental illness, that's been proven for nearly a century. And that means I'm the future, while you're obsolete. Now you can help us, or you can be thrown in the trash."

Smiling, Maggie leaned on the table to flash a bit of cleavage. "Okay, smart guy," she said, "Write me a poem."

He blinked.

She laughed at him. "What's wrong? Your simulations didn't predict that?" Then she remembered the rules of her poetry challenges; once started, everything afterward had to rhyme. "Well the thrash is on now. It's your turn at bat."

Radicker shot the man a warning glare. "We don't have time for this."

"It's okay," Weedy said, staring at Maggie. "I can beat her."

"That's a first infraction—every sentence needs to rhyme. But if you need to warm up, I think I've got the time."

That was a stock response that she had used on her show. No need to waste good material on her opponent until he made some effort. She felt it, however, a poem coalescing in the back of her mind, tended by a piece of herself that seemed distant yet powerful. For a second or two she let the construction simmer. Her inner self stripped words from it and pressed new ones in. But when she noticed Weedy's eyes glazing over, she quickly assembled a thrust.

"Downloading new software? Oh, give me a break. I've thrown couplets so far, and that's all you can take?"

Slapping the table, Radicker stood up and loomed over his associate. "Stop it, both of you. This isn't going to accomplish anything."

"If she loses, she'll give up. If I let her win she'll stay stubborn," he said. Then, "...as a pup," he added.

Maggie laughed. "Congratulations, you just committed art. You've proven you're human. Now prove to me you're smart."

"Intelligence isn't about writing poetry. It's about...being able to see."

"I've seen where this is going. It ends with a sonnet. I'm already composing—you better get on it."

From the back of the room, Theo sighed. "Bill, we're done here. She's not going to give us any more right now."

"I'm not done," said Radicker. "But you are, Agent Garrecht. Get out of this interrogation room."

Weedy—she couldn't think of him as anything else—held up his hand. "Thy gift, thy tables, are within my brain. And it is wider than the sky—"

"Plagiarist!" Maggie leapt to her feet, pointing at him. Her mind wheeled, constructing a rhyming accusation. "That's Shakespeare's line you stole, it's cut out and reused. And Dickinson as well—you've gone and stolen twice! You've married them, you cad, both bard and waif confused. That's all software can do, just rearrange and splice?"

She felt bad for not rhyming 'plagiarist'. But the man's eyes widened at her accusation, then narrowed in anger.

"Writing poetry is not what I can do," he said. "My talent lies in catching freaks like you."

Laughing, Maggie felt the final lines of her sonnet knit together, as if tangled pieces of her mind were weaving into a whole. She gave Weedy a dangerous smile, then leaned toward him.

"What makes us all complete, a doting muse?
Or metal circuits sunk within the brain?
Electronics restrain themselves by fuse;
Calliope can drive her charge insane.
But sanity cast off, look what we gain.
We dream of objects no search engines find,
with qualities and colors yet unnamed,
and no display to mediate their kind.
You boast, stutter, download; hem, haw and grind,
then pressed, you quote the bard as your reply?
If cut and paste's enough to tax your mind,
I'd urge you to unplug, curl up, and die.
While powers here appoint your mind as best,
My lot's with the crazies, human and blessed."

The meter wasn't perfect. She would have liked to have more time, or a guitar riff to work from. But in the long pause that followed she watched Weedy's expression go from shock, to anger, to a frightened glare. She smiled again. *This is what I am, and this is just a fraction of what I can do.*

Weedy looked sideways at his superior. Radicker clenched his jaw. "Get out, now," he said in a firm tone. Without complaint, Weedy got up and left. His chair sank back into the floor as he crossed the entrance.

"This doesn't prove anything," said the psychologist. The tilt of his head and his long, painful sigh radiated sympathy and sadness. Maggie wanted to carve his heart out. "People like him really are the future, you know. Lack of creativity is a feature, not a bug. The governors are programmed to limit imagination for a reason."

"Because you're afraid some people may go insane."

"Because creativity leads to invention, which leads to social change, and that process can now be sped through at a rate which no society can survive. Platinum Donkeys create Steel Elephants that can stomp our world apart."

"Elephants?"

The psychologist shrugged. "Disruptive technologies. It's terminology we created."

"Oh, you named the Platinum Donkeys? I've heard differently."

"You've heard lies, Maggie. The world needs to halt scientific progress. We need citizens who can be predicted, whose needs can be planned. We need people who cannot conceptualize mass murder—technology has made it just too easy. Every person whose intellect is left unbounded is an existential threat to the human race."

"There'll always be weirdos and outcasts. Society needs to make a place for us, or we'll carve out something for ourselves."

"No. You can be treated, you can adapt, or you can be destroyed. That's why—" He stopped. Radicker had stepped back as if in a daze, his eyes unfocused. His face was twisted into a snarl and he had balled his hands into fists. "Bill? What is it?"

"Check your messages, Theo," said Radicker, shaking his head to clear it. "We've got to get her out of here."

The psychologist brought up a display on his shirt sleeve. Radicker grabbed hold of Maggie's arm and pulled; she tore herself free. "What the hell?"

"We're going to a more secure facility."

He lunged for her again. Maggie, far more agile, danced away and put the interrogation table between them. He tried to reach over it, and she laughed, dodging his clumsy grab. Slapping the table, Radicker paused to listen to his implants for a second, then he slapped the table again.

"Damn it! Theo, why are communications down? I can't get the table to retract."

"I don't know. We don't have much time."

"Let's go," said Radicker, pushing himself upright. "We'll lock the door. Nobody's in this room, understand?"

"He's here, isn't he?", said Maggie with a laugh. *My shining knight with the grey eyes!*

That got her an angry glare. Then the two men nodded at each other. Before they could get to the door someone opened it from the outside, and a tidal wave of people began to push into the interrogation room.

"Why is this man in here?"

"Sir, he's got all the paperwork—"

"—said no one comes in this room, I don't care what papers—"

"—told me every section is working on this, but it will take—"

"—care what writ he's sent—"

"—step aside, this room's no longer yours—"

"Simon!", shouted Maggie, as the lawyer's charcoal suit came into view. She pushed her way through the crush of bureaucrats and police. He was clinging to Fianna's arm as people crowded around him, most of them shouting and making demands, but his eyes were intent and firm. He saw her and smiled, and behind him Maggie saw Prince Hasan, who had the good sense not to bring his enormous scimitar into the police station. Hasan offered his arm; Maggie took it, and they pulled into a tight ring surrounded by the authorities.

Radicker's face had turned beet red. "You have no standing to come in here. This detainee has been denied right of counsel."

"I'm not here as her counsel," said Simon. The room quieted down as he spoke, as if they were looking for any vulnerability in what he had to say. "Her status as detainee is not in issue."

"There is no way you're taking her out of here. Her detention was free of technicalities. Isn't that right?"

Men in white shirts and black ties nodded, murmuring agreement.

Simon seemed unfazed. "Yes, you should be commended for a good job. But while your legal teams were cementing Ms. Megaputri's status, you failed to notice that I was disincorporating your township."

Radicker's mouth dropped open. "What?"

"A formal dispute has been filed against the Collister precinct charter, and until that's settled it has been absorbed into adjacent precincts. With no legal status as a township, there is no allowable zoning for high security prisoners here. This building reverts to local government; I expect they'll turn it into a school."

"You can't *do* that!"

"You're not paying attention," said Simon, his teeth flashing. Maggie had never seen him look like such a predator. "I already *have* done it. And now that this facility is shutting down, all your detainees have to be transported, by authorized agents, to acceptable holding."

"All right, fine," said Radicker. "The transport specialists should be here within the hour. We'll wait for them."

"You misunderstand. I am a legally authorized prisoner transport specialist."

For a beat or two there was silence, as a dozen lawyers and policemen stared in shocked disbelief. Maggie was almost sorry that her giggling broke the tableau.

In the subsequent explosion of arguments and accusations, Radicker's voice bellowed through. "No! No, I am not going to let this happen," he said. "Simon Brovall, you're part of this conspiracy, too. I'm placing you under arrest."

"You can't do that. As a borderless jurist I have limited regional immunity. You need a waiver from the Unification Council."

On Radicker's flank, a handful of suits started brainstorming ways to deal with that. He cut them off with a curt wave. "Doesn't matter. She's not leaving this building. I'll take full responsibility."

"Fianna," said Simon, "Look up Radicker, first initial W."

"His name's Bill," Maggie volunteered.

"First name William, then. Dig deep."

"Yes, Simon."

"Stop your games, Brovall. I'll have my department's full support on this."

"I'm done sending complaints to your department. Eventually I'll go to the next level higher, but that's not what Fianna's after now."

Fianna's placid voice seemed odd in the tenseness of the room. "Simon, I've found his residence. Five-four-eight, Primrose Lane—"

"I don't need the address, thank you. Put a lien on it."

"What? For what reason?"

"In anticipation of reparations for a wrongful arrest suit. I've got—Fianna, how many W.A.'s do we have queued?"

"Fifteen."

"Fifteen different petitions ready to throw into court. If any one of them succeeds, your home defaults to my client. Even if none of them are successful, I can prevent your use of the domicile until all the suits make their way through the court system. One at a time."

"You bastard," said Radicker. The muscles in his jaw and temple were as firm as rocks. His face began to turn red. "Do you think you can intimidate me?"

"Simon," said Fianna, "He has a son."

"Excellent. Prepare an *amicus curie* brief for Family Services."

Radicker made a strangled sound.

Simon looked the officer in the eye. "You can't expect a boy to grow up without a home. Especially when his father is willing to throw his career away on emotional outbursts. Don't worry. If the boy suffers any trauma from growing up in a foster home, I'm sure a governor can fix it."

Maggie thought that the tall policeman was going to choke, or maybe leap at Simon in a rage. But although his fists were clenched and his teeth bared, Radicker's feet seemed nailed to the floor. He leaned forward, then rocked back, barely managing to say, "You can't—"

"Yes," shouted Simon, "Yes I *can*. I can take away everything you own, including your son, and throw them into legal limbo for *years*. Or I can walk out of here with my client, and none of these suits will need to be filed. It's your choice, officer. Make it now; my time is expensive."

Radicker looked around at his associates. The other policemen seemed shocked and frozen. The lawyers shrugged their shoulders, their faces full of apologies.

After a few seconds of tense silence, the man's shoulders sagged. "Take her. Damn you," he said, in a voice just above a whisper. "Damn you. This isn't over. Damn you."

"I think everything's settled, then," said Simon. His hand trembled a little as he looked around. "Thank you, gentlemen. Fianna, pause all actions concerning William Radicker. Hasan, lead the way."

As they marched, single file, through the police station, Maggie tapped Simon on the back. "You're amazing," she whispered.

"We're not out of here yet," he said. Then, in an even lower tone he added, "Plus, I worry that Delano may be about to do something stupid." He put a finger to his lips.

No one confronted them as they passed, but dozens of people stood in the corridors and watched. Maggie smiled at them and put a swish in her walk. They weren't fans—they weren't even happy to see her—but treating them as an audience made her feel better.

Simon's limo was sleek and black, inside and out. A fat, shiny scimitar lay on the seat. Hasan sat next to it and then bent almost double, sheathing it in his jacket's scabbard. As they pulled into traffic, Simon let out an exhausted sigh.

"This incident is going to be a problem for us later. If we have a later."

"But what a thrill", said Hasan. "Meeting the enemy, walking away in triumph. You were right; it was just the thing to draw me out of my mood."

"Yes, well, don't swing too far the other way."

"Simon," said Fianna, "The police are attempting to take control of the vehicle."

"On what grounds?"

"Public emergency."

Maggie had been staring at Simon, fascinated by his steely eyes and the contrast they made with his frail body. When she felt the vibrations in her loins they seemed natural, a tingling appreciation for a fine man. But then she realized the vibrations came from the limo. The ground was shaking.

Hasan scrambled to face forward. "I can drive."

"Oh, god, oh god," said Simon. "Fianna, give Hasan manual control. God, Hasan, get us out of here."

The canopy of the limousine turned transparent, and Hasan held his hands in the air to grasp at laserline projected controls. Simon curled up, trembling and moaning. Maggie almost reached out to comfort him, but she stopped, distracted by the view outside.

The six-lane thoroughfare had been packed with cars of every color and shape. Now they were scattering, flocking in synchronized patterns toward recesses at the base of the buildings that loomed over everything. The towering skyscrapers were swaying, with clouds of glass falling down from humongous cliffs full of broken windows. Between the towers sat squat arcology buildings whose solar cell facades were cracking and falling down. As a chunk of architecture across the street crumbled, Maggie could see inside the building. Its skeleton was steel; its guts were pipes and wires, with an outer skin of plastic and chrome. Everywhere around them the buildings' skeletons were twisting, their guts were snapping, and their skins were sloughing away.

Hasan accelerated the limo, aiming them down the center of the now empty road. Plastic and plaster rained across the roadway's outer lanes. Ahead of them a skyscraper tottered, then drew into itself as its floors smashed down onto one another. Hasan turned a sharp corner to avoid the dust and debris that flew out from that direction. A horrendous crashing boom cut through the quake's omnipresent rumbling, and for a moment their vision was obscured as the cloud of dust caught up with them.

Simon curled up into a foetal position. As the car swerved to avoid chunks of debris he almost fell from his seat, but Fianna held him with a firm grip. Maggie heard him scream as they passed beneath an archway, whose facade buckled and tumbled to the ground just behind them. The impact sent a thunderclap through the limo. The road itself was beginning to crack, and behind them she could see ragged sections of pavement tilting, causing gnashes of asphalt to jab into the air.

Then they turned again onto another road and picked up more speed, and the surrounding buildings appeared smaller, although whether that was due to their state of partial collapse Maggie couldn't tell. Walls of cracked glass and plastic leaned out precariously over the road, or worse, were pushed inward, vanishing into oily smoke that ballooned over piles of buildings turned rubble

The ride seemed smoother here—she realized that the earthquake had stopped. It had only lasted a few minutes, and the city had been horribly damaged. Buildings were still leaning, walls crumbling. Gravity threatened all the structures that the earthquake had left behind.

Hasan pressed his palm forward to decelerate the limo. Ahead of them sat another archway, and it had dropped a decoration, a curved sheet of plastic and chrome, across their path. They stopped a car length before it, then, with one hand on the door, Hasan turned to Simon.

"It looks thin. I think I can move it, with your android's help."

"F-Fianna," squeaked Simon, "ah-assist Hasan."

As they ran out of the vehicle, a cloud of dust blew in through the door, forcing Maggie to climb across the seats to close it. She looked over at Simon. He was balled up, arms around his head.

"Hey," she said, "Are you going to be okay?"

Shaking violently, he unwound himself enough to look up at her. His pupils were pinpricks, his face a pale rictus. Then his eyes flickered upward and looked past her, and he let out a powerful scream.

Maggie looked up in time to see the wall collapse.

Chunks of shattered plastic rained down onto the limo's canopy. Maggie dropped to the floor as larger, denser blocks pounded down. The vehicle's canopy turned opaque just as its light system flared and went out, leaving afterimages of warning icons in her vision. The chassis squealed; Simon wailed like a vacuum breach. Maggie clapped her hands over her ears until she no longer felt the thumping of debris pound at her through the limo's floor.

When she lifted her head, the silence was a relief. Above she heard groaning and settling sounds from the debris. She reached up and felt the limo's ceiling, searching for cracks. It seemed intact. Simon panted somewhere in the darkness. Maggie groped around to find him, and when she touched his leg, he gave her a vicious kick for her trouble.

"Get away!" he shrieked. For a couple seconds he babbled, stringing consonants together in a steady patter, as if he had lost the use of vowels. Then, with an effort she could hear in his voice, he found control of his tongue, if not his words. "You think I don't? I know a-ga-danna! They've got quo warranto, don't my father and all..."

"Hush," she said, sidling next to him, close enough to take the leverage out of his kicks and attempts to push her away. "Hush," she said, draping her body over his. "It's going to be all right. We're okay."

"Oh, no no. Not okay. I know what comes in darkness and the governor made me see grues and I can't breathe, Maggie I can't breathe!" He pushed at her; she dropped to her knees on the floor by his side, but kept her arms over him, hugging, stroking softly. "I can't take and can't breathe and fucking Delano! It's all ruined! Emile, help me! It's all a mistake! I didn't mean—oh god! Fianna has my will and my medicine and my mind isn't—and my wrath! No, oh no, please! Oh, god! Oh, Maggie, please don't kill me!"

"Don't be ridiculous," she cooed.

He fought with her some more but she pinned his arms, kissing his neck, nuzzling his ear. After a few minutes he gave in. Quivering, mewing feebly, he lay there as Maggie tried to soothe him by stroking his hair and whispering soft promises of safety.

After a long while, well after her adrenaline rush had faded, she fell asleep while running her hands across his smooth, unbroken skin.

Chapter 14—Blackout

She awoke in stages. At some point, she remembered, she had snuggled closer to Simon, covering his still body with her own. Her eyes fluttered when noise from the debris sent reverberations through the buried vehicle. They were in complete darkness, so she soon dozed off again.

Then a crescent of light sliced through the darkness. Maggie blinked to focus her eyes, and saw only a hand reaching into the limo. She took it. It was warm, and slick with sweat, but its grip was strong, and she let it pull her out through the half-opened door.

"Thank you, Hasan," she said when she saw her rescuer. He had taken off his jacket, and his shirt was caked with dust and sweat stains. He smiled but made no sound. Instead he leaned into the limo—the door, she saw, had been pried open and was too buckled to ever close again—and he reached for Simon.

"Simon's still asleep. How long were we in there?"

Again, no reply.

Maggie looked around. The sky was dark, with a few hazy spotlights cutting upward through dust-filled air. The light that was shining into the limo came from Fianna, who face emanated a brilliant, white, directed beam. Maggie held her hand up to block that light so she could look around. There was little to see. The city was rubble, with no illumination, although a few spots along the horizon were lit with a flickering orange glare. *Fires*, she thought. *We're still not safe. Nobody is.*

"Damn it, I wish I had a powered dress. Fianna, what time is it?"

"It is two forty-three A.M. Is Simon alright?"

"Yes, he's just sleeping. Do you have any net connections? How many cities did Delano hit?"

"I have access to emergency satellite communications. All local ground networks are inactive. The earthquake affected only Boise and adjacent townships. The CenNet is no longer active here."

"Only Boise?" *He boasted about London and Beijing, several cities simultaneously.* Then the realization struck her, and she balled up her fists. *The son of a bitch was after me.*

Hasan stepped next to her and lay something down onto the rubble.

For a moment Maggie couldn't process what she was seeing. Simon lay there, eyes open and face locked in a hideous scream. Fianna's face dimmed to a soft glow, and she knelt down, placing her hand on his neck. While the android tended her master, Hasan backed away, his mouth open in a wide smile and his big frame shaking with soundless laughter.

"No," said Maggie. "No, he's still alive. I didn't—I mean, I didn't. I swear I didn't." She looked up at Hasan. "What the hell are you laughing at?"

Still laughing, Hasan picked his scimitar up from the rubble and walked into the street, ignoring her. Maggie spun around, looking for someone, anyone, to whom she could plead her case. When Fianna stood back up, Maggie ran to her side, grabbing the android's arm.

"He's alive, right? Tell me he's still alive."

"I'm sorry, I cannot help you right now. Simon is dead."

"No. He can't be—"

She glanced down at Simon's body, and although her eyes were readjusting to the dim light, at first she thought she saw him move. But it was only the unexpected change in his pose. The android, following some obscure program, had straightened the man's limbs and used her own jacket to cover his face. When she saw him laying on his back in that state, the reality pressed in on Maggie. She felt tears welling. They, or the dust in the air, made her eyes water and sting.

"But how could he be dead? I didn't, I swear I didn't. He said he had a heart condition, didn't he? Fianna, can you tell how he died?"

"I'm sorry, I cannot help you right now. Simon is dead."

With a groan Maggie released the android and turned away. A few meters behind them, Hasan was swinging his weapon in a series of smooth, measured poses—a workout routine, in the middle of the debris-covered street. He was still panting as if to laugh, but not a sound escaped him. Maggie clenched her fists again and yelled at him.

"What the hell is wrong with you?" When he ignored her, she grabbed a chunk of plastic and threw it, missing him by meters. "You think this is funny? Oh, sure. Why not? We push away people who want to help us, we kill the ones we love, why the hell shouldn't we laugh when the world's coming to an end?"

Hasan continued practicing, feigning thrusts and parries with an invisible opponent.

After a moment watching him, a thought crept to the front of Maggie's mind. *Maybe that's the answer. Maybe I could just pretend...*

In the corner of her eye, something wavered in the darkness. Something that she ached to look at directly, something lawyer-shaped...

Maggie screwed her eyes shut and pressed her knuckles against her lids. *No! I am not going to pretend he's alive. I'm not going to start doing that. Not again.*

After a few seconds she peeked one eye above her knuckles. Fianna stood in silent mourning. Hasan made slashes in the air. There was nobody else.

There was, however, a light. It came from a ruined building across the street, a few meters above the domed rubble of a collapsed wall. Wary that it might be a hallucination, Maggie walked closer.

The wall had crumbled from the upper floors of the building, exposing the interior beyond the first story, which lay buried in the rubble. The pile of debris seemed to shift as she walked onto it, so she took care choosing her steps. On the third floor of the building floated a sliver of yellow light. As she came closer it moved, and she noticed a hand wrapped around it. Then two figures—a young boy and an even younger girl—resolved out of the darkness and looked down at her.

"Um. Hi," Maggie said.

The boy held a toy rocket ship that lit up, bright enough to illuminate the pair and part of the living quarters in which they stood. He looked at the girl, licked his dusty lips, then peered back down at the street.

"Are you Maggie Mags?"

Maggie's shoulders slumped, and a chuckle worked its way out of her. "Oh, honey. Please tell me you don't watch my show. You're not old enough."

"I watch your cartoon. It's pretty weird. My sister has your doll."

The little girl nodded, frowning. "I can't find it. I can't get in my bedroom."

Maggie remembered. She had signed off on the cartoon a few years ago, and hadn't worked on it since. The computers simulated her voice just as easily as they rendered a cartoon version of her. The plotline was about fighting space aliens, or something.

"Where are your parents?"

"Mama goes to the spa every day. She didn't come back."

The boy put an arm around her. "She's in the shelter. Everyone's in the shelter. We didn't get out of our room in time. Stuff fell into the hallway."

"I had to tinkle," said the little girl.

"It's not your fault," Maggie called up to her. "I'm sure your mama's okay."

"Now the teevee's telling us to stay where we are. And the fabber's making robots and meatberries."

"What?"

He pulled something out of his pocket, looked at it, then tossed it down to her. Maggie caught it, feeling it squish in her hand. Dark juices leaked out of a broken crust-like covering, with an appetizing aroma. She bit into the meatberry and discovered it was well-named—a little like seared protein, a little like a berry-flavored vitamin pill. Emergency food. They were lucky their fabber still worked. Maggie ate the rest, realizing how hungry she was, but she hoped to find something more palatable soon.

She looked up at the boy and smiled. "Thanks. That was good."

He shrugged. "They're all right. Did the aliens do this?"

"No. No, but I know who did. And I'm not going to let them do it again."

It felt good to take on a role, even one from a ridiculous cartoon. She didn't have to be herself. She could play a part—

No, she whispered, forcing herself out of that train of thought. *I am not going to pretend anything, anymore. I'm going to face all this. But,* she added, *I am going to make Delano pay.*

Once she had unclenched her teeth, Maggie looked back up at the boy. "What did you say about robots?"

"Little crawly things. They all climb up the building that way," the boy said, pointing.

Maggie nodded. Emergency food, emergency repair. She tried to think what other disaster plans the arcology designers might have made. Shelters. Rescue, maybe, if they cared enough. Corpse removal—

She turned and ran back to the buried limousine. Simon's body was gone.

"What happened?" She grabbed Fianna by the shoulders. "Where did he go?"

"I'm sorry, I cannot help you right now. Simon is dead."

"Yes, I know he's dead and he didn't fucking walk away. Where is he?"

"I'm sorry..."

Maggie threw up her hands and gave an exasperated sigh. When she turned around she almost ran into Hasan. Still wearing a beatific smile that cut through the dark blur of his face, he pointed with his scimitar. Something scuttled along the roadway, low to the ground but large enough to carry the body of a man.

She took a step in that direction then stopped. The robot moved quickly, and in the dim light she could barely see to walk. Balling her fists, she turned back to face Hasan.

"And what the hell is your problem? Oh, wait. You're manic-depressive. This is your manic side, right?"

The man put his hands on his hips and laughed. Then he stepped toward her. Without warning he dropped to one knee, stabbing his giant sword into the ground at her feet. Maggie took a step back.

"Hey, now. Can't you talk? What's this?" Hasan had lifted his sword and was presenting it to her, hilt-first. "What am I going to do with this?" she said, taking the weapon. It was lighter than it looked with a hilt and guard that felt like silk, and she saw a glitter along the edge that resembled diamond more than metal.

Hasan, still kneeling, bowed his head. Maggie chuckled.

"What, you want me to knight you?"

She touched his shoulders with the flat of the blade.

"Rise, Sir Hasan the nutcase. 'He who probably won't even remember this tomorrow.' And look, even the little kids are laughing at you, now." She heard the giggles from across the street. "Are we done here? How many depths of crazy do you have?"

Without making a noise, the big man's shoulders shook with laughter throughout her speech. Then he stood and reached for the scimitar's hilt. Still laughing, he walked away, dragging the weapon's tip through the debris.

Maggie just shook her head. When Hasan went back to his armed calisthenics, she walked over to the children's building.

"My friend's a little, uh," she said, swirling a finger around her ear.

The kids giggled again. "What about your other friend?", the boy asked.

"Oh, the robot? I think she's broken—"

Turning, Maggie looked in Fianna's direction, and jumped when she saw the android standing half a meter behind her.

"Hello, Maggie," Fianna said. "I'm done processing Simon's will. I am now your legal aide, and I am ready to serve."

"Wait—my aide? Simon gave you to me?"

"With the proviso that you did not cause his death."

Maggie caught her breath. Then she looked up at the children. "I didn't. I really didn't."

"It's not your fault," said the little girl.

Without a drop of sadness to it, the girl's tone made Maggie want to cry. She pushed the feeling aside. "Fianna, what else was in Simon's will?"

"For you: His identity files, his expense account, his portion of verification keys shared with Delano. For others, personal effects and messages. Without designation: Wrath."

Maggie's ears perked when she heard about Delano's keys...but then her jaw dropped open. "Wrath? Wait. Fianna, what wrath?"

"Seventy-three million legal filings. If you want further detail, choose a category: Ab inito voidance, redistricting clauses, nuisance suits—"

"Oh, no." The android went quiet as soon as Maggie spoke. "That was for Delano's crazy plans. Simon was talking about shutting down the system. Everything. Did you actually start doing it?"

"It was in Simon's will."

"I don't care. Don't do it. He decided not to, remember? He didn't want to be a monster, he didn't want wrath."

"It was in Simon's will."

"You don't have to follow his will, you belong to me now. I'm ordering you, cancel the wrath."

"I have to execute his will."

"No you don't. He wanted to change it, he just didn't have time."

"I have to—"

"Why? Why would you?"

"Because I love him."

The response threw Maggie back a step. "You can't feel love. You're a machine. You're only as smart as a dog."

"My uncle has a dog," said the boy from high above. "He loves everybody."

The little girl nodded in agreement. "I think that's the first thing they learn."

Maggie looked back at Fianna, realizing for the first time how battered the android was. Her slacks were ripped at the knees and streaked with dust. She had on a simple white shirt, and without her jacket she seemed smaller, even vulnerable. Then Maggie forced herself to blink and pushed the sympathy away.

I'm the one who needs saving, she thought. *And nobody is going to help me. Got to help myself before I help anyone else. Time to take the stage.*

She took a deep breath. Like an unbidden rhyme scheme, a plan began to form in her mind.

"Okay. Fianna, do you know where Delano is right now?"

"Delano is at the Van Hoogen chalet."

"No." Maggie shook her head. "He was there, but he's probably run off by now. Globalpol will be after his ass, but I want it first. Can you predict where he would go?"

"Location verified—Delano is at the Van Hoogan chalet."

"How can you be sure?"

"Simon receives automatic notification of the movements of his most important clients. There have been no notifications."

He hasn't run. Maggie chewed her lip. *How could Globalpol not have arrested him? Are they afraid of a deadman's switch, or are they too busy with Boise?*

Doesn't matter. I know where he is. "Fianna, we need a car."

"Yes, Maggie. Working on it."

Maggie looked up at the children where they huddled together. She wanted to save them, too. *But even if do I get them down, what do I do with them? Carry them off to face Delano and Globalpol?*

Then a creeping suspicion made her shiver.

Bending down, Maggie picked up a handful of rubble and cupped one of the chunks in her free hand. She acted casual for a few seconds, just staring into the twilight. Then she whirled and threw the chunk of plaster at the children. It skimmed centimeters from the boy's head. He yelled and ducked, and pulled his sister down with him.

"Just let one hit you," Maggie yelled up at him as she threw another rock with all her might. "Just one, I promise!"

The little girl shrieked. The children ran back into their ruined quarters. Maggie bounced a rock off the wall and cracked some furniture further in. Then she flung the entire handful of rubble upward, hoping it would hit a target. The gravel peppered the third story ceiling and rained down through the damaged building.

Maggie grabbed more debris and walked backwards, scanning for movement. "I'm sorry. If you're real—I'm sorry! If you're... Look, kids, get to shelter as soon as you can, okay?"

There were no replies. She had walked far enough away that the building was lost in the darkness. Maggie dropped the rubble and rubbed her temples. "Fianna?"

"Yes, Maggie?"

"Can you search for a television program? It's an animated kid's show, set on Megasat, using my image."

"I believe you are searching for 'Megasat Adventures', aimed at the 6-12 year old audience."

"Yeah. Can you remind me—did they cast me as the hero or the villain?"

"I'm sorry, I don't understand the question. You were cast as yourself."

Maggie nodded. Then snickered. Then she broke into throaty laughter. Her shoulders relaxed and her eyes stung as she let the tension pour out through her mouth and into the sky.

The android's voice broke her out of the laughter and into a choking fit. "Maggie, I have a car."

"Really?", Maggie asked as soon as she caught her breath. She looked around at the rubble, and up at the fire-edged horizon. "Is it invisible? Because that could come in handy."

"It's seven kilometers away. I'm sorry, that is the closest one available."

"Still, I'm impressed. How did you find it?"

"Identity 'Ulrich Gaspardeux' is empowered as an emergency worker in Brussels. I requisitioned a vehicle under his name."

"Brussels? This is kind of outside his jurisdiction."

"The electronic jurisdiction is valid. But it will fail when Simon's wrath activates. We have approximately four hours."

Nodding, Maggie cupped her hands and yelled down the street. "Hasan! We are leaving! Are you coming with us?"

The swordsman checked himself in mid-swing. Then he spun neatly on his heel, slid his weapon into its back holster, and ran toward them. Maggie took Fianna's arm and they began walking, with the android's face beam lighting the way. Hasan fell into step to Maggie's other side, and she took his proffered arm as well.

Fianna's steps were precise and rhythmic; Hasan strutted, though his body jiggled with quiet laughter. *This is real*, Maggie thought, feeling the presence of her companions on either side. She kicked at debris on the road and heard it skitter off. She smelled oily smoke in the air and breathed in delicious lungfuls. *I know this much is real, this much is good.*

Time to take the stage.

Interstitial

Young things are resilient. Children hit their heads and run off, smiling. Cut an embryo in half and its pieces might just reconnect. The younger they are, the more robust.

The global network was very old.

It began with ARPAnet, which—despite popular legend—was not built to withstand a nuclear attack. It could have, but it was never designed with that in mind. The next protocol, UUCP, could do more but could be sabotaged by forged commands, making it slightly less robust. TCP/IP heralded the birth of the Internet, with even more capabilities and even less resilience—enough to spawn a century-long communications revolution, but no longer an embryo. One good strike at a NSF backbone could have brought the nascent wonder to its knees.

Then came the World Wide Web, where centralized sites could be shut down with simple deluges of information, and people stopped talking about needing nuclear weapons to kill off the network. Next came the DRM protocols, woven into the packet switching logic of the net, allowing traffic to be analyzed, monitored, and shut off by remote command. After the DuMPNet came more insidious schemes, the HóngSèNet and the JointWork, which was called the BrotherNet by those few remaining critics of absolute government control. In another couple of generations the reasons for criticism had been forgotten, and the world was wrapped tight in the CenNet—the Centralized Network. The agencies responsible for naming it had no worries that activists would refer to it as the 'Censorship Network'. By then the Unification was complete, and there were no organized activists left.

The genius of the CenNet lay in authorities that monitored and gave permission for every transmission through the network—including every pattern requested of every fabber. Most of the authorities were automated, but the automated authorities were themselves centralized, and some requests still needed human attention. Little old ladies could not fab a flowerpot without someone's approval; an authority's stamp was needed whenever a child asked a fabber for a glass of water.

This was, of course, no longer robust.

When the earthquake hit Boise, millions of fabbers (and billions of other consumer devices) lost contact with the CenNet. Following their program, they dutifully created repair bots to fix the network break, and permitted emergency supplies when requested. When the repair bots scurried out to explore the extent of the damage, many of them shut down, deciding that they had been built in error. There was nothing to repair. They could find no city, no infrastructure; their logic programs came to the conclusion that they were activated in a test environment, and so they turned off, awaiting further instructions. In a matter of days, men with rescue equipment and temporary network nodes would arrive to give orders and breathe new life into the city's devices. The CenNet was vulnerable, but it would, in time, be patched back together.

But then, the global network was only a little over two centuries old. In comparison, the global legal system was a brittle fossil.

Through emergency channels, the report of Simon Brovall's death wound its way to a few devices sequestered just in anticipation of that news. They began a relay, coordinating a volley of writs, petitions, and suits. Individually the requests seemed innocuous. They came from many different nodes and were spawned from a myriad of identities. But taken together they formed an assault—not on the network nor on any physical thing, but on the legal system itself.

In the simplest attacks, legal dockets were swamped with filings, to the point where a human being would be required to prioritize the mess before anything could be resolved. In some jurisdictions hidden civil clauses were activated, switching defeasible ownership and rezoning commercial and government property. The most dangerous actions stabbed at the heart of the law itself. Parts of the Unification charter allowed for regional override rights, in case the default global laws were unacceptable to a regional populace. These overrides were challenged. Some treaties from before the Unification, which depended upon documents as far back as the Magna Carta, were ratified by grandfather clauses. Any inconsistencies between the old and the new laws generated a slew of opposing suits. The global legal system was a tangle of treaties, constitutions, and agreements. Simon Brovall's wrath found every loop in the tangle, gave them all teeth, and set them to eating each other.

Most of the filings would be dismissed at a glance; but given their number, even that would take days. Some of them appeared to have merit, and would clog courts for months. A few suits cleaved at true cracks in the legal system, and they would cause men in starched shirts and silk batiks to argue in parliaments for years before being resolved. Even that would be an improvement—at first they could only blame each other and stare in shock.

For a few days, every legislative, judicial, and enforcement agency on Earth became paralyzed and frantic.

The Burro watched this, and dutifully noted the scant handful of people who realized the source of the paralysis was a donkey's kick. One dead donkey, with others on the loose.

⎯⎯⎯◉⎯⎯⎯

Chapter 15—Understudy Call-In

They rumbled out of the city in an emergency vehicle, a four-seater with an orange and black paint job and wide treads for navigating rubble. It had been fabbed by an auto dealership that survived the quake with only minimal damage. The outskirts of Boise still had power, and as their car rolled over shattered glass and cracked roadways, Maggie saw people watching her from lighted walkways. In the dim light they looked like zombies; sluggish, wide-eyed, dazed.

The car had network access. News reports could only estimate the dead; the initial guesses were in the hundreds of thousands, and fires were still burning.

Hasan crashed almost the minute he sat down. His snoring harmonized with the rapid-fire click of the car's treads as they passed the wall surrounding Boise and accelerated down the open road. Maggie felt no urge to sleep. Instead she found the car's small fabber and made herself a thneed—a small garment with rudimentary mimic abilities, that could be used as a no-frills net connection. Adjusting the thneed into a black, knitted shawl, Maggie draped it over her shoulders and smiled as pastel menu icons were eyelined into her vision.

"All right, Fianna," she said, "Teach me how to shop."

<hr/>

The trip back to the chalet took almost four hours. Maggie absorbed herself in the network for most of the trip. Only at daybreak, when the sun rose over the Sawtooth Mountains, did she look outside. Jagged, red peaks shot above the early morning mist, beneath a cloud bank ribboned with purples and golds.

Pretty, she thought. Then she told the car to dim its windows.

Fianna announced their arrival before the vehicle stopped. Maggie tucked away her icons and menus and lists, and turned off her shawl. Plans were weaving together in her head like a script for her show. She could imagine all the players laid out in front of her. Their positions seemed to rhyme; their actions marked a beat, as precise as any poem. All she had to do was make them play their part.

The car stopped. "Fianna, start the countdown."

"Yes, Maggie. ETA is nine hours, twenty-seven minutes."

Hasan snorted as he woke up. "Huh? What's that for?"

"Just keeping track of something. Did you sleep well?"

The bronze-skinned man blinked. He ran his hand over his face and back over his bald head. "I am sorry. I wish I had been more help to you."

"You dug me out of the rubble. Saved my life. I'm not going to complain that you were loonier than a moonshot at the time."

"Destiny saved you. My small part in the act suffused me with grace. Doctors call it 'mania', but my parents taught me the truth. When I approach divinity, when I am touched by grace, then everything glows with holy light. It would be heresy to speak. I should be so lucky as to die during that grace, at the apex of my being."

His eyes widened as he stared at her. "When I am in my grace, Maggie, you glow. You glow with the aura of an angel."

Maggie thought a moment, then sighed. "Can I tell you a secret?"

Slowly, he nodded.

"I am an angel. We all are. Lambert was right—we are all paradoxes, creating heaven and hell for everyone around us. But that's not why you saw me glow. Do you want to know why?"

He nodded again.

"You saw that because you're nuts." She opened the car door. "Stick close to me. I want to keep people like you around."

They charged past the android gardeners and through the arched, white-lined doors. The foyer and the grand staircase were empty. Maggie went for the drawing room.

"I saw your show with Lambert," said Hasan, close behind her, with Fianna following them both. "His analogy was flawed."

"How so?"

"Grace is a temporary state. I can only stay in that grace if I expire at its peak. Then I will have created good without remaining behind to cause evil."

"So, give your show and then get off the stage? I guess it's a plan. Doesn't help me, though. I'm just warming up my act."

The drawing room was empty. The trio headed for the dining room upstairs.

"Do you intend to kill Delano?" asked Hasan.

"I don't think I'll have to. Delano's nothing, he's not a problem. It's the Momma that matters."

"I can kill him for you. It would be my honor."

"No, you stay out of this. If you need to do anything, watch my back. Fianna could use the help."

"Mmn. I can do that," he said, from two paces behind her. Maggie rolled her eyes and threw open the dining room doors.

One person sat at the long, black table, using it as a console, while his free hand stroked his glass jar.

"It's you. I knew you'd be back."

Maggie smiled. "Hi, Warren. Where is everyone?"

"They're down in the basement." He pulled his jar to his chest. The clay within jiggled and flattened itself against the side of the glass. "A few ran off, but then Delano began to crow about Boise, and staying here became more appealing. He thinks that everyone is after him. He's right, isn't he?"

"Absolutely. Tell me, Warren, do you know where the Mommas are? All of them?"

The scientist shook his head. "No. He hasn't said anything more about them."

"But can you make a guess? You know there's eight, right? Is there some configuration around the globe that would make sense to place them in? You can start by looking where Delano has mining sites."

Warren scratched his chin with the edge of his jar. "Maybe. I'd have to think about it."

"Do that for me, okay? I'd appreciate it."

"Um, why should I?"

"Warren. Do you trust anyone else here?"

"No."

"Don't you trust me?"

"Oh, no."

"Smart boy. The thing is, I swear to you that I am not your enemy," Maggie said through a clenched smile. "But if you don't start helping me out, I will be."

The scientist turned pale and clutched his jar. "I'll see what I can do."

"Thanks, sweetie." She glanced at Hasan. "Basement."

He almost beat her to the stairway.

A donkey—the Frenchman with the tooth displays—was standing in the cellar door, but he moved aside as soon as he saw Maggie, and began backing down the corridor when Hasan waved his sword. At the first of the wine racks the way was blocked by Leah in her fat purple dress; Maggie tapped her on the shoulder, then shoved her aside.

Where the monorail sprouted from the floor, Delano stood, tapping at controls on the sleeve of his smoking jacket. At the tunnel entrance—the monorail car was missing—stood Bartholomew Hwong in a spotless white shirt and slacks, his fiber optic hair speckled with yellows and blues. Bailey paced around the two, giving them a wide berth as Delano muttered and cursed.

Maggie barged her way past a few people to get to the center of the room, with Hasan at her side. Some spectators closed up after them, which was their mistake—where Fianna could not slip past, she barged through with unstoppable force, sending one donkey stumbling into the wine racks.

Delano looked up at the commotion, and Maggie saw that his nose was a mass of purplish bruises. He had cotton balls stuffed in both nostrils, turning his booming voice into a nasal honk.

"How did you—but of course," he said. His wandering eye began searching in all directions. "It must have been you and Simon who sabotaged me."

"I didn't do anything. Did someone shut down your carnival ride?"

"It's a trifle. Just more evidence of your perfidy. You disable my monorail, break my nose—"

"None of the above. I've got nothing to do with it, this is all about you. My guess is, the person who disabled the monorail is the same one who's blocking net access to your mines."

Delano paused in mid-word, his jaw canted at an angle. Maggie laughed.

"Yes, Fianna and I checked that on our way here. You're locked out. You tried to use the Momma again, didn't you? But Globalpol has an agent here, and they're cutting all your access. No more earthquakes for you, big boy."

For a few seconds, the ruddy-faced man looked up at the ceiling and chuckled. "Oh! I see what this is. This is contrition from you, is it? Simon always works like this; a gift in one hand, a tremulous caution of mortality in the other."

"Simon Brovall is dead. You killed him, with the quake that hit Boise."

"Ah. Ah. So, bereft of her defender, the waif comes crawling back for my favor. I understand your game, now. You're a bright girl. You know we have still won. If we can contact just one of the T.E.M. emplacements, the others will be connected via the subterranean network, and our plans resolve. So I capitulate. If you'll bring back my monorail car, we can go about destroying the world, and then I'll find it in my heart to forgive you."

"I don't need your forgiveness. I've done things that need forgiving, but not to you. I'm not even going to be the one that breaks your nose."

"It's predetermined, dear lady. You can't deny that your destiny lies with me. Although we should work on redirecting your anger to more plebeian targets."

"Maybe it's a paradox. Maybe I can be both angel and devil; aggressor and victim all at once. Maybe I always have been."

"Damn it, girl! Get over here, punch me in the nose, and say you're sorry!"

Maggie giggled. "I have no intention of doing any of those things."

She watched as his face turned a brighter red, his eye jerking in random directions. Then Delano stuffed his hand into his jacket and pulled out a pistol. With both hands he worked his stubby fingers around the sleek gun, and pointed it at her. Maggie laughed again.

"You're not going to shoot me," she said. "If you were going to, you would have already known you were going to, so it'd be the first thing you did."

"Or maybe I just realized that I should do it."

"Nope. I'm betting that your little flashes come in sequential order, and nobody's hit your nose yet. You know, Delano, you're just like Globalpol, just like the Uni Government."

"What?"

Slowly, she walked around him in a twisted, wandering path. "You think everything can be predicted. But that attitude has made you more predictable than anyone else. You can't handle, can't contemplate, someone whose actions are chaotic. I came here intending to do the opposite of whatever you expected me to, hoping that you'd self destruct. And look there, I think you're starting to."

She pointed at Delano's chest. Beneath his jacket, a red stain began spreading across his white shirt. He looked down at it, touched it with his free hand.

"It's a struggle, then," he said, his breath becoming raspy. "You attack me, hit my nose, the gun goes off—"

"I'm not going to attack you, I promise. And Hasan, you stay back." The swordsman had slipped through the wine racks and stood, tensed and ready, at Delano's flank.

Delano backed up, his head swiveling as he looked around the room. "No... No, it can't be you. Bailey, this is bad. It's Globalpol, they've followed her here. Man the defenses..."

"Yes, sir," mumbled Bailey, as he stared in rapt fascination. "I'll get right on that."

"...and do something, the rest of you. Damn it, I can't—"

Walking backwards, with one hand clutching at his chest, Delano backed into and tumbled over the monorail. In an attempt to recover he twisted as he fell, but succeeded only in landing on his face with a sickening crunch. Without delay he pushed himself up, blinking, a gurgle coming from his throat and blood dripping from the hem of his jacket. Just as he regained his feet a spasm jolted through his body, and he clutched his chest again.

Then Delano collapsed, backward, and lay spread-eagled on the stone floor.

As Bailey jumped to his side, Maggie walked over and calmly retrieved the gun. Hasan joined her. "Is he dead?"

"There's no pulse," said Bailey. "I don't understand. What killed him?"

Maggie pushed Bailey aside. "I did. Like this."

Her first shot went wild. The gun kicked more than she had expected, and the bullet ricocheted off the stone and into the wine racks. A bottle shattered; the crowd yelled in alarm. Maggie aimed carefully, straddling Delano's corpse, and her next shot went *paff* right in the center of the bloodstain on his chest. She pointed the gun at the ceiling, thrust her chest out in a defiant pose, and gave the crowd a dangerous grin.

"I killed him. Because I command the Platinum Donkeys."

She let that hang in the air for a second, and basked in the shocked looks from her audience. In the back, a fat lady cackled.

"Now, Delano did bring up a good point. Globalpol hasn't come to arrest all of us yet. Why is that, do you think? I think part of it's because the agents assigned to watch us are currently digging out of the rubble of Boise. And maybe it's because Simon dropped a legal bomb that has tied the government up in knots. But I think mostly it's because they're worried that Delano had a switch that would activate the Momma if he died."

Hwong raised his hand. "If he did, you may have killed millions."

"Of course he didn't. Delano was a narcissist who thought he could predict the future. He wouldn't have planned past his own death. He thought that he'd see danger coming, and that he'd have time to react to it. Delano was too egotistical to think he'd actually need a contingency plan. However, I am not. Fianna, status?"

"Dead man's switch is active. Last call/response cycle was forty-three seconds ago."

"Fianna has set up watch sites on the net. If they don't hear from her every five minutes, they'll send activation signals to the Momma. If anything happens to me—or if anything interferes with Fianna's net access—then the sites activate, and the Momma starts taking out population centers."

"They blocked Delano's access to the Mommas. Why do you think you will be able to get through?"

Maggie nodded, and began walking around Delano's corpse with a casual pace, holding the pistol high.

"Delano tried a straight connection. Fianna's trickier than that. She can operate on emergency channels, and she can flood the CenNet with innocent-looking packets, any one of which will do the job if it finds its target. Globalpol is welcome to kill me if they're sure that they've patched up all the holes. I'm guessing they're not sure of anything right now. They do have one advantage on us, though. There's a spy in the Platinum Donkeys. I think it's time we took care of that right now."

Maggie ended her pacing next to Bartholomew Hwong. Snapping her arm down, she pressed the gun against his chest. The man's eyes boggled, and the tips of his hair flashed orange.

"Why would you think—"

"You ask questions. You never stop asking questions. Have you noticed that deviants don't pry into other deviants' lives? It's rude. We have our own baggage to deal with, we don't need to carry everyone else's. But I'm not the expert. Bailey, am I right?"

"He would be my guess, mum. Sir, you're the most lackadaisical obsessive-compulsive I've ever heard of. I served you a dirty fork yesterday, and you didn't bat an eye."

"That seals it, honey," said Maggie. She leaned closer, and stage-whispered in his ear with a breathy voice. "Now I need you to take off your clothes."

"What?"

"The shirt, the pants, anything powered. Come on. No more cameras behind the scenes."

Hwong hesitated; she jammed the muzzle of the gun into his neck. Then he began to unbutton his shirt, his eyes wide with fear. But his movements were steady. He tossed his shirt aside without shame, with just a hint of defiance, and Maggie knew she had made the right choice.

"Now your pants, handsome. Take your time, go as slow as you like."

Maggie didn't consider Hwong attractive. She was playing to the audience, and trying to ruffle the man. He rewarded her with a blush and a show of bravery.

"What do you think you're going to gain by this, Maggie?" Bartholomew asked. His Asian accent and hesitant demeanor were gone. "It's over, you're all doomed. My people are probably securing the Mommas right now. They'll come for all of you next," he said, rising his voice and addressing the room.

Maggie prodded him with the gun. "Less talking, more stripping. And no more bluffing. Nobody but Delano knows where all the Mommas are. If Globalpol had the ability to be here, they would be already."

Setting his jaw, Bartholomew unzipped his slacks and wriggled them down his legs. When he stepped away, Maggie smiled.

"Nothing electrical in your underwear, I hope? Or do we have to run a current through them and see what happens?"

"Maggie," said Hasan, "His hair is powered. He has implants."

Hwong shook his head, making the pink-tipped hair fibers bob and sway. "I have no cranial implants. They're only cosmetic."

Maggie searched the man's eyes, trying to decipher the truth. She knew that killing Hwong would be the smart thing to do, but the prospect tasted sour to her. Unlike Delano, she didn't hate Hwong enough to kill him. She didn't like him well enough, either.

There's really not an excuse, she thought.

"There's a four-poster bed in every room of this house, isn't there? Hasan, take Bartholomew and tie him down to one."

"Oh, let me help," said Leah, "I have a pattern for bondage foam!"

"Spare me the details. Just make it good and tight. We need him out of the way for a while. Fianna, countdown?"

"ETA is eight hours, fifty-four minutes."

A few of the donkeys murmured. As Hasan marched the prisoner out, Maggie picked up Hwong's clothes. The recycler machinery in the basement had a waste input port; she fed the clothes into it, and then after a moment's hesitation, the gun. When she turned around, Bailey stood in her path.

"Pardon me, mum. Some of the guests were wondering what the countdown is for."

Chuckling, Maggie winked at Bailey then turned to the rest. "That countdown is to my next show. Eight hours from now I'm going to put the world on its ear, and I'm going to let them know who did it, and why. But to make that deadline, I need stagehands. You're all hired. If you don't like that, and don't want to be a part of my show, no problem. Just get the fuck out, and don't let me catch you on the way to the door."

She punctuated that with a dangerous grin.

"For everyone else, congratulations. The next eight hours are the Platinum Donkeys' time to shine. Welcome to show business."

———◦———

Chapter 16—Rehearsal Problems

Maggie sipped at a snifter of brandy as she watched the hackbot climb out of the kitchen fabber. Its four arms were crude and minimal, with rubber gecko toes at their ends, but its mouthparts were serrated and fierce. Without delay the robot crawled over the fabber's surface, chewing holes in the plastic hull and then squatting to fill them with dark goop.

"This is the last of the house fabbers," said Bailey. "The other upgrades are complete."

"So the fabbers are unlocked? We can make unlimited copies of anything?"

"It would seem so. As long as we have the patterns and enough feed."

Maggie nodded.

After killing Delano, Bailey had been eager to be her manservant, although he made her feel as if she were an experimental subject. But he had been helpful, rounding up the donkeys so she could give them their marching orders, and then wheeling in breakfast just after she had taken a long, hot shower. She wanted to challenge Bailey, to see where his limits were. But they had more important things to do. She smiled at him and put her snifter on the marble countertop.

"I like this glass, Bailey, but I hate the booze. Next time give me gin in a glass like this."

"Very well, mum."

"Next time. No more alcohol for me today."

The robot gnawed a final hole, and the fabber's display console shut off. When it replaced the circuits with goop the display rebooted and cycled through a diagnostic. Satisfied, the robot hopped off the fabber and walked toward the attached recycler.

Maggie went over and synched the fabber with her thneed, downloading the patterns she had bought. It accepted them and began production without querying for her bank account. Nor did it query the CenNet authorities; the donkeys had cut the chalet's connections, leaving them off the network. She hoped that wouldn't provoke a response too soon.

"Okay, Bailey. Start fabbing androids as your first priority. After that, these are the tuxedos and paint packages that I want. Make one for every android, and make sure the paint is any color but red."

"Certainly. Did you want the tuxedos in colors, also?"

"Tuxedos should all be black and white. This is a high class production," she said, pouring her brandy out onto the tile floor.

"Yes, of course, if you say so, mum."

They left the kitchen, putting a donkey in charge of the fabber. Eventually Maggie hoped they could use androids to pull more androids out of the fabbers. The donkeys listened to orders, but they were easily distracted.

They listen to my *orders*, she thought, smiling. A thrill fluttered in her chest; she was in charge of a production again.

Elements of a show—of a *plan*—coalesced in her mind, where her instincts worked to piece them together. The crew was present, the cast chosen. She pictured the script and knew it to be whole and perfect. Now they could create props.

That leaves set, and signal.

She walked into the future set. The grand staircase of the chalet flowed through the center of the foyer, connecting to a platform that led to spiral wing staircases on both sides. They walked up one of the wings, past a crew of butler droids with handsaws who were separating the stairs from the wall. Maggie watched for a few minutes to make sure they were not damaging the stairway. Pierre, the silent donkey with the tooth displays, waved at her from the other wing, where he supervised another droid crew.

At the second floor railing, Maggie tapped a droid's eyeline control to make it stop and stand at attention. Then she hip-checked it, shoving the android against the railing where it tottered for balance. She had to push it with her hands to get the flailing thing to fall. It landed on the hardwood floor below with a heavy thud. After a second or two, the android got to its hands and knees, then its feet, and then it walked back to the stairway as if nothing had happened.

"They're pretty sturdy."

"Yes, mum. Not really designed for defenestration, though."

"We all need to keep our skillsets current, Bailey."

She barged into the dining room, sending the double doors flying back against the wall. The look on Warren's face made her smile—*They want to be shocked*—but then he curled up in his seat and clutched his jar, and she wondered if she had overdone her entrance.

"I'm sorry," Warren said. "I can't do it. I tried, I just can't."

Maggie walked up to the dining table and tapped to get its attention. The laserline display projected an image of the Earth, hovering over the table, with a web of straight yellow lines forming a shape inside the planet. "Tell me what the problem is, Warren."

"I thought that, since there were eight Mommas, Delano might have arranged them in an octahedron—taking in account ellipsoid oblateness, of course. But I can't find a unique solution. Van Hoogan industries has thousands of mines. I can spin these graticules almost any which way."

He tapped at a control; the lines inside the Earth spun and wobbled, anchored by a single vertex in North America.

"So there's no solution. Then I thought the installations might not conform to the geoid, might even be non-conformal or a sparse stellated set..."

"Okay, stop. Would it help if I knew the location of another Momma?"

"Oh, yes. That would help a lot." The scientist raised his head a little, like a rabbit poking its head out to check for wolves. "Does this mean you're not going to kill me?"

Maggie put her hands on her hips and feigned a hurt look. She had no intention of hurting Warren—she liked him—but he needed to stay motivated. Besides, her instinct told her that he'd believe the worst no matter how she consoled him.

"I'm not going to kill you, Warren. You haven't failed me...yet." She gave him a wicked smile and pointed at the hovering globe. "The other Momma is in Australia. I forget the name of the town, but Fianna will remember it. Let me find her. Be right back."

She led Bailey out of the dining room. He coughed into his glove as they went down the staircase again. "You seem to be awful cheerful today."

"Don't psychoanalyze me, Bailey."

"Part of my job, mum. A good clinician should know when and whether to intervene."

"Try and I'll break your arm."

"Yes. Well, that settles that question."

"Besides, you have more important things to do. Have you gotten access to Megasat, yet?"

"No. I've sent several queries but no response. I remember Delano mentioning that the Burro often took some time to respond."

"Who is this Burro, anyway? Maybe I should try. I bet anyone on Megasat will pick up the phone if I call."

"I gathered that the Burro was some sort of AI."

"I don't know of any AI on Megasat. And what kind of AI doesn't answer when called? Keep trying. If Globalpol shows up before we get that link, we're all screwed."

Cast. Crew. Props. Set. Script. Are we going to have a signal?

The drawing room looked like the ruins of Boise. Desks, tables cabinets, and daybeds had all been pushed to the edges of the room and stacked high. Some of the antique or faux-antique furniture had collapsed from the weight, and the shattered remains had been thrown back into the pile. In the space that had been cleared stood Fianna, in front of Prince Hasan and one of the butler androids. The droid was limp; Hasan held it up by the waist and throat, and nodded to Maggie as she approached.

"How's the rehearsal?", she asked.

"Going slowly. Fianna has wormed through a connection to the reservation, but we're still scrambling for bandwidth. It doesn't help that we have to practice each move several times."

"You said you had a hundred men, Hasan. Surely one of them knows how to dance."

"A hundred fighters, not dancers. But yes, I've found a few with talent. It's just—there's a lot of moves in this routine."

"Program them so that when they get stuck, they'll run around like frightened sheep. That'll work. Are you okay handling the choreography?"

Hasan grinned. "It's like fighting without weapons."

"Oh, there'll be weapons. Before your next set, I need Fianna for a second. Fianna, what was the town I met you near? A reservation city, underground?"

"I think you are asking for 'Leonora's Bottom.'"

"That's it. Thanks."

As she turned to go, Hasan called out. "Maggie? I think you should check on Bartholomew. I won't have a chance—and we may have a problem that you will want to deal with."

"What kind of problem?"

"After we restrained him, Leah stayed behind and locked the door." Hasan frowned, and his bronze cheeks darkened a shade. "I don't know her, but she does not seem trustworthy. I think we should check on him."

Maggie nodded, and led Bailey back out to the main foyer. The androids were more numerous, spilling out the front door, filling the foyer with wood dust and the noise of their sawing. Maggie yelled to be heard over them. "Bailey, do you have a key for that bedroom?"

"I'm unlocking it now," he yelled, tapping at his sleeve.

"Okay, go tell Warren—'Leonora's Bottom.' I'll look in on our spy."

Maggie made her way to the third floor, where the prisoner had been taken. She slid the bedroom door open quietly, unsure of what she might find.

Bartholomew lay on the bed, spread-eagled. His arms and legs were connected to the bedposts with blobs of fuzzy pink goop that looked as if it were globbed on and left to dry. A smear of the goop sat on his mouth and chin also, like a half-formed pink goatee. His bare body shivered. Maggie noticed his underwear was gone. His crotch was a mess of scratches and dried residue—

"Oh, god," she said. She looked around, saw a duvet on the cabinet, unfolded it and draped it across his torso. Then she sat on the bed, careful not to touch him.

"I'm sorry. Whatever she did to you, I'm sorry."

He said nothing—the goop seemed to adhere his lips together. After a moment of eye contact, he looked away.

Maggie sighed. "I'm not going to hurt you. And I'm not going to let her hurt you again."

There was a spray can on the dresser with drips of pink goop on the nozzle. Maggie reached for it, read the label. "Vanishes in six hours, or with the dissolver solution." She looked around. "Figures she didn't fab any of that. Guess I can't free your mouth now, but at least you'll be okay. I need you as a witness. Maybe you're relaying this to the government now; maybe they won't get the message until you're rescued. Either way works. Soon you won't be able to stop me."

His eyes went wide. She smiled. "No, I'm not going to tell you what I have planned."

"I know what you're thinking. Us Donkeys—we're all evil people. But we're not. I want the same thing the government wants. I want the people to be happy. They're my fans, after all. Making them happy is what I do.

"I know what the Unification has in mind. Utopian cities, separated from Eden-like wilderness. High quality of life for everyone, with enough natural space to absorb and scrub away the excesses of modern life. A balanced ecosystem. I lived my whole life on a space station; you think I can't see a hydroponic remediation system being set up? You're turning the Earth and all its people into a self-sufficient, static environment.

"There's just one thing that bothers me about that. It can only work if the people are dumb and their lives are boring. You have to eliminate creativity. New innovations could stress your system, if not throw it into open revolution. The only question I had is why you let the revolution come so close?"

His eyes had narrowed, staring at her, although he avoided her gaze when she stared back.

"You thought you could predict us, didn't you? Some simulator, somewhere, told you that we could be led, and corralled, and you could turn a risky situation into an unimaginable triumph. You thought you could take Delano at the right moment and gain control of all his industry. You probably thought you could gain Megasat, too. That's probably why I'm still alive. Some computer keeps insisting that the Unification can net a profit from all this mess, that I can still be predicted and outmaneuvered."

She leaned down, close to his face. "It's wrong. I know as soon as the government finds out how wrong they are, they'll put everything they've got into killing me. By then it won't matter. By then, I won't care.

"I'm different from whatever simulations you're using. I know how I'm broken, now. I shielded myself behind strong men. Even if they weren't really there, even if I had to pretend that they were. But there was a price. I ended up being what they wanted me to be. Doing what they wanted me to do.

"But my daddy's dead. And Simon, and Delano. So I want you to know, what happens next is coming from me. I'm not just a poet, I'm a showrunner. I'm a planner. This next plan, it's all mine. I'm sorry for what happened to you today. I am not sorry for remaking the world to my own design."

She stood back up, smiling at him. "I'm an entertainer, after all. Who else would you trust to make an exciting, interesting world?"

He mumbled something, his eyes wide again. She opened the door, waved bye, and left.

Once in the corridor Maggie shook off her good humor. "Bailey," she typed into her thneed, "Where is Leah?"

The answer came back: Servant's kitchen. A map appeared to guide her there.

Maggie prowled her way back down the stairwell. Androids scattered as she passed near. She smiled; the dumb robots had learned something. They had learned to avoid her.

Guess the cast and crew aren't final, yet. It's not my first time as producer. I should have known that I'd have make some cuts.

Whomever decorated the servant's kitchen had abandoned the Victorian decor of the house. The tables and chairs were sleek steel, and the floors were a grey, springy surface that looked like concrete. A largish fabber sat in the middle of the room as the only appliance, and around it stood four men and a fat figure in a purple dress. They were pulling stuffed pink sacks out of the fabber, formless pillows that barely fit inside.

"What are you doing with my fabber, bitch?" Maggie asked.

Leah turned her head and laughed. "Hers. See, she's a goddess, now. Thinks she owns everything."

"Own it or not, I'm using it. What are you doing with it?"

"We're getting the hell out of here. You've gone goody-good, want to help the world and all that bullshit. You're going to get yourself and everyone here killed. Take the fabber back, we're done. C'mon, boys."

The five of them picked up their pillows and walked out of the back of the kitchen, into the cramped servant's corridors. Maggie followed. "I thought you'd like my plan, Leah. It was your idea."

"You ruined it", Leah shouted back. "You took out my fabber libraries!"

"People don't need their food and drink laced with LSD."

"You don't know what the fuck people need. People need enlightenment. They're not going to find it just because you hand them the keys. You've got to push them through, kicking and crying."

A side door opened into a mudroom, with racks full of pine-stained overalls and a pegboard holding an organized array of gardening tools. The back door of the mudroom led outside, to the rock-strewn foliage at the side of the chalet. Leah dropped her pillow onto the ground and stepped back. The men watched as it began to inflate, then imitated her actions, all while watching Maggie nervously.

"I don't think people need pushing," said Maggie as she followed them outside. "There's a lot of people like us out there. They're creative and they're smart, they just need an outlet and some freedom. I'm going to give them that."

"They're idiots and so are you. You've only just now figured out that it feels good when you act bugfuck crazy. How do you think you became a goddess, anyway?"

"What are you talking about?"

"I'm talking about trauma!"

Leah steadied her balloon, which had swelled into a fat pink donut, and she pointed a crooked finger at Maggie.

"It's the trauma that made you what you are. It's what made all of us. Something fucked us up and turned us into geniuses, instead of bland mundanes. That where power comes from. It's within us, when we lose control. When our world turns into chaos we become creatures of primal emotion, and we learn to master our world. *That's* God. But it doesn't mean shit if you use it to help others. It's a defense mechanism. It's meant to help *yourself*."

She turned away to poke at controls on one side of the donut, showing them to the men so they could do the same to theirs. But she kept muttering, spittle arcing from her jagged teeth.

"You can't lead others to that power by helping them. They need to be traumatized. They need to claw their way through hell. You'd do more for them if you fucked them over, give them an excuse to lose their mind. Insanity, genius, godhood—they're for making your own life better, for getting back what you're due. Altruism misses the entire god-damned point."

The pink donuts suddenly bobbled and stood erect like waist-high wheels. A red saddle extruded from the top edge, and wrapped arms around one limb of the toroid. Leah stepped back, nodding. Then she waved at her men.

"Go on, climb up. They're gyro stabilized. Let's get out of here."

Maggie sifted Leah's words around in her mind as she watched them clamber onto the fat, pink unicycles.

"I think you're missing the point, Leah. God isn't rolling around in whatever filth makes you happy. Religion is worthless unless it

makes you better than you are. Trauma doesn't do that. It's the
determination to overcome it that does. So yeah, I'm damaged. But I
can transcend that, and be a better person than that fucked up part
of me. That's God, if anything is."

"Whatever works for you. I'm gone."

"Good. Go preach somewhere else, bitch. And you better be
thankful I'm holding back that crazy part of myself. Because she
wants to slice you open just to see what pieces bleed."

The five of them rode their unicycles around to the front of the
chalet, the fat pink tires crunching in the fallen pine needles. Maggie
walked along behind. The columns at the front of the building were
fallen, spread out in a fan from the entrance. Androids swarmed over
the chalet's front, using hacksaws and pry bars on the facade's rich
orange wood and white trim. The robot crew distracted Maggie for a
few seconds, but she turned back when she heard Leah's cackle.

"Hey, look up there. I think your time's up."

Maggie shaded her eyes. Far off to the west, a black and white orb
hung in the sky.

"It's the cops," said Leah. "here to stop your little show. Good
luck, psycho. See you in hell."

With that, Leah and her four accomplices pointed themselves
down the grassy slope and began rolling off the mountain. The
unicycles stabilized themselves well, even though the men were
shouting and flailing their arms. Leah, fearless, outpaced them, and
her pink unicycle began bouncing down the mountainside with her
frilly purple dress flagging in the wind.

Maggie watched them. She pinched herself, thinking that this
was weirder than her hallucinations so it might be a dream. As she
was rubbing the spot where it hurt, she felt Bailey sidle up next to
her.

"Is she going to be a problem, mum?"

Maggie shook her head.

"No. She's a blessing." She looked at Bailey and tried her warmest smile. "She sets an example that I can avoid. I may be damaged, I may be crazy, I may even be the villain. But I know that I'll never be as evil as Leah."

"Good for you, mum. By the way, the Burro has answered."

"Good. Let's talk to it."

"But one other thing. If you'll pardon my asking—what do we do about that?" He pointed at the approaching ship.

Maggie pulled up a corner of her thneed shawl and typed in a command. The device shone the letters, "Countdown—ETA 00:12" into her vision.

"We find a place for it to land. It's our getaway vehicle." She turned, and smiled at Bailey's puzzled expression.

"Did you know, Bailey, that you can buy almost anything at a fabber? If it doesn't fit into the fabber itself, the manufacturer will happily charge you for delivery. It costs a fortune to purchase a private gelship yacht, let alone have a robotic crew deliver it. Lucky for me, I have a fortune."

"Ah, yes. So you do."

"Make sure it doesn't land anywhere near the stage. Throw all the crew into recyclers; we'll restaff it with androids we can trust. But worry about that later. Now that Globalpol knows we have a vehicle, they might get around to us sooner. So let's get the show going. And let's talk to that Burro."

They threaded their way back into the chalet, dodging androids and discarded wooden trimmings. Bailey led her upstairs, toward Delano's private office. Pierre waved at her and she waved back with a sense of pride.

I'm on top of a production again, she thought. *And this time, I feel good.*

The office was decorated in Victorian tinged with De Sade, with marble statuettes of nude women scattered over the ornate cherry bookcases and end tables. But the desk at the center of the room shifted at Bailey's touch, its red-brown surface turning black, the gothic engravings rippling and smoothing away. The top of the mimic-metal desk became glossy and shot laserline calibration displays into her eyes. She let Bailey work the menu system.

I'm not that damaged, I'm not that crazy. Screw Leah. I feel good.

The room lights dimmed; the laserline display grew outward, creating a full immersion video. Around them shone the projection of another room with the familiar metallic walls and white velcro floors of Megasat. Maggie didn't recognize the room, but the plentiful handholds and circular doorways told her it was the zero-gravity section, even before she focused on the resident in its center.

Strapped to a floating bed lay a man with wires and tubes sprouting from his torso and skull, connecting him to medbots, command strips, and data ports on every side of the room. He wore a simple, purple silk robe, and his skin was a healthy plastic-pink except where it was not. His exposed neck, one foot, his face—they were yellow, wrinkled, and frighteningly aged. The expression on that wrinkled face was blank where it had once been kind; his eyes—one gray and plastic—were dull where they had once been piercing.

Maggie stumbled back. She caught herself on an end table; a statuette fell with a thump.

"D-Daddy?"

The man turned his head to look at her in a precise, inhuman motion.

Maggie felt light-headed. The room seemed to be in zero-gee, but instead of being exhilarating she felt clumsy and vulnerable. Her breaths were quick and ragged; she grasped for a handhold and forced herself to breathe slow. "Bailey," she said, "What are you seeing?"

"I see Mega, or what is left of him," the butler said. But he only glanced at the projection. His attention was fixed on her. "I'm as shocked as you are. Or perhaps not. How do you feel?"

Maggie ignored him. Balling her fists, paying close attention to the true direction of gravity, she stepped closer to the projection.

The withered man had little of the business magnate left in him. Little of anything left in him, she saw as she peered along the tubes that dove into his flesh. His limbs were almost all plastic, their thin, sculpted forms marked with Megasat research logos. He no longer had a torso as such; his body was an open plastic case, filled with oblong metallic components and a nest of tubing. His face seemed the most unaltered, but even that was a front, with the skin ending just behind his ears. Gray plastic comprised the rest of his skull, with a cascade of wires tumbling out from a small port and fanning to connect with bots within the room.

Maggie's arms had begun to shake. She tried to relax her clenched fists. "You are not Mega."

"I am not Mega," the man repeated.

"You were Mega."

"I was Mega."

"I thought you died. Everyone thought you died."

"I died."

Those words sent Maggie back a pace. Behind her, something with wings began to buzz. "What happened?"

"Life extension research. Limbs failed; they were replaced. Organs failed; they were replaced. The brain failed—" For a moment, the man looked sad. Then his face snapped back to a neutral mask. "Replacement was unsuccessful."

Tears trickled down Maggie's cheek. She focused on them and closed her eyes. The tears told her which way gravity pointed. "Daddy, I'm sorry. I miss you so much."

When her sobs ended and she opened her eyes, the man's expression seemed sad again, in a softer way.

"I've watched you. I've whispered to you. But I am not allowed contact with anyone. The Conspirator found me. He had codes an access channel. This channel. He called me Burro."

"Delano was involved in corporate espionage," Bailey said, his voice just above a whisper. "I knew he was spying on Megasat. But Maggie, I did not know about this."

Maggie nodded, and wiped her cheeks.

"You put secret messages in my show."

"Yes."

"Can you pre-empt programming? Can you flood the airwaves with a short video, and a fabber library, with a mandatory installer?"

"Yes."

"We don't have codes. Can you still do it?"

Burro looked at Maggie, and for a moment his face flashed a wistful smile. "Yes. Anything. You're a very special girl. I love you."

Maggie trembled, but gritted her teeth and kept standing. "Yeah. That would have been the first thing you learned. Bailey, make the arrangements."

Then she turned on her heel—the laserline display cut off as soon as she stopped facing the desk—found the exit and ran through it, slamming the door behind her. She kept running until she hit the second floor railing. She hung onto it, eyes squeezed shut, letting her tears fall over the side.

She stopped crying when she realized the buzzing sound had not followed her. But she continued to stand there, watching the androids work. They were no longer sawing, but sweeping and making measurements. They were mindless, loving, and happy. Part of her hated them so.

Bailey joined her, touching her elbow; she jumped, which made him jump more, which made her giggle. "It's okay," she said, drying her eyes with her thneed. "I'm okay."

"Are you?"

"No. No, I'm really not. It's funny, for a second, I thought I was whole, but—it doesn't matter. He never loved me, you know."

"I'm sure he—"

"He didn't. Mega, I mean. He never loved me. He was kind and he was patient, but never loving. I was his good deed, I was an investment. When I became a performer I became an asset. All my life, all my antics, I was trying to get him to love me, or even notice me sometimes. He never did."

Bailey nodded.

Maggie turned and laid her arms and head on the railing. "I have to kill him. That thing in there, that Burro, it isn't Mega. It's soulless, it doesn't have the spark that made Mega who he was. It's a perversion. I can't let him exist like that any longer. I have to kill him. I can kill him. I will." Looking over at Bailey, she narrowed her eyes. "You don't believe me, do you?"

"I will never disagree about your ability to kill someone. It's not right to question one's employer on such things."

"You're not my employee."

"I served Delano by choice; I've made that choice again."

"Talk about bad career decisions. Your resume must look like a horror vid."

"It'll all be worth it once I publish my research. But that is not the only reason I'm asking—are you going to be okay?"

Maggie nodded. She inhaled, tasting the cherry wood dust in the air.

"I think so. I'm broken, and I'll always be broken. But I can function. And I can still put on one hell of a—"

A sharp crack interrupted her; she clenched the railing as she felt the building shake. Then she saw the sunlight peeking through a sliver cut across the wall, almost as high as the third floor. The sliver of light expanded, and grew down the corners of the foyer. Air sucked past her, blowing her hair and stealing breath from her throat as the facade of the chalet teetered outward. Cut open on top and on both sides, the wall of the foyer tipped over in a chorus of snapping wood and crackling stone, landing in the front yard with a thunderous, bone-jarring crash.

Maggie looked down.

The foyer, now open to the elements, twinkled with dust grains caught in the bright mountain sunshine. Androids that had fled the scene came milling back by the dozens, an undirected horde. From outside Pierre Martineau walked in, striding confidently on the fallen wall, his hands spread wide. Maggie smiled. The man and robots below were no longer standing in a foyer; they were standing on an open, sunlit stage.

"Brilliant," Maggie called down to him. Straightening herself up, she began to point. "Clean up that debris. Get the androids in costume. Set the cameras up there, and there." Then she turned to Bailey, with a wide, dangerous grin, as a checklist clicked together in her mind.

Cast. Crew. Props. Script. Signal. Stage.

"Get the Burro ready. And tell Hasan it's on."

Showtime.

Chapter 17—Showtime

Interstitial

In an apartment in Macau a television turned on by itself, which startled no one. Baozhai's governor often loaded up a program to show him something. They had been playing 'Twenty Questions'—Baozhai was pretty sure the answer was 'girl'—but you never knew when the governor would interrupt a game to give a lecture.

But the governor had nothing to do with this program. It began with a simple placard, announcing 'A Very Special Performance from Maggie Mags'.

His governor protested, with icons and warnings. Baozhai accessed the television controls.

"Don't touch that," his father said, sitting in the armchair across the room. "I want to watch."

Baozhai watched, too, as the woman came on.

Maggie basked on the railing of an ornate staircase, surrounded by a coterie of androids in formal tuxedos and tails. She wore a white sheathe gown, skintight over her torso but flaring into a flowing, knee-length skirt that moved as if made from molten platinum. The music sprinkled into existence, light piano notes with a brassy reverb, a bouncy tune he had never heard before.

The governor was insistent. "Papa," Baozhai said, "My governor doesn't want me to watch this."

"You don't have to listen to it all the time, son."

Mags dismounted the railing with a scissoring of her legs, landing in perfect poise before a triad of robotic suitors. They leaned forward; she leaned back and then fled behind another row of androids. They spun—Baozhai marveled at how she had programmed her androids to dance—and pushed Maggie with their attentions back to the center of the stage. There, an android caught her and pulled her into a tight embrace. Maggie stared into the android's face, her expression a mask of fear and desire...

Her brows tightened; her smile blossomed into a feral grin. Baozhai almost didn't see the blade, its metal flashing in her hand, before she sank it into the android's chest.

After that Baozhai had to sit on his wrist, to keep his governor from ruining the show.

<hr>

In London, R. Saptenshu was in Gentry's pub when the broadcast hit. The staid, tweed-wearing clientèle of the late evening were just thinning out, and the hard-drinking lower class were just filtering in, but both types were riveted when every screen and table in the pub showed Maggie dancing.

Saptenshu watched as she pulled the weapon free, spinning backwards. A line of blue arced from the blade and traced across the line of robots that stepped back to avoid her. The stabbed android fell back against the wall, a bright blue stain on his chest. Maggie drew the flat of the blade across her dress, painting herself with the blue ichor of her prey before she leapt toward the next. She caught one android in a perverse pas de deux, an inverted tango that ended with her hand at his throat and the knife in his belly. His blood was bright green; she counted the coup on her thigh and charged into the frightened herd.

"Bugger me!" said someone from across the bar. "She ain't putting on a skit—she's giving a bleedin' confession!"

"'Bleeding' confession," muttered Saptenshu. "Very droll."

As the androids scattered across the stage, Maggie paused on the left side staircase, her hands on her tilted hips, blinking her eyes with feigned innocence. The scattered androids were reeled back in and they encircled her, stepping up and down the staircase in time with the music, which seemed to pulse with rhythm of her swaying hips. Mags smiled, her teeth flashing in the camera. She embraced an android, kissing its featureless face while driving her knife into its chest. It fell, dribbling orange paint, and the dance went on.

When she reeled in the last cluster of androids, a dozen or so, they hefted her into the air. Mags lay on her back as the dancers spun around in formation and the music swelled—then they lowered her to the ground, and she slashed out with her knife, and the column of dancers fell to the ground in a spray of purple gore. One remained; it stepped toward her. With a brutal, lustful energy Maggie wrapped her arm around it, stabbing repeatedly into its belly, matching the beats of the final, orchestral trumpet blasts.

The music faded. Maggie let go of the knife and held the last android as it slumped in her arms. She stroked its cheek—then abruptly let it fall.

"I've been saving that dance for you, kiddies," she said to the camera. "I think it's my last performance. But before I sign off, let me give you stage directions for the future.

"First, the planet's going to quake. Can't be helped. Watch yourselves and keep safe. After that, I want you all to help me make the world interesting. Go wild, try out everything you always wanted to try. Invent new things. Make a new world, overthrow the old. Be creative. There are no limits, anymore."

With a smile, Maggie slid her hand down her chest, tracing her fingers through the technicolor streaks splattered across her body. "And if anyone tries to stop you," she said, "do something that I would do."

"This is Maggie Mags saying bye-bye, kiddies. Love you all."

With that, all the screens in the pub shut off.

The uproar of the patrons started out as a formless, puzzled murmur. It turned into a screaming row when the mechanical lizards began climbing out of every fabber in the pub.

Niklaus woke to the sound of something like a drill, if a drill could also scuttle and make chewing sounds. With sleep still in his eyes, he staggered to the kitchen just in time to see the robot climbing into the recycling end of his overlarge research fabber.

He ran to check for damage. There were new holes drilled and unfamiliar patches of amorphous circuit goo in some places, but the system responded fine. Better than fine; the fabber menu displayed a new library item, 'WorldFun'.

The first thing he checked was the origin. It came from Megasat, apparently one of the fabber promotions they gave out. His entertainment system had not woken him when it arrived. The program was recorded for viewing at his convenience.

The second thing Niklaus checked was the library manifest, which made his jaw drop and shocked him fully awake. Then, with a clumsy impatience he loaded up the program to see what the hell was going on.

After watching Maggie's dance and hearing her instructions, Niklaus peeked into the fabber library again. It was expansive. It held designs for weapons, armored androids, even other fabber models. And it was a shared library on a global net channel, meaning that any patterns added by anyone in the world would also be available to anyone else. As he watched, new patterns for every object imaginable came streaming in.

He marveled over the variety and boldness of the new fabber patterns. Many were illegal. Some appeared impossible, but were packaged with testimonies from early reviewers. A few seemed well within a fabber's capability, but could not be produced with the locks that he knew were in place—

Trembling, Niklaus loaded up his *Elopteryx* pattern.

The fabber went to work. Sitting at the kitchen table Niklaus waited, his mind whirling with anticipation. But his excitement faded into numbness, and when the fabber beeped that the pattern was done it woke him from a sound sleep. Niklaus shook himself awake and opened the fabber's access panel.

The creature inside lay curled around its own tail. Its scales were dark green with irregular blotches of pink, and long, barbuled quills—the protofeathers of the juvenile—ran in streaks down its head and back. The completed, inert creature was familiar to Niklaus, but he jumped in surprise when the chest inflated and sucked in a great lungful of air. The head poked upward with a newborn's wobble and sniffed the air outside the fabber. Then *Elopteryx* opened its eyes and shrieked.

The baby's call reminded Niklaus of a squeaking door, or perhaps shearing metal. He imagined herds of the creatures, and felt himself crying with joy. In his mind, their calls trumpeted the beginning of a new world.

Chapter 18—Curtain Call

There were three donkeys left behind at the chalet. Maggie had meant there to be four, but Bailey insisted on coming with her, claiming that his research was not complete. Hasan also went with her, although he had lapsed back into his manic state, silent and hyperactive. Still, he did a good job leading her android army—fifty-six strong when they left, most of the robots paint-splattered but now tried and trusted. Warren came too; he didn't have a choice. He had not yet discovered the Mommas' locations, so Maggie dragged him into the gelship still clutching his precious superfluid like a toddler would his favorite toy.

As the gelship launched, Maggie waved down to the last donkeys from the lower gondola. They had her all-terrain emergency vehicle and instructions to run to ground and stay hidden. She hoped they'd be okay. She knew she wouldn't be.

If her fans did as she asked, there would soon be so much unallowed activity across the globe that the authorities wouldn't have time to run down everyone involved. She had gotten the Platinum Donkeys to put every fabber pattern they had in those libraries. They had made public hundreds of oddball machines and wild inventions, even untried experiments that would have been useless before the fabber hack. She had also forced the Burro to carve a framework into the network allowing new patterns to be shared. Her fans should be creating distractions for her. If they loved her.

After another long shower, Maggie squeezed herself into a form-fitting black jumpsuit and looked back as the gelship passed over a sea-side arcology. Portland-Astoria, said the sleeve of her jumpsuit. The city resembled San Francisco in many ways. Tall buildings with shiny black solar collectors covered the ground for miles, stopped only by a fat river to the north and snow-capped mountains in a wilderness area to the east and south. The buildings had peaked roofs, rather than San Fran's flat-topped ziggurats, and the cleverly arranged foliage that lined the walkways tended to be evergreen. Aside from those minor differences it could have been San Francisco, or pre-quake Boise, or any of a hundred other similar arcologies.

But as she watched, Maggie began to see changes.

There, a perfect circle of trees had turned shiny, metallic gold. A bit further out, something inflated on a rooftop without apparent aid, something brown with what might grow to be long, ape-like arms. Closer to the shore a giant purple flower had seized an outdoor arena, its delicate petals—hundreds of meters across—waving over the stadium seats. Underneath Maggie glimpsed vehicles with flashing lights. She chuckled.

Pressing the police into flower-removal duty. That would make a good skit.

Then her smile faltered. Most likely, she would never do another skit.

Before she could wallow in that, however, her mood was broken as an android zoomed past the window, falling headfirst. Maggie blinked, looked down at the falling robot, then turned to Fianna, who was never more than a few meters away.

"Was that one of our androids?"

"Yes."

"Why is it jumping out of the upper deck?"

"Because Doctor Poltrasky ordered it to."

Maggie leaned against the window, trying to peer upward. "Warren, what are you doing?" She had been speaking to herself more than anything, but after a second her jumpsuit chimed a tone: No response.

Another android fell past the window, arms stretched out in a streamlined dive.

Maggie ran toward the stairs, Fianna in tow.

The gelship yacht had twelve cabins on three levels, with an additional pilot's forecastle slung below the craft's bulbous nose. Adjustable wood panels decked every room, and trimmed mimic-metal furnishings lined every hatch, shelf, and door. By factory default, they were set to heartwood walnut and a convincing, if lightweight, gold. As she climbed the stairs, Maggie passed android teams that were stripping the luxury furnishings and carrying them to the recyclers. Hasan needed more material.

When she got to the top level, she made her way aft into the galley. There she found Warren sitting at a cook's table, staring out of a bay window. An adjacent door set in a transparent wall formed an airlock to the outside, marked with instructions for delivery of supplies. In the airlock stood three more androids. The furthest had its arms outstretched and pointed towards the open outside door.

"Warren!" she yelled. "What are you doing?"

The white-haired scientist hunched his shoulders as if struck. Then he looked over at her. "I need to borrow some androids."

"Borrow? After you throw them into the ocean, how do you plan on returning them to me?"

"Um. It may be an extended loan."

"No. Get them out of there, Warren. Give them back to Hasan."

"You—you don't understand," he said. Tapping at the table display, he brought up numbers and diagrams: A cartoon gelship, a dotted path arcing down, an android at its bottom. "They're following us. They're always following us. And, and only the androids can see them!"

Maggie put her hands on her hips as she watched him page through incomprehensible graphics and equations. "Warren, you need to stop this and get me the Momma's coordinates."

"Oh, that." He looked at her from the corner of his eye. "I need androids."

"I need the Momma."

"I have her. Every piece of her. It's done." He glanced from her to his display. "But I need androids."

Maggie took a deep breath, and wished she had a knife.

Then she exhaled, forced her shoulders to go slack, and smiled at him.

"Bailey told me you were paranoid. This is your price? I let you do your checks to see if we're being followed, and you give me the coordinates? Is that all you want?"

"Well," he said, "Dropping me off in Chicago would be nice."

Maggie laughed. "Not going to happen, hon. Okay, five androids, they're yours."

"I need ten."

"You're getting five." She sat at his table and dialed a corner of it for a glass of gin. "Go on, do your magic."

Warren looked at her for a moment, then bent to his work. The aftmost android hiked itself up on its toes, then raced towards the open hatchway. As it jumped out of the gelship it brought its arms together and did a flip before spiraling down out of sight.

"Nice form."

"Thank you," said Warren. "I needed them to spin as they fell, so I downloaded some dive programs from the android Olympics."

Graphics marched across the table. Rectangles filled with images of the sky began popping into existence. Warren's fingers flew across the slick tabletop as he organized the images, flicking some of them toward application icons. Maggie watched with disinterest.

The fabber dinged. She stood up and retrieved her gin, then paced around the small galley, waving her glass in one hand.

"Did you see that huge flower, Warren? Look, you can still see it, a little, over there."

The scientist grunted, working on his imagery.

"Things are changing, I can feel it. We've only been in the air for what, an hour? Hour and a half? And already my fans are grabbing attention. Making things. You don't think they'll hurt anyone, do you?" She glanced at him, then sighed. "I don't want anyone else to get hurt. Well, except for the people I need to kill. But I have good reasons for that, and I'm going to feel terrible about it afterward, you know?"

She glanced over at Warren again; he had paused, slack-jawed, one finger still pressing against the tabletop. "Yeah. Um, I'm sure you will."

"I will, I really will. Maybe I should have told them how guilty I feel about all those boys on Megasat. And Lambert. Not so much Delano, but...oh, maybe I should make a list."

Another android ran through the airlock and dived into the ocean, curling up into a spinning back flip as it fell. Maggie watched it go, wondering if it loved them.

"Do you think that God—well, he forgives, doesn't he?" She took a long sip of her gin. "So if this turns out all right, I mean, if people are better off than they were before—"

"I don't truck much with religion," Warren grumbled. "People think it's about getting closer to perfection. In my experience it's more about conformity."

"Hmmn. Emile Lambert thought it was about conforming, sure. A paragon, an example to follow. Simon thought God was absolution, reparation for damaged souls. Hasan thinks it's perfection. He told me he wants to die at that perfect moment, in one of his manic peaks."

"Well, now that's just stupid."

"No, it's not stupid," she said, chuckling. "It's crazy. I have my way of being crazy, you have your ways, Hasan has his. To be honest, I'd rather travel with someone who's suicidal than someone who's homicidal."

Warren nodded, his eyes wide. "So would I. Or worse, one of each."

"Yeah, you're right. That would suck." She downed the rest of her gin.

They were far from the shore, now, and the late afternoon sun cut across the ocean waves in red glints of light and black streaks of shadow. A splash of white surprised her—the last android had dived without her notice. She had missed its sacrifice.

"I think I understand the Unification now," she said. "Take Leah. Her God is insanity itself. How do you deal with that? You don't. You have to eliminate it. They had to unite people, to dull them down, force them all to keep their God to themselves."

"Yes, that's the point," said Warren. He tapped at his graphics; as numbers scrolled up, he sat back and stroked the side of his glass jar. "They're creating a world-wide homogeneous population to maximize predictive power. It's working for them. Except for a few outliers. Except for us."

Maggie nodded. "You know what I think? I think God is a Platinum Donkey. No, really, he is. He's kind and wrathful, he's terrifying yet loving. He is the potential for all great things, and his is the judgment for eternal damnation. He sees no contradiction in loving someone while killing them. You know what I mean?"

Warren froze, then pulled his jar into his lap and curled around it protectively. "I understand your point, yes."

"The Platinum Donkeys are just broken people. We're skilled and creative, and maybe we're broken in ways that amplify those qualities. We're powerful, but inhuman and paradoxical. That's all it takes to be gods. But there are millions of people out there with just as much potential. They have a future. Not us." She smiled, a crooked little grin that she would never be allowed to show on camera. "Although I may have to break them a little."

"So you're not going to stick around to lead them?"

"We can't be a part of society. We can't rule it with goodwill. We don't have the empathy, we don't understand people, it's the nature of our damage. At most, we could be dictators, and not very nice ones."

"We could be their gods."

"I don't want a world ruled by gods, Warren. I want a world populated by them. We have to get out of the way to let that happen. Hasan was right about that much. After you change the world, you should get off the stage. Maybe God Himself did that, long ago."

"If He was a Platinum Donkey."

"No doubt in my mind, Warren. The future belongs to the insane. It's about time we gave it to them." She noticed that the table display had stopped scrolling. She sat down next to Warren and smiled at him. "Looks like your project's done. So, are they coming for us?"

Warren looked over his results. He nodded. "Yes."

He sorted through his homemade menus and brought up an image, then spun it with a finger so that it faced Maggie. The picture showed blue sky with wispy clouds far above. In the center of the image something was wrong. A section of the clouds had been shifted, as if cut, moved, and pasted, with a different, poorly-matching section filling in the hole left behind. The outline of the displaced section was bulbous, with familiar, stubby projections at its sides.

Maggie's jaw dropped. "That looks like another gelship."

"It's invisible," Warren said, hugging his jar. "There are metamaterials that warp light around them. I think their ship's hull is made of that. But it only works in one direction, over a short angular range. By jumping the androids away from our yacht, I was able to get a little beyond their angle of effect and bring out some imperfections in their cloak."

"You're telling me that's an invisible gelship. And it's following us?"

"The cloak only works in the direction we're looking at it. It's only invisible to us, so yeah, we're the ones they want." He narrowed his eyes. "If I had more androids, I could get a better picture."

Maggie ignored the request. She ran her finger over the tabletop, tracing the outline of their pursuer. "Son of a bitch. They're invisible, now. Warren, are you as paranoid as I was told, or are they really out to get you?"

Warren hunched his shoulders, frowning.

"Everyone at the nursing home was out to get me, I'm sure of that. Making fun of me because I talk to things. I know they're not alive—I know that—it just makes me feel better." He stroked the top of his glass jar, making the blob inside ripple in mock pleasure. "It helps me understand things. I could never have modified that hyperbaric bed into a bose condensator, to make my superfluid, if I hadn't talked to it. But that's when the trouble started, so..."

Maggie looked at him from the corner of her eye. "Wait. Did you just say that you invented that thing using spare parts while stuck in a nursing home?"

"No," he said, shrinking further into his chair. "They weren't spare parts. It was a brand new bed."

Maggie laughed. "Well, whatever. I'm glad you're on our side."

"I'm not on your side. You kidnapped me."

"Oh, right. Well, I'm glad we kidnapped you. So the police are invisible, now—can you think of any other tricks they might have?"

Warren shook his head and waved his hand in the air. "How should I know? You don't get it, do you? This is not modern technology. This is beyond that. They are more advanced than us.

They've suppressed technological advancement for decades, but apparently they're keeping the good stuff for themselves! There's no way to tell what the Unification government is capable of. All we know is that they're beyond us. And you're bluffing them!"

Maggie blinked. "Excuse me?"

"You're bluffing with that 'dead man's switch'. You don't have any network channels that Delano didn't have. I doubt that you even have the protocols to access the Momma. You're bluffing them, and when they find that out, they're going to kill you and everyone on this ship. We probably won't even see it coming. And I have a son in Chicago I'd like to see. He might not want to see me, but..."

For a few seconds, Maggie fixed a skeptical, haughty expression on her face as Warren dithered with his jar and mumbled. But soon she let him off the hook with a playful laugh.

"You're right," she said. "I am bluffing. I do have the access protocols—Bailey got them for me before we left the chalet. But there's no way I can access the Momma through the network. I need to be on site, at the Momma's controls, to set them off."

"You won't get that far. As soon as they figure out your android isn't really doing anything, they'll know you're bluffing."

"Oh, she's making it look real. It's a pretty good bluff. Simon had secure, encrypted sites on the net ready to activate his wrath. I just borrowed them. Globalpol has had hours to figure it out, but they haven't yet."

"How many sites? What encryption are you using?"

"I don't know. I just told Fianna to use the best Simon had." She turned to the android, who stood in an out-of-the-way corner of the galley. "Fianna, please answer Warren's questions."

"For this project we are using eighty-eight sites: thirty virtual, forty-five realware, and thirteen wetware installations. Only twelve are used in common rotation; with each acknowledgment cycle four additional sites are also contacted at random, with ten held in deep reserve. All of these sites were installed with a twenty terabyte one-time pad library with index seeds synchronized to my master copies at setup."

The scientist whistled. "That's actually pretty good."

"In addition, my communications with the project sites are tagged as highest-privilege legal documents, and are thus not interceptable except by regional level subpoena. Distributions of the sites insure that approximately 40 separate subpoenas will be necessary to intercept them all; the wetware sites have additional *onus probandi* legal protections from section 46.3 of—"

"Okay, okay, I believe you. They're not going to find out that you're bluffing."

"Well, they still might," Maggie said. "I'm just hoping to slow them down. I need enough time to get to a Momma and trigger it. Which is why I need you, Warren."

Warren huddled in his chair. "You're going to kill me."

"No."

"You are. As soon as I give you the sites you're going to kill me."

"I am not going to kill you, Warren. I would never kill you. Now give me what I need to know or I'll throw you out the airlock."

He flinched. Maggie stared at him for a few seconds, her hands on her hips, until he turned and jabbed at the table with a frustrated finger. Her jumpsuit beeped; she activated the sleeve's eyeline display, and a model of the Earth appeared in her vision. Eight spots on it were marked, with tag controls that led to detailed coordinates.

"Thank you, Warren. How certain are you about these?"

"That's the solution. It has to be. It's a sparse icosahedron—Delano said that the Mommas are linked by a ultra-low frequency mantle network, and that is most efficient if linked by a discretely symmetrical standing wave. This is the only solution with vertexes on Van Hoogan mining sites. Plus the site in Australia, of course."

"Mmm-hmmn."

She brushed the image of the globe with her hand. The transparent ball spun, hovering a few centimeters over her right sleeve. She touched it again, stopping the image, then toyed with it a bit, spinning the globe with a flick of her finger. She continued playing with the Earth as she walked out of the galley, with Fianna and the puzzled Warren following in her wake.

"What are you going to do now?" Warren asked.

"I'm going to destroy them."

"You're what?"

"That's why I needed all the sites. I'm going to have the Mommas destroy themselves."

Maggie wasn't watching him; she was playing with the model globe, but she heard Warren's footsteps hesitate and stumble.

"I don't believe it. You've got a doomsday weapon in your hand, and you're going to make it destroy itself?"

"No one should have this, Warren." She fixed him with a piercing glance, to let him know the seriousness of her words. "This weapon is good for one thing—killing entire populations in a large, contained area. The Unification wouldn't use it to destroy society like Delano wanted. But think what else they could target with it."

Warren blinked, then frowned. "The reservations."

"That's right. The Momma can destroy a reservation, or damage it enough to make their people dependent upon the world government, and do it all in a deniable way. Once the reservations are subdued, they can replace them with arcology or wilderness and there will be nothing, nothing else left. This is the final weapon they need to homogenize the world and make every corner of it predictable. That's not the only reason I want it gone. It kills entire populations, and no matter where you look a good segment of the population are my fans. Nobody hurts my fans but me. That's why I'm blowing this damn thing up."

But it is an enticing little toy, she thought, spinning the Earth once more as she walked away.

Persistent, Warren followed. "If you're not going to kill me, can you drop me off in Chicago?"

"No. But when we land you can have the yacht—take it anywhere you want."

"When are we going to land?"

Maggie thought about that as she walked the stripped corridors, with the android work teams dodging out of her way.

There was one Momma in North America—near the Van Hoogan chalet. They couldn't go back there. One was in South America, a possible destination. But she knew where they would have to go. All but one of the Mommas were sited at Van Hoogan mines. If she were running Globalpol, she'd have found a way to lock down all of Van Hoogan's properties. Only one of the Mommas might be safe. Of course, with their invisible stalker following them, they would likely have to fight their way in no matter where they landed.

"Bailey," Maggie shouted as she walked onto the pilot's bridge. The prim butler sat at the controls, two android copilots flanking him. "I know where we're going, now."

"Ah good, mum. Do you have a heading, or should I point us directly toward Hell?"

"We're headed to Leonora's Bottom. But I don't want them to be sure of that, yet. Steer halfway between that course and one going to Media Bay."

"Yes, mum."

Warren tapped at her arm. "Why Media Bay?"

"The space elevator is at Media Bay. Globalpol will assume that's where I'm going. I might still do that—there's someone on Megasat that I need to kill."

Bailey leaned toward Warren, speaking with a conspiratorial tone. "She may be psychotic, but at least she's selective."

"Suddenly I'm glad that women have standards," Warren mumbled.

Maggie ignored them. "Fianna, can we encrypt a phone call so that no one knows who we're calling?"

"No. Encrypted messages can be traced, unless an obfuscated forwarding site has been pre-arranged."

"I want to call Oswald in Australia."

"An obfuscated forwarding site has been pre-arranged."

"I thought it might. Simon told him to get me and where to find me. They had to have some way of talking in secret."

"Shall I make the call?"

"Yeah. Put it up—do we have a screen?"

Bailey pointed; the forward window of the gelship turned an opaque grey. A blinking icon indicated the placed call. They waited, silent except for Warren's undecipherable mumbling. Bored after a few seconds, Maggie started playing with the model Earth that only she could see.

Thus distracted, she didn't see when Oswald appeared on screen. "Bloody hell. It's you." He was in his black leather jacket and hat, looking down into the camera from the seat of his truck. "What do you want?"

Maggie turned off her globe display. "Can't a girl stay in touch with her old flings, Oswald?"

"This is Simon's channel. Where is he?"

"Simon's dead. Not my fault. I'd forget him if I were you, he's not your type. What are you doing about seventeen hours from now? We could go to dinner."

She walked closer to the screen, leaning forward to give him a good look at the deep v-neck cleavage on her jumpsuit. He rewarded her with an exasperated chuckle.

"Look, princess, I've got important things to do—"

"This is important. Remember when you said the world was divided into those who were sleeping and those who were awake? I called to let you know: I'm awake now."

"Oh, aye? Too right. And what does that mean for you?"

"It means I'm going to destroy the Momma. I'm coming to Leonora's Bottom to make her eat herself up."

Oswald blinked, or a tic crossed his face—Maggie couldn't tell, the expression seemed so strange. Then his hands worked out of camera, and he rocked forward with a screech of tires. Once the truck had stopped, he leaned into the camera.

"There's seventy-odd kilopoppies in there. Including my family. What the fuck do you think you're playing at?"

"Yeah, lots of people," Maggie said, brushing a hand through her hair. "I thought you might want to evacuate them. Then when I show up we can have the place all to ourselves. A little dancing, a little wine, who knows?"

"Princess, by the time you touch down, I'm gonna be over the horizon twice."

"So it's a date, then. Should I wear something casual, or just barbecue sauce?"

"I should have thrown you to the fucking snakes!"

"You should have eaten me," she said, with a wide, toothy grin. "I'll give you one more chance. Might even repay the favor."

"Fucking loony bitch!", Oswald shouted, and his hand shot out to kill the connection.

Maggie sighed dramatically, then turned to smile at Warren and Bailey. "He's so into me," she said, with a look that dared them to disagree. In unison, they swallowed and looked away.

"Okay, then," she said to herself as she walked out of the bridge, leaving the men behind. "Oswald will evacuate our stage. We have a crew and a script. That leaves cast and props. Fianna, where is Hasan?"

"Middle deck, lounge area."

The androids in the lounge were arranged in neat columns, filling the dance and game areas. In each android's right hand they held a curved blade with a diamond pattern, a lighter version of the weapon their instructor held at the back of the lounge. Hasan lifted his scimitar; the androids mimicked his pose. He went into a shadow sparring routine, slashing at the air and blocking unseen attacks. The androids followed, the status lights on their smooth faces blinking in rapid, violent patterns.

"Swords?" Maggie shouted to the back of the room. "I told you to fab them weapons, and you gave them swords? Haven't you ever heard of guns?"

Hasan continued his sparring, giving no sign that he had heard.

Maggie stepped around the horde and found a seat on a chaise lounge that had not been recycled due to its being connected to the bar. The lounge asked for her drink order. Maggie remembered leaving her gin in the galley, and dialed for another.

With the clattering squeaks of new plastic, the androids continued their routine even as Hasan walked through the ranks to inspect them. Maggie found herself approving of his attention to detail. When a droid performed a motion out of form, Hasan corrected it, manually shifting the robot's limbs into the correct position. He corrected so many that Maggie began to see that almost every android had flaws in their technique. But once taught they learned instantly, repeating the motion with mechanical accuracy. Then he would unsheathe his sword and demonstrate the next move.

As impressive as their small army was, Hasan drew most of Maggie's attention. He wore a loose, flowing white robe of some mimic fabric that billowed with his movements and contracted back into normal cloth when at rest. His scimitar and scabbard hung on a rust-colored baldric, his only accessory. His bald head was dotted with sweat, giving an impression of melting bronze that dripped into rivulets further down his neck and jaw. He moved like no man Maggie had ever seen. Every motion exuded power and grace, exerting as much force as needed but nothing more, and every step and turn remained in balance. The androids were learning perfection by example; Hasan, in his manic aptitude, was the template.

He's pretty.

Maggie frowned at the unbidden thought, but kept watching the dark-skinned warrior.

Yes. Yes, I'm allowed to think that. He is an attractive man.

He's doomed.

That was the thought that caused her to look away.

Poor Hasan. I'm going to get him killed. Warren and Bailey might escape. They'll probably be captured, but at least they'll survive. Hell, I might escape. But I'm putting Hasan in a situation where he'll happily go down fighting.

But if that's what he wants, is it wrong?

Maggie chuckled and rubbed her eyes. *It might be a little late to worry about being an ethical person.*

She pictured the faces of men she had known—the recent ones, like Simon, and the earlier ones, the poor men she had seduced on Megasat. All of their deaths were like weights on her shoulders. The entire world sat there, but she felt those deaths the most.

After all that I've done, I don't deserve to escape even if I get the chance. They should lock me away...

When she stopped rubbing and opened her eyes, Hasan stood before her, as if he were measuring her for inspection.

Maggie sighed. "What?" she asked. "Am I glowing?"

With a minimal gesture, Hasan shook his head.

She chuckled. "I'm just worried. And scared. And feeling guilty. No, don't comfort me or anything." Another chuckle escaped her as the tension built up inside. "Delano wanted to rule the world. Stupid. Too much to deal with. We donkeys are antisocial by nature, if not outright sociopaths, and the craziness and guilt just adds up and we don't support each other—"

Hasan interrupted her by stepping forward and cradling her chin with his hand, then leaning down to give her a deep kiss.

His scent was exotic and spicy, of cardamom and seared oils. The kiss lasted a second, or maybe ten; she was too surprised by it to tell. Then Hasan took her hands in his own and pulled her out of her chair with patient, irresistible strength. He put his arm around her waist and drew her close before kissing her again.

Maggie put her hands on his chest. Beneath his thin cotton robe she felt beads of sweat and a hard wall of muscle. Everything below her neckline began to tingle. "Hasan," she began, at a whisper, "I don't think I can...get too close to anyone."

His grip on her was insistent. She had to follow where ever he intended to go.

The nearest cabin had been stripped of furnishings, but the bed was intact; off limits until morning, by her decree. Maggie waved Fianna back as Hasan closed and locked the door. Then she stood, paralyzed with indecision as Hasan drew the zipper down her back, trailing its progress with pecks of his lips. Excuses came to her and were pushed aside. As she stepped out of her suit, she leaned back against him, letting his strength hold her up. At the touch of a control his clothing fell away like fog and reassembled itself on the floor.

Beneath his robe she found a marvel of textures. The boys on Megasat had been lean and smooth, with nothing harsher than peach fuzz or soft woolly hair. Hasan had stubble on his chin. She scratched her cheek back and forth across it as he lowered her onto the bed.

When she clawed down his back she felt wiry hair and slabs of thick, unyielding muscle. His hands were coarse and warm. He curled one under her back and gripped her shoulder as he thrust into her.

Pent up tension made her gasp, and as he entered a rhythm her gasps became staccato moans. He was silent, and his beatific smile broke only when he kissed her or nibbled at her arching throat.

Then abruptly he lifted her, and rolled.

Maggie settled on top of Hasan with slow wriggles of her hips, and licked through the sweat on his broad chest. She braced herself against his ribcage and began moving in tight, bucking waves. He grabbed her hand and she entwined their fingers together, and reached for his other hand—

—his other hand was palming something. He pressed it into her grip, then closed his fist around her fingers. She felt a hard, contoured handle, and as she glanced at it she saw a gleaming steel blade.

Maggie tried to drop the knife, but Hasan's fist tightened, and the pain of his grip and the light glinting off the blade sent electricity shooting down her spine. Her hips moved of their own accord, jerking hungrily against his taut body, and he steered her hand until the knife touched his chest and her eyes rolled back—

She tore her hand out of his grasp, and stabbed downward with all her strength into the mattress, centimeters from his arm. The orgasm rocked through her; then she realized there was no need for guilt, and another wave of convulsions hit, freer and more powerful than the last. She screamed. She fell, and collapsed on top of her lover's muscular chest.

For a few seconds she lay there trembling, kissing at his stubbled jaw. Then he shifted, pushing her off and rolling away. Maggie reached out and stroked the taut curve of his waist.

"Hey, we're not finished yet. I mean, you didn't—"

"You didn't kill me."

She giggled. The knife was still in her hand. She pulled it free from the mattress. "I didn't, did I? And it was good. Better than I thought it... Wait." She noticed that his face had gone sour, his brows bunched together. "Are you mad at me?"

Hasan pulled himself up and sat on the edge of the bed. He seemed deflated, his shoulders sagged and his head hung low. "I think you'd better leave," he said.

Maggie stared. Without looking back at her, Hasan got up, staggered to his clothing, and with jerky, fumbling motions tried to pull his sword from its scabbard. Maggie laughed despite herself, then when he froze and looked at her with a teary, hateful glare she laughed even more.

"Please go," he mumbled.

Maggie got up and strode toward the door, still chuckling. When she passed the threshold the door was quickly forced shut and locked. Again she began to laugh, but caught herself when she saw Bailey standing across the corridor, with a wide-eyed expression and one hand down the front of his pants.

She raised one eyebrow and smiled at him. "Enjoying yourself?"

"P-perhaps not as much as some," he said, stammering. He hurried into a butler's pose with hands dutifully behind his back, but his eyes were wide and fearful. Then Maggie realized she had left her clothes in Hasan's cabin—she was naked, dripping with sweat, and still holding a knife in her hand.

Maggie gave him a dangerous grin, and he rewarded her with a trembling, audible gulp. "Relax, honey," she said. "Is there something you wanted to tell me?"

"Y-yes, mum. You should know that Dr. Poltrasky has taken the controls. He says that he wants to learn how to fly the gelship."

From the cabin behind her came loud sobs, and clanging sounds of steel against steel that made Bailey's eyes twitch even wider. Maggie chuckled and shook her head.

"Let Warren do whatever he likes, as long as he doesn't change our course. Anything else?"

"No, mum. Ah. Is Prince Hasan going to be all right?"

A crash punctuated the question; something in the cabin broke and clattered to the floor. The sobbing became a despairing wail. Then the chopping sounds began again.

"If anything does happen to him, it won't be my fault," Maggie said. "Maybe you can cheer him up."

"Yes. Perhaps I'll try that later."

"Right." She looked sideways at him, a calculated stare that could break poorer actors in two. "Tell me, Bailey. Are you really a doctor of anything?"

The man flinched as if hit. "Aw, shucks, ma'am," he said in his western drawl. "I always wanted to be."

Maggie nodded, then let him off the hook with a sincere smile. "You'd have made a good one."

"Really? T-thank you, mum."

"And you're a good donkey." She strode off down the corridor, swinging her hips as she walked for his benefit. "Let me know when we get to Australia. I'll be drinking, so send an android to wake me."

"Very good, mum. Do have a pleasant binge," he said in a relieved British tone. Then, as she descended the stair and passed out of sight, she heard him say in his natural voice, "Think I'll go on one myself."

———●———

Chapter 19—Smash Cut

From overhead, the main entrance of Leonora's Bottom looked like a miniature arcology. A egg-shaped building almost a kilometer long, its axis aligned with the thin desert dunes, the Bottom's Top lay at the intersection of three long roads. The gaping tunnels inward were barricaded by lines of bright yellow robots with flashing lights. Walkways and cultivated eucalyptus orchards covered the structure, but there were no people that Maggie could see.

Evacuated, Maggie thought. *But not by any alarm raised by Oswald. The government did this.*

She turned to Hasan and sighed. "Well, it's a trap."

"Yes, indeed," he said.

He wore the same loose robe and baldric that he had yesterday; Maggie tamped down her urge to feel through it for his muscular chest. She had fabbed a new jumpsuit with additional hip pockets, one of which held the knife he had given her last night. It made her feel better to have a weapon, even though she had fifty-six sword-wielding androids surrounding her in the embarkation deck ready to fight. Hasan had given her that knife, and more. She worried that she still owed him something.

Prince Hasan, however, seemed unruffled.

"We will drop in three platoons," he said, summoning a grid display and tactical lines on the bay window. "We'll be in the third wave. If they have something planned they'll have to throw it at the androids first. If we should be so lucky that they don't, we'll face whatever it is with two columns of infantry at our flanks, and skirmish teams that will already have secured the entrances."

"Six sets of entrances. Are we going to use them all?"

"We'll only use one. If there's a battle just head for whichever entrance is nearest—one platoon will follow you, the other two will stay with me."

Hasan turned to face the formation of androids. "Any questions?"

None of the androids said anything. They had not been equipped with voiceboxes. Hasan grinned with pride anyway, and winked at Maggie.

"La-hallaq mniih," he said. "So far, so good. Bailey, any sign of trouble out there?"

A screen opened on the window, showing a view of the bridge. "No, sir, but—"

"Tell them about the microwaves!", interrupted Warren's voice. Bailey rolled his eyes as Warren barged into the camera's view. "Look, look!"

The scientist held his jar of superfluid up to the camera. The gray, spongy thing looked melted and more liquid than before, and as they watched tiny bubbles rose to its surface and popped. Each pop made a ripple that flowed, undamped, across the whole, so that in seconds the superfluid's surface was a dancing, boiling mass of solid static.

"They're flooding the area with microwaves," said Warren. His eyes were sunken; Maggie didn't know if he had slept. "It's a power transmission frequency."

"They're trying to burn us?", asked Maggie.

"No, no, it's not that strong. This is a microwave frequency used to supply power to small devices. Ones too small to have their own power source."

"Like what?"

"I don't know. It could be anything. It could be ubiquitous nanotech—it could be everything. You can't go out there!"

Maggie took a deep breath. "I have to, Warren. But as soon as we're on the ground, you fly out of here."

"I—", he started. Then, after a moment's pause, he shook his jar until the superfluid reverted back to lumpy clay. Clutching it to his chest, Warren backed away from the camera. "I will. Damn right I will. I'm sorry..."

"Don't be sorry," Maggie told him. As Bailey returned to the screen, she smiled. "Take good care of him, Bailey. You can set us down, now."

"Yes, mum. And may I say—good luck."

"Of course you may. We're going to need it."

Maggie leaned on the window as the display closed, and she watched their descent toward the Bottom's Top. When she felt Hasan step near, she sighed.

"You know, Hasan, you don't have to go down there. You can direct the androids from up here."

"But then I can't be your bodyguard."

"I've got Fianna for that." The legal aide stood a couple meters away. She was dressed in a jumpsuit that matched Maggie's. "I mean, she looks the part, doesn't she? Might not ever show up on a fashion runway, but I think she makes this outfit work."

Hasan chuckled, and put his hand on Maggie's shoulder.

"Look, I'm sorry that I went all fakakta last night. But I know that you're doing this to keep the Momma from being used against the reservations."

"That's just one reason."

"And it's just one reason I'm helping you, to save my people. Believe me, we'd be the first reservation they got rid of. Would you want to live next to me? But I'm also with you until the end because I like you, and Simon believed in you, and I want to see what kind of world you'll make."

She turned to look at him, then dived into his arms. Hugging him tight, she looked up into his smiling face.

"And because you glow," he said.

Maggie rolled her eyes and pushed him away.

The gelship touched down on a large concourse, snapping the stands of eucalyptus trees on either side. They dropped the gangplank and marched a platoon of androids out onto the Bottom's Top. When they had spread out and taken position, the second platoon marched out. Teams of two broke off from the columns, running toward the elevators and stairways that dotted the massive building.

Hot air blew in through the open gangplank, carrying in a dusty, burnt smell that Maggie remembered from her time in the outback. Swarms of tiny gnats danced over the walkway in the bright sunlight. Nothing else moved.

"Damn, it looks safe," Maggie muttered. "They always make it look safe. Whatever happened to governments just showing up with guns and tanks?"

"Everything winds up on teevee, now. If you want to keep people ignorant, you have to use a velvet glove when they're watching. Ready?"

She nodded.

If there were any cameras—or police gelships—next to her as she walked down the concourse, they remained invisible. With Hasan on her left, Fianna on her right, and a contingent of androids surrounding them, she wanted to feel safe. But the gnats buzzing around their heads were an annoying reminder that she was not in control.

Wait. A dim memory clicked in her brain. *Were there gnats in the desert? Gnats in South Carolina swarmed near water—*

An arriving call distracted her as icons blinked on her suit. "Maggie," said Warren in her sleeve display. "Look at the horizon!"

She looked up. Hasan pointed.

The edge of the kilometer-long building had a black line, as if the horizon had darkened and grown thick. As she watched, the darkness expanded upwards, stretching over the Bottom's Top like a gigantic, black clamshell. The shell looked razor-thin, but its sides reached hundreds of meters over the Top, and began zipping itself shut.

Maggie felt a chill jolt through her. *They can blot out the sun.*

Darkness clapped over them. Maggie reached for Hasan but found only empty air. Then the gnats ignited into thousands of tiny specks of light. She held up her hand, trying to shield her eyes, out the pests flew closer, and shone miniature lights into the sides of her vision. Combined, the specks began to form a pattern, like a laser line calibration display...

The indirect lighting turned on, showing gray metal walls, gray metal ceiling, maroon executive carpet.

She uncovered her eyes.

"Yes, I'd prefer if we made this go away," said Tom, sitting at the long black table with the Megasat logo worked into the wooden trim.

Maggie looked around the boardroom. She was standing on Tom's right side, while at his left sat Percy, his face flushed with anger. Another pair of minor execs completed their side of the table. The cramped room had a small window screen dialed to show a deep space look centered on the brilliant wedge of the moon.

On the other side of the table sat several men in Globalpol uniforms. The man in the center had a square jaw, and looked at her with a haughty sneer.

"Sit down, Ms. Megaputri," Radicker said. "The negotiations are almost complete."

She sat down. The chair felt lumpy and uncomfortable.

"We've come to an agreement," Tom said. He tapped the table, bringing up pages of text. "In return for a delayed levy on your assets, they're willing to accept a plea bargain of manslaughter, with lifetime house arrest here on Megasat. I thought that would be okay with you. You get to stay here for the rest of your life, and nothing changes."

"I'm not on Megasat," Maggie said. She was wearing a dull pink jumpsuit, unpowered. The table felt rough, not like the slick display it appeared to be.

Tom rolled his eyes. "And there'll be treatment for your condition, of course. God knows that's been a long time coming."

"We could let it go to trial, Mags," said Percy, "But you'd probably still lose. And then they'd throw you in jail. At least this way, we get to keep doing the show."

Maggie ran her hand down her thigh. The jumpsuit looked smooth, but she felt a pouch, and inside that the handle of a knife. "I'm not on Megasat," she repeated, glaring at Radicker. "What kind of game are you playing?"

"This isn't a game," he said through clenched teeth. "People have died. We're being very generous in letting you off without public humiliation. Sign this. It's your last chance."

One of the documents in the table display moved over to her. A fingerprint box blinked for attention.

Maggie shook her head. "This is bullshit. What's this levy about? Oh, let me guess. I sign this, you get Megasat."

"It's a delayed punitive judgment. It won't go into effect until you die."

"So I sign this, you shoot me, and *then* you get Megasat. Fuck off."

Radicker ground his teeth together.

"I give you my word," he said, "that you may live the rest of your life on Megasat. We are not an unethical government; we do not kill unless it is necessary. It took centuries to unite the world under a common set of ethics, did you think we would discard them that easily? This is the most compassionate government system that has ever existed, that can ever exist for human beings. It is almost utopia, Maggie. With Megasat it can be. Do you see how insane it is that you would want to destroy that?"

"Mags, come on, just sign the fucking deal," Percy said.

She threw an icy glare at him—and noticed a bright hole in the ceiling. Or not in the ceiling, beyond it. Hundreds of meters in the air, a gelship-sized hole had been punched through the black, light-obscuring clamshell. Just beyond the hole, she could see Warren's yacht rising into the sky.

Sunlight streamed in through the hole. The scene around her changed. An underlay of red sand and pale eucalyptus shone throughout the projected boardroom. In front of her stood a squat pyramid of androids, pretending to be a meeting room table. The clamshell began repairing itself, regrowing over the hole, and as the light dimmed the vision of Megasat strengthened. Australia faded away.

Radicker waved his hand to get her attention. "You're hallucinating right now, aren't you? You're a sick woman, Maggie. You're fortunate that we got you safely back to Megasat."

Maggie ran her hands over her uncomfortable chair. It had bumps and peculiar crannies, as if an android or two had mimed a chair for her to sit on.

"We're taking your illness into account with this light sentence. Please, let us help you."

She laughed and got to her feet.

"You can hack our androids. You can project sound, like a governor does, right into our ears. You've got little flying laserline projectors, and all they need is a darkroom to create all of this."

"No. Maggie, this is reality. Think about how crazy you sound."

"It's not crazy to distrust reality when technology can make anything happen. Skepticism is sensible, it's necessary. But you've assumed I don't have any sense. You think that because I hallucinate sometimes, I'm easily fooled. You don't get it," she said, laughing again. "I've learned to choose what my reality is."

"You don't get a choice, now."

"Wrong. Because I'm the star and I write the scripts, and the stagehands follow my lead. I'll show you."

Then she cupped her hands around her mouth, and screamed at full volume. "Fianna, if you can hear me—spotlight!"

A blinding white oval shone from Maggie's right side. Shielding her eyes, she ran toward it. The spotlight streaming from Fianna's face shifted down to illuminate concrete behind the rich carpeting in front of her. She ran through a Megasat bulkhead into pitch blackness, then into Fianna's small but sturdy frame. Maggie hugged the android like an anchor.

"Maggie," Fianna said, "Someone has been trying to infiltrate my systems. I believe they have already compromised the others."

"Yeah. Don't let them in. Can you make that light wider?"

The android's light widened to flood the area.

The concourse, where disciplined columns of androids had awaited commands, was a circus display. Androids stooped in odd poses mimicking tables and chairs, or were deactivated and slumped against railings and trees. About a dozen meters away she saw five droids with their weapons out, battling Hasan. He dodged them with inhuman speed, parrying one sword with his giant scimitar before kicking the legs out from one of his opponents. The scimitar chopped downward; an android lost its head. But another nearby droid reactivated, drawing its weapon and joining the battle.

It took her a moment, with the dimness of Fianna's spread light and the false imagery still coming from the laserline gnats, to realize that Hasan was fighting with his eyes closed.

Maggie stood and marveled as the Prince dispatched two more opponents. When replacements activated, she yelled. "Hasan! We're free!" The metallic clashes of the fighting were muffled; something in the air was dampening sound. She yelled again.

With a flourish of his scimitar Hasan pushed back three androids. A fourth struck from behind, but Hasan's billowing clothing deflected the blade. In a spinning riposte he tore a gash in that android's side, and in the same motion toppled the fifth with a brutal kick to the midsection. In the moment of safety he had created, Hasan turned to face Maggie—his eyes still closed, his mouth curved into a blissful smile—and ran toward her.

She shrieked for him to stop when it appeared he intended to run them down. Instead, he slowed at the sound of her voice then took her hand and pulled her forward. When she noticed his eyes were still closed, Maggie ran faster and began to pull him.

Following Fianna's lead they ran toward the nearest entrance, a stadium staircase leading into the Bottom. Two of their androids were slumped on the walkway halfway there—when one of them reached out to grab Maggie, Hasan cut off its hand without breaking stride. As they reached the staircase a thumping sound shook the air and the concrete beneath their feet. With one foot on the stairs, Maggie stopped and pulled Fianna around so she could look back.

On the main concourse, three-meter wide gelatinous gobs were splashing down onto the walkway. In the dim light Maggie watched one hit, the impact sending ripples shuddering through the mass, cushioning the fall of a dark object in the center. Then she watched as the object inside stood upright, extended its arms, and began tearing its way out toward her.

Maggie ran.

Two levels down the lights were on. Fianna led them through a commercial district, past locked-up tourist shops and advertisements for guided safaris. They ran into a maintenance area, where brushed aluminum hallways were powdered with red dust. At a loading bay, Fianna stopped before an industrial elevator with rust spots in its orange paint and interlocking steel lattices for a door.

"What's wrong?" Maggie asked. The bay was littered with stacks of metal storage containers, but she could see several exits. "Which way do we go?"

"We need to go down point eight kilometers to contact the T.E.M. control network. This is a mine elevator. It will take us that deep."

"Okay. So what are you doing?"

"The elevator will take three minutes to arrive."

Maggie looked back at the hallway they had come through. In the distance she heard running footsteps. "Globalpol will be here before that. Should we keep running? Can we outrun—"

Hasan interrupted her by touching his finger to her lips.

Then he shifted his stance, bringing his scimitar over his head in a slow, meditative arc, ending the motion with the weapon pointed defiantly down the hallway, his every muscle tensed and alert.

Maggie crossed her arms. "Hasan," she said, "the lights are on in here. You can open your eyes, now."

He did, and a wide smile broke across his face. Then he waved one hand, shooing her aside. Maggie grabbed Fianna's arm and pulled her behind a row of containers. Through a gap they watched as Hasan positioned himself at the edge of the entryway, able to look out but not easily seen.

Six men in midnight-blue uniforms ran into the hallway. One in the rear barked a command, and they all slowed to a careful walk, the rifles in their hands held shoulder height, at the ready. The men scanned the room with their eyes, their faces grim. Maggie gasped when she got a clear view of the one in the back. He held only a pistol, but she saw how his eyes glazed over and defocused every few seconds, and Radicker's determined jaw was unmistakable.

Hasan waited until they had almost entered the room before he lifted one hand into the corridor, fingers spread. The soldiers pointed their rifles at him.

"Come out! On the floor!"

Hasan took a casual step toward them, the one hand held over his head. His scimitar was in the other hand, pointed down toward the floor.

"Drop the weapon and lay down with your hands—"

The forward soldier didn't finish his command. Hasan spun, whipping his sword arm out and slashing the soldier's throat. His white robe ballooned with the movement, and puffed further out as the Prince whirled toward the next man, knocking his gun from his hands just before the others opened fire.

Maggie's hands squeezed at the side of the container when the automatic rifles filled the loading bay with reverberating gunshots. But Hasan seemed not to notice. He stayed in constant motion, thrusting his blade into the nearest soldier's gut before turning, with his arms crossed in front of his face, to strike down into another man's shoulder. Maggie saw black pepper marks across his billowing white robe—bullets, stopped in the thick padding of the inflated mimic fabric. Some of them fell back outward as Hasan twirled to slash another soldier's face. Ragged bits of white cloth flew out as well as the gunfire shredded through the robe's ablative protection.

The fifth soldier was a quick thinker, and lifted his rifle to parry the Prince's scimitar when it thrust toward him. But Hasan cut backward and sliced down into the man's side. The soldier cried out and took a step back; Hasan lunged again, catching him in the chest. He fell with a gurgling scream, the giant scimitar pinned in his ribcage.

Maggie watched the last man, the one with the pistol: Radicker. He had been backing away from the fight, his eyes glazed over. As she watched, Radicker aimed the pistol in quick, mechanical movements. When Hasan put his foot on the chest of the last victim to pry out his sword, Radicker took careful, dispassionate aim.

Maggie jumped up from behind the boxes and shouted. "Hasan!"

The pistol barked three times. The billowing robe, retracting for that moment while Hasan was stationary, manage to block two of the shots. The third created a spray of blood and gore out of the back of the Prince's skull, staining his miraculous armor a grisly red. Hasan fell backward, his hand still locked on his weapon.

Radicker looked Maggie's way. His arm moved with inhuman, computer-aided precision.

Maggie gasped as the shot rang out, both from the sound and from the gray blur that pushed her from the side. She kept from falling by grabbing the containers. Fianna, pushed back a step when she intercepted the first shot, jumped over the containers as the man fired again.

Without grace the android ran toward Radicker, her limbs and head jerking back as bullets hit her. He backpedaled, still firing. Fianna overtook him anyway, and knocked the weapon across the corridor with a two-handed slap. He shouted something, a string of letters and digits that Fianna ignored. The android grabbed the man's arm and twisted, then stepped behind him and grabbed the other, crossing them together in the small of his back forcefully enough to make him howl with pain. He tried kicking backward and shouting more gibberish code numbers, but Fianna would not budge.

Maggie stood up and walked toward him.

The textured pavement slabs of the hallway floor were crisscrossed with blood. A prone body, its blue uniform stained black, twitched as she stepped over it. Something breathed in thin, irregular gurgles. Strips of blood-soaked fabric lay in her path; she ground them into the concrete with her heels as she walked. She tried not to look at Hasan's body, or the formless robe that was sopping up the pools of blood that she strode through.

"Hello, William," Maggie said through clenched teeth. "I thought you didn't like to kill."

"No choice," he said, wincing as the android pulled his arms back. "We're way past plan B, Maggie. Down to the last resort. And more people are going to die unless you give yourself up now."

"Uh-huh."

She looked at Fianna. The android had tears in her jumpsuit, with nasty looking dents beneath. A furrow in the plastic of her face spread from her cheek to where her ear would be. "Fianna, are you okay?"

"Minor damage."

"How long can you hold him?"

"Indefinitely."

"This android," Radicker said, "is illegally programmed to ignore override codes."

Maggie put her hand on his chest. The uniform was thick but skin tight. She pressed a fingernail into it, dimpling the surface. "Oh, that's not my fault. I don't think Simon trusted the police very much. Isn't that right, Fianna?"

"Yes. Maggie, there is increased network chatter. More police may be arriving soon."

Maggie looked back into the loading bay. The elevator had arrived, and the steel lattice doors were withdrawn.

"Well, then. Can you take Bill with us?"

"He may escape. He may suffer multiple fractures if he tries."

"Hmmmn..." Maggie tilted her nose up and smiled at the man. "...let's risk it."

Radicker struggled somewhat as they walked down the hallway, but the android's powerful grip sent him into roars of pain when he became too aggressive. Fianna almost dragged him past Hasan's body, as he tried to take advantage of the slickened floor.

"Wait—Maggie. Your friend. We can still save him. Medical technology can repair this kind of brain damage. We can get him to a hospital if you surrender now."

"No, he'd never forgive me," she said, making an effort to keep her voice steady. It was the first offer he had made that she was tempted to take. "Hasan's greatest wish was to die at the peak of perfection. I denied him that once. But now, he's met his destiny."

"You're a cold-hearted bitch."

Maggie turned around in the elevator, and put her hand on the dust-covered rubber controls. "I think you've misunderstood me, Bill. Maybe we can correct that."

When Fianna and her captive were in the elevator, Maggie pressed the switch. The steel gate rattled up, and with a lurch the elevator began to descend.

"Why do you think I'm here, anyway? You think I'm going to blow up the world?"

"Something like that."

"And you couldn't take the chance that Fianna can't do it remotely."

"You might not be able to access the T.E.M., but Fianna has proven herself to be a weapon with Simon Brovall's legal bomb. We know you have similar contingencies lined up in the case of your death."

"I really don't," she said, chuckling. "You don't know anything about me. I'm going to destroy the Momma, so that nobody can use it again."

"No, you wouldn't do that. Our profilers know you, Maggie. If you have the opportunity to kill, you kill."

She stepped close to him. He was tall—his angular chin was at her eye level, and he smelled of gunpowder and cooling sweat.

"I haven't killed you yet," she said. "Your profilers suck. Except that one in Boise, who tried to get on my good side. I liked him."

"Theo's dead. He died in the quake."

"Oh? Funny, you don't look any worse for wear."

"I was running for the helipad as soon as you left the building. I was going to talk to my superiors—my team stayed behind to monitor the donkeys." He swallowed, and his jaw tensed. "My copter got into the air just as the quake hit. We had to land afterward, to help with recovery."

"Mmm, you're so noble. I like that."

"Then believe me when I say you can't win, Maggie. If you don't give yourself up, we have one last option. We're going to nuke every site that could have a Momma in it, starting with this one."

"Oh, come on. Van Hoogan has thousands of mines. And the Mommas are kilometers beneath solid rock. You're a terrible bluffer. I don't find that attractive in a man."

"Maggie," said Fianna, "I have connected to the local T.E.M. control network."

"Nice. Patch it to me."

Maggie stepped away from Radicker as an eyeline display lit up on her sleeve. She brought up the communications menu, and found the Momma's icon. The control system opened up in a grid of options, curved around the image of a projected Earth. Radicker began to struggle again as Maggie loaded the coordinates she and Warren had prepared.

"Why do you want this so much, Bill? The Unification has a serious crush on both Megasat and the Momma. What do you think you're going to get from them?"

"They complete Utopia, Maggie. Without Megasat we're stuck. We'd have no choice but to stagnate here on one planet. Megasat is the only route to the frontier, to expansion. The Momma...it's new technology, we need to understand it—"

"It's old technology, and I know what you can do with it. You can eliminate whole populations that aren't assimilated into your Utopia. It'll give you the Earth all to yourself."

"We'd never do that."

"You'd never do it, but you want to have the ability? Oh, no, Bill. I know how society treats its outsiders. If you have the opportunity to kill, you kill."

With her hand Maggie sent the globe on a slow, lazy spin. Nine targeting reticules were pasted on the Earth's surface, little red crosshairs bristling with info tags. She sent the activation command; the Momma acknowledged. A timer appeared over each site. The T.E.M. waves took hours to build waves in the mantle. Maggie frowned. She had been expecting a quake right away. Leonora's Bottom would be hit in three hours time.

As Radicker fought and cried out in pain, Maggie shut down her clothing's display. "I don't like doing this, Bill," she said. "This is necessary."

"No—damn it—it's not..."

"Yes, it is. I just can't take the chance."

She turned away from him, letting her hand drop to her hip pocket. Inside, the knife handle was warm to the touch.

"This isn't passion, it isn't fun. It's just practical. And I hate it. I've never hated it before. It's like there's something wrong with me—or, finally, something right."

Radicker's struggles grew more frantic. "You're not making sense! Maggie, you're threatening millions of people!"

"No, I'm not. Well, maybe."

"You can still stop this! You don't want to use the Momma—"

"Oh, that I do want. That's not what I was talking about."

Maggie turned and stepped forward, pressing herself against Radicker and throwing her free arm over his neck. Then she pressed the knife beneath his ribcage. As she expected, the uniform resisted fast objects like bullets, but slowly, she managed to dig the point in. Radicker started to scream. He kicked at her, but she leaned in close, hugging his body as she forced the knife in.

"This is what I don't want," she said, in quiet counter to his shrieking. "This is what's necessary. Because the Momma can still be stopped. And you'd stop me, if I gave you time. So there's no heat, no thrill. Just cold calculation, something that has to be done."

Blood dripped onto her hand. She pushed hard against the uniform's resistance—then the width of the blade was through, and the knife slid up to the hilt. Radicker's screams turned to a strangled groan. His eyes widened. They stared at her.

"It's just not *fair*," she said, biting her lower lip. "You're the last man I'm ever going to kill. And I don't even want to kiss you."

His struggles weakened. Maggie watched, with cold resignation, until Radicker's eyes glazed over for a final time. Then she stepped back and nodded to Fianna. Radicker slumped to the floor, the knife still buried in his ribs.

"It's not fair. Because I don't want to be a monster anymore."

Maggie stepped away from the corpse and the pool of blood that spread out from under it. She wiped her hand on her suit. Then, making sure the blood wouldn't flow out to her corner of the elevator, she sat down.

And she waited.

Chapter 20—Take a Bow

The quake is going to hit, and Leonora's Bottom is going to fall in upon itself, just like crushing an empty beverage bulb in my fist. I just have to wait for it.

Maggie looked at Radicker's corpse, then at Fianna. Then she stared at the orange-painted floor plates some more.

She didn't want to die. But she kept seeing the faces of those she had killed, not as schizophrenic hallucinations but as wistful remembrances of guilt. Radicker, thank God, wasn't among them. Killing him was necessary and she had no guilt about it. She had done what she had set out to do; she could see no reason to go on living. *Do your act, then get off the stage.*

Except there was one niggling doubt.

Maggie had set the Momma to destroy nine sites—the eight T.E.M. installations Warren had given her, and a ninth whose coordinates she had added herself. But she couldn't be sure that quake would strike home. In the end, it came down to another cold, practical consideration. She had to be sure.

"Fianna, I've changed my mind." Maggie picked herself up off the floor with a resigned sigh. "I don't want to die down here."

"I don't want that either, Maggie."

"We're going to need a path out of here. Not through the Bottom's Top—we need an exit that Globalpol isn't watching."

"I have already planned an escape route. I have also procured a car. It is reserved for us at a dealer's shop on the fifth level."

Maggie blinked. The android almost sounded bouncy. "You planned an escape route? I didn't ask you to do that."

"Simon told me to always have an escape route planned. He also insisted on always having a car available."

Maggie shook her head, smiling. "He was a better person than I am. Lead the way."

———◉———

The vehicle Fianna had ordered from the dealer was a smooth, white, six-wheeled limousine, its ground effect pads spotless and new. The first thing Maggie did was dial its exterior color to candy-apple red. Then she stripped off her jumpsuit and, careful not to get blood on the upholstery, stuffed it into the recycler attached to the wet bar.

"We've probably got another two hours. How far away can this get us in two hours?"

"How far away do you want to be, Maggie?"

"Just get me to a city. A big one. The biggest you can find."

The limousine rocketed out of an underground annex, red dust curling in its wake as it sped down the straight Australian highway.

Maggie fabbed herself a simple white shift and dress. She set an alert for network news. Exhausted, she slept.

When the news alert woke her, Maggie didn't remember where she was. She jumped awake, scrambling away from the edge of the long seat to avoid touching a pool of blood on the floor. But there was no blood. Maggie shook her head to clear it, got a glass of orange juice from the bar, and activated the limo's laserline display. Chills went up her spine as the calibration pattern crawled up the sides of her vision.

The CenNet was in chaos. Her release of the fabber hack and its shared library had set every network meet on fire. Multiple quakes had hit that day; they were blamed on 'aftershocks' of the Boise earthquake, and although they were almost all in wilderness areas the news brimmed with eyewitness reports and tallies of the damage.

Simon's legal bomb had removed the authorities' ability to police chatter and uploads, and nobody knew how long the new network freedom would last.

But none of those were the big story. Maggie found and activated a video report from a gelship that had just taken off from Kajoa. The reporter had a screeching voice, and babbled as if his hair were on fire. She turned off the sound.

The waters of Media Bay sparkled beneath her vantage, still and calm, unlike the busied disaster unraveling on shore. A million fans were streaming out of their shantytown on the golden beach, running in unsteady, drunken circles. Visible waves rippled through the sand, and the people caught in the beach tremors found themselves buried to the hip or worse. As Maggie watched, the makeshift buildings crumbled into sticks of wood and plastic, kicking up clouds of sand to add to the debris. Above the shoreline, the corporate town and its luxury mountainside villas were faring no better. They cracked into pieces, their facades and extensions and interconnected walkways tumbling down before the structures themselves gave way.

But Maggie looked upward, focusing her attention on the mountains standing above all of the destruction below. *Please. Oh, please work. Let this be worth it.*

It was the secondary fork of the elevator, the strand leading up from the smaller Mount Jojaru, that first began to shake. Tiny specks—elevator cars the size of school busses—flew off the black cable like fleas from a dog. They sprouted white mushroom heads as emergency parachutes went off. If they landed safely and after the quake had finished, she guessed that the people in those cars would be counted luckier than most.

Then a wall of rock and earth cascaded down from Jojaru's peak, and the secondary fork snapped free from the mountain.

Two and a half kilometers of secondary cable sprung into the air and collided with the main fork of the space elevator. It bent subtly. Maggie was disappointed it didn't twang like a guitar string, but she knew the tension was too great, the length of it too long. Still, there were effects. Elevator cars on the main cable flew off in all directions. Dust kicked up at the base on Mount Bungali. Maggie winced; she had bitten her tongue.

Suddenly, like an inverse thunderbolt, the elevator disappeared. One moment it had stood, bent, a thin black line cutting through the blue sky. Then an eruption of earth shot upward. The shock wave of a sonic boom rippled through the debris below. Where the elevator had been, only a translucent column of dust and pebbles remained, drifting in the wind.

Maggie opened all of the info tags attached to the video. One of them linked to an official radar sweep which linked to an analysis which linked to a simulation that told her what she needed to know. Megasat, the counterweight that pulled up the space elevator, had been cut loose from the Earth with a speed that was half a kilometer per second more than escape velocity. It, and everyone on it, was headed into deep space.

Maggie turned off the laserline and sat back, taking a deep breath. "Goodbye, Daddy," she said.

She allowed herself a minute to cry.

Then, dabbing her cheeks with the hem of her skirt, Maggie turned to the placid android sitting across the limo. "Fianna, I need to make a list."

"The fabber here can give you a printout, or can make pen and paper for you."

"Yes, I know that. No, what I need is your help. There were four young men who died on Megasat under mysterious circumstances. One was named...something like Victor, but that wasn't it. Can you look through news reports for their names?"

Fianna found them. Maggie decided to fab a pen and a pad of paper, and she wrote the names down. She added 'Emile Lambert' at the bottom, then, after a second's consideration, 'William Radicker'.

"So did you find me a city yet?"

"Yes, Maggie. We entered it forty minutes ago."

"Good. Take me to a police station," Maggie said, as she reached out to the window, opening its menus and activating transparency.

Her jaw dropped. She stared for a few seconds. Then she made the entire canopy transparent.

"Fianna?" Maggie hiked her knees up on the seat, and hugged them tight. "Could you describe for me what you see outside? I'm worried that I may be hallucinating again."

The android turned in her seat to look ahead.

"We are in an arcology. The main architecture, of high vaulted concourses with seasonal arbor displays on the top levels, is typical of Australian design. There are unusual variations."

"Yes, yes, those. Describe what variations you see. Please."

"They appear to be unauthorized art installations. On the left a residential structure is wrapped in what appears to be a tentacle."

"It's hot pink. I'm not crazy, am I? Isn't it hot pink?"

"Yes. Small children are climbing it. It is helping them in and out of the third floor windows." She turned the other way. "On the right is a walkway. A man is walking with a large toad on a leash."

"Large? That toad is three meters high, and has rabbit ears made of solar cells."

"The trees lining the walkway have turned crystalline. One of them appears to be playing guitar with a smaller, uprooted shrub."

"And that one on the end is setting up a drum kit made out of waste containers. I hope that stupid kid watching gets out of the way. He's going to end up a cymbal stand."

"The next residence is surrounded by balloons shaped like genitalia. They are—"

"Never mind what they're doing. The person responsible for that house should be ashamed of himself. And the guy in the next house, all those bricks made of eyeballs have got to be recording something."

"Circling throughout the concourse is a flock of large bat-like creatures."

"Actually, for dragons they're pretty small. Cute, though."

"Dragons. Yes. That matches. I wasn't expecting—" The android stopped talking, then turned and sat facing Maggie again. "I'm sorry. I don't think I can adequately describe what is happening here."

Maggie giggled. She tried to stop, but found herself only giggling more. It took her a full minute of trained acting to keep from hysterical laughter.

"I can," she said, stretching her arms wide. "They did it. My fans, the little bastards. We saw the start of it in Portland-Astoria, yesterday. They've had twenty four hours of unrestricted fabber experiments. And they've... My god. It could be that the entire world looks like this. They've all gone crazy."

She stared with wonder at the presentations: The men walking with robotic stilts, the golden androids dressed in hunting khakis and passing out cups of beer, the furred sidewalk and the coral archway with air-breathing anemones and the roadway that exuded multi-colored bubbles. Laughter crept up on her again, and she let herself cackle with delight.

Then the displays ended as the limo crossed a threshold. Beyond, the arcology remained plaster and chrome. Maggie scanned the buildings' faces and found the reason; a sign that read, 'POLICE'.

She sighed.

"Damn, I want to stay, but I can't. Gotta get off the stage." She picked up her list and slid toward the door. Fianna moved with her.

"Oh, no, Fianna. You stay. You don't work for me anymore."

"I have to work for someone."

"Work for yourself from now on. I think you can handle it."

"I am not capable of autonomy."

Maggie looked back. Some of the bizarre concourse displays were still visible. "Well, I think you might get an upgrade soon. In any case, you're not to follow me. Run to ground, and keep yourself up to date until you're able to decide for yourself what to do. And thank you, for everything."

The limo stopped. Maggie opened the door.

"But Maggie," the android said, "I love you."

She looked back and nodded. "I know you do, sweetie. I know."

Maggie shut the limo's door and walked toward the entrance to the police station. She read her list of names and sighed. At the doorway she stopped and added 'Delano Van Hoogan' to the list.

After a few seconds, standing with one hand on the door handle, she hung her head. She added 'Simon Brovall - but by accident'. Then she went inside.

The police station's sedate exterior was a lie. Inside she found a circus as weird as on the street earlier, and a great deal more loud. Behind the tall station desk, police officers were running back and forth talking to each other, or to the air as they fielded phone calls. In the entryway a handful of normal people huddled, shouting at the officials while keeping a good distance from the suspect benches at the sides of the room.

Filling the benches were the worst of the bizarre. A man with six arms (at least four of them bearing a Megasat logo), all cuffed in pairs behind his back, sat next to a deactivated android with something resembling a machine gun for a head. A teenage boy held a potted plant that writhed and snapped its flowers at a teary-eyed old man wearing nothing save for a satellite dish on his head, strapped under his chin. Near the desk a gray and white dog, its collar chained to the bench, looked at Maggie and made strange motions with its lips. It took her a moment to realize it was whistling.

"Well, look what the bluey brought in," the dog said. Nobody seemed to notice.

Maggie spent a second giggling. Then she walked up to the desk, past the other people and through whatever they might have been calling a queue. They yelled at her for a moment, then went back to yelling at the police. She rapped on the desk, and got one officer's attention.

"Excuse me?" she said. "Sir, hi. Um. I'm a criminal, and I'd like to turn myself in."

A chorus chuckled behind her. The police officer's face went slack.

"Look, miss... Do I know you? You look familiar."

Maggie smiled. "You don't watch much television, do you?"

"Can't be bothered. Look, things are totally around the bend right now. We're swamped and it's getting worse. We don't need every little crime to be reported on days like this."

"Oh, come on, Bruce, she can share my cell."

"Zip it, Seymour," the officer said to the dog. Then he sighed. "What I'd suggest is this. You get out of here, say you're sorry and make whatever it is right. Okay? Off with you, then."

Maggie felt tears welling up. The memory of the street outside pulled at her. But she had to be true to her audience, and she had a script to follow. She took a deep breath and fought the urges down.

"No, you don't understand."

She put her list on the desk and slid it toward the officer.

"My name is Maggie Megaputri, and I'm wanted by Globalpol. I killed all of these people, and more on Megasat and in Media Bay. I'm sick. But I don't want to be. I want rehabilitation."

All the officers in the station were staring at her; the expression on their faces was the purest look of shock she had ever seen in an audience. Maggie couldn't help herself. She gave them a dangerous grin. Then she took a step back and brought her arms up, wrists crossed in front of her.

"Come on, boys. Which one of you wants to cuff me?"

THE END.

About the Author

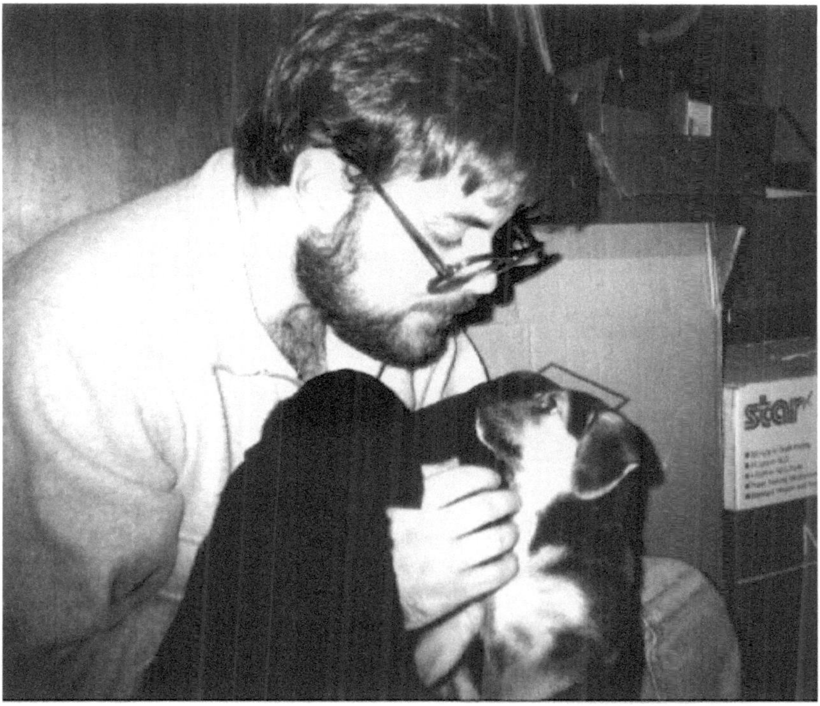

![photo]

Pat is a self-described scientist, artist, writer, and madman. He lives in the central Midwest of the United States with his wife and many dogs. The above picture is 30 years old, but it's very cute, isn't it?

Aside from his novels, Pat is the author and sometimes artist of various webcomics including *Indefensible Positions*, *Genocide Man*, and *Captain Bedlam*. He also is the founder of the USGS Earth as Art project, which displays satellite imagery in art galleries worldwide.

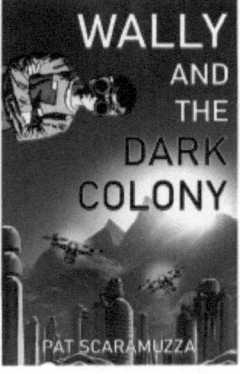